THE GRAND MASQUERADE
BY AMANDA HUGHES

DEDICATION

This book is dedicated to everyone who helped us escape.

ACKNOWLEDGMENTS

Thanks again to Madeline for lending an ear.

Chapter 1
Natchez Trace, Mississippi
1831

Sydnee was worried. Margarite was too drunk to conjure the spirits. She had fallen asleep in the shed with her head on her arms at the table used for divination. Her Madras *tignon* was askew, and she was snoring loudly.

She looked at the old slave and bit her lip. It was obvious the woman had been drinking for some time because candle wax was running down onto the altar cloth. She would have to set things up for the reading all by herself and do it quickly.

The fourteen-year-old girl looked around the shed frantically. In the corner, she found a burlap bag and took out statues and skulls arranging them on the altar in front of a standing crucifix. Next she ladled water from an earthenware jar into a wooden bowl and then scattered fresh flowers everywhere from a basket, all to prepare for a Hoodoo reading, a blend of Roman Catholicism and Voodoo.

Sydnee Sauveterre looked up. The rain was drumming hard on the shed behind The Devil's Backbone tavern on the Natchez Trace. Her father had opened the tavern on this heavily traveled, dangerous thoroughfare almost twenty-five years ago. His customers were flatboat men, nicknamed "Kaintucks" who brought goods down the Mississippi River to sell in New Orleans.

Sydnee worked frantically to get ready for the customer who was up at the tavern drinking. Everything had to be set up in proper Hoodoo fashion before Margarite could begin her divination. The most difficult part would be to shake the whiskey from the old woman's brain. Margarite had been sneaking more and more "white lightning" lately, and Sydnee did not want her father to give the slave another beating.

"Margarite," Sydnee said, shaking the old woman's shoulders. "Margarite, Papa will be angry. You must wake up."

Beads of perspiration broke out on the girl's forehead. She pushed the damp, brown hair off of her forehead and stepped over to an earthenware jar. She took a ladle of water, pulled back the collar of the slave's threadbare gown and poured water down her back.

Margarite jerked her head up, slurping her drool. Wiping her mouth with her sleeve, she mumbled an oath in French and looked around with bleary eyes. Her face was lined with wrinkles and ritual scarring from her early days in Martinique.

"We must hurry," warned Sydnee, placing a chamois bag of cat bones on the table. "The man will be here any minute. Here are the bones for the reading." The girl reached out and straightened Margarite's *tignon*.

"*Ma chère,* you tire yourself," the old woman said, pinching her chin.

Wind chimes by the altar flooded the room with an eerie jingling. They looked up at the decoration made out of old keys swaying in the corner. Margarite murmured in French, "The spirits are here. They will protect me. Now go, child."

Reluctantly, Sydnee nodded. She cast one more look around the dark room. A crucifix was set out and seven candles were guttering on the white altar cloth. Water was in a bowl ready as a medium for the spirits to enter the room, and floral offerings were strewn for the ancestors.

Sydnee looked up at the chimes. She too felt the presence of the spirits and was comforted by it. The moment she opened the door to leave the shed, several cats raced toward the steps trying to get inside out of the rain. She slammed the door quickly behind her and dashed for the woods. Squatting down in the wet brush, she watched the man enter the shed.

The rain ran down Sydnee's face and soaked her clothing, but she did not notice. She had grown up in the elements and was accustomed to all kinds of weather. Put to work from the moment she could walk, Sydnee grew slowly. At last, she was the correct height for her age, but she was as thin as a skeleton and as dirty as a street urchin. Her hair had been washed only a few times in her life, and her clothes were nothing more than shreds hanging on thin bones. Quiet and withdrawn, taking to animals rather than people, Sydnee was reclusive and shy. With wispy hair, freckles and high cheek bones, the girl was a mere waif. The only thing remarkable about her was her large, brown eyes.

"The eyes of a doe," Margarite would say affectionately.

When Sydnee's mother died giving birth to her, Victor Sauveterre purchased Margarite. It was a convenient arrangement for him in every way. He could use the slave to do the heavy work and satisfy his sexual needs as well.

From the first day Margarite arrived at The Devil's Backbone, she had been a mother to Sydnee. She fed her, nurtured her, and taught her, but as a slave, their relationship was limited. Sydnee's father exercised complete authority over the two females and dominated all decision making in the household. He firmly believed women, slave or free born, were his property, and he did not hesitate to punish them with violence if necessary.

The only source of power for the females was through Hoodoo, and Margarite and Sydnee were proficient at it. Margarite learned it as a child in Martinique and carefully schooled Sydnee in the arts from an early age. Victor Sauveterre encouraged the divination because it made him money at the tavern or "stands" as they were called on The Trace.

For years The Devil's Backbone thrived. The Kaintuck boatmen traveled downriver in flatboats loaded with goods from Nashville to New Orleans. Once unloaded, the men would break up their boats, sell them as lumber and then come north again on foot to drink and carouse in Natchez. After their revelry in the bordellos and taverns of Natchez Under-the-Hill, they would start their four hundred mile overland journey on the Natchez Trace back up to Nashville. Along the wilderness trail, they would patronize stands like The Devil's Backbone for food, drink and whores. Once in Nashville, they would purchase flat boats and goods and start all over again. The journey was dangerous, and the men were too.

A rush of wind blew into the room as the customer stepped into the shed for his reading. The candle flames blew horizontally, and the wind chimes jangled nervously. The moment Margarite laid eyes on the man, she sobered up.

He stepped into the doorway and stopped for a moment, looking at Margarite with his head lowered. His grey eyes glowered at her under a heavy brow. The stranger was tall and lanky with rounded shoulders and sunken cheeks. He wore a long, threadbare greatcoat with the collar up, and heavy boots. Although he was bald, he had a ring of long, thin hair at the base of his skull.

Margarite met his gaze and swallowed hard. Something did not feel right. The man shut the door, never taking his eyes from her. She felt the hair rise on her arms. Sitting down at the table, he continued to stare at her.

Margarite pushed the chamois bag toward him. When he reached out for it, his long, bony fingers swept lightly across her wrist. Margarite jerked her hand back.

Still watching her, the stranger shook the bag and threw the cat bones onto the table. He was obviously familiar with Hoodoo. Margarite looked down at the bones and stared with horror at what she read.

Suddenly, she felt sick to her stomach, and dizzy. She clutched at the table to steady herself, and her eyes rolled back. Like a black veil dropping over her head, darkness enveloped her, and she slipped into a swoon.

Something felt wrong to Sydnee as she waited in the woods. She could feel it. Squatting like an animal in the brush, she watched the shed, her knees apart and her bare feet on the soggy ground. The spirits were trying to tell her something. She pressed her eyes shut, straining to see into her mind's eye. Nothing came to her, nothing but darkness. She closed her eyes again. This time she clutched a charm around her neck and murmured a prayer. Over and over she chanted, "Hail Mary, full of grace--"

A blur of light came to her at last, and gradually, it sharpened into the image of a flame. Sydnee could see candles on a white cloth. She heard something scatter on a table. Her breathing quickened. There was danger. But what was it? She must relax. She must relax or the visions would not come. Sydnee put her head back and opened her mouth to breathe slowly. Over and over she petitioned to the saints for second sight and protection for Margarite.

"St. Michael, stay with her," she murmured. "Our Lady of the Assumption protect her. St. Gertrude watch over her."

Sydnee hesitated a moment, feeling the chill of danger. Summoning the greatest of Hoodoo powers, she uttered, "Danbala, I invoke you."

The mist lifted instantly, and Sydnee saw Margarite sitting in the shed with the stranger. Cat bones were scattered on the table. The guttering candles cast dancing shadows across the room. She saw Margarite's head roll back, and her jaw drop open. Then like a rag doll, she slumped back into her chair. Sydnee's heart jumped. She knew she must run to Margarite, but she could not move.

The stranger put his hands on the table and stood up slowly. His body unfolded like a mantis, and he took a gutting knife from his belt.

"I must go to her!" Sydnee's mind screamed, but she was paralyzed, a prisoner of her vision. She saw movement on the floor of the shed. The long body of a snake slipped under the door and began to glide toward the stranger. As it stretched out to its full length, Sydnee could see the diamond pattern on its back.

"Cumptico!" she cried. Her head snapped forward, and her eyes opened.

Sydnee jumped to her feet and bolted toward the shed, her feet splashing in the mud. When she threw the door open, she saw the stranger standing over the body of Margarite. Between the man and Margarite was the coiled form of Cumptico, ready to strike. The front portion of his body was upright as he challenged the stranger; his tail rattling ominously, and his tongue darting out.

Margarite raised her head and screamed.

From the doorway, Sydnee said with strained reserve, "Cumptico, my thanks to you. Your job here is done."

The snake did not move, nor the man. The stranger looked at Sydnee with hate in his eyes.

"Danbala, I beseech you," she said, with her hands upturned.

At last, the snake dropped down and slithered out the door.

With a crash, Victor Sauveterre stormed into the shed. "What the hell's going on here?" he roared. Grossly overweight with a shock of red hair and skin the color of a fish's underbelly, Sydnee's father was massive. "What happened?"

"It was a snake, Papa," Sydnee said quietly.

He turned to Margarite and roared, "I told you to keep your goddamned creatures out of here!"

Suddenly assuming an obsequious air, he straightened up and said to the stranger, "I apologize for my nigger. She will be punished for this. How can I make this up to you, sir?"

Putting his knife away, the stranger pushed past him toward the door.

Victor Sauveterre grabbed Sydnee. "You may have my daughter for no charge tonight."

Sydnee dropped her eyes to the floor. This was her job, but tonight she was afraid.

Margarite blurted suddenly, "*Mais non*, Master! The girl is about to give birth."

The innkeeper turned and back handed Margarite across the face. "Shut up!" The force of the blow sent her staggering.

Changing back to faux gentility, he added, "Have the girl, with my compliments, sir. She is a little bigger than normal but I assure you, she will satisfy."

Sydnee held her breath and waited. The wind chimes moved slightly, sending a tinkling sound through the room.

The stranger looked at Victor Sauveterre and then at Sydnee. He shook his head and left The Devil's Backbone.

Chapter 2

All was quiet at The Devils Backbone the next morning. Sydnee tiptoed past her father who was on his pallet snoring in the corner of the cabin which doubled as a tavern. After his drunken rampage, he passed out and would not be awake again for hours.

She glanced at the tattered blanket thrown over a rope in the corner where he slept. Sauveterre talked about adding bedrooms onto the cabin one day, but it never happened. Sydnee slept in the loft and Margarite in the shed. The cabin was furnished with a table and a few rickety chairs, but the room was used seldom by customers. They preferred sitting on the front porch since the Mississippi backwoods were often oppressively hot.

Today promised to be another suffocating summer day. When Sydnee stepped outside, two dogs crawled out from under the porch to greet her, a large English mastiff named Baloo and a powerfully built terrier named Atlantis. As she sat down on the step, the dogs dropped down beside her. Sydnee treasured her mornings. It was the only time she had to herself, and today in particular, she dreaded her father waking. She knew that he would be in a foul mood.

After the stranger left last night, Victor Sauveterre raged for hours. "You and your creatures!" he bellowed at Margarite. "A goddamned rattler!"

Then he turned to Sydnee. "And if you weren't such an ugly slut," he roared. "I could have made some money!"

With eyes lowered, the females stood before him on the porch listening to him rant until he dropped into a chair and began guzzling from a jug of whiskey. "Now get the hell away from me, both of you!" he roared, flinging his meaty arm in the air.

The past few years, business had been slow at the stand. The stranger last night had been the first Kaintuck to stop in days, and Sauveterre blamed the two females for driving him away.

Taking a deep breath, Sydnee looked up at the morning sky. Already the air was thick as pea soup. She reached down and stroked Atlantis' head. Sydnee loved the dog's pink nose and the matching pink skin inside her ears. Although she was bred for bear baiting and exhibition fighting, the lean muscular bull terrier was anything but vicious. Victor Sauveterre won Atlantis in a card game a few months ago, but when she did not perform well in the ring, he had beaten her senseless. It took weeks, but Sydnee nursed her back to full health and was rewarded with a loyal loving companion. Sweet and sensitive, Atlantis took everything to heart.

Baloo was another matter. Slow and plodding, always several paces behind everyone, he was easy going and gentle of nature. He appeared at the stand one evening years ago and never left.

Margarite named him "Baloo" which means bear. With a dark wrinkled face and a fawn-colored coat, the dog was soft to the touch, slow to anger and born old. He had been with Sydnee as long as she could remember. Baloo loved to be hugged and was always ready to lend an ear when she was feeling gloomy.

A large crow swooped down out of a tree and landed on Sydnee's shoulder. "Good morning, Vivian," she murmured to the bird.

Vivian was a large, bossy crow that she fostered as well. One morning, some months ago, Sydnee heard a terrible outcry in the oak tree above her head. Looking up, she saw a snake gorging himself on baby crows in a nest. The mother bird was gone, and the hatchlings were squealing with terror. Outraged, Sydnee showered the serpent with rocks. She missed repeatedly, but at last, she managed to smash it squarely on the head. Stunned, the snake dropped out of the tree, hitting branches all the way down until it tumbled into the grass, and then it slithered away into the woods. Sydnee hiked up the tree finding one baby crow left. Nestling it in her gown, she took it to a safe place and nursed the hatchling back to health. It found a perch on a tree near the cabin, and Vivian remained there ever since.

Much to the dismay of the dogs, Vivian had an indomitable maternal instinct. She believed it was her duty to supervise and reprimand the canines at all times. Whenever the dogs would romp or play, Vivian would swoop down and peck at them parentally, reminding them to act with maturity and mind their manners.

All day long, Sydnee would have to break up their fights. This morning was no exception. After settling in on the girl's shoulder, Vivian looked down at the dogs.

"Nooo," Sydnee warned. "Let them be."

Even though the bird looked away, the canines stole glances at her warily. They were afraid of Vivian.

A light breeze blew Sydnee's cinnamon-colored hair. "Let's go," she said, slapping her hands on her knees. Vivian flapped her huge wings and returned to her favorite tree. Sydnee rolled off the step clumsily. Her belly made navigation difficult lately.

She started down an overgrown path. The Sauveterre claim was a heavily wooded piece of land on the Natchez Trace in southern Mississippi. Their one room cabin was nothing more than a shack, covered with a crumbling moss covered roof. It had one window and crooked front porch. The cabin faced Plum Creek which was spanned by a rickety bridge that Victor Sauveterre built twenty-five years earlier.

Plum Creek was a picturesque little waterway lined with weeping willows and swamp grasses. It drifted lazily along, twisting and turning until it joined the Pearl River to the East and eventually the Gulf of Mexico to the south. The terrain was flat and thick with tangled underbrush, oaks, claw footed cypress, soggy marshland, and a myriad of water fowl and wildlife.

Hacked out through this wilderness, the Natchez Trace ran in front of the Sauveterre stand. After twenty-five years of heavy traffic, deep ruts had been ground into the thoroughfare.

In spots, a man could not see over the banks of the trail because the path had been carved so deeply into the earth.

In fourteen years, Sydnee Sauveterre had not left her father's homestead in the Mississippi backwoods. The child's knowledge of the world beyond The Devil's Backbone was limited, and she had experienced more than a lifetime of privation. Hard work and using her body to earn a living was a way of life for her.

In 1807, her father erected the stand along The Natchez Trace to sell food and liquor to travelers, but the past few years, business had declined.

"Those rich bastards in New Orleans ruined everything," Sauveterre raged. "Their goddamned steamboats took my living. No one uses The Trace anymore."

It was true. For years, stands like The Devil's Backbone prospered along the 400 mile path from Natchez to Nashville. "Coon Box Stand", "Buzzard Roost", "Shoat's", "French Camp", over fifty stands in number, dotted the rugged trail. But with the invention of the steam engine, there came a new and easier way to travel on the Mississippi; by paddle wheeler, and the golden years of the Natchez Trace came to a close.

Sydnee walked over the little bridge and then up a path alongside the creek toward her favorite spot under a willow tree. She brushed aside the long green tendrils of the tree and sat down. Baloo and Atlantis ducked in after her.

Sydnee eased herself down onto the moss. The verdant chamber was the only place she felt safe. With the green curtain surrounding her, she could lower her guard and allow her imagination to soar. Ever since she was a small child, she would come to this hideaway, armed with stories from Margarite about Martinique and a city called New Orleans.

"The ladies gowns are the color of the finest flowers," Margarite told her. "Fabric as blue as cornflowers, reds like christmasberry blossoms, and yellows as brilliant as the flowers on lily pads."

Sydnee would listen with her chin cupped in her hand, memorizing every word.

"And the houses, child," Margarite would continue. "They all have balconies bordered with lacey iron railings and courtyards filled with magnolias and camellias."

Sydnee would try to imagine the big river to the west, called the Mississippi, where the "Trace" began in Natchez. She had never seen a cake, but Margarite told her that the paddle wheelers on the river looked like gigantic, white layer cakes, all trimmed in gold.

"Someday I will see it all," she murmured to the dogs.

As she mused, a crane caught her eye. She could see him just beyond the green strands of the tree, strutting in the shallow water. Sydnee loved all creatures but particularly birds. It was because of her love of birds that Vivian had come to her.

Sydnee dropped back with her hands behind her head, thinking about life in the city to the south. Margarite had spoken also of her life on the sugar cane plantation in Martinique. Sydnee knew this was where Margarite was born and where she received her training in Hoodoo, and her ritual scarring. These stories were not as beautiful though. In fact they were frequently disturbing. They often ended in talk of cruelty to slaves and people using Voodoo for dark purposes, a practice which Margarite abhorred.

Suddenly she heard the bell ringing from the porch of the cabin. It was her signal to return to the house. As she rose, she felt the muscles of her abdomen spasm. She recognized this feeling from her first pregnancy. It was her belly practicing for birth.

As she headed down the path with the dogs, she stopped to check her turtle traps. She had six holes, about ten inches deep, along the banks of creek to lure turtles. Sydnee would entice them with worms around the ridge of the hole, placing the juiciest morsels at the bottom of the hollow. Greedy for the best worms, the turtles would drop down to the bottom of the hole and be trapped. The catch was small today. She scooped up the few turtles she found and held them in the skirt of her dress. She would take them home to Margarite for soup.

As she walked down the path in her bare feet, Vivian landed on her shoulder. Baloo lumbered behind her as Atlantis dashed in and out of the creek, scaring up waterfowl. The birds would burst out of the marshy grasses with their wings thundering. On one occasion, the terrier put her nose underwater and then yelped. She was investigating a snapping turtle too closely.

When Atlantis returned to shore, she stood in their path and shook her coat, spattering Sydnee and Vivian with water. Sydnee blinked but Vivian swooped down giving Atlantis a punitive peck on the head. The dog immediately dropped into a crouch and ducked into the bushes.

When Vivian landed back on her shoulder, Sydnee commanded, "Come!" and Atlantis came out to the path once more. Sydnee reached up to dry her face with her sleeve. Her dress was nothing more than a rag. It had been a well-made gown at one time, but now it was threadbare, faded, and ragged around the hem. Her clothing came from a Kaintuck whose wife died along The Trace several years back. The man gave them three dresses, a sun bonnet and an apron. Prior to that, Sydnee had worn only the garments left by her mother. Victor Sauveterre did not think it was necessary the females have fabric for clothing. He thought they should make-do with sack cloth or burlap and that footwear was a luxury, so Sydnee never owned a pair of shoes.

Margarite was hanging Victor Sauveterre's clothes up to dry. She was wearing her faded turban or *tignon* and a brown gown with a dirty, white apron. A string of shells hung from her neck, and she had one hoop earring in her ear. Sydnee could smell the rice and gravy simmering in the Dutch oven on the campfire near the cabin. It was too hot to cook inside the house this time of year.

Chickens scattered as the dogs raced up to greet the old woman. She bent down stiffly to pet them, murmuring endearments as she scratched their ears. Margarite always moved slowly, but lately her crippled hip caused her to move even slower because of increased pain. Sydnee knew this was one of the reasons she was drinking heavily.

Sydnee and Margarite managed to hide the drinking from Sydnee's father thus far, but her failing health was hard to disguise. Sydnee noticed the woman's appetite was decreasing and that she was drinking more and more corn whiskey instead of eating. Margarite had access to the alcohol from a still in back of the cabin. Since it was one of her tasks to make "white lightning" for customers, she was around it constantly.

Sydnee dropped her skirt full of turtles into a bucket of water and started toward the cabin to see if her father wanted breakfast.

"He is gone to Buzzard Roost already," Margarite called to her in French.

Sydnee was relieved. Victor Sauveterre went to George Broussard's stand frequently to play horseshoes and drink. Many days he was gone from sunrise until sunset.

She turned and came over to help hang up clothes instead. Margarite put her wrinkled hand to Sydnee's cheek and said, "Good morning, my leetle girl."

Sydnee murmured, "Are you well after last night?"

Margarite shrugged her shoulders, not wishing to discuss the incident with the stranger. She changed the subject. "I picked an egg for my reading today."

Sydnee lowered her eyes and frowned.

Margarite looked at her and dropped her arms from the clothes line. She continued in her French patois, "What is it?"

Sydnee thrust her jaw open and strained to speak, but no words came. Mute until the age of nine, Sydnee had been speaking for only the past five years. When she at last spoke, Margarite was amazed at her mastery of both English and French. It was further confirmation that Sydnee had a fine mind.

"Why don't you want to do my reading?" Margarite pressed.

"I-I am not good at egg readings," Sydnee said in English, but she was lying. The truth was that she was afraid of what she might see in the woman's future.

Margarite narrowed her eyes. She knew that Sydnee was lying. At fourteen, the girl was the most proficient diviner she had ever known.

"Well, I want you to try," the old woman said, pursing her lips. She started to the back of the cabin toward the still. Sydnee knew that she was going to start drinking again.

After pinning the last of her father's shirts onto the line, Sydnee picked up a bucket and a knife and started down The Trace into the woods. When the creatures tried to follow she commanded them to stay back.

She felt another tightening in her stomach as she trudged down the dirt road, bucket in hand, but she ignored the sensation. It was a fine summer morning, and she enjoyed her peaceful walk. Years ago, she would have met all sorts of people traveling this thoroughfare, but now it was unusual to see anyone. A meadow opened up on her right and Sydnee left the trail to cross the sun-drenched field of grass. She wiped the perspiration from her brow and slowly approached the hollow remains of an oak tree. Bees swarmed around the trunk, but Sydnee continued toward them.

As she walked, she began to chant. The words and their meaning were unknown to her, but the bees seemed to be charmed into submission. The chant came to her from the spirits one day years ago. Gradually the bees landed on the trunk of the tree, mesmerized as if asleep, allowing her access to the hive. They looked like a large fur coat on the oak.

Sydnee set the bucket down, still chanting, took the knife and shaved off a large hunk of honey comb. Dripping with liquid gold, she dropped the comb into the bucket. Leaning over and looking at the bees, she bowed once in gratitude and then backed away. She crossed the meadow, sucking the delicacy from her fingers.

The first few times Sydnee tried to harvest honey, Margarite told her to use smoke to subdue the bees. Although an ancient technique for bee charming, she found it ineffective. She believed if she simply approached the colony, chanted the incantation and asked for permission, the bees would share their honey with her.

Like with so many creatures, Sydnee had an uncanny ability to communicate with them. From an early age, Margarite taught her to respect and love all living things and to use the power of Hoodoo to do good deeds. Sydnee's whole world revolved around this simple philosophy of living.

Before she left the meadow, she put the bucket of honey down and pulled a flat blade of grass from the ground. Pressing it between her fingers, she blew on it making a loud screeching noise. In a matter of moments, she could see the dogs running up The Trace with Vivian soaring above them.

As the group ambled back toward the cabin, they met Margarite on the road. She was carrying a basket of produce on her head. It was filled with onions, okra and plump red tomatoes which she had just picked from their garden. Sydnee reached up and carefully transferred the basket to her own head.

Margarite took the bucket of honey and limped along beside them. "I found the plant we need to ease your pain when the baby comes. It is over there near the indigo bush." Well versed in the use of plants for Hoodoo potions and medicine, Margarite was frequently in the woods searching for flowers, barks, and herbs. "How do you feel today, my beauty?" the old woman asked.

Sydnee smiled. This time the words rolled quickly off her tongue. "I know this baby will live. It kicks more than my first one."

"Any pains?"

"No, but I feel my stomach practicing."

"Get your craw fishing done early, so you can rest this afternoon. Your father will be gone until late tonight."

The dogs dragged along behind Margarite and Sydnee, panting. The air was steadily growing more humid in the green darkness along The Trace. Two redwing blackbirds darted in front of Sydnee, one chasing the other through the trees. The girl smiled. She loved the woods, the creek, the swamps and all of its creatures.

"Bon jour to you my little Cumptico," said Margarite suddenly.

Sydnee looked down at a rattlesnake sunning himself on a rock along the side of the road.

"Thank you for your protection," the old woman continued. "May your day be filled with peace and harmony."

They continued past the snake with the dogs giving Cumptico a wide berth.

"You have taught me so many things," Sydnee said. "Will you teach me how to be a mother?"

Margarite's eyebrows shot up. She stopped walking and looked at the girl. Her wrinkled face looked like the head of an old apple doll. "You know that I have no children."

Sydnee said, "You have me."

Margarite brushed a lock of hair off the girl's face affectionately and murmured. "You are right, leetle one. It is true that motherhood is not just about giving birth. *Oui*, I will help you."

When they reached the cabin, Baloo crawled under the porch where it was cool, Atlantis waded in the creek lapping water, and Vivian flew to the shade of her favorite oak tree.

With a sigh of relief, Margarite sat down in the rocker on the porch, a mug of white lightning in her hand. She could never have rested if Victor Sauveterre was home. Sydnee went into the cabin to get some mint tea out of a jar. She came out and eased herself down onto the step, drinking out of a gourd.

Margarite rocked back and forth, fanning herself. "Your name has given you a good start at motherhood."

Sydnee looked up at her quizzically.

"The name Sauveterre, did I never tell you, child? *En français*, it means safe haven."

"That is what Papa's name means?"

Margarite frowned. "The name belongs more to you. You live by it. He does not."

Sydnee drained the ladle and pushed herself up. "I am going craw fishing now."

"Good," the old woman said draining her cup too and starting inside to make turtle soup. "Soap making tomorrow," she called, but the girl did not hear her. She was already headed along the creek with Baloo.

Carrying her net and bucket, Sydnee found a slow back wash of water under a cypress tree and squatted down. The muddy creek bottom was alive with the creatures. Prodding them gently with a stick, scores of crayfish backed into Sydnee's net. In no time, her job was complete.

She sat down on the bank and put her arm around Baloo's big neck and kissed him. "Margarite does not like Papa very well, does she?"

The dog rolled his brown eyes up at the girl adoringly.

"He has never been very nice to her, but I think it is because he is lonely. I think he misses Mama."

Baloo rested his chin in Sydnee's lap while she scratched his head. She said nothing for a while, deep in thought. "This baby will make Papa feel better," she declared, nodding.

Sydnee told Baloo everything. In fact, he was the first creature to ever hear Sydnee utter a word. The girl was seldom lonely but when she did see other children her age, she felt awkward. The Devil's Backbone was very isolated, and when a customer brought youngsters to the stand, Sydnee was too busy cooking and doing chores to play.

"Let's go," she said to Baloo, picking up her bucket.

They rested that afternoon during the oppressive heat of the day. Sydnee was glad her father had not returned. She felt guilty thinking it, but things went more smoothly when he was not around. Everyone was on edge when he was home. She was also secretly grateful when no customers came to the stand. Inevitably her father would offer her body to the men, and when they accepted, she had to endure their heavy, sweating bodies upon her behind the hanging quilt in the cabin. Most of the time they did not look at her, but on occasion the customers wanted her to look into their eyes while they did vile things to her.

She had seen the animals of The Trace mating, and she found it a natural and functional way to procreate, but the customers of The Devil's Backbone changed all that. They made the act filthy and depraved.

That evening after the sun set and their chores were complete, Margarite told Sydnee it was time for her egg divination. They went to the shed and lit one candle. Usually they burned strings in cups of grease for light, but a divination was special and called for a candle.

Sydnee felt sick to her stomach. She knew the reading would not be good. She felt it in her bones.

Before they sat down, she poured a ring of purifying salt onto the floor, around the table and sat down. Margarite sat across from Sydnee, holding the egg. Solemnly, she swept it around the outside of her body to cleanse her aura. She started over her head and then moved the egg down over her arms, legs, under her feet and then up the other side of her body. When she was finished, she handed it to Sydnee who quickly cracked the egg and let the white drip through her fingers into a clear glass bowl of water, discarding the yolk into a small crock at her feet.

Sydnee looked to the heavens first with her palms raised to thank the Lord for life and pray for guidance, and then she moved the bowl forward. They waited in silence as the egg white settled into the water. The sounds of night were all around them. Crickets were singing in the woods and toads called to one another in the swamps.

At last the divination began to unfold. The first thing Sydnee saw was a thin veil of translucent white that resembled a shroud, dropping gently over an oblong mass at the bottom of the bowl. She swallowed hard and clenched her teeth, staring at the bowl. Next long threads began to rise up like spires on a church. They were beautiful slender filaments, like the gates of heaven. Next she saw bubbles resembling the stars and the opaque form of a woman draped in white, her arms raised in welcome. Lovely as it was, this was not what she wanted to see.

She looked up at Margarite who was studying her.

"Oh, my dear one," the old woman murmured. "I know what you are seeing. I have known for some time." She shook her head. "I was wrong to have you divine this. *Peut-être* it was my way of telling you."

Tears welled up in Sydnee's eyes and rolled down her face. The girl sat rigidly, not looking up from the table. She did not want to admit that Margarite was dying.

Suddenly a crippling pain clutched Sydnee's abdomen, and she cried out. Margarite grabbed her hand. When the pain passed at last, Sydnee looked up at her panting, with sweat drenching her brow.

When the chimes tinkled in the corner, a slow smile spread over Margarite's face, and she said, "The spirits are speaking, my beauty, a life for a life. It is the way of it, and it is good."

Chapter 3

The ancient oak tree above Sydnee's head stretched over her like a canopy. She examined the heavy black branches with their verdant foliage and then looked down at the dappled sunlight at her feet. She felt warm and protected as if she was enfolded in the arms of a loving mother. She longed to stay but something compelled her to keep moving.

When Sydnee started down the paved walkway, she frightened away two song birds that were drinking from a stone basin on a pedestal. Walking closer she saw that the basin was filled with water. Something in her memory stirred. Margarite told her of such a decoration. She called it a bird bath.

What beautiful and peaceful place is this?

The grass felt soft and luxurious under her feet. She walked a little farther and paused by a small waterfall to watch water tumble over a staircase of rocks. A warm breeze moved her hair. Unsure whether this place was real, she reached down and stroked moss on the rocks. It was as soft as Vivian's feathers.

Suddenly everything went black, and Sydnee was consumed with excruciating pain. She gasped for air and heard Margarite's voice, but it was far away. She opened her eyes and saw a blurry light. When her vision cleared, she realized that she was looking at candles. She was on Margarite's bed in the shed. She heard water splashing in a basin as if someone was wringing out a cloth. Then the pain came again. It started in her abdomen and swept up her back. She lurched forward and screamed.

The next time she opened her eyes, the pain was gone, and she was standing by a pond. But this was not like the wild marshy ponds of The Trace; this was a pristine and perfectly round basin with a rim around the edge. The rim was so large you could sit upon it. In the middle of this pond was a metal statue of a girl who was half human, half fish. She was holding a tall lily that spewed water high into the air which splashed back down into the pond.

Sydnee looked up realizing that she was surrounded on all sides by a white two-story home bordered with pillared walkways and lacy, iron railings. Tall palm trees rose majestically over her head. Bushes with large white flowers grew in the courtyard and wisteria vines encircled the pillars. This was a place Margarite told her about. She was standing in the courtyard of a Creole home in New Orleans.

Suddenly, without warning, red hot pain shot through her body again, and she was sick to her stomach. She was back in the shed again. She heard Margarite mumbling an incantation and shaking a rattle charm. She raised Sydnee's head and gave her a sip of herb tea. "Take this. It will ease the pain and make you dream," she said.

The pain subsided again, and Sydnee looked around. This time she was in a different garden bordered by tall arborvitaes and fragrant flowers. She looked down at the green grass and flowers at her feet. There were yellow daffodils planted in straight rows, dappled coleus, and bushes with pink roses, and purple phlox. Suddenly the colorful flowers grew taller and taller and changed into women dressed in vivid ball gowns. They were held by gentlemen in dark suits who danced them around and around a pool filled with lily pads and swans.

Sydnee watched spellbound as the guests whirled past her. She could smell lavender on the ladies, cedar and spice on the men.

Gradually the dancers melted away, and she found herself standing in front of a tall, white iron gate. It reminded Sydnee of the gate she had seen in the glass bowl during the divination. It was large and arched high over her head.

The wind moaned sadly in her ears. The sun was setting as she pulled the gate open. On the other side were rows of small stone houses set in straight lines. Eucalyptus trees shaded these tiny enclosures. When Sydnee came closer, she saw statues of angels and lambs adorning the doors with tiny marble crosses on the roofs.

She realized suddenly that this was a cemetery. Margarite had spoken of these Cities of the Dead, where they buried their deceased above ground in vaults.

Panic flooded her. She had to get out of this place. She did not want to be here. She did not want to think about death. She started to run but stopped abruptly, doubling over in agony. Pain shot through her belly again and began to wrap around to her back. She could not endure it. She dropped to her knees in a faint.

The Grand Masquerade

When she woke up she heard a baby crying, and Margarite was near. She cooed, "My leetle girl has a leetle girl."

When Sydnee opened her eyes again, she was back under the sheltering arms of the oak tree. She was tired, but she felt safe. She leaned back against the trunk of the tree and rested.

Somewhere down by the swamp she heard a baby crying. Sydnee listened. The crying continued. She walked down to the marsh and waded into the water, parting the swamp grass, looking for the child. Her skirt plumed out around her in the water as she searched. Wading through the reeds, she remembered a story Margarite told her long ago, about a babe found in the bull rushes who grew up to become a great leader.

At last she found the baby in a basket floating among the cattails. The child stopped crying the moment she saw Sydnee. She was a beautiful little girl, with eyes the color of robin's eggs. A thrill of wonder shot through Sydnee. Smiling, she reached down carefully and picked the baby up. She took her up the hill to the bird bath where she unwound the swaddling clothes and slipped the child into the basin to bathe her. As she scooped water over the child, they stared at each other in wonder.

"Give it to me goddamn it!" a voice roared.

Startled, Sydnee clutched the child to her breast. Dripping with water, the baby started to howl again. Sydnee scanned the woods desperately. All was quiet. With a sigh, she calmed the baby and lowered her again for her bath. Suddenly her jaw dropped. The bird bath changed into a font for divination and there before her eyes, in the water, a scene was unfolding.

Sydnee's father was arguing with Margarite and shaking his fist at her. They were in the shed, and it was dark. "You stupid nigger!" he roared.

"Non!" Margarite screamed, backing up with a baby in her arms. "Not again!"

Victor Sauveterre scowled and with one swift movement, he covered Margarite's face with his hand and sent her toppling backward into the wall of the shed. She stumbled and tried to remain standing but fell into the corner. In spite of the fall, she did not let go of the child.

Sauveterre reached down.

Margarite screamed "Non," rolling away from him, holding fast to the baby.

Straddling the old woman, he jerked the child away from her and thrust the screaming infant under his arm. Throwing open the door of the shed, he strode out into the night.

*   *   *

Sydnee's eyelids fluttered. She felt sick to her stomach and confused. *Where am I? What happened?* She recognized the shed at last, but something was banging. When she raised her head, she saw that the wind was slamming the shed door open and closed. She rubbed her eyes. *Where is Margarite?*

With great effort she raised herself up on one elbow. Except for a cup of grease guttering on the altar, it was dark. The blankets of her bed were soaked, and she pushed them off, sitting up gingerly. She was sore all over but particularly between her legs. Then she remembered that she had just delivered a baby.

Pulling her dirty shift over her head to cover herself, Sydnee carefully stood up. Shuffling over to the altar, she lit some tapers and looked around. The bed was rumpled and soaked with blood. The wind continued to bang the door, making the flames jump and the wind chimes jangle.

As Sydnee pulled the door shut, something caught her eye, and she started. There in a rumpled heap in the corner was Margarite.

"*Ma mère!*" she cried.

Hanging onto the wall, she stumbled over and dropped to her knees, putting her hands on the woman's face. "Wake up!" Sydnee cried, turning her head toward her. "Please wake up!" she begged. Margarite opened her eyes and mumbled something, but Sydnee did not understand.

Mustering her limited strength, she crawled behind Margarite and lifted her under the arms, pulling her over to the bed on the floor. Panting, she ran her eyes over her but found no injuries.

"Where is the baby?" Sydnee asked anxiously.

Gently she shook Margarite, and she opened her eyes.

"The baby?" Sydnee repeated, looking at her desperately.

Margarite stared at her. She grimaced and then murmured apologetically, "*Mort.*"

Sydnee blinked in disbelief, dropped back onto the blanket, covered her face and shook her head from side to side. *Another baby born without life. How can this be!*

All night long and all through the next day, she stayed on the bed, stone faced and mute by Margarite. She bore her despair in silence, letting Margarite sleep. She knew that the woman was exhausted from helping her give birth, and it was not until the sun began to set that she turned and looked at her. Margarite was on her back, her breathing quick and shallow. Her cheeks were sunken, and her eyeballs were yellow when she turned to look at Sydnee. Moving her lips, she tried to speak, but no words would come.

Sydnee waited, afraid of what she was about to hear. At last Margarite whispered, "Pain. Help me, my leetle one."

Sydnee squeezed her eyes shut. She did not want to do what she knew Margarite was asking.

"*S'il te plaî?*" the old woman pleaded.

Reluctantly, Sydnee nodded and pushed herself up off the bed. Still weak and sore, it took great effort to rise. Her hair was matted and dried blood was caked over her legs. The heat in the shed was oppressive and the air thick with illness. When she stepped outside, the damp air of the swamps filled her lungs, and the dogs dashed out from under the porch to greet her. The sunset glowed red as it filtered through the tangled webs of Spanish moss.

The first thing she did was scan the yard for her father. All was quiet. She hung onto the shed, gathering strength to walk to the cabin. She took a deep breath, mustered her courage and walked up the path.

The cabin was empty, and she sighed with relief. Sydnee took a plate of hush puppies and scooped a bowl of nuts from a barrel and then ducked out back to the still where she filled a jug with whiskey. She returned to the shed as quickly as her legs would allow. She was afraid her father would appear at any moment and demand work from her.

The white lightning seemed to put new life into Margarite as Sydnee held her head and poured the alcohol into her mouth. Margarite dropped back onto the bed and sighed, much relieved. It seemed to warm her core and ease her pain.

Sydnee felt guilty giving whiskey to Margarite. It was the very substance that was killing her, but she knew that it was too late. It was all the woman had to dilute her pain for her last few hours on earth.

She gulped some from the jug herself, ate some hush puppies and then pulled back the greased paper on the window to look outside. Vivian was perched on a branch nearby. She cocked her head when she saw Sydnee and then went back to watching over the shed diligently.

When Sydnee eased back down, Margarite took her hand. It was difficult for her to speak, but the old woman whispered, "Leave here."

"Leave you and Papa?"

"You are not listening to the spirits. They want both of us to leave. I am a slave. Passing to the other side is the only way for me."

Biting her lip, Sydnee rolled her head away from Margarite. She had indeed heard a whispering in her ear lately, but she had not understood it.

Margarite is wrong. The spirits would never tell me to leave. Someone has to take care of Papa.

"*Saint-Christophe* appeared to me last night," Margarite said hoarsely. She gasped for breath, licked her dry lips and said, "He is waiting to carry me across the big river. He waits to guide you away from here too."

Ignoring the words, Sydnee stood up, poured fresh water into a basin and soaked a cloth. Kneeling down stiffly, she started to sponge Margarite's face. When she finished, the old woman said, "Go now to the creek and wash the blood and dirt from your own body."

Nodding, Sydnee retrieved a crock of soft soap and rags from the homemade wooden cupboard where Margarite kept her herbs. Before she stepped out the door, she looked back. Margarite was watching her with a faint smile on her lips.

Baloo and Atlantis accompanied Sydnee to a private spot on Plum Creek where the water ran deep and the trees joined overhead like a giant green umbrella. Vivian seemed to know that Sydnee was weak and did not try to land on her shoulder. Instead she flew from tree to tree as they walked along.

Sydnee took her shift off and waded in the running water, splashing her body and lathering her skin. It felt good to wash again. Atlantis hopped about chasing frogs, Baloo snapped at flies and Vivian stood guard in an oak tree overhead. The creatures were relieved to be near Sydnee once more. They were frantic all night, hearing her screaming in the shed, but when she emerged at last, they were overcome with joy. Content now just to be near her, they occupied themselves happily.

Sydnee plugged her nose and dropped back into the water and then lathered and scrubbed her scalp vigorously. When she was done, she scrubbed her blood-soaked shift in the creek, putting the damp garment back on when she crawled out. The moisture would keep her cool until it dried. She tied several rags between her legs to catch the blood still running from childbirth and started back along the creek toward home.

It was getting dark now, and the bugs were getting thick. She hurried back to the shed, eager to rest again, at least for a while before her father returned. She could feel the energy draining from her body with every step she took.

When she pulled open the door of the shed, Margarite was looking at her with the same faint smile on her lips.

"Papa is still not back," Sydnee said. "I am going to try to sleep again."

No response.

Sydnee looked at Margarite. The woman did not move. She did not blink, the smile frozen on her face. Sydnee's lips parted, and she stared. Margarite was gone. Dropping to her knees, she sobbed, "*Non, non*! How can I go on without you, *ma Mere*?" she cried.

Sobs wracked her body for what seemed like hours, and when she looked up at last, she realized that Margarite died the moment she stepped out of the shed. They joined eyes *and* souls at that moment.

Something caught Sydnee's attention, and she looked up in the corner. It was the wind chimes jingling in the corner of the room. Margarite was saying goodbye.

Chapter 4

Victor Sauveterre returned after dark, shortly after Sydnee finished washing and sprinkling Margarite's body with oils. He entered the shed as she was starting to wrap her. His huge frame filled the door. "Jesus Christ, she's dead?" he asked.

Sydnee looked up into his heavily-freckled porcine face and nodded.

Sauveterre threw his hands up, exclaiming loudly, "Well, that figures. Now I'm out a nigger!"

Sydnee dropped her head, afraid to aggravate him further. She buried her hands in the pockets of her blue smock.

"God damn it, she stinks. Get me a lantern. I'll find a spade."

Even though it was dark, the sultry weather made it imperative they bury Margarite immediately. Her father chose a site behind the shed for a shallow grave. When he finished the hole, he returned to the shed drenched in perspiration. His broadcloth trousers were covered in dirt, and his shirt clung to his meaty flesh.

"Well, help me," he demanded, taking Margarite's upper body.

Sydnee reached down and took the feet, staggering from the weight. As she walked, she could feel a rush of blood soaking the rags between her thighs. They carried the body to the back of the shed where the lantern cast an eerie golden glow under the trees.

A pain shot through Sydnee's abdomen. She dropped Margarite's feet and doubled over, but she did not make a sound.

"Oh, Christ!" her father grumbled. "I'll do it myself."

He pushed Sydnee out of the way and hoisted the corpse over his shoulder. Before she could protest, he had thrown Margarite into the grave like a sack of rotten potatoes.

A man's voice called from the cabin, "Hello? Is anybody here?"

A customer was at the cabin. Wiping his hands on his pants, Sauveterre ordered, "You do the rest."

He yanked an earthenware flask out of his pocket, threw his head back and emptied the contents down his throat. Wiping his mouth on his sleeve, he called; "Coming!" and then turned up the path.

Sydnee watched him disappear into the darkness, relieved that he was gone. She wanted to be alone to say farewell to Margarite. She bent down, tossed the first bit of earth into the grave asking St. Christopher to guide Margarite safely to the other side. Then slowly and reluctantly, she picked up the spade and started to fill the grave

*　　　　*　　　　*

Sydnee could hear men talking and laughing with her father late into the night. The customers came just in the nick of time, saving her from one of her father's tirades. He would have ranted all night long about the loss of a slave and how bad luck only happened to him.

Sydnee understood that he was worried. She was all that he had left, and she wasn't much. He never recovered from the death of her mother, and then The Devil's Backbone fell onto hard times, and now the death of Margarite. It was a lot for him to bear.

Sydnee tossed the blood and urine soaked blanket outside and put a clean blanket on Margarite's bed. At last she could drop down, exhausted from the grief and sorrow of the day. She knew that sleep would not come easily, but she had to try.

The spirits blessed Sydnee at last with some rest, but after a few hours she was awakened again with a jolt. "Girl, get up here!"

Sydnee sat up, her heart hammering.

"Girl!"

It was her father roaring for her. Sydnee stumbled to her feet. Bursting out the shed door, she ran up the path in the rain, splashing mud everywhere. The dogs scrambled out from under the shed and followed.

Lamplight glowed inside the cabin, and she saw two donkeys tied up in front. She ran up the steps and stopped, quickly realizing that her father and the customers were there on the porch. Her father was in his rocker; one customer was in a chair with his leg slung over the arm, and the other leaned on the porch railing, swinging a leg and paring his nails. All of their faces were in the shadows.

"These here men would like some company tonight," her father said, wiping his mouth with his sleeve. He passed a jug to the man in the chair next to him.

Sydnee stood before them panting. Her hair was wet and plastered to her head, and her smock was soaked. She felt their eyes on her and heard the rain running off the roof of the porch.

"Well," her father said in a businesslike tone while he rocked. "Who wants to go first?"

There was a bright glow from the pipe of the customer as he drew smoke, looking at Sydnee.

Sydnee was scared. She knew the pain would be too much to bear so shortly after childbirth.

The man sitting on the railing quit paring his nails, slipped his penny knife into his pocket and stood up. "I'll go first," he said in a husky voice.

Looking at her father frantically, Sydnee blurted, "Papa, you forget, it was just yesterday I delivered a baby."

Silence. The only sound was rain spattering on the ground.

The man looked at Victor and drawled, "You said she was fresh as the mornin' dew."

Sauveterre sputtered, "But--"

The other customer stood up, put on his hat and announced, "Come on, Rufus. Let's go to Shoat's. He's got girls."

"No, no," pleaded Sauveterre, jumping to his feet. "My girl is fine and dandy and ready for some slap and tickle. She's just a little shy. That's all."

The men mounted their donkeys with Sauveterre at their heels. "There's no call to leave," he pleaded.

They kicked their donkeys and headed up The Trace in the pouring rain.

Sauveterre watched them leave, and then whirled around, back-handing Sydnee. The force of the blow sent her staggering.

"You had to open your goddamned mouth!" he barked.

Panting, he looked at the men leaving and then started into the cabin. Changing his mind, he marched back down the steps and slapped her again, this time even harder. "I'll teach you," he snarled.

She toppled a few steps backward again and covered her head with her arms. Grabbing her hair, he drew back and slapped her again and again, following her down the path as she retreated.

Suddenly he exclaimed, "What the--"

Baloo and Atlantis leaped of the woods and charged him.

Sauveterre had forgotten. He had always given beatings inside the cabin to avoid the dogs. Baloo was the first to reach him. The massive dog took a running jump and toppled Sauveterre over into the mud. Next Atlantis was upon him, clamping onto his throat and thrashing back and forth, snarling and tearing at the arteries of his neck. Baloo ripped at his groin, and legs.

Sydnee was stunned. She screamed for the dogs to retreat, but in their fury, they did not hear her.
Somehow Sauveterre kicked off Baloo and struggled to his feet. Atlantis was harder to dislodge. She continued to dangle from his neck, like a huge goiter. He tried to free himself by clawing at her jaws and swinging her around, but it was no use. The ancestral memory of her breed was at work, and she hung on tenaciously. Blood was soaking his pants and running down his neck.

Baloo began tearing at his legs again. The snarling of the dogs rose to a crescendo. Sydnee rushed forward to help, but her father swung Atlantis around and smashed her in the face with the dog. She tumbled back onto the ground, hitting her head on a rock. The last thing she saw before she blacked out was Vivian watching the attack passively from a tree. For the first time in her life, the crow seemed to approve of the dog's behavior.

$$* \qquad * \qquad *$$

The sun was up when Sydnee recovered consciousness. She was covered with dried mud, and her head throbbed. Vivian, ever vigilant, remained in the tree watching over her. It took a moment to sweep the cobwebs from her mind, but then she remembered.

She looked around frantically for her father. There was blood on the ground and shredded garments everywhere, but no trace of the man. The dogs were missing too.

Maybe Papa got away. Maybe he is up at the cabin.

Sydnee staggered toward the shack and then stopped. There was a trail of blood on a path of crushed weeds as if something heavy had been dragged into the woods. Her eyes followed the path. At the edge of the tree line, she saw feet.

Her legs turned to jelly, and her palms began to perspire. She could see from a distance that her father had on only one boot. The other foot was bare and bent at an unusual angle. He was on his back, and his pants were shredded.

Reluctantly she approached the body. Terror seized her as she leaned forward, pushing back the brush. One glimpse was all she needed to know that he was dead. The contents of her stomach rose into her mouth, and she retched. Sydnee was stunned. Everything happened so fast in the past few days that she was in shock. Her entire world had changed, and suddenly she was all alone.

Taking a deep breath, she waded through the weeds back to the cabin. She returned with a blanket, rolled her father onto it and then dragged him into the meadow.

Drenched with perspiration and nausea, Sydnee dug a hole. Several times she stopped and dropped to her knees panting, wondering why she felt no sorrow. She was burying her father, her own flesh and blood, but there were no tears. There was no despair. She felt nothing, except shame for not caring.

When she was almost done, she dropped the spade, put her hands on her hips and arched her back. She was trembling from exhaustion, and her head ached. Adding to her misery was the fact that her breasts had engorged with milk and were tender and sore.

Sydnee brushed the wet hair from her eyes and picked up the spade again. Something caught her eye. The dogs were watching her from the woods.

*   *   *

Sick and exhausted, Sydnee collapsed into bed that night. She decided to sleep in the shed inviting Baloo and Atlantis to join her. The dogs approached her cautiously, unsure of her feelings after the attack. They eased down stiffly beside her on the quilt, stealing furtive glances at her. It was not until she snuggled up beside them that they relaxed.

All night long she felt the presence of Margarite and her father. They were not at peace, and she could feel their restlessness. Sydnee could not find the rest she needed until late the next morning, and then she slept steadily for almost two days. It was a heavy, dreamless sleep while she healed from the tribulations. She rose only to eat, feed the dogs and relieve herself.

Late on the second night, the scream of a panther awakened her. The dogs were immediately on guard with their ears perked. The sound was not uncommon, but it always alarmed them. Sydnee listened outside for a long time, but all was quiet.

She stared at the ceiling considering her future. It was comforting to know that at least she had The Devil's Backbone to fall back upon. She could feed herself off the land, and Vivian, Baloo and Atlantis provided the companionship she needed. She would never be hungry *or* lonely.

Nevertheless Margarite's words nagged her. "Leave here. You are not listening to the spirits."

Sydnee sat up and ran her fingers through her hair. Anxiety flooded her. "Why must I leave?" she blurted. "I have nowhere to go. I don't understand, and I am scared, Margarite."

Swallowing hard, she threw back the covers, retrieved an egg from the cupboard and then ladled water into the glass bowl on the altar. After sweeping the egg over her body, she cracked it quickly and dropped the white into the water.

Taking a deep breath, she prayed and watched. The egg white dropped slowly in a solid mass to the bottom of the bowl. Fragments of something began to unfold, but it was not clear to her yet what the egg was divining. She closed her eyes, asking the spirits for guidance. A sudden draft blew into the room as if someone opened a window. The wind chimes moved, and Sydnee's hair blew.

She let her head roll back and closed her eyes. She was about to have a vision. The scene unfolded at last. Margarite and her father were arguing. Victor pushed the old woman backward, and she fell to the floor. She saw him yank the baby away from Margarite and walk out the door.

Now it was clear. What she dismissed as delirium the night she gave birth, had been true. She had actually witnessed her father taking her newborn.

Horror shot through her like a bolt of lightning. Her head snapped forward, and her eyes opened. She grabbed the roots of her hair and screamed. The dogs jumped to their feet, terrified.

Sydnee burst out of the shed and ran up the path toward the water. The sun was just rising over Plum Creek as she plunged into the water searching madly for the remains of her child. She traversed the stream, back and forth, up and down, searching the muddy bottom for the body of her little girl. At last she collapsed on the grassy bank and sobbed. In the end, she gained nothing except the revelation that her father had indeed been a monster.

*   *   *

By afternoon, a cold determination settled over Sydnee. She took what she needed from Margarite's cupboard, rolled the crucifix and wind chimes into a blanket, and tied the bundle to a sturdy branch.

After putting food into packs and strapping them to the dog's backs, she went into the Sauveterre cabin one last time. On her father's bed, where she endured the groping of so many strangers, she started a fire and then stepped outside to watch. Smoke belched out of the window and then poured out the door. Flames climbed quickly up the brittle walls to the moss covered roof and climbed into the morning sky.

In a matter of moments, the house was an inferno. With Vivian on her shoulder and the dogs at her feet, Sydnee turned her back on The Devil's Backbone and left forever.

Chapter 5

Every step Sydnee took away from The Devil's Backbone, she felt stronger. The darkness that hung over her like a decaying shroud had lifted. It was replaced with warm sun and vivid color. She raised her face to the clear sky with a smile on her lips as she watched birds careening overhead. Her joy was contagious, and Baloo and Atlantis trotted alongside her happily. Vivian came too, flying from tree to tree, swollen with importance, overseeing the journey.

Sydnee knew very little about her future, but she did know that her destination must be the big river to the west, the Mississippi. This great water, of which they spoke, is where all life seemed to originate.

Overhearing customer's talk, Sydnee knew that The Trace would end in the town of Natchez where she would find the great waterway. It was said that Natchez was the wealthiest city in the United States. The rich soil yielded huge cotton crops, and fortunes were made there every day. Located on the mighty Mississippi, Natchez exported goods around the world, making the residents fantastically wealthy.

Although she was still weak from childbirth, Sydnee walked for hours that first day without stopping. She was trying to put as much distance as possible between her and The Devil's Backbone. The day was hot, but they were surrounded on all sides by lush green darkness. The trees formed a canopy overhead, sheltering them from the blistering sunlight of midday.

When the air grew sultry, they stopped to bathe in a small lake. It felt delicious, and it was tempting to linger, but Sydnee spied an alligator slide silently into the water looking for a hearty meal. She had to whistle briskly for Atlantis, who was frolicking in the water, to come ashore quickly. Before continuing, Sydnee applied a solution of cloves, alcohol and oil to her skin to repel the onslaught of bugs along on the densely forested trail.

Late in the afternoon, steep banks rose up on either side of the path as they walked. The embankments were from ruts carved deeply into the soft earth by countless wagons, mules and horses traveling on The Trace. The scars were so deep one could not see over either side of the hills.

The dogs went instantly on alert as they passed through the dark furrow. Sydnee was on guard as well. She heard these places were hideouts for bandits and cutthroats who preyed upon unsuspecting travelers. Luckily, they were unmolested. It seemed that too few people passed this way anymore for it to be a profitable haunt for bandits. Sydnee breathed a sigh of relief. All day long they traveled without incident, seeing only one man who merely lifted his hat and said, "Howdy, ma'am".

The dogs carried packs on their backs, loaded with meat, cornbread and eggs. Sydnee slaughtered and cooked chickens before they left, but the meat would have to be eaten shortly. There had been no time to smoke it or salt it properly. The journey to Natchez would take a week, and she had to ration the food carefully.

When the sun set at last, Sydnee found a small clearing, well hidden from the trail, and draped a quilt over a low branch. Clipping one end shut with clothes pins, she draped a long veil of muslin netting from a hat she found on the trail, over the other end of the tent to allow air to circulate. After strewing pine needles and soft leaves on the ground, she snapped a quilt open for their bed and then invited the dogs in for the night. They slept heavily until the sun rose the next morning, at which time Vivian nagged and cawed at them to rise.

Sydnee stepped out of the tent and stretched. She rubbed her eyes and gazed up at the clear sky. She had never felt such happiness. For the first time in her life, she was at peace and felt safe. Although Margarite was gone from this earth, Sydnee could hear her voice encouraging her and giving her direction. She felt the spirits with her too. Their presence was everywhere, particularly in the sheltering arms of the trees.

Sydnee ran her fingers through her hair and put on her hat. It was a man's hat, dirty with a wide brim that lost it shape and drooped, but it protected her from the sun and the bugs, particularly when she draped the veil over it. She winced when she took a step. In spite of years without shoes, her bare feet were still sore.

She took down the tent, rolled everything up and tied the bundle back onto her stick. Next she built a fire and cooked some eggs and Johnny cakes in the small cast-iron pan that she brought along. She made enough breakfast for the dogs as well.

Vivian resented the dogs receiving a free handout. The crow walked around the fire glaring at Sydnee, looking for her share. Nevertheless Sydnee gave little to the bird. The crow foraged and scavenged successfully all day long, whereas the dogs would have to hunt if Sydnee did not feed them. There was little time for that undertaking.

They passed many stands like The Devil's Backbone on their journey, but they had all been abandoned, remnants of an earlier time when overland travel was the only way to the north. It was a lonely sight, doors left open, roofs caved in, split rail fences crumbling, and nature reclaiming the landscape. Sydnee considered entering these stands to search for discarded tools or clothing and then reconsidered. She did not want to surprise any wildlife inside or risk injury from the shacks collapsing.

At sunset on the third day of their journey, they passed an active stand. There were men sitting on the porch, drinking from jugs and smoking. They were dressed in rags and had long tobacco-stained beards. When they saw her, they hooped and hollered, whistling and shouting profanities. They told her to come and drink with them and take turns pleasuring them.

Sydnee held her breath and walked past, not making eye contact. Even Vivian and the dogs did not acknowledge the men. They walked by quickly and cautiously, and much to their relief, the men did not follow them. Even though Sydnee knew the dogs would protect her, the canines were no match for firearms.

There was a lot of time for Sydnee to consider her future as she walked along The Trace. At the top of her list was earning a living. When she reached Natchez, she decided that she would find work on one of the plantations. Maybe she could pick cotton, plant or help with household tasks. In a town the size of Natchez, there was sure to be employment.

She also took time to appreciate the beauty of The Trace too. It was midsummer, and the wildflowers were in bloom. Thick hedges of purple flowers that looked like thistle lined the trail along with yellow daisies, wild roses, and orchids. The smell of the air was thick with fragrance, especially late in the afternoon, when the air was heavy. At night the moonlight dappled the floor of the forest, illuminating white wildflowers as the crickets sang.

A day never passed without rain, but Sydnee welcomed it and found it refreshing. It cooled the heavy coats of the dogs while it soaked her clothing and skin. On two occasions when the wind was right, she thought she heard a whistle blowing in the distance. But she could not imagine what this could be and put it down to fancy.

On the fifth day, they heard a woman calling from her stand on a hill. She was an old lady, hunched over with age with skin like brown leather. Her cheeks and lips were sunken, but her smile was warm and friendly.

"Howdy, lil darlins'," she called. "Can you see fit to keep an old woman company? I ain't seen no one now for near seven days."

Sydnee lifted up her veil and climbed the hill, smiling. "Of course."

The dogs trotted up to the woman, and she stroked their heads.

"Come take a load off. The name's Nell Patchett," she said, pointing a skeletal hand at a porch chair.

Sydnee sat down with a sigh. She had not been in a chair for almost a week, and her back was grateful. The dogs dropped down beside her. Vivian landed in the yard searching for grasshoppers.

"I don't have much food since my husband died a month ago," the old woman said, easing herself down stiffly into a rocker.

"W--we have plenty for us all," Sydnee said shyly, embarrassed of her stutter. She had never been comfortable with strangers, but she forced herself to ask, "Y-you have lost your husband?"

"Yezum, a month ago. I miss him terrible," she said, her voice cracking.

Sydnee turned in her chair to look at the decrepit cabin. It was in worse shape than The Devil's Backbone. One side of the shack had caved in, and a straw mattress was on the floor in the opposite corner. They were no farm animals and no chickens in the yard.

Sydnee built a fire under the tripod in the yard, and using the old woman's crucible, she cooked up a chicken stew. They sat on the porch and ate.

"You sure are a pretty little thing," the old woman said, gumming her corn bread and looking at Sydnee.

Embarrassed, Sydnee smiled and looked down.

"You headed to Natchez?" Mrs. Patchett asked.

"Yes, is it close?"

"Almost a week's walk."

Sydnee looked up abruptly. "A week?"

Her heart sank. She had enough food for only three more days. Nevertheless she was more concerned about the old woman. She rehearsed her words in her head and then said, "How w-will you make it here all alone? Come with us."

The old woman cackled. "These ol' legs can barely make it down to get water. No ma'am, I lived here, and I die here," and she held out her bowl for another helping.

Sydnee nodded and brought her more stew. The sun was starting to go down, and the old woman suggested they stay at her stand for the night. Sydnee agreed and pitched her tent over a limb in the yard.

The next morning, they said farewell. It rained off and on for several hours, and when the sun finally came out around midday, Sydnee decided to rest and eat. She sat down on the banks of a creek and took the pack off Baloo's back. When she flipped it open, the bag was filled with rocks.

Sydnee's jaw dropped. She leaped to her feet and opened the pack Atlantis was carrying. It too was filled with rocks. She realized then that the old woman had taken their food during the night and put rocks in the packs instead.

Sydnee put her hands to her face. What would they eat? They had a week of traveling left. She knew that she could fish and the dogs could hunt, but this all took time. She took her hat off and rubbed her brow. She felt a headache coming on. She dug inside her pack for a net. She would have to craw fish, if she wanted to eat.

Sydnee tried to swallow her fury at the old crone. She knew she was needy, but she had stolen everything they had brought along.

"Howdy!" a voice called. A stocky man with a big stomach waddled across the rickety creek bridge. He was leading a mule. The wood groaned under the strain of the weight. He had a closely cropped beard and a bald head.

Sydnee nodded coolly and went back to sweeping her net on the creek bottom. She'd had enough of strangers for one day.

"Which way you headed?"

"Natchez," she replied.

The man looked at the rocks strewn on the ground near the packs and whistled. "Hew-wee! You musta met up with Nelly Patchett."

Sydnee looked at him sharply. "We did."

"She's all that's left of the old time Trace swindlers. She still using the Conklin Stand?"

Sydnee stared at him, dumbfounded.

"The one with the side caved in?" he continued.

She nodded.

The man began to laugh, his belly bouncing. "God damn! I bet she told you that her husband just died and that's her house. Well it ain't! She lives in a nice little place down by Jackson. By the looks of ya, she didn't get any money. That's what she's really after."

Sydnee's jaw tightened.

"Well, it does my heart good to see that there is still a few of 'em left. Those were the good ol' days, you know," the man reflected wistfully. "The days when The Trace was alive and full of good folks."

He did not notice Sydnee gathering up her things.

He shook his head, as he reminisced. "There was Hoppin' John Tate and Harry Spoiler--" Suddenly he realized, she was leaving and he called, "Hey little lady. Why are you leavin'? "

Sydnee did not look back.

*   *   *

Traveling was more difficult now thanks to Nell Patchett. Sydnee had to stop and fish, forage for berries, and the dogs had to hunt. It did not take the canines long to understand they had to fend for themselves. On the second day of their ordeal, Baloo presented a squirrel to Sydnee for her supper. She was touched by his gesture, and her eyes filled with tears. Squatting down, she hugged the dog's neck and murmured, "You're a good ol' boy."

After that Baloo and Atlantis did not consume their kills, rather they brought the meat to Sydnee for everyone to share. She cooked rabbit or squirrel along with fish every night followed by a dessert of berries. The portions were not huge but the group managed to survive.

The journey now seemed endless to Sydnee. The remainder of the trek should have taken a week, but because of hunting, the time now doubled. Everyone in the group was losing weight. Tempers ran high as well, and spats broke out regularly between the dogs and Vivian.

Late one afternoon when the sun was setting, Sydnee allowed the dogs to run ahead. Vivian had been squabbling with them all day, and Sydnee needed a break.

Sydnee was walking along unconcerned when suddenly there was a blood curdling screech behind her. Turning abruptly, she saw Vivian pecking at the head of a large, burly man. He dropped into a crouch as the bird pecked furiously at his eyes and pulled out his hair. He had been about to attack Sydnee.

The man ran into the woods, terrified as Vivian swooped at him and screeched. Hearing the commotion, the dogs charged, but Sydnee stopped them. She did not want to witness another kill like her father.

Sydnee smiled as Vivian soared back through the trees toward them. She raised her arm, and the crow landed on her. Sydnee kissed her head, praising her for a job well done.

The next day, it was apparent that they were getting close to Natchez. They passed more people on the trail, and there were more crossroads with active stands. Around midday they came upon a couple traveling to market with fresh produce. The young man was pulling the cart and his wife was riding in the back, her bare feet dangling. She held a tiny baby in her arms.

"Howdy," she called to Sydnee, swinging her legs. She wore a faded yellow bonnet, an old blue dress, and a gray apron. Her feet were dirty, but her face and hands were clean.

The young man put the cart down and turned around to greet Sydnee too. He was dressed in rags as well, but his hair was clean, and his demeanor was friendly. His lifted his tattered straw hat, mopped his brow and nodded a greeting.

"Where you come from?" the girl asked.

"Devil's Backbone Stand on The Trace," Sydnee replied.

"Come far?" the young man asked.

"Over two weeks walk." Sydnee said. "Would--would you know of any work around Natchez?"

The girl studied her a moment and said, "You sound French. You French?'

Sydnee shook her head.

"I reckon San-Souci plantation might need help," the young man said. "Head left at the fork. You'll be off The Trace, but keep followin' the trail. It'll take you right down to the plantation."

"Thank you," Sydnee murmured.

"God's speed," the girl called.

Sydnee turned left at the fork feeling hopeful about the future. *Perhaps it is cotton picking time, or maybe there are vegetables to harvest. Surely these large plantations have work.*

She spied a patch of blue beyond the trees, and her heart lurched. Is it possible? And she walked a little farther. "There it is!" she cried.

Sydnee began to run, stopping with a jolt before she fell down a steep embankment. Throwing her hat, she dropped her pack and grabbed the trunk of a tree, swinging forward to look at the Mississippi River. Her mouth dropped open in awe as it stretched out before her in all of its glory. Never had she seen anything so magnificent! The panorama was breathtaking. White clouds climbed overhead like huge ghosts ascending to the heavens, with the wide river rippling noiselessly below. The sun seemed to glimmer on the surface like sparks of white fire.

She slid down the riverbank, clutching branches and trees for support. The underbrush was thick with orange tiger lilies, and when she reached the shore, she stepped out onto a large boulder, putting her hand up to shade her eyes. The dogs joined her as Vivian soared overhead, riding the air currents.

Sydnee had never seen anything so beautiful, and she fell in love with the Mississippi instantly. A light breeze lifted her hair and tossed it around her face. The air was cool and tinged with the scent of fish.

Suddenly there was a blast of noise more deafening than any clap of thunder. Terrified, Sydnee dropped into a crouch, covering her head. The dogs charged back up the hill in a panic. There was a rhythmic splash, splash of water and a deep rumbling.

Cautiously, Sydnee stood up. There in front of her, gliding on the water, was a moving mansion which was propelled by a large red wheel churning water from the back.

There was another blast and black smoke belched from a tall, fluted stack on the roof. Sydnee covered her ears, but this time she did not crouch. She knew that she was seeing her first riverboat. The stern-wheeler was white and several stories high, all trimmed in gold.

So these are the famous steamboats of the Mississippi.

The women strolled carelessly on deck with colorful parasols, resting on their shoulders as the gentlemen leaned on the railings, dressed in fine suits, smoking cigars.

Sydnee memorized every inch of the riverboat as it went by. She noted the white shuttered doors and the gilded arches, the red paddle wheel, and the two black smoke stacks. When she spied a square piece of fabric, flapping atop a tall pole, she shaded her eyes to see more clearly. It had a curious design of red and white stripes next to a blue square with a circle of stars. It was pretty.

Sydnee dropped her hand and sighed. More than anything else in this world, she wanted to ride a riverboat. It was the most beautiful thing she had ever seen. As she watched it fade into the distance, the smile faded from her face as well.

Just as she was about to climb back up the hill, she saw another boat come around the bend. She heard about these crafts all her life, but this was more than she expected. A massive floating barge, the Mississippi broadhorn was more than two stories high. Sydnee blinked in amazement. She spied cows and goats on board, pens of chickens, spinning wheels, tables and chairs which were lashed to the roof. There were small tents down below and even a loom. Men stood with oars at the sides of the massive raft, guiding the floating village. Sydnee noticed women preparing food in a fire pit right on board the boat while others hung laundry up to dry. Some of the children were fishing off the side and one of them waved to her.

These were different from the privileged people of the exquisite paddle wheeler. Their clothing was homespun, worn and faded, and the children had no shoes, but Sydnee heard laughter, and the children were singing.

Sydnee sat down on the bank to see what else may turn up on this busy waterway. After a few moments, a dugout canoe came by paddled by Indians, and then a keelboat sailed around the bend with a young man playing music. He sat on the edge of the boat with his feet dangling in the water, clasping a box which he collapsed in and out. Sydnee had never seen or heard anything like it. The box created a whimsical wheezing sound, and the music rolled across the water as clear as a bell. The dogs were fascinated and listened with their heads cocked.

Sydnee shook her head in amazement at the traffic on this great river. She could pass the entire day watching this endless parade and never become bored. Reluctantly, she turned to go, and the dogs bounded up the riverbank behind her with Vivian in the rear.

Chapter 6

Deep ruts lined the path to the San-Souci plantation. The day was coming to a close, and when they reached the outskirts of the plantation, it was dusk. Sydnee stayed in the bushes to survey the grounds before approaching anyone. Snapping her fingers, she signaled for the dogs, and they sat down quietly behind her.

She ran her eyes along the open field. Rows of black slaves were bent over hoes, chopping and plucking weeds from the rich black soil. They were in shabby homespun clothing and sweat glistened on their dark skin. Most were as thin as skeletons, and their faces were heavily creased. Some of the women wore *tignons*, a few wore bonnets, and the men worn ragged straw hats.

Watching them work, Sydnee realized that she missed cotton planting, but perhaps they were starting a different crop. Taking off her hat, she smoothed her hair, straightened her dress and stepped out into the field.

The hands stole looks at her, but they did not stop their hoeing. Several of them glanced around for the overseer, but they did not call to him. Sydnee caught sight of the big house in the distance. It was a sprawling two-story dwelling with white pillars and galleries wrapping around the top and bottom floors. A graceful stairway ran up either side of the entrance and candlelight twinkled in every window. Sydnee's heart fluttered; never had she seen such grandeur.

"Say there! What's your business?" someone barked.

Sydnee jumped, and the dogs stiffened as a white man strode up with a whip in his hand. He was short but massively built. The sleeves of his sweat-stained shirt were rolled up, revealing strong arms covered with curly black hair. He was frowning.

Sydnee stuttered, "I-I was wondering if you have—have work?"

"Not for trash like you," was his abrupt reply. "Now git," he ordered, gesturing toward the woods. "Or I'll give you a taste of this whip!"

Sydnee stared at him a moment, and then turned away. She could feel the eyes of all the field hands upon her as she walked back to the woods. Standing for a long time in the trees, Sydnee tried to quell her humiliation. The dogs sat down, leaning against her legs. Lifting her chin, she took a deep breath and started to walk again.

Over the next three days, Sydnee was met with rejection after rejection. Up and down the river road she traveled, stopping at plantations, going to small farms, asking strangers for work. She heard the same reply again and again, "We got our niggers. There's no work for you."

Frustrated and afraid, she considered returning to The Devil's Backbone. It would be easy to live off the land and lead the life of a recluse, but her bitter memories returned, and she dismissed the idea.

Hungry and discouraged, Sydnee headed for Natchez. Searching in town was her last resort. Even though her homespun demeanor and backwoods speech would be met here with scorn, she was desperate. Her stomach yearned for food, and she was getting frantic.

Just before town, Sydnee ducked under a willow by the river and pulled up her legs, resting her chin on her knees. She needed to gather her strength. Baloo and Atlantis sat down beside her, sensing her despair. The green drapes of the willow swayed gently as Sydnee opened her being to the spirits, filling her lungs with the sweet breath of the tree. She closed her eyes and listened. The voices grew stronger. "Have faith," they whispered. "We will take care of you. Your path will be revealed."

Sydnee sighed and opened her eyes. At the top of the tree she could see Vivian riding a branch in the wind. She remembered something Margarite told her once about the birds of the air. *They neither sow nor reap; yet the heavenly Father feeds them.*

"I will find work today. I can feel it," she said to the dogs, planting a kiss on each of their heads. When she stepped out from under the tree, Vivian dove down and landed on her shoulder.

When Sydnee arrived at last in Natchez, she was overwhelmed. This town was no cluster of cabins hastily constructed along the Mississippi River. There were no barns, sheds or shabby outbuildings littering this landscape. Instead the streets of Natchez were lined with trim, thriving businesses and lavish estates. Manicured boulevards wound past plantation homes bordered by wrought-iron fences and gates which opened onto gardens bursting with flowers and fountains. Lush lawns swept up to palatial estates which were monuments to cotton, slavery, and the power of the Mississippi. Like San-Souci all the homes had porches with white pillars and tall, shuttered windows stretching from floor to ceiling.

Leaning on the ornate iron gate of one of the homes, Sydnee closed her eyes and took a breath. The sweet fragrance of flowers filled her nostrils, and the breeze whispered as it moved through the dogwood and hawthorn trees.

It was the middle of the afternoon, and all activity ceased in the town during the heat of the day. She spied two boys walking toward her eating apples and carrying burlap bags. One had red hair and freckles, and the other had a pug nose and shaggy hair. They were about her age.

She didn't notice them elbow each other when they saw her. She mistook their smirks for smiles.

"*P-pardon*," she stammered in her French patois. Swallowing hard, she started over. "I beg your pardon. Would you know of any work?"

The boy with the pug nose mocked her. "W-well, yes we do. Y-you are in luck."

Sydnee's heart jumped, and she looked eagerly from one to the other.

"Tell her, Will," the pug-nosed boy said, poking his friend in the ribs.

The freckled-faced boy looked confused, and then his friend nodded toward the big house. He perked up and said, "Oh! Go right up there, knock on the door in the back, and ask for Angelique. She'll have something for ya'll."

Wide-eyed, Sydnee nodded and said, "Thank you."

Starting for the gate, she hesitated.

The pug nosed boy waved in the direction of the house. "Go on!"

Telling the dogs to stay, Sydnee reluctantly opened the gate and walked up the service driveway to the back of the house. Her mouth was dry, and her hands were shaking. It was terrifying approaching such a grand home, but Sydnee mustered all her courage and walked on. When she reached the back of the house she hesitated, wiping her hands on her smock. She did not want to knock on the door.

The moment she raised her hand, the door flew open and a tall slave with an angular face loomed over her.

The woman scowled. "What you want?"

Sydnee opened her mouth, but no words would come.

"I just ask you. What you want?"

It was like Sydnee's tongue was glued to the roof of her mouth.

The woman's eyes narrowed. "We got nothin' for you here. Riff-raff like you belongs Under the Hill!"

Before Sydnee had time to turn around, the woman took a dish towel and started to shoo her away like she was a stray dog. She started to run, and the woman chased her all the way down the driveway. Mortified, she could hear the boys in the distance howling with laughter and calling her a "Kaintuck."

Panting, Sydnee turned toward the river. She didn't know where she was going, but she knew that she had to get away from this part of town. She did not feel good enough to be among these fine folk. Tears began to run down her face. The road ran parallel to the river and sloped sharply downhill. It was lined with businesses and warehouses, and it took several hairpin turns before it reached the busy landing where five steamboats were moored and flatboats as well.

With her ragged hat pulled low, Sydnee never looked at anyone. She was blinded by humiliation and rage at the boys who played her for a fool. She did not stop until she reached the base of the hill by the river. Standing for a long time with her heart pounding, she realized at last that she was in the shade of a building which stood over her head on pilings. All the businesses on the landing were on stilts along the river. Hastily constructed shabby structures, the buildings teetered precariously over mounds of debris and garbage. Sydnee wrinkled her nose at the decaying fish and feces. She realized suddenly that the dogs were nosing around in the trash, and Vivian was picking at fish bones.

"No!" she called to them.

Atlantis began retching. "Come!" Sydnee commanded and then turned and walked briskly back up the hill with the dogs trotting behind her.

For the first time, Sydnee realized the area was alive with activity. *This must be Natchez Under-the-Hill.* She looked up at the bluff overhead lined with fine homes and then down at the decrepit whore houses, saloons and warehouses on the muddy road below. Mules strained up the hill, pulling wagons full of barrels and crates from the riverboats. Draymen snapped whips barking orders at the beasts. Riverboat men lounged in the shade. All of them were heavily-built men with thick muscles and leathery skin. They watched the activity on the streets and exchanged news while chewing their tobacco which they would spit in long brown streams.

The sun was setting and Sydnee saw whores coming out onto porches, fanning themselves and starting to solicit business. Advertising to customers walking below, they would pull up their skirts and put a leg up on the railing so the men could look at their privates. Boys whooped and hollered, while older men acted amused.

All of these images were familiar to Sydnee. These were the people who frequented The Devil's Backbone. *The house darky at the plantation was right. Natchez Under-the-Hill is where I belong.*

Sydnee squeezed her eyes shut and took a deep breath. She made her decision. Someday she would find other work, but for now this is what she must do. She scanned the storefronts for possibilities. Many of the whorehouses had saloons on the street level, and Sydnee decided against these. Walking into a drinking establishment alone was not an option.

At last she saw a *fille de joie* escort a john up a short set of steps and into a wooden building with shutters and a sign out front. A young, black boy sat on the step guarding the customer's horses.

Sydnee took a deep breath and stepped up to him to ask about work. He nodded and said to ask for Miss Magdalene. Sydnee told the dogs to stay and knocked on the door.

A large man with a black mustache appeared and escorted her down a dark hall to the back of the building. It was hot and stuffy inside the house, and Sydnee felt queasy. The man told her to wait in the hall and disappeared into a room, shutting the door behind him. She could hear a female inside the room scolding someone. Her voice grew louder, and then there was a string of obscenities from someone else and a smashing of glass. Next there was the shuffle of feet, more swearing and a door slammed.

Sydnee swallowed hard and waited. The man opened the door at last. He jerked his head and said, "Madame Magdalene." Sydnee walked into the room as he walked out. It was a small office with two upholstered chairs and a desk. It smelled of smoke and heavy perfume. A tall, thin woman with extremely white skin and long smooth black hair was emptying broken glass into a waste bin. She wore a red wrap tied loosely around her waist. She turned and opened the window drapes. The room was instantly flooded with the red glow of the setting sun. Sydnee could now see Madame Magdalene more clearly. Although her body was slim and erect, she was not young. The corners of her eyes were lined with wrinkles, and there were frown lines around her mouth. Her thin lips were painted a blood red which stood out against her white skin and jet black hair.

Madame Magdalene looked at Sydnee at last. Lighting tobacco, she asked quietly, "You want work?"

"Yes, Madame."

"You have done this sort of work before?"

Sydnee nodded.

"Take off your hat."

Sydnee complied.

Madame Magdalene bent over and grabbed Sydnee's chin, turning her face from side to side.

"Any disease?"

"No," Sydnee replied.

The woman put a hand on her hip. "Where were you working?"

"For my father at a stand on The Trace."

The woman chuckled cynically. "For your father," she said, taking a puff of tobacco and blowing it out. "Well you are in luck. I am down a girl. You can start tonight. Come back in a few hours, and I will get you something to wear. Stop at the kitchen and get something to eat before you go."

"Thank you," Sydnee murmured.

The cook gave her a turkey leg, corn on the cob, and some biscuits. She almost swooned when she smelled the food. Racing down the steps, she found Vivian and the dogs, and they joyfully rushed to the shade of a tree to consume their meal.

When Sydnee was done, she sat back against the tree and sighed. Tonight she would have to work for her food, and she began to feel sick. The thought of men sweating and groaning over her made her want to retch.

Several hours later the torches were ablaze at Natchez Under-the-Hill. The revelry was in full swing as night fell. A steady stream of men roamed the streets, laughing and cursing, drinking and carousing. As Sydnee walked up the stairs to Madame Magdalene's establishment, she passed a tall immaculately dressed black man coming out of the house. He held a lace hankie to his nose, his hair was graying at the temples, and he wore an emerald-green frock coat with light pantaloons.

Sydnee was surprised to see someone of his gentility here, but she gave him no more thought and continued up the steps.

When he reached the sidewalk, he lowered his hankie and said, "Say there!" in French.

She turned around.

"What is your business in that place?"

Sydnee looked over her shoulder, unsure if he was addressing her.

"Yes, you," he stated sharply.

"I start my work here tonight."

He looked her up and down and said, "Come here."

She walked back down the stairs warily.

The man put the hankie back to his nose and ran his eyes over her, looking at her again. He cocked his head from one side to the other, looking first at her hair and then at her eyes. He walked around her several times appraising her figure and then asked, "How old are you?"

"Fifteen."

"Hmm, you need a bath," he observed. "Have you committed any crimes?"

She shook her head.

He continued to address her in French. "Disease?"

"*Non.*"

Lowering the hankie from his face, he said, "Although you have a patois, your French is tolerable."

Putting his fist to his mouth, he started to pace. He walked for so long he seemed to have forgotten her. Merry-makers staggered past him, tilting bottles to their lips, shouting and laughing. Whores could be heard hawking customers in the distance. Down by the landing a firearm discharged.

After a while Sydnee assumed he was done with her, and she started back up the stairs.

"Come back here," he barked.

Sydnee approached the man once more.

With his lip curled, he asked, "How would you like a job working for only one customer?"

"What would I do?"

"This filth," he said, nodding toward Madame Magdalene's house.

Sydnee blinked and asked, "Will I work for you?"

"No thank God," the man said, rolling his eyes. "For my master. He has sent me to Natchez to find—to find—a girl of your sort."

Swinging his cane, he said, "Come, we will talk elsewhere."

They pushed through the streets, torches blazing outside of every establishment. The thoroughfares were muddy and crowded as patrons zigzagged in and out of every saloon. Clearly disgusted by the rabble, the man picked his way delicately through the throng. Sydnee, Vivian and the dogs followed behind him in a line. When they got to the river, the man stopped and asked, "Are you aware that there are creatures following you?"

Sydnee nodded and said, "These are my friends."

"Well, tell them to wait here."

He turned and nodded to an attendant who was guarding the ramp of the paddle wheelers and said to Sydnee, "Come along!"

Sydnee thought she would be happy to be boarding a paddle wheeler, but instead she was nervous. Lanterns were hanging on the deck, shedding a dim golden light as she followed him onto the boat. The paddle wheeler was quiet and deserted. The man picked up a smoke pot to ward off mosquitos and set it by a table. He sat down, crossing his hands over the head of his cane and looked at her.

Sydnee stood before him, her eyes wide with expectation.

"First things first. My name is Maxime. I am acting on behalf of my master who lives in New Orleans. I have been instructed to find a--tutor—for his sixteen-year-old son. The boy has some habits which are unnatural, and we *do not* approve."

Maxime pursed his lips. "Although there are women of your sort in New Orleans, I have come all the way to Natchez because this is a matter of utmost secrecy. My young master's reputation is at stake as well as his father's reputation. You will live in New Orleans with the family, take a room in the servant's quarters and visit the young man as necessary in his *garçonnière*.

When Sydnee looked confused, he explained. "The *garçonnière* is a small building in back of the main house where young gentlemen reside."

"What will I teach him?" Sydnee asked.

Maxime clenched his jaw and looked from side to side. "*Mon Dieu!* Must I be explicit? The art of love—passion," he hissed, clearly embarrassed. "Most importantly, you will teach him to desire females."

They fell silent a moment. Sydnee could hear the river splashing gently against the hull of the steamboat.

"How old are you?" he asked.

Remembering that she just had a birthday within the past few weeks, she said, "Fifteen."

Maxime put the hankie back to his nose and said, "Well, the first thing you must learn is to bathe regularly and wear becoming clothes."

Sydnee nodded.

"Very well," Maxime stated, standing up. "Come back tomorrow at dawn. We will be taking this packet to New Orleans."

*　　　　　*　　　　　*

Sydnee found a private spot outside of town in the woods where she pitched a tent over a low branch. All night she was awake, listening to the dogs snore beside her. The thought of leaving her friends was torture. They were all she had in this world, and they had saved her life time and time again. Now she was betraying them. Yet the alternative was to stay in this filthy town and sell her body in a bordello. She would live day in and day out in squalor, risking disease and beatings, eventually dying in the street. Tears rolled down her face as she stroked their fur. The dogs thumped their tails and then drifted back to sleep, oblivious to her quandary.

At sunrise, Sydnee gave the last of her food to Vivian and the dogs, rolled up her pack, and headed for the landing. She felt as if her heart was being ripped from her chest.

Natchez Under-the-Hill was bustling with activity once more. Draymen were driving teams down the hill, overseers barked orders to slaves as dock workers loaded firewood, crates and barrels onto the riverboats. Cargo swung overhead, being loading onto the paddle wheelers that were parked at an angle along the shore. Whistles blasted, announcing riverboat departures, and each time the sound erupted, Baloo and Atlantis would drop into a crouch. Peddlers hawked their wares, pushing carts loaded with fresh produce and flowers. Servants and slaves pushed past Sydnee carrying steamer trunks on their backs bound for other river towns.

Most of the travelers at Natchez Under-the-Hill were boarding vessels headed upriver to Vicksburg, Memphis and St. Louis. They were trying to avoid not only the stifling heat and humidity, but the yellow fever and malaria which plagued the low country during midsummer. Once they arrived in the north, many paddle wheelers would drop anchor until the autumn. Then, once the river regained a safer depth, they would return the residents back to the south, after the oppressive heat ended and danger of contagion was past.

Black crew members in snappy uniforms stood officiously at the ramps, checking off passenger's names as they boarded the steamboats one by one. Sydnee blinked in amazement at the elegant gentlemen with ladies on their arms, looking cool and fresh in the latest fashions from Paris. *Marchandes,* or female peddlers, waited for them on deck, eager to sell nosegays of violets to the ladies and pralines to the children.

The only paddle wheeler headed to New Orleans was the *Vidalia*, and Sydnee stopped there. Maxime was standing at the railing, wearing an Aylesbury hat, cream-colored frock coat and dark pantaloons. His hands were gloved and folded on the head of his cane. He did not acknowledge Sydnee, but he knew she was there.

The whistle on the *Vidalia* blew. It was time for her to board, and her stomach was in knots. She swallowed hard and bent down in front of the dogs. Sensing something was wrong, they stopped panting and looked at her. Vivian sat on a mooring nearby watching.

"I must leave you now. It is our only hope."

The dogs stared up at her.

"You cannot come with me. Not this time. But I will be back for you, so you must never go far."

Tears pushed at her eyes. Sydnee stood up and looked at Vivian. "I leave you in charge. Take care of them and don't be too harsh."

Sydnee's chest heaved, and the dogs moved closer. Dropping down, she hugged their necks and said, "Thank you for saving my life--so many times."

The whistle blew again, and she stood up, abruptly cupping Vivian's head with her hand. "Goodbye."

When she started up the landing stage the dogs began to follow, and she ordered, "No!"

Maxime nodded to the crew member who allowed her to pass. Her dream had come true. She was on a magnificent paddle wheeler, but she didn't notice. She did not care. All she could see were Baloo, Atlantis and Vivian sitting on shore watching her leave.

The crew began to make preparations for departure. Orders were shouted, ropes were untied and people began to wave farewell.

Maxime saw the tears streaming down Sydnee's face. How ungrateful, he thought. *How incredibly lucky this dirty little waif is, and she doesn't appreciate it.* He shifted from one foot to the other, sniffing and looking away. Over and over he told himself that he was being so *very* magnanimous giving this child a fine home in New Orleans, but her tears bothered him.

The whistle blew for the final time, and he barked, "Oh, *Mon Dieu!*" Approaching a crew member, he said, "See those dogs down there? Put them on the next flatboat to New Orleans."

Sydnee whirled around and stared at Maxime with wide eyes.

"Yes, they are coming," he growled. "You spoiled little child."

Sydnee put her arm up, and Vivian landed on her sleeve.

"And keep that filthy bird away from me," he declared.

Chapter 7

The crew hoisted the landing stage, the whistle blew, and the big red paddle wheel started to churn. A sense of elation swept Sydnee from head to toe. She raised her head to catch the scent of the fresh river air, and a breeze blew through her hair. *At last I have direction. At last I have a future. The spirits had been right all along. I did find my way, and Baloo, Atlantis and Vivian did too.*

Shortly after they cast off, Maxime shooed Sydnee down to the lowest deck to be among the slaves and lower class passengers. He remained above to talk with the riverboat Captain, a man he had known for years.

Sydnee stood at the railing in the morning sun watching the paddles turn round and round and listening to the soothing splash, splash of water. She shaded her eyes to see the flatboat on which Atlantis and Baloo rode. She could just make out the dogs sitting side by side. It appeared as if the crew member found a little boy to watch them, and the child had his arm around Baloo's neck. Sydnee smiled. The dog was twice the size of the child.

Vivian was soaring overhead, coasting on the river winds keeping both the flat boat and the paddle wheeler in sight. Sydnee put her arm up, and she swept in for a landing. The crow landed gently on her forearm, and Sydnee stroked her head. "You are a good girl, but you must be on your best behavior. We are going to a beautiful new home, and we must make a good impression."

Vivian cocked her head, listening. They stood together for a long time watching the muddy water of the Mississippi and the green shoreline littered with fallen trees. Suddenly a young crew member jumped into a skiff and started rowing to shore. When he reached land, he jumped out and ran to a tree that had a red box nailed to it. Pulling out a piece of paper, he stuffed it in his shirt, jumped back into the skiff and returned to the paddle wheeler before it left him behind.

"The pilots leave notes for one another," Sydnee heard one of the passengers say on the deck above.

"Why is that?" a woman asked.

"To let each other know about river conditions or hazards ahead."

Sydnee smiled. Eager to see more of the paddle wheeler, she tossed Vivian back into the air and walked toward the bow. She edged her way through mounds of firewood, barrels, crates and bundles. Slaves and working class folk were sitting on the lower deck in the shadows of this cargo, playing cards, throwing dice and murmuring quietly to each other. They were not to disturb the fine ladies and gentlemen riding on the decks above.

Sydnee was glad for the fresh air when she reached the bow. This deck had an apron which thrust out in front of the boat where the landing stage was mounted. Sydnee walked to the end of the apron and turned around to see the other decks. The second deck had a lacy white railing and was lined with state rooms. Sydnee assumed these cabins were unoccupied because she overhead someone say the journey to New Orleans was only a day trip. She wondered what luxuries were behind those fancy white louvered doors. She imagined there to be soft feather beds with sumptuous linens, perfumed pillows and rich carpets.

The next level on the stern-wheeler was lined with beveled glass windows, and she wondered if this is where first class passengers were getting the cool drinks that they carried in frosty goblets. Sydnee did not dare gawk at these fine folk, but she did notice that the ladies wore grand gowns with huge puffy sleeves. Although the dresses were of lightweight, cool material, they were cinched tightly around the waist and dropped in heavy folds around the legs. They all wore wide brimmed bonnets as well, decorated with ribbons and flowers. These hats framed a sort of funnel around the ladies' faces, and she heard someone call them poke bonnets.

The men wore frock coats with crisp linen shirts and colorful waistcoats. They smoked cigars and moved about on the promenade deck with an arrogant authority, as if the world belonged to them. She noticed, for all their fine clothes and grand manners, none of them cut as elegant a figure as her patron, Maxime. She had never met anyone with so much style and dignity. It did not seem to be in keeping with being an enslaved gentleman.

They rode the river all afternoon and well into the evening. Maxime had a basket of fruit and bread sent down for her midday meal and red beans and rice for supper. She had no desire to mix with anyone, so she sat outside on the deck watching the river and the flatboat carrying Atlantis and Baloo.

Sometimes she would gaze up at the very top of the paddle wheeler where the pilot house was located. It amazed her how the crew could maneuver a huge boat with such skill, avoiding the fallen trees, rocks and snags, especially when they navigated into a landing.

Many times the *Vidalia* stopped at plantation landings to drop off or pick up passengers and goods. The crew would blow the whistle and children would come running, shouting, "Steamboat a'comin'!"

These landings were nothing more than docks with wooden platforms below the cotton fields. Sometimes peddlers would be waiting and board the boat to sell melons, chestnuts or newspapers. Sometimes they would sell the crew firewood to fuel the boilers.

As they came into one landing, Sydnee could see the white plantation house overlooking the river below, its tall pillars towering majestically over the rolling fields. It felt cool as they coasted into shore. The riverboat slid into the shade of the overhanging trees, lowered the landing stage and started to unload supplies. It surprised Sydnee when the flatboat with the dogs pulled up to the landing as well. They too had supplies for this planter.

She saw the little boy jump onto shore with the dogs right behind him. It was time to stretch their legs. Sydnee stood by the railing and watched, laughing as they chased each other back and forth along shore. The little boy threw a stick into the river, and

Atlantis launched herself in the water to fetch it. This game went on until the boy's father called for them to return to the flatboat, but the dogs did not respond. They sighted a rabbit and were chasing it.

Sydnee watched the child call to them repeatedly until at last, she shook her head in disgust and gave a sharp whistle. Two heads popped up from the brush and looked at her. "Go on!" she called, and flung her arm toward the flatboat. Atlantis tore toward the boat with Baloo lumbering along behind her. They jumped onto the craft just before it set off.

Evening was Sydnee's favorite time on the stern-wheeler. The river shimmered with a golden light, each ripple reflecting the slanting sunset. It was peaceful watching the herons strutting along the shore and the geese overhead, but what pleased Sydnee the most were the torch baskets and lanterns on the paddle wheeler when it was dark. It was beautiful to see the flames reflected in the river and watch the light dance over the deck. She spied several couples stealing kisses in the shadows.

Since it was dark, Vivian was able to fly in and rest on Sydnee's shoulder. She knew that the bird was tired from following the boat all day. They sat together in a dark corner on deck and dozed, listening to music from the deck above.

Suddenly Sydnee heard the bell ring from the pilot house followed by the whistle. She opened her eyes and saw the riverboat approaching the shore again which was ablaze with light.

Maxime was standing over her holding his valise. "You and the albatross follow me," he said.

Rubbing her eyes, she struggled to her feet with Vivian on her shoulder. The crow and Maxime were eye to eye. He glared at the bird and then turned and walked down toward the front of the boat where the first class passengers were disembarking. He waited until all of the white passengers were off the riverboat and then proceeded to walk down the landing stage with the slaves. Sydnee stayed close to him. The city of New Orleans seemed so large, and there were so many people.

The boy who was taking care of Baloo and Atlantis found Maxime, received payment and skipped off. Overwhelmed by the noise and activity, the dogs stayed at Sydnee's heels. The group pushed their way through the throngs of people on the docks, and entered a large square bordered on three sides by the biggest buildings Sydnee had ever seen. She thought that the structure in the center must be a church. It had three tall towers and a cross. She had no idea about the other two buildings. They were large imposing structures with many windows and a gallery along the street.

While she was gawking at the buildings, she bumped into Maxime. "Pay attention," he scolded.

They turned down a dark street, dimly lit by oil lamps on tall poles and lanterns hanging from buildings. Paved with cobblestones, the streets were lined with two-story town houses made of brick or stucco. Each adjoined the other and most had wrought-iron balconies and floor to ceiling shuttered windows. They passed enclosed courtyards hidden from view by tall stone walls and foliage. Sometimes Sydnee could hear fountains and the murmur of voices from within these gardens.

At last Maxime stopped to unlock a tall iron gate in front of a large stucco home on a corner. With Vivian still on her shoulder, Sydnee looked up at the second story. Each room had its own lacy balcony with green louvered shutters and French doors. They walked along a narrow carriageway which opened up into a lush courtyard with a three tiered fountain. The heady scent of flowers surrounded them. Moonlight filtered through the oaks and magnolias.

At one end of the courtyard there was a small stable where Maxime had Sydnee put the dogs. After she settled Atlantis and Baloo in for night, she tossed Vivian into the air where the bird nestled into a tree.

Maxime pointed out the necessary house by the stable and then gestured toward the other end of the courtyard at a building with a chimney. "That is where you will eat. It is the kitchen, and over there is *le garçonnière*. That's where the young gentleman resides."

Sydnee looked at the hexagon shaped two-story dwelling. Although it was separate from the main house, *le garçonnière* was decorated in the same style. It too had stucco siding with French doors, green shutters, and a second story with a miniature balcony.

Maxime took Sydnee into the house through the service entrance where he stopped at a cupboard to show her where the candles and lamps were stored. He handed her a small pewter container filled with whale oil and lit it. Sydnee marveled at the light that burned. It was smooth and smokeless, not like the nervous sputtering flame of a candle. Maxime carried a cut glass lamp and led Sydnee down a carpeted hall.

She sighed with pleasure as her feet sank into the plush Oriental rug which lined the hall. It reminded her of walking on a bed of moss. The house was quiet except for a ticking sound coming from a tall wooden box with a glass face standing in a corner. Sydnee wanted to examine this curiosity more closely, but she did not dare delay Maxime. She followed him up the stairs where a tawny-skinned woman was waiting with her arms crossed over her chest. She was tall with high cheekbones and heavy lidded, sultry eyes. Her stomach protruded slightly from pregnancy.

"So, you return at this ungodly hour and expect me to dance attendance on this little tart?" she exclaimed haughtily.

"I thank you to do your job without comment," Maxime replied. Turning to Sydnee, he said, "I leave you now with Giselle. But Mademoiselle, I must advise you to think long and hard before you steal anything from this home. Its value will never equal the opportunity you will find here."

Sydnee stared at him, wide-eyed. Maxime disappeared into the shadows, leaving Sydnee alone with the woman.

"This way," Giselle instructed, taking her down the hall. "This is where you will stay," and she opened the door to a bed chamber. It was a small room but lavishly appointed. The highly polished hardwood floors were covered by an Oriental carpet. The fireplace was black marble, and there was a four poster bed with a turmeric yellow duvet and sheer bed curtains to match. Sydnee was thunderstruck. She had never seen such luxury.

At one end of the room there was a set of French doors standing ajar. They opened onto a small balcony which overlooked the courtyard. Sydnee wanted to rush out and look over the railing.

She moved cautiously around the room and stopped at a large metal container near the hearth. "That is for your bath," Giselle explained. "Now help me get water."

The two females made several trips down to the cistern bringing buckets of water upstairs for Sydnee's bath. When the tub was half full, Giselle left a crock of soft soap, a towel, and some clothing for Sydnee. "I want you to scrub your hair and every inch of your body. We will burn your clothing tomorrow." Handing her a shift, she said, "Wear this to bed."

Next Giselle hung up a corset and a gown in the wardrobe and left her a pair of shoes adding, "Dress in this tomorrow morning. We will fit your gown properly later. I will call for you at dawn."

The moment the slave left, Sydnee dashed out onto the balcony. The moonlight shimmered on the water splashing in the fountain and illuminated the walkways that wound through the petite garden. She spied a stone bench under a trellis and a small table and chairs among the ferns. She ran her hands over the wrought-iron spirals and *fleur-di-lis* of the railing and then rushed back inside.

She opened the wardrobe and looked at the gown Giselle left. Wiping her hands on her smock, she pulled the garment out to look at it. It was forest green with a print of dark floral bouquets and had a black belt and large sleeves. She couldn't wait to put it on in the morning.

Shedding her ragged clothes, Sydnee stepped into the bath. It felt wonderful to shed the dirt from travel and to massage her scalp with the soft soap. When she dried off, she slipped the shift over her head and went back out on the balcony. She looked for Vivian but it was too dark to see her in the trees.

Then something caught her eye. There was movement in the upstairs window of the *garçonnière*. Sydnee could see shadows dancing on the curtain. She blinked and looked more closely. The shadow looked like the profile of a tiny dog. Sydnee realized that someone was in the room doing this puppetry with their hands. The dog bounced back and forth and then dropped down out of sight. She blinked and smiled slowly, wondering if the puppeteer was the young gentleman.

Another silhouette popped up in back of the curtain. This time the shadow seemed to be a bird with a long graceful neck. It turned its head from side to side and dipped repeatedly as if drinking water. Next an alligator appeared and then a deer, and a rabbit.

At last the light was extinguished. It seemed that the puppeteer had gone to bed. Regardless of all the excitement, it was time for Sydnee to rest too. She crawled into the plush feather bed and smiled as she dropped off to sleep. Tomorrow she would meet this young gentleman.

*   *   *

Thoroughly excited, Sydnee was up before dawn. She dropped the green gown over her head and walked to the mirror. Sydnee had never seen herself in a full length mirror before, and she turned from side to side thrilled with her new dress. Although it was a day dress, the material was a polished green with a black floral print. It had a wide neckline which ran out to the tips of her shoulders with large sleeves and cuffs. The gown was too big for her, so she pulled the black belt tightly around her waist.

Sydnee was not familiar with dressing her hair, but she found some pins in a drawer and put it up. After she rolled her stockings up her legs, she stepped into her shoes. It was awkward walking, but she was determined to learn the ways of a lady.

As she walked back and forth, there was a knock on the door. When she answered, Giselle walked in and ran her eyes over her. "Turn around," she demanded.

When Sydnee turned, Giselle pulled a small sewing kit out of her pocket and began tucking and pulling the material, making basting stitches here and there, adjusting the garment to Sydnee's figure.

"There," she said, straightening up. "That will do for today. I will alter it permanently tomorrow." Opening the door, she said, "Now go to the kitchen for food. Monsieur Maxime will meet you there."

The tall windows flooded the house with sunlight as Sydnee walked down the stairs out to the courtyard. Someone had let the dogs out of the stable, and they sat side by side at the door waiting for her. They ran up to her the minute they saw her. She only had time to give them a quick pet before walking to the kitchen.

The first thing she saw when she stepped in was a large fireplace filled with trammels, cast iron pots, trivets, and frying pans. In front of the hearth was a large wooden table where two dark-skinned women stood, rolling and cutting biscuits. They looked up at Sydnee and then over at Maxime who was finishing his breakfast. He wiped his mouth and stood up, examining her appearance. "Have Giselle show you how to dress your hair, and for goodness sake, have the dress altered."

Gesturing toward the cook's table, he instructed her to take some biscuits and gravy and ushered her out to a stone bench by the fountain. He stood before her and paced while she ate.

"In a moment we will go upstairs, and you will meet Monsieur Tristan, but first I must explain your new identity. You will keep the name Mademoiselle Sydnee Sauveterre, but we will tell everyone that you are the young gentleman's distant cousin. He is aware of this arrangement and has been informed about your employment here. Tristan's father, Monsieur Saint-Yves, is the owner of this home and several other properties. We will say that your mother has recently died and you have come here from the Mississippi Country to live. No one will ask questions. This is a very quiet household. Only Monsieur and Madame Saint-Yves and their son live here. Visitors are infrequent. You will meet Monsieur Tristan's parents later. At present they are in the North avoiding the midsummer heat and fevers. They did not care to have their son join them this year."

Sydnee noted a tone of disapproval in Maxime's voice, but he quickly resumed his reserve and continued. "This morning you will attend tutoring with Monsieur Tristan in the *garçonnière*. There is a break in the afternoon during the heat of the day, and then I resume lessons again with Monsieur Tristan until the evening, at which time you will--" again he paused. "You will begin *your* work with the young gentleman."

Sydnee looked down at her plate. The subject made her uncomfortable. She finished her breakfast, and they started into the *garçonnière*. She shuffled behind Maxime, trying her best to move gracefully in her new shoes. He stopped suddenly and looked down at her feet. "What is the problem?"

"I am not used to shoes, Monsieur Maxime."

"First of all, never call me 'Monsieur'. Address me only as Maxime. Next take those shoes off and carry them. We will find something more suitable for you later."

Maxime opened the door of the *garçonnière*. Sydnee's hair was falling down, her gown was too large, and she was in her stocking feet. Swallowing hard, she stepped inside.

A young man looked up from his writing, and Sydnee's lips parted. He was the most beautiful human being she had ever seen.

Tristan Saint-Yves had the ethereal beauty of an angel and the gentle demeanor to match. He stood up and smiled at Sydnee, his blue eyes sparkling. She stared at him in wonder. He put his hand up self-consciously smoothing his wavy blond hair. Smiling, he mumbled, "Welcome, Mademoiselle Sydnee," and kissed her hand.

Feeling incredibly gauche, Sydnee tried to hide her feet under her gown, putting one foot awkwardly on top of the other. He saw what she was doing and laughed. She realized then that it didn't matter. She found a new friend.

Chapter 8

The first floor of the *garçonnière* was converted into a classroom with several desks, a chalkboard, and shelves lined with books. There was even a small nook by the window with old wing back chairs for reading.

Maxime lectured on the history of Rome and discussed several of the emperors, but Sydnee was not interested in this lesson. She was curious about the instrument Tristan was using to write. He sat at a wooden desk scratching figures onto paper dipping a sharp object into an ink pot. He used the elegant bone handled instrument to produce exquisitely beautiful sweeping and flowing figures on paper. She loved not only his writing but the industrious sound of the scratching and the smell of the ink.

Latin was the next lesson Maxime taught. This subject caught Sydnee's attention immediately. She recognized many of the words and was pleased that she could understand some of the language even though she did not know why the words were familiar.

Maxime paid no attention to Sydnee at all, focusing instead on young Tristan. A very strict teacher with high expectations, Maxime had no tolerance for mediocrity. He firmly believed that under his tutelage a student would excel, so he gave Tristan all of his attention expecting the best from him in return.

Sydnee watched Maxime strut back and forth proudly in the classroom, moving with a haughty demeanor. Tristan was not intimidated by him though. He asked questions and initiated dialogue freely. Maxime, in turn, was eager and willing to answer questions and feed the boy's hungry mind.

In the afternoon, Maxime allowed Sydnee to get up and look around the classroom. With her hands behind her back, she looked at the colorful books, maps and pictures in the room. Formal education had never been a part of Sydnee's life. In fact, she met few people who had ever gone to school. Like most girls, Sydnee was well versed in domestic duties. Margarite had given her expertise in the still-room, an appreciation of nature, and a deep sense of spirituality, but academic tutoring had been non-existent. Since Margarite was a slave she was not allowed to read, so as a result, Sydnee could neither read nor write.

Occasionally there was an exception to this rule, and Maxime was an example of this phenomenon. He came from a long line of scholars and educators from Maryland. Although enslaved, his ancestors were known as the finest pedagogues in the country, and for this reason, Monsieur Saint-Yves purchased him.

Sydnee did not know it, but Maxime watched her as she moved around the room. He studied her as she drifted along the book shelves and examined the globe. There was something about the waif that fascinated him.

Tristan was distracted by Sydnee too. He would write a few words, steal a look, write a few more words and steal another look at her. He liked everything about Sydnee; her quiet demeanor, her large chestnut eyes but especially her little stocking feet peeking out from under the green dress.

"It is time to dismiss for our rest period," announced Maxime, closing his book and standing up. "We resume at four."

Sydnee bit her lip, unsure how to tell when it was four o'clock. Maxime did not notice her quandary, but Tristan saw it. Immediately he knew that she could not tell time. He said, "Just in case you fall asleep, Mademoiselle Sydnee, I will come for you at four."

Breathing a sigh of relief, she said, *"Merci."*

*   *   *

True to his word, Tristan came for Sydnee at four, and they spent the rest of the day listening to Maxime talk about ancient philosophers and the great art of the Renaissance. Promptly at six, Maxime gathered his books and left Sydnee and Tristan alone together in the classroom. The moment he left, the two became self-conscious. Tristan fiddled with his pen while Sydnee looked at her hands in her lap.

At last he asked, "How old are you?"

"Fifteen," she replied.

"Oh, I'm sixteen."

Sydnee kept her eyes on the floor, tongue tied.

"What manner of books do you--" and he stopped, remembering that she could not read. "Oh, I am sorry." There was another long pause. He swallowed hard and said, "I saw your dogs."

Sydnee's face brightened, and she looked up into his blue eyes. "Do you like dogs?"

"Yes, I do" he said rather loudly, eager that they found common ground. "I especially like large dogs."

"Would you like to meet them?"

"Yes indeed," Tristan said, standing up.

The moment they stepped into the courtyard, Baloo and Atlantis bounded up. Tristan bent down and rumpled their fur, talking to them. She noticed his fine blue vest and his white silk shirt. His pantaloons were crisp, and his shoes were a rich brown leather. She found it hard to believe that anyone so refined and genteel would speak with her. Her favorite part about Tristan was his hair. The soft curls grew just over the tops of his ears and were the color of sunshine.

Sydnee walked to the fountain. The water bubbled out of an ornamental pineapple, overflowed the first basin and then splashed down into the second and larger third tier.

"Has anyone shown you the house?" Tristan asked, coming up alongside her.

"No, not yet."

"We will start at the front door as if you are a guest."

They went out through the carriage gate and up the front steps. He pushed open the heavy front door, covered with brass fixtures, and took Sydnee into the entry where the tall wooden box stood. This time she stopped to examine the small painted landscape on the face.

"That is our grandfather clock," Tristan said. He leaned close to her ear and said confidentially, "I will teach you how to read it."

Sydnee looked at him and smiled.

Walking into a huge corner room, Tristan explained, "This is where we entertain guests, if they ever come."

Sydnee gasped. Floor to ceiling windows lined three walls of the parlor. They were adorned with long, sheer curtains which moved slightly in the breeze. The walls were painted a cool white, and a huge, gilded mirror graced one wall reflecting the crystal chandelier overhead and several *girandoles* on the walls. Chairs and divans upholstered in colorful patterns were grouped around two fireplaces.

Sydnee leaned into the room, not daring to step inside.

"Come in," coaxed Tristan, standing by a piano. "You won't hurt anything."

Cautiously Sydnee stepped onto the plush patterned carpet, walked over to the piano and then looked at the porcelain figurines on the mantel. One was a basket of flowers and the other was a tall elegant woman with a dog.

"Come along. There is more," Tristan encouraged.

Doors were open across the hall so a breeze could pass throughout the first floor. They crossed into the next room. This was the library and had a more masculine look. "This is where my father takes brandy and smokes with the men," Tristan explained. The walls were lined with books, and the furniture was darker, sporting a more solid appearance. "This is nice, but I prefer the library at *Saint-Denis*." he said.

"What is *Saint-Denis*?" Sydnee asked.

"That is our plantation home on the river. I will take you there."

Joining the library was a drawing room for the ladies which was lighter and airier in feel. They crossed the hall again into the dining room. The room was dominated by a heavy walnut table, sideboard and a large, black marble fireplace. The drapes were a light green and dropped in luxurious folds onto the floor. The carpet was a light green with a beige pattern.

"In there," Tristan said, gesturing toward some doors, "is the pantry and wine room. Upstairs are the bedrooms. Most of them are at rest since my parents are gone."

Sydnee did not know what "at rest" meant, but when she peeked in two of the bed chambers earlier, there was no bedding on the beds and much of the furniture was covered with sheets.

"Where is Maxime's room?"

"The quarters for darkies are over the stable," Tristan explained.

They returned outside and took their supper at the little table in the courtyard. It was a great relief for Sydnee not to worry about finding food, and she was at peace knowing that Vivian and the dogs were gorging themselves on table scraps by the stable. She noticed that they had been sleeping a great deal, renewing themselves after the journey.

Tristan and Sydnee were at last able to talk more easily with each other. He was eager to hear about life on the Natchez Trace and asked her many questions. She told him about the beauty of the back country, the wildlife, the people, and her life with Margarite, but she carefully avoided her job at the stand satisfying men. She knew that Maxime told him her role, but she was not comfortable speaking of it. She was extremely anxious about approaching Tristan as a paramour. They were becoming friends, and it did not feel right.

Tristan told Sydnee about his life in New Orleans and on the plantation. "I have no siblings so I read a great deal. I read all kinds of books. I also like to study insects, particularly butterflies. Do you like butterflies?"

"Very much," Sydnee responded. "There were many butterflies around the stand where I lived."

Tristan said suddenly, "I am glad you have come. There was a boy schooled here before you came. Our fathers were business associates and we became friends," and his face reddened. "But he was sent to Paris to finish his education."

Tristan lowered his eyes as if ashamed. Sydnee wondered if this boy had something to do with the reason she was here.

Trying to cover his embarrassment, Tristan said brightly, "But I have another friend who lives on a plantation next to *Saint-Denis*. I want you to meet her. She is our age, and her name is Isabel."

The sun had gone down, and it was starting to drizzle. "Come see where I live," Tristan said, jumping up. She followed him up the staircase in the *garçonnière* to a hexagon-shaped room. There was a small fireplace with a sitting area and on the opposite wall was Tristan's bed, an intricately carved half tester with snow-white bed linen. There was a large oak wardrobe and a small balcony with French doors.

Sydnee walked to a window and looked out over the courtyard. "Was that you doing a puppet show last night?"

Tristan's eyes grew large. "You could see that?"

Sydnee grinned. "It was good. I liked the swan the best."

Tristan started to laugh. "I didn't know I had an audience. Shall I teach you?"

She nodded and he dashed over, dropping the curtains to darken the room and lighting candles. They sat side by side for over an hour making shadow puppets and laughing. Sydnee was glad she had come here to live.

* * *

The next day, Maxime informed Sydnee that she was to help the women beat carpets outside and not attend class. Tristan was indignant. "But Maxime, she is my new friend. I want her to attend class with me."

Maxime lifted his chin and stated, "Out of the question. She is a female, and I am here to give *you* an education not some mendicant from the back country."

"Yes, but she is supposedly my cousin. How would this look, you sending a family member to work with the darkies?"

Maxime sucked in his cheeks, clearly annoyed, but he knew Tristan was right. If they were to convince everyone that Sydnee was a cousin, she must be treated like a cousin.

Seeing that he was gaining ground, Tristan added. "I will help teach her, Maxime. If I instruct her, I will learn as well."

Maxime sighed and said, "I don't like it. I don't like it at all, but I will allow it only if you spend extra time on your own studies."

"I promise," Tristan said, his cheeks flushed with excitement.

Sydnee returned to the classroom, this time in a proper-fitting beige, floral print day dress and shoes. She was thrilled to be a part of the classroom and listened eagerly to Tristan's alphabet instructions. Maxime resisted teaching Sydnee, but Tristan was overjoyed and took charge. By the end of the day, she had painstakingly reproduced half of the alphabet and could tell time on the clock. Maxime loaded Tristan with extra reading and Latin exercises, but the boy didn't care. He adored his new pupil.

After several days, Maxime relaxed his resentment about teaching Sydnee and started tutorials for her. This pleased Tristan. He appreciated the fine skills Maxime had to offer, and he watched Sydnee move, in a matter of weeks, from fundamental identification of letters to entire words and then sentences. They introduced basic arithmetic to her, geography and even some Latin. Maxime coached her in speech, helping her with her stammer and gradually Sydnee began to speak more fluidly.

Every evening Sydnee would join Tristan in his room and together they would work on assignments. One afternoon, when class was dismissed, Maxime asked Sydnee in private, "Are you fulfilling your obligations with the young gentleman?"

Sydnee paused and then nodded hesitantly. In reality there had been no physical contact between them.

"I notice that you visit him in his room every evening. *Tres bien,* I am glad there is progress. I shall write to Monsieur Saint-Yves apprising him of the situation."

Sydnee nodded, swallowed hard and walked away.

*   *   *

Sunbeams filtered through Tristan's blinds, casting stripes of light on his bed in the *garçonnière.* The boy rolled over and opened his eyes. Today there was no school and after daily Mass, he crawled back into bed. He stretched, hearing voices in the courtyard below. Throwing back the sheet, he walked to the French doors and listened.

"You must do something about the stench," he heard Maxime say.

Tristan looked outside. Maxime stood below the balcony with a handkerchief to his nose, talking to Sydnee. The dogs were sitting at her feet.

"I want these creatures bathed immediately. It is to be done by the time I return."

"Yes, Maxime," Sydnee said.

Tristan yanked the sheet off the bed, and draped it over his nightshirt. Dashing out onto the balcony, he made sure Maxime was gone and then called, "I will help you."

Sydnee looked up, nodding as she put on her apron.

Tristan pulled on his clothes and raced downstairs.

"You will ruin those," she said.

Tristan looked down at his silk shirt and pantaloons. "I don't care."

Sydnee smiled and shrugged.

"What do we do first?"

"Have you ever washed a dog?"

"I have never done anything like this in my life," he announced with excitement. "A young gentleman must never dirty his hands," he said and rolled his eyes.

"Well, we need soap and plenty of water. Are there wash tubs?"

"Yes, by the laundry."

"Get some rope to hold the dogs, and I'll get water," she ordered.

Tristan ran into the stable, and Sydnee walked to the back of the house with the dogs behind her. There was a laundry area with large crucibles, wash tubs and a clothes line. It was getting warm, and Sydnee was grateful for the large fronds giving her shade. She gathered soap and rags and started to fill the tubs with water from the cistern.

One of the kitchen workers walked past and said, "Don't use that good water from the cistern, Mademoiselle Sydnee. Them barrels over there is full of river water. Use those."

Sydnee nodded. She hoped the woman would not tell Giselle. The head housekeeper did not like anyone touching her supplies.

"I have rope," Tristan announced coming around the corner.

"Good, help me finish filling the tubs, and then you wash Baloo, and I will wash Atlantis."

After filling the tubs, they started. Unsure of himself, Tristan mimicked Sydnee's every move. He was clumsy and fumbled with Baloo, trying to get him to step into the tub. He pulled him with the rope, and then pushed the dog from behind, but the mastiff would not budge.

Sydnee stopped washing and yanked Baloo's rope sharply. "Come!" she demanded, and the dog stepped in the tub.

Tristan sighed and said, "Yes, now we begin."

Rolling up his sleeves, he poured several buckets of water over Baloo. The dog instantly shook all over him. The boy's shirt was soaked, his pantaloons were wet, and dirty water was spattered all over his face.

Sydnee started to laugh. Tristan wiped the water from his eyes and laughed too. "We are going to do this, Baloo," he said with conviction, and the dog looked at him warily. Tristan poured soap all over his back, buried his hands in the wet fur and started to scrub him briskly.

In her own wash tub, Atlantis stood stiff-legged and resentful while Sydnee washed her. The water was black as mud.

Suddenly Tristan yelled, "No!"

Baloo had jumped out of the tub and was running into the courtyard with the rope trailing behind him. Tristan dashed after him. At last, he cornered him and threw himself on top of the dog as Sydnee grabbed the rope.

Wet and covered with mud, Tristan stood up, victorious. "I did it!"

An hour later they were finished.

"What's next?" Tristan asked with enthusiasm.

Sydnee pushed her damp locks off of her forehead. She was tired and hot. They were sitting in the courtyard on the ledge of the fountain. "Aren't you tired?" she asked.

"No, I've never had so much fun!"

Vivian swooped down and landed on her shoulder.

"Will she sit on my shoulder?" Tristan asked.

Vivian seemed to know what he wanted and glared at him.

"Let's see." Sydnee reached up and Vivian stepped onto her forearm. "Now hold my hand," she said to Tristan reaching out to him. She tilted her arm upward, hoping to get the crow to walk down her arm onto Tristan.

Vivian did not move. Sydnee shook her arm and said, "Go, Vivian."

Vivian rode up and down, not moving. When Tristan reached up to touch her, she burst into a mass of flapping wings and pecked at him.

"Well, maybe later," Sydnee said.

"Do you want to look at insects?" Tristan suggested. When Sydnee agreed, he ran up to his room and returned with a large magnifying glass. He handed it to her and said, "Now look through it."

Sydnee bent over and looked at an insect darting around on the surface of the water in the fountain. "Oh!" she exclaimed. "Look at that!"

She wandered off, and Tristan spied Vivian sitting in a magnolia tree. "What kind of food does Vivian like?" he called.

Sydnee was on her knees examining something on the ground. Sitting back on her ankles she said, "Oh, I don't know, anything, corn if you have some, or meat. She's a crow. They eat everything."

Tristan went into the kitchen and returned with an assortment of treats on a plate. The bird was watching him closely. He held a piece of pork in the palm of his hand. "Come here. Look what I have," he cooed.

Vivian did not move from her perch in the tree.

Next he held up a handful of corn and made kissing noises. Still the bird did nothing. Determined, Tristan picked up the plate and moved under the tree where Vivian was sitting. Holding up some cornbread, he murmured, "Good bird. Come and get it."

Vivian flapped her wings and hopped around. Tristan was pleased. He believed that she was finally warming up to him. Just when he thought she was about to fly down to his arm, she turned around, lifted her tail and dropped feces onto his neck with a splat.

"Damn it!" he exclaimed, pulling his collar up to wipe his neck. "Damn it all! So that's the thanks I get! Well, here is your food," and he threw it at Vivian.

Unconcerned, Vivian flew to a different tree.

*   *   *

In the afternoon, Sydnee and Tristan moved into the school room to work on a play about ancient Rome that Maxime had assigned. Sydnee loved activities that had to do with school. Her quick mind combined with her enthusiasm for learning made her an excellent student. First they practiced their parts, and then they made costumes. They tied old sheets over their clothes for togas and made wreathes for their heads out of vines.

When Maxime returned from his errand, he heard them practicing and smiled. He was impressed with Sydnee, and it was obvious that Tristan adored her.

The cooks made bread pudding that evening, and Sydnee and Tristan took their dessert and orgeat drinks to the courtyard as the sun was setting. They sat down together on a wrought-iron bench when suddenly wings flapped around Tristan, and black feathers hit his face. He blinked and ducked, dumping his drink.

"Oh!" Sydnee gasped. When she realized what was happening, she laughed and exclaimed, "*Zut alors!*"

There sitting on Tristan's shoulder was Vivian.

Tristan sat stiffly on the bench, his eyes like saucers. The crow sat there proudly, looking down at Sydnee with a haughty attitude.

"She has never done that for anyone but me!" Sydnee exclaimed. "It is official, Vivian is now madly in love with you."

Chapter 9

As the summer wore on, the heat and humidity became oppressive, and everyone grew out of sorts. The kitchen workers were surly and on edge. Giselle was glaring at everyone like a wildcat ready to pounce, and Maxime was a holy terror. His patience evaporated in the heat, and he would flare up at Sydnee and Tristan without cause. Even the dogs were crabby.

One morning after Mass, when they did not have school, Tristan whispered, "Sydnee, let's go for a walk in the city."

"What?" she said, surprised. "You told me that we cannot leave here unchaperoned."

"I don't care. I have only seen New Orleans from the window of a carriage. I must escape for a while. It will only be for a short time. We will take the dogs to keep us safe."

Sydnee looked around furtively. "Where is Maxime?"

"Composing his weekly letter to my father and going over his accounts. Please, please, please?"

Biting her lip, Sydnee nodded.

She gave a short whistle, the dogs came bounding up, and Vivian landed on Tristan's shoulder. He reached up and stroked her feathers. Looking around cautiously, they stepped out of the garden sanctuary onto Rue St. Louis. The street was glaringly hot and silent. Sydnee put her sleeve to her nose. In the heat, the odor of horse dung was overpowering.

"You forgot your gloves," Tristan said.

"I must wear gloves?" Sydnee asked.

He blinked. "I think so. Never mind, let's go," he said taking her arm.

They walked down the cobblestone street with the dogs behind them. Rows of houses were lined up, one flush against the other, painted in pastel hues with shutters of contrasting colors. A man came around the corner pushing a heavy cart. He stopped at each doorway dumping refuse into it.

Sydnee looked around. It was thrilling to be out of the confines of the courtyard. As much as she relished her new life at the Saint-Yves household, she missed being out in the open air. She missed the wind on her face and the trees whispering to her. When she was inside, the spirits were quiet and their voices indistinct.

Tristan was excited too and looked around smiling. "We will go down to market."

"Is that where everyone is?" Sydnee said, looking at the empty street.

"Everyone abandons New Orleans this time of year, but the market will have more people. Most families leave for the North because of yellow jack, but there is very little fever this year."

Sydnee wanted to ask why Tristan's parents left him behind but reconsidered.

Almost as if he was reading her mind, he added, "I have already had the illness, so there is no danger for me. That is why I did not go with them."

Nevertheless Sydnee felt there was another reason.

They walked several blocks and at last turned down a street with more activity. Dusky women walked with baskets on their heads, men lounged in doorways smoking, as children ran with sticks and hoops.

Tristan thought better of having Vivian on his shoulder and tossed her into the air, so she would not attract attention. Sydnee noticed people staring at him as he walked along anyway. He was unaware of the admiration in their eyes. She knew they were impressed with his beauty in the same way she had been taken with it that first day over a month ago.

The *trottoirs* were uneven, and when Sydnee wasn't paying attention, she tripped. The root from a huge tree had heaved the sidewalk up, cracking the bricks. Tristan caught her, and they laughed. As they walked, they stayed under the galleries for shade, keeping the dogs at their heels.

Near Jackson Square there was a long stucco building Tristan called the *Halles des Boucheries*. It was the meat market, and the dogs sniffed the air. Men speaking Italian wearing white aprons haggled with shoppers over the rows of cutlets, roasts and seafood. Chickens, hams and sausages hung from hooks as slaves brushed flies away with palmetto fans. Sydnee had never seen so much food and activity. She could not imagine the market on a busy day.

"Hey!" shouted one of the workers in a thick Italian accent. "Watch your dogs!"

He gestured toward Baloo whose snout was on the same level as juicy pork cutlets resting on long trays.

"Come, let's go to the Vegetable Market," suggested Tristan.

The *Halles de Legumes* was another open air building lined with cream-colored columns and green awnings. Wagons were backed up to the stalls in neat rows where the vendors unloaded and arranged colorful produce. Baskets of peanuts, onions and apples lined the walkway, next to bunches of herbs, trays of yellow peppers, bright green okra, and red potatoes. Sydnee stopped and examined a palmetto broom that was for sale next to large baskets filled with dried Spanish moss for stuffing mattresses. She closed her eyes and inhaled the dark scent of the herbs and the sweet aroma of the fruit.

Farmers called to shoppers, describing the juiciest of fruits and the freshest of vegetables. Black women with baskets over their arms and *tignons* on their heads wove up and down the aisles scrutinizing the produce and haggling with the grocers. Some carried babies tied onto their backs while others had children trailing behind them in a row.

Tristan stopped at a stand and picked up a handful of brittle brown sticks in a small basket. When Sydnee drew closer she realized they were dried grasshoppers.

"For ze birds," the old woman said with a toothless smile.

Tristan nodded, reached into his pocket and gave her a picayune.

"For Vivian," he said to Sydnee, wrapping a handful into his handkerchief. The crow was nowhere to be found, but they knew she would reappear when they left the chaos of the market.

Sydnee smiled. "Why do you do it? That bird already loves you."

They walked to the levee to sit on the grass. Long rows of empty docks stretched out before them. There was only a few riverboats on the landing, and they watched the men unloading crates and barrels. Sydnee ate a pear Tristan had purchased for her.

"Any other time of year this landing is filled with paddle wheelers and flatboats," Tristan explained, popping a fig into his mouth. "It is usually loud and filled with people."

Vivian swooped down and landed on the ground in front of them.

"Look, Vivian," he said. "I have a treat for you," and he opened his handkerchief, handing her a dried grasshopper. The bird walked over and plucked it from his hand crunching it in her beak.

"Maxime calls her 'The Albatross'," Sydnee said.

"Yes, it is from a poem. She is *my* personal 'Albatross'," he said laughing and put the rest of the grasshoppers back in his handkerchief.

Vivian cawed loudly in protest, but Tristan was firm. He swept his arm into the air signaling her to leave, and she flew up into a tree to sulk.

A fashionably dressed couple walked past them arm in arm. The young woman had on a pink gown with white lace frills and twirled a sea foam green parasol on her shoulder. The young man wore a cream-colored coat with tan pantaloons. When he stole a kiss from her, Sydnee and Tristan looked away.

"Sydnee," Tristan said, pausing. "I know why you are here. Thank you for not trying to--" and he broke off.

Sydnee stared straight ahead. When he looked at her, she nodded, keeping her eyes down.

Tristan bit his lip. "I don't understand myself. I am sixteen years old, and I should like to kiss girls, but when Isabel and I were practicing last summer, I-I didn't like it. I couldn't wait to wipe my mouth."

He sighed and stood up. With his hands in his pockets he walked toward the river. He bent over and threw a rock. Turning suddenly, he came back with tears in his eyes and exclaimed, "But when Lucien did it, I liked--" and he choked, not finishing his sentence. His chest heaved. "I don't understand myself, Sydnee. I am so ashamed."

He looked at her, his eyes red-rimmed. "When my father caught us, he beat me and sent Lucien away. He called me depraved. Am I depraved, Sydnee?" He looked at her beseechingly.

She started to speak, but words would not come. Tristan stood over her, his hands in fists, waiting for an answer.

"I-I do not know the meaning of that word," she uttered at last. "But I do know that you are the finest person that I have ever met."

Tristan squeezed his eyes shut and turned away.

Suddenly Vivian dropped down onto his shoulder. Startled, he half laughed and half sobbed. Reaching up, he stroked her head and sat back down on the grass by Sydnee.

"And what of your mother? How is it with her?" Sydnee asked.

Tristan looked surprised. "My mother? I don't know. She never takes notice of me. Especially since my brother died."

"I thought you had no siblings."

"Not anymore. My brother, Guy sailed for Paris several months ago. There was a storm, and he was lost at sea. My mother is convinced he will return, so she has a light put in the window for him every night."

Sydnee remembered the lamp lit by Giselle in the bed chamber every sunset.

"What should I do about how I feel?" Tristan asked desperately.

"What do the spirits tell you to do?"

"What do you mean?"

"The voices that comfort you, guide you."

"You mean God?" Tristan asked, rubbing his forehead. "I don't know. I can't hear anything."

"Sometimes I cannot hear them either, but they are always there. For me they are in the wind and the trees and sometimes the creatures around me. Look how Vivian landed on your shoulder to give you comfort when you needed it."

Tristan laughed. "Oh, that was just Vivian." He looked up at the crow in the tree and then looked back at Sydnee. "This talk does not sound like something Bishop de Neckere would like."

"Margarite taught these things to me."

Tristan remembered how awkward Sydnee had been in Mass, and he realized now that she had never been to church. "Are talking about Voodoo, Sydnee?"

"No, it's Hoodoo. We say the same prayers and speak to the same saints as you do at St. Louis Cathedral."

Tristan rubbed his eyes. He was suddenly very tired. "I want to hear all about it, but not today. Maxime will be finishing up soon," he said. "We should go home."

*   *   *

There were many more excursions after that day. Tristan was eager to experience freedom from the walls of his townhome on St. Louis Street. He was tired of schoolrooms, *garçonnières* and courtyards. He wanted to fish, watch riverboats on the Mississippi, hear music on the landing, and eat food from street vendors.

Slipping away proved to be quite easy. Before every excursion, they would go into Tristan's bedroom, lock the door and then crawl down a tree into the courtyard where they would slip out onto the street. Maxime would not disturb them, thinking that Sydnee was teaching Tristan the sensual arts.

Some days they would simply walk through Jackson Square and talk, other afternoons they would run with the dogs to the outskirts of town looking for butterflies. The old grand-dames would shake their heads at Sydnee as she darted through the streets of New Orleans with no bonnet or gloves, disgracefully showing her ankles as she ran alongside Tristan Saint-Yves, but the youngsters did not care. Tristan and Sydnee were having too much fun.

Tristan's favorite activity was to fish the Mississippi. After catching an abundance of catfish and crappies, they would collect branches, build a fire, and fry their meal upon the riverbank. Sometimes they would bring okra or onions to sauté and add a freshly baked baguette to accompany their meal.

One Sunday afternoon at the end of September when Maxime was bookkeeping, Tristan and Sydnee stole away to their favorite field off Orleans Street to run the dogs. It was a beautiful open area just outside the city with groves of large oak trees. Sometimes they would watch boys playing *raquettes* or catch insects to examine under the magnifying glass but this time, as they drew near, they heard singing and drumming. Slaves and Creoles of color were flooding the streets, laughing and talking, carrying children, baskets of food and blankets. Some of the men had bright sashes tied around their waists and women wore colorful skirts and *tignons*. Everyone seemed to be going in the direction of the open field.

When Tristan and Sydnee arrived, they were amazed. Their favorite field had been transformed into a festival attended by the black residents of New Orleans. Only a handful of spectators were white townspeople. Perhaps four hundred souls turned out for the shopping, music, and dance.

"I have heard the kitchen women speak of this," Tristan shouted to Sydnee over noise. "They call it *La Place Publique,* or Congo Square, but I didn't know that it was here."

Keeping the dogs close, they wound through the crowd, stopping to watch groups of black men and women dancing to the rhythm of drums and gourds, dressed in free flowing garments trimmed with ribbons, bells or shells. They would jiggle and jump to the music, stomping in time to the music. The women would shake their shoulders seductively as the men beat a frenzied rhythm on the drums.

Sydnee could feel the sound of the drums resonate in her bones and began to tap her foot. They walked from one end of the field to the other watching performances. One group plucked stringed instruments and tapped *agogos*, chanting and singing songs in an African dialect. Another cluster of people chanted and clapped while participants took turns shimmying under a pole.

Scattered throughout *La Place Publique*, vendors had booths where they sold yarn dolls, brightly colored scarves and wooden jewelry. There was food for sale too including fruit, nuts, gumbo, and fried catfish.

Sydnee noticed Hoodoo charms, candles, and herbal remedies for sale. Practitioners and spiritualists spread their wares out on blankets and consulted with customers, shaking rattles, chanting or doing readings. Margarite told her that Hoodoo was practiced widely among the slaves and free people of color in New Orleans. It all seemed very innocent but a voice whispered to Sydnee that some of the practitioners here indulged in the dark arts.

Tristan tugged on Sydnee's sleeve. It was time to go back. His parents were returning to New Orleans that night on a riverboat.

When they arrived home, the dogs loped to the trough to drink water, and Tristan grabbed Sydnee's arm. He looked concerned.

"What is it?" she asked.

"I am worried about the dogs. My parents will not tolerate them. They may even have them shot."

Sydnee's stomach lurched. "Then I must leave."

"No, wait. I have been thinking all day, and I have an idea." He took her wrist and led her to the stable. "Mortimer?" Tristan called.

There was no reply.

"Mortimer Gish?"

"Coming, Monsieur Saint-Yves," someone said, from the courtyard.

Sydnee turned and looked. Walking quickly toward them on the flagstone path was a boy about Tristan's age. He was tall but thin to the point of emaciation with unkempt brown hair and a sallow complexion. The characteristic which was so unusual about the boy was his curious gait. Mortimer did not swing his arms when he walked, and he always kept his head down.

"Mortimer, I want to ask you something," Tristan said as the boy drew nearer. He still did not look up. "Would you consider taking Mademoiselle Sydnee's dogs with you to the livery? I will pay Monsieur Schinden their boarding."

Mortimer stole a look out of the corner of his eye at Sydnee and then looked back down at the ground. "Yes, I like Atlantis and Baloo," he murmured.

Sydnee's eyebrows shot up. He knew their names.

"Mortimer is our groom, and he has an uncanny ability with animals," Tristan explained. "He seems to understand what they need, and they always like him." Turning back to Mortimer, he asked, "You are sure that Monsieur Schinden will not mind having the dogs at the livery stable?"

"No sir, not if you pay him, and I take care of the dogs myself."

"Sydnee," Tristan said, turning to her. "The stable is just down the street. Would you be comfortable with this?"

"Yes," she said with relief. "I will get the dogs."

*   *   *

Tristan's parents returned that night, and instantly a dark cloud fell over the Saint-Yves household. Sydnee sat in a wing back chair by a window in the schoolroom, trying to read. Her efforts were unsuccessful though. She was too preoccupied listening to Tristan pace back and forth overhead, getting ready for supper. Tense and stiff, he descended down the steps at last. He was dressed in a light blue frock coat and dark pantaloons. On any other day, his eyes would have shown bright blue, but today they were a pale gray. He swallowed hard and said, "I am going into supper now." He looked at her empty plate on the end table. "I would have much rather eaten with you. I'm so sorry. Everything will change now."

She nodded.

At sunset, Giselle called for her to come to the back entry. "Monsieur wants to look at you."

In anticipation of this, Sydnee had washed her hands and face and put on a fresh apron. She stood up, straightened her skirt and took a deep breath. The moment she stepped inside, she saw Monsieur Cuthbert Saint-Yves. Although the light was dim, Sydnee could see that he was a tall thin man with a long face and sunken cheeks. He wore a black frock coat, and his hair was thin and gray. He frowned and looked down his sharp nose at her.

"Madame Saint-Yves!" he called loudly, keeping his eyes on Sydnee. "Here. Now!"

"I will find her, Master," Giselle murmured and brushed past them. She returned with Madame Augusta Saint-Yves. Cuthbert jerked his wife around in front of him so she could see Sydnee, holding her by the arm. She was a woman of middle age with narrow eyes and ivory skin. The dark haired Frenchwoman exclaimed, "Oh!" and put her hanky over her nose and mouth.

Sydnee blinked. She was confused. She had been bathing regularly, and her clothes were clean.

Turning her face away, Madame Saint-Yves murmured, "Yes, now I have seen her."

Monsieur Saint-Yves let go of her, and she swept back down the hall.

"Out," he said to Sydnee, jerking his head.

Sydnee stumbled out into the courtyard. It had been worse than she thought. She stood for a long time, trying to calm her beating heart. Until now she had been happy, but in one evening that had all changed.

She wanted to run to her room and hide, but she dare not enter the house. The schoolroom was not private enough so she went to the back of the stable to hide under the stairs in the dark. She sat down on the floor, hugging her knees.

Sydnee had to ready herself for the worst. She relived the meeting with Tristan's parents, the curled lips, the look of repugnance, and Monsieur Saint-Yves' harsh dismissal. She knew now that there would be no more meals with Tristan. She would be banned from the schoolroom and maybe even turned out onto the street again.

She put her head down, wanting nothing more than to escape into a dreamless sleep. Suddenly she was awakened by a door opening overhead. The faint light of a candle shone through the wooden stairs. "Don't be foolish, Giselle," she heard Maxime whisper in French. "If you run, they will find you."

"Let go of me," Giselle hissed.

There was the rustling of skirts on the stairs, and Sydnee held her breath.

"I should have run away months ago. My baby is the last link with her dead son, Guy. That woman will steal my child the moment I give birth. Then she will sell me."

"You don't know that for certain," Maxime countered.

"Of course she will," Giselle said. "She still grieves for him. Every night I must light a lamp for him."

"Tell them it is the master's baby."

Sydnee recognized the voice of Manon, one of the cooks.

"That won't work, you fool," Maxime hissed. "The master can sire no children. Have you forgotten that the Saint-Yves children are foundlings from the Ursulines?"

"Even if I wanted to say that it is the Master's baby, she wouldn't believe me. She caught Guy after me in the pantry."

"Come back upstairs, and we will talk," urged Maxime. "There must be another way."

"No!" said Giselle. "Escape is the only answer."

"Well not tonight, it isn't. Come back to my room for some tea. It will help you sleep, and we will consider everything tomorrow."

Sydnee heard Giselle sigh. There was the sound of footsteps, the door shut, and all was dark in the stable once more.

Chapter 10

Tristan dined alone with his father that night. Madame Saint-Yves left supper after the first course, pleading a headache. Father and son sat rigidly at the table eating trout with butter sauce. The table was draped with a fine white linen tablecloth and fashionably set with floral patterned Limoges china and Baccarat crystal.

After a long silence, Monsieur Saint-Yves announced, "I am dismissing that girl in the morning,"

Tristan looked up at him, thunderstruck. "Mademoiselle Sydnee? No, Father! Why?"

Cuthbert Saint-Yves sipped his wine. "Maxime has written to me that the girl has been visiting you privately for some time, and it has gone on long enough. We have returned home now, and quite frankly, we don't want to look at her. Your mother finds her presence in this house repugnant, and so do I."

"But you invited her here for me, and now she has become my friend," Tristan pleaded.

"Friendships are not possible with the lower class. She was here for one reason and one reason only. Her term of employment is over."

Tristan looked down at his dinner plate. His stomach was in knots, and his hands were shaking. He must think of something quickly to keep Sydnee. He pushed the remains of his dinner around with his fork.

His father continued, "We will be announcing your betrothal to Isabel Trudeau shortly. This must be done before you leave for Paris for your studies and the Grand Tour."

Tristan could find no words.

One of the kitchen slaves came in with more carrots and potato soufflé. Tristan's father waved her off, and she left the dining room. Finished with his meal, Monsieur Saint-Yves put his napkin on the table and stood up.

"Father," Tristan said.

With cold, gray eyes he looked down at the boy.

Swallowing hard, Tristan continued, "I am not—ready."

Monsieur Saint-Yves' eyes narrowed.

"I have not," the boy stammered. "Mademoiselle Sydnee, we have not--"

His father pursed his lips.

Tristan looked down and mumbled, "I would not want to disappoint Isabel when we wed."

"So," his father said coldly. "Your tastes are still for the—unnatural?"

Tristan jumped to his feet and pleaded, "By the spring I will be ready, Father. I promise."

"Spring!" his father barked. "You need the entire winter as well? Out of the question!"

"But you and Mother will be at *Saint-Denis* for the Christmas season and then in Natchez until April. You will not even see Mademoiselle Sydnee. In April, you can announce the engagement. I will be completely cured by that time. Isabel will notice nothing out of the ordinary when we wed, and of course, she will then have no complaints for her family."

This was Tristan's trump card. He knew that maintaining appearances was of the utmost importance to his parents. He held his breath. The dining room was silent as Monsieur Saint-Yves stared at him.

At last his father said, "That *creature,*" and he paused. "Is to stay out of sight until your mother retires at night and be out of the house before she rises in the morning. Is that clear?"

Tristan nodded and murmured, "Of course. Thank you, thank you."

His father looked at him with distaste, shook his head and left the room. Tristan gasped and collapsed into a chair. He had just bought more time with his best friend, Sydnee at least until springtime.

*   *   *

Every day at the livery Sydnee would visit Atlantis and Baloo. They were well fed, content and secure in the care of Mortimer Gish, and for this she was grateful. She was relieved that they had escaped the shroud of hatred and despair that had recently fallen over the household on Saint Louis Street.

Everything changed with the return of Monsieur and Madame Saint-Yves. Although Sydnee was allowed to stay, and she was allowed once more in the schoolroom, Maxime was tense and had increased the amount of homework. There was no more free time for adventures to the French Market or fishing expeditions on the Mississippi. Vivian could no longer land in the courtyard to visit her, and Tristan never smiled anymore. The surliness caused by the heat wave a month ago seemed like Carnival compared to the funereal atmosphere pervading the household now.

Even though Madame and Monsieur Saint-Yves were seldom seen, their presence was felt everywhere. Each morning after Mass, Tristan's father would leave on business, and Madame Saint-Yves would breakfast in her bed chamber alone. Most days she would remain cloistered there until supper. Even though it was common knowledge she had been drinking excessively after the death of her son, everyone knew that she was still watching and listening to everything. On one occasion, Sydnee actually saw her in the bedroom window watching Giselle cross the courtyard. It gave her a chill to see her black eyes tracing the steps of the young woman. When Madame Saint-Yves noticed Sydnee looking up at her, the lace curtain dropped back into place.

In the evening, when Monsieur Saint-Yves was home, everything revolved around his needs. He sat at his desk in the library, making demands of Maxime. Maxime was constantly answering the bell and working late into the night poring over books and accounts. The tension was visibly wearing on him.

Giselle was starting to show signs of strain as well. Her face was drawn, and she had dark rings under her eyes. Her skin developed a sickly, gray pallor, and except for her belly, she appeared thin and brittle. Sydnee believed that she was making preparations to run. She understood too well the panic she was feeling because she too had lost newborns to a monster.

The morning of All Souls Day, it rained. It added to the general malaise of everyone as they dispersed from Mass at St. Louis Cathedral. Tristan's father was out of town on business, so he attended Mass with his mother.

Sydnee never attended the Celebration of the Eucharist with them. Monsieur and Madame Saint-Yves did not want her around them, and if anyone inquired about her, they said she was ill. Sydnee was happy with this arrangement. Sitting with the Saint-Yveses in church would make her anxious, and she would be unable to feel the spirits and recite her prayers.

Thunder rumbled off and on all throughout the entire day. It was dark and candles were lit early because of the foul weather. Sydnee was busy with homework and household chores and could not visit the dogs until late that night. She ate supper and dashed over to the livery stable, returning home well after dark.

The wind rustled the trees as Sydnee stepped inside the courtyard and locked the gate. She shuddered as shadows fluttered across the stepping stones. She picked up her skirts and ran toward the house. Just as she reached the entry, someone stepped up beside her. She jumped back, startled. It was Maxime.

"I must speak with you," he whispered.

"Yes, Maxime," she replied.

He led her to the stable and up the stairs to a sparsely furnished bed chamber where Giselle was laying on a bed. Her knees were drawn up under a threadbare quilt, and she was holding a rag between her teeth. She looked at Sydnee wildly with bloodshot eyes. Clarice bent over her, dabbing her forehead with a damp cloth. Looking up quickly, Clarice nodded at Sydnee and then wrung the rag out in a bowl. The room was dimly lit with one candle.

"Giselle is frantic," Maxime said. "She has been in labor since early this morning. She does not want Madame Saint Yves to be bothered, so she stifles her cries with a rag."

Sydnee looked from Maxime to Giselle and back again.

Maxime continued, "Although Clarice knows how to midwife, Giselle wants her mother to attend her. The woman is well versed in Hoodoo remedies if needed."

Giselle spit out the rag. "You know," she said panting, "the power of Hoodoo. I know because I found the gris-gris in your room."

There was a rumble of thunder.

"Slaves cannot go out at night in New Orleans, not without a pass," Maxime said. "Can you find Giselle's mother and bring her here?"

Sydnee rubbed her forehead. "But how can *she* can go out at night?"

"She is a free woman of color," he replied.

"Where will I find her?"

"It's All Souls Day, so she will be at Saint Louis," Giselle said weakly.

"The Cathedral?" Sydnee asked.

"No, the cemetery--Basin Street."

Sydnee drew in a breath and looked at them reluctantly. She had observed the cemetery only from a distance, and it was just as she had seen it in her nightmare. It scared her, and she did not want to go near it. She also remembered the dark aura from some of the Voodoo practitioners in Congo Square. She did not want to see them either.

Sydnee rubbed her forehead. She suspected Giselle wanted potions from her mother to hasten the birth so she could flee with the child.

"Ask for Anouk. Anyone there will know her," said Giselle, breathlessly.

Sydnee bit her lip, nodded and left the room. Everything about this endeavor felt dangerous. When she stepped out into the courtyard, she looked up at the house and then at the *garçonnière* to make sure she was not being observed. Tristan was in bed. The lamp was out in his room. There were no candles burning in the main house, except in Madame Saint-Yves' room. Suddenly she realized no one put a lamp in the window for Guy.

This was Giselle's responsibility and would be a sure sign that something was amiss.

She dashed across the yard and ran up the steps into the entry. Pulling open the cupboard, she hastily lit a taper. Taking the carpeted stairs two at a time, she held her breath as she passed Madame Saint-Yves' room. She could hear the woman mumbling inside, as if in prayer, and the sound raised the hair on her arms.

At last she stepped into Guy's room. It was dark and smelled of camphor. Her palms began to perspire as she fumbled with the glass lampshade. After lighting the wick, she glanced at the tiny clock on the nightstand which read four thirty, and it confused her. Then she remembered what Tristan told her. It was the custom to stop clocks at the time of death while in mourning. This must have been the time when the Saint-Yveses had received word of Guy's drowning. Sydnee shuddered.

She looked over her shoulder furtively. She had the funny feeling that she was not alone. Nevertheless, the room was empty.

Slipping noiselessly back down the stairs, Sydnee stopped at the cupboard, replaced the candle holder and lit a lantern. It was raining and she put her shawl over her head. It was late and the streets were deserted as she walked. She wished fervently the dogs were with her. There was laughter from the taverns and inns on the wharf, and although it was comforting to hear, it grew faint as she approached Basin Street. She could identify the cemetery blocks away. Lanterns flickered warmly on buildings everywhere but there. The St. Louis side of the street was black as ebony.

Sydnee finally reached the cemetery and stopped at the entrance. She did not want to go inside. The black wrought-iron gates stood ajar. Squaring her shoulders, she tentatively pushed them open and held up her lantern. In the dim light she could see rows of crypts. They looked like little white houses lined up, one next to the other.

So this is the City of the Dead, Sydnee thought, just as Margarite had described it. Taking a deep breath, she stepped inside and started down an avenue. Suddenly she became dizzy, and her palms began to perspire. She stumbled to the wall for support, a change sweeping over her. Her head was buzzing with a droning sound that was growing steadily louder. She realized with horror that a vision from malevolent spirits was about to begin.

Her eyes closing, Sydnee saw darkness and heard moaning. A vortex of wind like a hurricane commenced, and it grew stronger and stronger, sucking her hair upward. She saw phantoms rising and swirling into the air with faces of fiery white, and their arms stretched upward. They were clothed in hooded shrouds and winding sheets. They were pleading for mercy, and their cries were growing steadily louder and more insistent. Soon they were screeching.

Sydnee put her hands to her ears to block the unholy sound. It continued on and on, the vacuum trying to suck her upward.

"St. Expedite help me!" she screamed.

Then as abruptly as it had started, the vacuum of resurrection stopped, and all was quiet. The phantoms had vanished.

Panting, Sydnee swallowed hard, trying to catch her breath. She stood for a long time collecting herself. As she recovered her senses, she started to smell moisture and earthworms. The air around her felt cool and damp, and she realized with a jolt that the evil spirits were not yet finished with her. This time she was inside a stone crypt with a decaying corpse. Before she could scream, she was vaulted from one crypt to another. She saw old people stretched out in shrouds, clutching crucifixes. There were children in tiny coffins, and young soldiers decomposing in mass graves. Although Sydnee could hear their cries of anguish and despair, the corpses and skeletons remained motionless. She flew from one crypt to another, faster and faster as if the dead were summoning her to suck the life force from her body. She was growing weak, her knees barely holding her, and tears streamed down her face.

Suddenly she felt bony fingers clasp her shoulder. It was one of the phantoms trying to take her, squeezing her shoulder tighter and tighter, gouging her skin. When it shrieked in her ear, Sydnee thought she would swoon. Her head snapped forward, and she awoke from the hallucination.

Her eyes focused, and she realized that it was not a phantom at all but Vivian clutching her shoulder. The bird had followed her. When at last she gathered her senses, she understood the vision. It was the Feast of All Souls today, and she had channeled those lost in Purgatory, pleading for deliverance. She had experienced first-hand the agony and suffering of souls not at peace.

Sydnee fought the urge to wretch. Weary beyond belief, her strength and her spirit were spent. "My loyal friend," she panted, as she stroked the crow's soft feathers. "You saved me."

Vivian clung hard to Sydnee's shoulder, determined to keep her grounded, away from the chasm of despair. Sydnee sighed. More than anything else she wanted to leave this place and go home. She knew that in the morning the spirits would be at rest, but tonight they were restless and in agony.

"Come, we must find this woman quickly," she said to Vivian. She knew Giselle was depending on her.

Holding the lantern high, Sydnee walked up and down avenues calling, "Madame Anouk? Are you here?"

The mausoleums and crypts looked macabre in the lamplight, many of them crumbling. Dead flowers and wreaths littered the walkways as well as stones and rubble. Sydnee stumbled several times but kept on driving deeper and deeper into the cemetery. Vivian riding on her shoulder gave her strength, and she summoned her best spirits to guide her and to keep her safe.

Suddenly, she heard a rattle, and she swung around, thrusting her lantern high into the air. A black-skinned woman with long tangled hair was crouching by a crypt. She was dressed like a gypsy with beads, ruffles and large earrings. Although

Sydnee could feel a dark aura from her, she was not afraid. The best of her spirit guides had formed a circle of protection around her.

Sydnee raised her chin and asked, "Are you Madame Anouk?"

"What do you want from Anouk, little girl?" the woman hissed.

"Her daughter gives birth this night. She wants her mother."

The woman's eyes narrowed as she scanned Sydnee. There was no question, this creature would do her harm if given the chance. The woman looked at Vivian. The bird ruffled her feathers and returned her gaze. Growling at the crow, she shook her rattle again.

"I will tell her," she said and disappeared into the darkness.

Sydnee started to quiver. She knew there were more like her lurking in Saint Louis. "We are done, Vivian," she said turning to go, but Sydnee realized that she had come far into the maze of the dead and had no idea how to get out. She picked her way down the avenues, turning this way and that way, until at last Vivian flew ahead of her, leading the way to the gate.

When she landed again on her shoulder, Sydnee stroked her feathers and said, "Good girl!"

When they reached home, the rain stopped, and she perched Vivian in a tree for the night. "Sleep well, my friend. Tomorrow I will find a big treat for you."

"Giselle's mother just arrived," a voice said behind her.

Sydnee jumped. It was Maxime.

"I am glad," she replied.

"I want to thank you sincerely," he said.

Sydnee looked up at Giselle's window and nodded. "Is she well?"

"Yes, she is well."

"Good night," she whispered.

"Good night."

Weary and fatigued, Sydnee climbed the stairs to bed. She slept heavily for several hours but was disturbed suddenly by a nightmare in which she heard Giselle screaming. In the dream there was a violent storm, and she looked out the window at the deluge. When lightning flashed, she spied Madame Saint-Yves rushing through the courtyard with a bundle in her arms.

Chapter 11

When Sydnee awoke the next day, she was weary and drained. She dressed and listened at the door before leaving her room. The house was quiet. Still groggy, she stumbled down the stairs and outside to the kitchen. It was empty, and the work table was clean. She found it curious because the kitchen was seldom unattended.

She found Maxime arranging books and papers in the schoolroom. There were dark shadows under his eyes.

"Why is no one in the kitchen?" she asked.

"The women made breakfast early so they could prepare the body for burial."

Sydnee's eyes grew large. "What body?"

"Giselle died last night."

She gasped. "But you said she was well!"

Maxime dropped his eyes. "There was a turn of events. She started bleeding and--"

"The baby?"

"He survived but was very weak. Madame Saint-Yves took him away to be attended to."

Sydnee covered her mouth with horror. So there had been no escape. Madame had won. "Did Giselle see her take the baby?"

Maxime pressed his eyes shut and nodded. Suddenly he found it curious that Sydnee asked this question. He looked hard at her and asked, "Why?"

"No reason."

Sydnee's knees felt wobbly, and she slid down into a chair. She realized that the nightmare last night had indeed been a reality. She *had* heard Giselle screaming, and she *had* seen Madame Saint-Yves whisking the baby away. She believed that

Giselle had lost her will to live after her child was taken from her. Memories flooded her, and her eyes filled with tears.

"I will be tutoring Tristan in mathematics privately today," Maxime said. "I suggest you do reading and geography on your own."

"Yes, Maxime," Sydnee responded, without looking up. She gathered her books and went back to her room to study.

It was difficult concentrating on her schoolwork, but she managed to finish by midday. When Sydnee picked up her noon meal, the women in the kitchen were quiet. Everyone seemed mute and stunned.

She ate by the fountain, and when she finished she brushed off her apron, tied on her green poke bonnet, and walked down to give Monsieur Schinden money from Tristan to board the dogs.

Schinden's Livery Stable and Undertaking Establishment was two blocks down from the Saint-Yves home. It was a large brown stucco building with huge wooden doors. It smelled of hay and horse dung. The dogs bounded up to see her the moment she walked into the stable. She bent down and hugged them before walking into the dark office.

Carl Schinden, a stout, middle-aged Prussian with huge arms, looked up from his desk with a scowl. *"Ja?"* he barked.

"I have payment for the dogs," Sydnee murmured, holding out coins in her gloved hand.

He snatched the money from her, tossed it inside his desk and looked back down at his ledger without another word.

Returning to the stable, Sydnee stopped and looked at the black hearse parked in the corner. She peeked through the glass at the empty chamber. The window was draped in dark velvet, and the curtains were tied back with black tassels. She looked at the identical white hearse standing nearby. This vehicle was for children's funerals. Sydnee chastised herself for looking at the hearses. This was the last thing she needed to see after the events of last night.

"Gish!" Schinden roared suddenly behind her.

Sydnee jumped.

The Prussian walked past her, calling to Mortimer in a thick accent, "I go out now. You be done when I get back, or I beat you to an inch of your life!"

"Yes, Mr. Schinden," she heard Mortimer mumble. The boy was in the back of the stable, brushing one of the horses. He had on a soiled smock and leather apron. The dogs were sitting beside him.

When Schinden walked out the door, Sydnee went over. The dogs bounded up, and she squatted down to hug them.

"Good afternoon, Mademoiselle Sydnee." Mortimer said, still brushing the horse.

"Hello, Mortimer. The dogs seem happy," she said. "I can tell that you are good to them. Thank you."

He looked down at them with a smile, his long dirty hair dropping down in front of his face. "They are easy to get to know except for Madame Vivian."

Sydnee's jaw dropped. "Vivian comes here?"

Mortimer nodded. "She sits outside in that tree. I have tried to coax her inside, but she refuses."

Sydnee chuckled and said, "You are getting to know Vivian. She *is* stubborn."

She walked around the livery looking at the horses. Most of the stalls were occupied. Although it was dark and stuffy, the stable was clean.

"You do all this by yourself?" she asked, coming back and scratching Baloo behind the ears.

"Yes."

She spied a cat in the corner, panting as if it was in pain, and she heard a horse wheezing. "Are some of these animals sick?"

"Yes."

"You take in sick animals too?"

"Yes, I try to help them."

Sydnee remembered Tristan saying that Mortimer had a way with creatures. She shook her head. "There is much work here."

"I have many friends. It is a fair bargain," he said.

Sydnee smiled. She understood him completely. She watched him for a while as he moved around the stable. His gait was so unusual. When he was not carrying something, Mortimer's arms hung limply at his sides. He never swung them, and his head was always lowered.

He walked over and removed a bridle and some black plumes from a rack. "I apologize, Mademoiselle Sydnee, but I must get ready for a funeral. I am short on time."

Sydnee realized that he was gently telling her he had no time to talk. She started to leave and then reconsidered. She dreaded returning home. "Mortimer? Would you like some help?"

"Mr. Schinden would not allow it."

"But he is gone. If he returns, I will act as if I had taken the dogs out for a walk and just come back."

Mortimer hesitated, looking down at floor. He said at last, "Very well."

For the next few hours, Sydnee helped Mortimer attend to the sick animals, groom the horses, and clean the stalls. Just before Schinden returned, they finished hitching the team to the hearse and securing the black plumes to the horse's heads.

Sydnee hid in the shadows as Schinden marched in, examining everything. He berated Mortimer for the poor shine on the horse brasses and for not tying back the drapes properly in the hearse. After spitting tobacco juice onto the sick cat, he pulled on his black undertaker's coat and barked, "Get my hat!"

The boy scurried over to a peg returning with a black mourner's hat. The squat Prussian climbed onto the hearse, belched and snapped the reins. He disappeared down the street to the funeral of an elderly woman.

Sydnee stepped out and asked, "Can you rest for a while?"

He nodded and said, "Let's sit with Lady Rowena."

He walked over and sat down by the sick cat who had fallen asleep. He took a rag from his pocket and wiped the spittle from her fur.

"This is Lady Rowena?" Sydnee asked, sitting down beside him.

"Yes, I took the name from the book *Ivanhoe*."

"You read?"

"I do. Monsieur Tristan brings me books."

"He does? How old are you?"

Mortimer shrugged. "I am not sure. I think I am about your age."

"How did you come to be here?"

"My mother couldn't feed us so she apprenticed us all out to merchants. I ended up here at the livery stable. It was a long time ago."

"Did your mother teach you to read?" Sydnee asked.

"No, I taught myself," he said, fiddling with some straw.

She blinked in amazement. When he leaned forward, she noticed purple bruises on his arms and face, and she suspected Schinden beat him. The two sat for a long time in silence petting the cat. There was little need to talk, but at last, Sydnee asked, "What do you want to do when you grow up?"

Mortimer cocked his head in thought and said, "I want my own stable."

"A livery?"

"Sort of," he said. "But mainly a stable to take care of sick animals."

Sydnee nodded thoughtfully. "My mother taught me the ways of the still room, potions, remedies and such. Maybe I can help you."

"Maybe," Mortimer said. "What about you?"

Sydnee put her head back on the wooden stall and said, "I want to ride in a paddle wheeler as a fancy lady someday. That's what I want to do."

*　　　　　*　　　　　*

There were many visits with Mortimer Gish after that day. Sometimes Tristan would accompany Sydnee too. It was difficult for him to get away with his parents in residence, but he always seemed to find a way. On days when Schinden was gone, the three youngsters would work together in the livery; taking care of the animals, grooming and cleaning the horses and caring for sick creatures. They became close, sharing their hopes and dreams and sometimes their worries and fears with each other. Each of them had been lonely, and at last they had companionship.

"Mortimer, why don't you swing your arms when you walk?" Tristan asked, one afternoon in December.

"I do swing my arms," the boy said with surprise.

"No you don't," said Tristan, and he demonstrated how Mortimer walked with his arms hanging at his sides.

Sydnee was sitting, leaning against one of the stalls eating an apple and listening. Mortimer peered out from under his stringy hair to watch Tristan.

"Here," said Tristan. "I'll help you." and he walked along Mortimer's side, helping him swing his arms.

Mortimer tried it on his own, several times. He was stiff and clumsy as he experimented, and he seemed to walk even more awkwardly.

Tristan stood back and watched thoughtfully. He put his fist to his mouth and cocked his head, observing him. He gave several suggestions, and each time Mortimer tried to swing his arms, his walk looked worse.

At last, Tristan shrugged said, "Well, Mortimer, this is just who you are."

Sydnee nodded in agreement, finishing her apple. They never discussed it again. Unconditional acceptance was the cornerstone of their friendship.

On many occasions, Sydnee helped Mortimer minister to the sick animals. The boy taught her how to help with births, treat mange, and set broken bones. She in turn shared Margarite's recipes for ointments and tonics, salves, and poultices. She imparted the wisdom of Hoodoo and explained the healing power of the spirits to him.

Tristan was included in the exchange as well. Mortimer taught him how to groom and shoe a horse, swing a hammer and sew leather. Tristan in turn brought the boy books and taught him how to write.

*   *   *

Three evenings a week, Sydnee and Tristan attended Madame Picard's School of Etiquette and Dance. "This is New Orleans's finest school for young people," Maxime told Sydnee. "Madame Picard, an acquaintance of mine, has been gracious enough to allow you in her classroom even though you cannot pay."

Sydnee noticed that Maxime had been treating her differently since she had delivered the message to Giselle's mother on All Soul's Day. He took a personal interest in her education and began to mentor her. He spent more time with her in the classroom and tailored much of the coursework to fit her needs. Sydnee was grateful for all that he was doing. His attention pleased her immensely, and more than anything, she wanted him to be proud of her.

The afternoon before the first etiquette class, Sydnee was nervous. She was afraid that she would act gauche and unrefined in front of Madame Picard, so Tristan tried to calm her fears. He told her that, although Madame Picard was the most famous quadroon and free woman of color in all of New Orleans, she was gracious and patient with all of her students.

Although in her middle years, he admitted that she was still a beauty and had the bearing of a queen. In her youth, Madame Picard had been the most sought-after woman in all of New Orleans, and eventually she became the consort of the most powerful and handsome planter in Louisiana. Her salon on Royal Street still hosts the *crème de la crème* of New Orleans' society, he explained, and to this day, her fashion and taste is emulated throughout the South. In spite of all this beauty and refinement, he assured Sydnee, you will find no one more charming and kind. Tristan leaned close to her ear and whispered, "*And* it is common knowledge that the great love of her life is Maxime."

Sydnee's eyebrows shot up. "Really?" she gasped.

"Indeed," murmured Tristan, nodding his blond head.

Suddenly Sydnee was eager to attend the school. She wanted to see this beautiful woman who could move mountains. She put on her royal blue gown, her silk bonnet and her finest gloves.

Madame Picard's town house on Toulouse Street was a modest, peach-colored, two-story stucco structure. It had petite balconies that were encircled by black filigree iron railings and matching black shutters on the windows. The sidewalk to the front door was bordered with autumn flowers; pink asters, snow white mums, blue hyssops and red firecracker bushes. When Tristan and Sydnee stepped inside the house, they were shown to the parlor where class was to be held. The room was fashionably appointed in the Second Empire style with two low sofas and several chairs upholstered in deep blues with cream accents. The windows had heavy drapes of the same color and a table was set for tea in front of the fireplace.

Using manners he learned the year before in class, Tristan introduced Sydnee to Madame Picard and all twelve of the students.

Sydnee was awestruck. Madame Picard was even more beautiful than she imagined. She was tall and willowy with smooth dark hair streaked with white. Her lips were full and sensuous, her eyebrows arched and her skin was the color of amber.

"Welcome, Mademoiselle Sauveterre," she said. "My dear friend Maxime speaks highly of you."

Sydnee felt her face flush, and she dropped her eyes. "Thank you, Madame Picard," she mumbled.

The students all stared at Sydnee. They were her age and children of the finest families in New Orleans. They were curious about this cousin from Mississippi and followed Madame Picard's example being gracious and welcoming to her.

As Sydnee stepped back, trying to hide from inquisitive eyes, she wondered if Madame Picard knew the truth about her previous life. Maxime told Sydnee that Madame Picard judged people on the content of their character rather than their pedigree and this was just one of the many reasons she was considered a great lady. If she *did* know about Sydnee's background, she treated her no differently from the rest of the class. She included her in everything and addressed her as she would any other student.

"Come, let us begin," Madame Picard announced to the group.

That first evening the students worked on introductions, conversational skills, and the etiquette of tea. Although shy and self-conscious, Sydnee sat on the edge of her seat listening to every word Madame Picard said, watching her every movement.

Just before they dismissed for the night, Madame said, "The next time we meet, we will work on the language of flowers and the fan. Gentlemen, this is necessary for you as well, so you receive messages properly from the ladies."

On the way home, Tristan said to Sydnee, "When you weren't looking Madame Picard was studying you tonight."

Sydnee started. "Oh no, I don't fit in!"

Tristan looked at her with surprise and then continued walking, deep in thought. "No," he said at last. "I don't think that was it. I am not sure what it was."

"She will not be inviting me back," Sydnee said, crestfallen.

Contrary to her fears though, Sydnee was invited back, again and again. Madame Picard, just like Maxime, had taken an interest in her.

*   *   *

Weeks turned to months as Sydnee and Tristan worked during the day with Maxime and in the evening with Madame Picard. In their free time, they would practice their dancing or simulate fetes to polish their manners. Sydnee was even learning to play the piano forte.

A week before Christmas, school was dismissed, so the youngsters traveled to *Saint-Denis* for the holiday. Tristan's parents decided to go to Natchez early, so they left an aged cousin to chaperone Tristan and Sydnee at the plantation over the holiday.

"Her sight is poor and so is her hearing," Tristan said with a smirk about Cousin Agnes.

When Sydnee raised an eyebrow, he countered with mock indignation, "Of course we will do nothing wrong."

"Of course not," Sydnee replied.

Sydnee was excited when the landau turned up the long driveway lined with ancient oak trees. *Saint-Denis* was a sprawling cotton plantation. Like other grand estates along the Mississippi, the manor house was a large, two storied structure with soaring columns built in the Greek revival style. What set it apart though was a white pillared veranda which arched out gracefully in a semicircle to welcome guests. It was a beautiful addition to an already grand structure. In anticipation of Christmas, boughs of evergreen were draped over the black iron railings on the upper and lower level of the gallery.

It was early evening and candles winked in the windows as they pulled up. The carriage stopped at the veranda, and the youngsters jumped out. Christmas wreathes made of myrtle and sprinkled with red cassina berries hung on the two doors of the entrance.

Tristan took Sydnee by the hand, and they raced inside. The entry was large and dominated by a broad sweeping staircase. Sydnee's lips parted, and she gasped.

"Look where you are standing," Tristan said, and he pointed up at a kissing ball over her head. He darted over and kissed her cheek. "Come, I will show you around," he said.

The slaves lit candles in all the rooms to welcome them. He opened two heavy double doors and took Sydnee into the parlor first. It was the grandest room she had ever seen. The walls were a pale yellow with elaborately scrolled white cornices. The chairs and sofas were upholstered in gold, and a huge gilded mirror hung over the fireplace with green boughs of myrtle and holly on the mantel below it. Gold candle holders with crystal tear drops ornamented either end of the arrangement. A large glossy piano forte stood at attention by two tall windows which were draped in a sheer white voile.

"We can practice our etiquette in here," Tristan said.

All of the rooms on the main floor were grand and designed for entertaining. There was a drawing room for the ladies, a smoking room for the men and a grand dining room, but by far the most elaborate chamber was the ballroom. "Here is where we can practice our dance steps," Tristan said, sweeping into a bow in front of Sydnee.

She ignored him and ran her eyes over the room with a gasp. The room was dressed all in bright white. There were white pillars, white walls and a white marble floor and fireplace. There was a shiny black piano forte in the musician's alcove, floral chairs in the corners and a portrait of Monsieur and Madame Saint-Yves over the mantel.

"I'm hungry. Let's see what cook has for us," said Tristan, tugging on Sydnee's sleeve. "Come on. This is just a room."

Reluctantly, she followed him out into the hall and asked, "When is Mortimer coming out with the dogs?"

"In a few days. Schinden is making him scrub the entire stable before he leaves. He is angry that my father stole him away permanently."

Several days ago, Monsieur Saint-Yves sent word that he was purchasing racehorses. He told Maxime to hire Mortimer Gish immediately to be *Saint-Denis'* head groom.

"There is no question my father knows talent when he sees it," said Tristan. "Maxime is the best educator in the South, and Mortimer will be the best groom in Louisiana."

"I'm glad Mortimer will be free from Schinden," said Sydnee. "He will never be able to beat him again."

"Indeed," said Tristan.

After supper, Sydnee raced upstairs to see her bedroom. It was similar to her bed chamber in New Orleans except for the view. When she opened the French doors and walked out onto the gallery she could see a small lake glistening in the moonlight, surrounded by lawns as soft as velvet and the Great River in the distance. She swept her eyes over the landscape and spotted Vivian sitting in a tree outside Tristan's room. The crow would not let the boy out of her sight. Sydnee marveled at how much her life had changed in the past year. She had come a long way since her life on the Natchez Trace. She wondered how long this dream could last.

Chapter 12

The next morning a carriage pulled up to *Saint-Denis,* and the footman helped an elderly woman step out followed by her granddaughter.

Cousin Agnes Saint-Yves came down the stairs of the plantation house to welcome her long-time friend, Sophia Trudeau. Kissing cheeks, the two elderly women started up the steps slowly. They were in black satin gowns with black lace caps on their gray heads.

"It has been too long, Sophia," Agnes said, taking her friend's elbow. "We have so much to talk about. We will have tea and catch up on all the news."

Sydnee gave Madame Trudeau her best curtsy while Tristan steadied the women up the stairs. He wondered why they always wore black. He assumed that they were forever attending some funeral or other. He looked over his shoulder at Isabel, Sophia Trudeau's granddaughter, who gave him a dazzling smile.

When Sydnee saw the girl, her eyes grew wide. She looked like Tristan's twin. She was about his age, her eyes were a bright blue, and her hair was golden. She had it parted in the middle with a knot on top of her head and long golden ringlets on either side of her face. Her gown was mauve with large *gigot* sleeves, and she wore a matching ribbon around her head. "Hello, Mademoiselle Sauveterre," Isabel said, turning to Sydnee. "Tristan has been writing to me about you. I feel as if I know you already."

Sydnee dropped into a curtsy. "It is my pleasure," she murmured. "Please, Mademoiselle Trudeau, call me Sydnee."

Isabel took both of her hands and said warmly, "If you call me by my Christian name, Isabel."

Isabel picked up her skirts and dashed over to pinch Tristan on the arm as he escorted the ladies inside. He made a face at her over his shoulder. Sydnee followed them into the house feeling as plain as a sparrow in her gray and black plaid skirt and charcoal jacket.

"You children run along now," Cousin Agnes said, as she ushered Madame Trudeau into the drawing room.

"What shall we do?" Tristan said to the girls as they walked down the hall.

"Is Mortimer here yet?" Isabel asked.

"No later today."

Isabel looked back to include Sydnee in the conversation. "Tristan said that you know Mortimer too. We will all be great friends."

"You know him?" Sydnee asked.

"Oh, I have known Mortimer for as long as I can remember. We always board our horses at Schinden's when we are in New Orleans, and my father has even had him out to the plantation to attend to our sick animals."

"Now he will be here all the time," said Tristan.

"I am so glad. We can talk books endlessly," Isabel said wistfully.

Tristan stopped and looked down the hall furtively. Lowering his voice, he whispered, "Let's take the rowboat out."

Isabel's jaw dropped. "Cousin Agnes wouldn't object?"

"She would. Why do you think I'm whispering?"

"You have only done it once, Tristan. Will you remember what to do?" Isabel asked.

Tristan put his chin up indignantly and said, "Of course I remember."

The three raced to the shed by the lake and pulled the rowboat down to shore, resting it on the grassy bank under a weeping willow. Tristan took his boots off and rolled up the legs on his pantaloons. He stepped into the water, pulling the boat out onto the lake.

Isabel tossed her parasol into the boat and said, "You get in first, Sydnee."

Unsteadily, Sydnee stepped in, and the craft rocked. It was her first time in a small boat.

"Stay low," Tristan instructed.

She sat down and looked back at Isabel who hopped in, followed by Tristan. Sydnee's face lit up as they glided out smoothly onto the lake. Isabel put her lace parasol up and asked, "Are we going around the island first?"

"Yes, we will show Sydnee everything," Tristan said, starting to row.

The lake was bigger than it looked. It curved around and joined up at one end with a lazy little stream and at the other end it melted into thick marshland. Ducks and geese paddled on the open water and herons strutted among the lily pads and reeds. Most of the shore surrounding the lake was for cotton and even though there were no crops in December, *Saint-Denis'* slaves were still busy tending cattle, repairing fences and keeping the lawns and gardens manicured.

The marshy side of the lake was wild and heavily forested. It was dark and thick with bald cypress, tupelo and iris. It reminded Sydnee of the back country of Mississippi.

The three spent the entire afternoon rowing lazily around the lake. They took turns with the oars, and when they weren't visiting, they were dozing in the sunshine. The water was as blue as a robin's egg and the sky as well. Sydnee had never felt such peace. The spirits were everywhere; in the water, overhead in the sky, and especially in her young friends.

"This is heaven," Isabel said, lounging in the front of the boat. "It is not often we can break away from our chaperones to have fun," she said to Sydnee. "But it sounds as if lately you have managed to steal away. Tristan wrote to me about why his father brought you here and how instead you sneak off to see New Orleans in the afternoons. I'm jealous," she said with a pout. "But now I have you too. I am so tired of boys. It is always Tristan, Mortimer or my older brothers."

"I've never had a girlfriend," said Sydnee.

"Nor I," said Isabel, dragging her hand through the water.

Sydnee marveled at how smooth and white Isabel's skin was and how perfect the features were on her face. Her nose was tiny and turned up ever so slightly like a sprite, and her eyebrows arched gracefully over her blue eyes.

Suddenly Isabel sat up straight, rocking the boat.

"Whoa!" exclaimed Tristan, grabbing the sides.

"Look," Isabel said. "There he is!" There was no mistaking Mortimer as he walked to the stable with his arms dangling at his sides and the dogs loping behind him. "Let's go back, right now," she exclaimed.

Tristan picked up the oars and rowed back. The moment they pulled up to shore, Isabel lifted her skirts and hopped out, running for the stable. Sydnee watched in amazement as she dashed up the hill, and then she looked at Tristan. He shrugged and shook his head. "For as long as I can remember, she has been in love with him. I don't expect it will ever change."

*   *   *

Sydnee explored every inch of the plantation. Every day was a new adventure with Tristan. They would exercise the horses with Mortimer, read books under the elms, play with the dogs, or examine bugs with the magnifying glass. Even when Cousin Agnes had them help with household duties, they would invent stories or turn their chores into an amusing competition.

Sydnee liked Cousin Agnes. Her face was as wrinkled as a prune, and she smelled heavily of lavender, but she never had a harsh word for them. Frequently she would invite them into the drawing room for Christmas ribbon candy which she kept in a glass jar on the mantel. She loved the dogs too and would sneak treats to them throughout the day.

One afternoon Sophia Trudeau and Isabel returned for a visit. The first thing Isabel asked when she jumped out of the carriage was, "Are the cooks out of the kitchen? I want to bake a cake."

Tristan's eyebrows shot up. He said with surprise, "You want to bake?"

"Yes I do," she said firmly.

They walked back to the kitchen house. The cooks were just finishing preparing tea for the ladies and allowed them one hour to bake.

Isabel tied on an apron and handed one to Sydnee. "We are going to make a birthday cake for Mortimer."

"What?" Tristan exclaimed. "He told me he didn't know when his birthday was."

"That's right," said Isabel. "We are declaring today his birthday."

Sydnee laughed. "That's a fine idea!"

Isabel and Sydnee pulled out crocks of all sizes filled with ingredients and set them on the long wooden work table while Tristan shoveled coals into the hearth oven. Isabel measured and cracked eggs into a large blue pottery mixing bowl while Sydnee stirred.

"What kind of cake is it?" Tristan asked sticking his finger in the batter for a taste.

"A pound cake," Isabel said. "Hand me another egg."

Tristan reached in a basket and gave her a brown egg.

"Tristan, are you coming to the fox hunt on Christmas Day again this year?"

He nodded. "Of course."

"Fox hunt?" Sydnee asked.

"Yes," Isabel said. She pushed a strand of hair away from her forehead with her wrist since her hands were sticky. "Every Christmas, my father hosts a fox hunt for other planters in the county. Mother and I stay back to supervise Christmas dinner. Will you come and help us, Sydnee?"

She nodded and smiled. It all sounded very exciting.

Isabel walked over to the oven, swung the door open, thrust her arm inside and started to count. When she reached three, she withdrew her arm and said, "It's ready."

Tristan leaned on the table and said to Isabel as she worked, "Mortimer told me that your father hired him to help in the stables the day of the hunt."

"He did. So we will all be together on Christmas."

Isabel poured the batter into a pan and handed it to Tristan. "Put that in the oven, and we'll fetch it later."

*   *   *

That evening when the sun began to set, Tristan went to the stable. "Mortimer?" he called. "I have something to show you."

Mortimer came shuffling out, wiping his hands on a rag. "Yes, Monsieur Saint-Yves?"

"You can dispense with the formalities," Tristan said. "No one is around."

With his head still lowered, he rolled his eyes up and looked at Tristan through his stringy hair.

"Follow me," Tristan said.

Mortimer stuffed the rag into his pocket and followed him down a path into the woods. Baloo and Atlantis fell into step behind them. They walked deeper and deeper into the woods as the sun was setting. When they reached the banks of *Saint-Denis'* little stream, it was dark. It was difficult to see the lazy little creek, thick with brush and overhanging trees.

Tristan whistled loudly, and Mortimer looked at him with surprise. He ran his eyes over the woods and then looked up at the sky with curiosity. Suddenly, there was a blaze of light floating down the stream.

Mortimer blinked, and his jaw dropped. "What is it?"

Tristan was grinning broadly. "It is a birthday cake for you with candles."

Mortimer stammered, "A--a cake? It is not—I don't know when--"

"I know, but we are declaring today your birthday. This is Isabel's idea, but we helped too. We baked the cake earlier today, and the girls launched it upstream."

Mortimer continued to shake his head slowly in amazement as he stared at the blaze floating down the creek. Isabel and Sydnee put the cake on a large piece of barn siding, and it wound downstream toward them.

They could hear the girls giggling as they ran through the brush toward them. They burst from the woods, laughing and cried, "Happy birthday!"

"So you did this?" he mumbled to Isabel.

"Yes," she said. "But I had plenty of help. Are you going to just let it float on by?"

Mortimer ran toward the creek. Wading out into the water, he brought the cake onto shore. Sydnee spread out an old blanket on the bank, and Mortimer set the cake down.

"Don't put all the candles out or we'll have no light," Isabel said to Tristan as he started to take off candles. She cut a piece of cake and handed it to Mortimer.

He sat down heavily on the blanket and said, "I've never had a birthday cake."

"You've never had a birthday before--that you know of," Sydnee said. "Until now."

The dogs sniffed the blanket for crumbs as Mortimer stared at the candles. They glowed brilliantly against the dark background of the forest, casting a soft light on Isabel's face. Mortimer gazed at her for a moment and then he looked away quickly as if ashamed of himself. "Thank you," he murmured.

*   *   *

"'If we stayed in New Orleans there would have been a *Reveillon* tonight," Tristan told Sydnee as they walked down the stairs to the dining room on Christmas Eve.

"What's that?" she asked.

"Everyone goes to Midnight Mass on Christmas Eve and then returns home for a feast called the *Reveillon*. We usually stay up all night. But here at *Saint-Denis* we go to bed early, so we can attend the fox hunt in the morning."

"I am eager to see this fox hunt," Sydnee said, stopping to tuck a loose strand of hair back into place. She donned her best gown tonight, a floral and stripe print with *gigot* sleeves and tiny green bows at the shoulders.

They met Cousin Agnes in the hall outside the dining room. "Merry Christmas children," she said as Tristan bowed, and Sydnee curtsied. They walked into the room, and Tristan held his cousin's chair. Sydnee waited until Cousin Agnes was seated and then sat down herself. Tristan noticed immediately that the matron was not wearing black. She wore a silver gown with lace at the neck and an amethyst necklace. He was glad to see more festive attire on Christmas.

Just as they began their meal, there were gun shots in the distance which startled Sydnee.

"Don't be alarmed, dear," said Cousin Agnes, looking toward the window. "They are shooting off firecrackers and guns at the Trudeau plantation. Many families do this on Christmas Eve."

Tristan jumped up and pulled back the drape to see out.

"Do come and sit down Tristan. Your food will grow cold. You did not ask to be excused."

Tristan returned to the table and sat down. "I apologize, Cousin Agnes," he mumbled.

They dined on oyster soup, shrimp remoulade, okra and rich brioche. When they finished, they moved to the parlor for rum cake and chocolate to drink.

Sydnee's eyebrows shot up when she saw one of her long stockings hanging by the hearth.

"Don't forget to put holly in your stockings for *Pere Noel*," said Cousin Agnes with a wry smile.

"I am guessing she has gifts for us," Tristan murmured to Sydnee.

Although Margarite explained the tradition of gift giving at Christmas, Sydnee had never experienced it. There had never been the money or the time for gifts at The Devil's Backbone.

The next morning, when they returned from Mass, there was indeed a gift in each stocking. Cousin Agnes put a shiny new jack knife in Tristan's stocking, and Sydnee received a tiny maple music box which played a Chopin mazurka. Sydnee was entranced. Listening to the delicate notes drift up from the tiny box seemed like a miracle. She held it in her lap with reverence.

Cousin Agnes watched her and said, "Well I declare, child. You act as if you have never received a gift."

Sydnee said with a shaky voice, "Thank you, Cousin Agnes. Thank you for all your kindnesses."

The woman stared at her.

Fearful that she may suspect something about Sydnee's identity, Tristan jumped up and announced, "Come it's time to get ready for the fox hunt."

They excused themselves and rushed up to their rooms to change clothes. Sydnee put on her new dark blue riding habit and looked in the mirror. Even though she was not participating in the fox hunt, she would be riding horseback to the Trudeau plantation with Tristan. Running her hands over the fine fabric, Sydnee turned from side to side. She adored her new clothes and vowed to learn as much as possible about fashion from Madame Picard. Slowly her figure was filling out, and she was glad to have a waist and a bosom at last.

Tristan looked dashing in his mustard-colored jacket, dark breeches and tall black boots. Sydnee studied him as he walked down the stairs. He was indeed a handsome and poised young man. She was glad that her feelings for him did not go beyond friendship. She knew that females held no appeal for him and that any young woman who desired him would be sorely disappointed.

It was a short ride to the Trudeau plantation. The sky was clear, and the morning air was cool. Mortimer greeted them when they arrived, taking their horses. "They are ready Master Tristan. I have saddled Serendipity for you."

Tristan put on his hunting cap, mounted Serendipity and joined the others. Sydnee dismounted and stepped out of the way to watch the men assemble for the hunt. She saw Mortimer and the stable hands adjusting saddles and checking shoes. Many of the horses were dancing around nervously. They were eager to be off, but their riders kept them reined in, laughing and shouting greetings to each other as they assembled. Everyone was in crisp new riding attire. Sydnee was amazed to see so many wealthy well-bred residents in one place.

A slave wound his way through the horses holding up a tray up so the riders could take brandy before departure. Fox hounds circled the area with their tails wagging. They were filled with anticipation for the chase.

At last a bugle sounded, signaling that the fox had been released, and the hounds started to bay loudly. There was a huge commotion, the clatter of hooves on flagstones, and they were off. Sydnee strained to see Tristan, but he was lost in the chaos as the group raced up and over the hill.

With a sigh, she turned and headed for the house to look for Isabel. The Trudeau plantation house was similar to *Saint-Denis,* built in the Greek revival style, and set near the river. The main house was brown brick with a white two-story gallery in front. The stables and kitchen were brick as well, but the slave quarters and out buildings were constructed of white-washed wood.

"Come in, Sydnee," Isabel called from a side door. "I want you to meet Mother."

As the girls walked down the hall, a woman came down the stairs holding a garland. It was Isabel's mother, Madame Trudeau. The first thing Sydnee noticed was that she was an older version of Isabel. Although her hair had darkened into a sandy brown and her face was careworn, the resemblance was obvious.

"Thank you for coming, Mademoiselle Sauveterre," she said to Sydnee. "Isabel told me that you are kind enough to help us with the Christmas festivities today."

Sydnee curtsied and said, "With pleasure, Madame Trudeau."

She followed Isabel into the dining room to arrange decorations while Madame Trudeau went outside to the kitchen to supervise meal preparation. The layout of the home was identical to *Saint-Denis.* The rooms had floor to ceiling windows for ventilation and were lined up and down on either side of a long hall.

The dining room table was set for dinner, so all that was left was dressing the windows with garlands and decorating the mantel with fruit, myrtle, and holly. When they were done, Isabel looked over her shoulder and whispered to Sydnee, "Let's go to the stable to see Mortimer before everyone gets back from the hunt."

When they arrived at the stable, they found Mortimer already busy. He was examining one of the horses and looked worried. Tristan was there too, helping a young man sit down on a bench. The youth had his arm over Tristan's shoulder and hopped on one foot. When he sat down, he took his hat off and ran his hand through his black hair in a gesture of frustration and pain.

"What happened?" Isabel asked.

Tristan looked up. "His mount stumbled and threw him."

Tristan bent down to ease the young man's boot off. The youth put his head back and held his breath. He had fine aristocratic features and pale skin which grew whiter as Tristan eased off the boot. He winced and drew up his shoulders.

"I'm sorry, D'anton," Tristan said, setting the boot aside. "I know it hurts." He stood up and looked at Isabel, "Would you ask your mother to come down here please?"

"Of course," Isabel replied. She picked up her skirts and ran toward the house.

D'anton sat back with his eyes closed. Tristan took out his handkerchief and dabbed the perspiration from the young man's forehead.

Madame Trudeau came down to the stable immediately and examined his ankle. She dressed it with eucalyptus salve, wrapped it tightly and had the young man taken up to the house to rest.

"There is no question, he will be staying with us until the swelling subsides," Madame Trudeau said to Tristan later in the house. He could see D'anton over her shoulder in the library. He was propped up in a chair with his foot on a stool. "There will be no walking and definitely no riding."

Suddenly the front and rear doors of the house burst open and riders began to flood into the hall. Madame Trudeau smiled and swept down the hall to attend to her guests. The hunt was over, and it had been a great success.

There was a flurry of activity as everyone began to dress for the midday Christmas feast. People were running up and down the stairs, laughing and greeting each other, discussing the hunt and asking about D'anton. Those who did not participate in the hunt began to arrive in carriages, including Cousin Agnes who brought dinner attire for Sydnee and Tristan.

Sydnee went up to Isabel's room and put on her best gown again. She fixed her hair up on her head with a matching ribbon and started downstairs. Isabel met her on the landing. She looked stunning, dressed in a dark pink gown trimmed in white lace. Her gigot sleeves were fashionably enlarged with sleeve plumpers. "Mother has excused us from dinner so we can take our meal with D'anton," she announced. "Tristan is in the library with him right now."

Sydnee was relieved. She was not ready to attend a formal meal yet, even though she had been practicing her manners in class.

When the girls walked into the room, the boys had their heads together, looking at a book. D'anton was sitting in a leather chair with this foot on a stool. Tristan was on a corner of the stool. D'anton looked more at ease now, his foot bandaged and elevated. He had changed out of his torn riding breeches and jacket into a dark frock coat and trousers. The suit was set off by a waistcoat of burgundy brocade. Tristan was in evening dress too, wearing a dark blue frock coat and trousers with a gold waistcoat.

He jumped up and introduced the girls to D'anton Delacroix. The young man greeted them in a heavy French accent. Sydnee noticed that he was indeed a dashing young man with bright green eyes, a slim physique and curly dark hair.

"D'anton has moved here recently from Paris," Tristan explained. "He now lives in New Orleans on Chartres Street."

"And for Christmas, are you staying in the River Country?" Isabel asked him in French.

"*Oui*, I stay at the Aurora Plantation," he replied.

"Not anymore," Tristan interrupted, looking at Isabel. "Now he stays with you."

Sydnee watched the young men as they conversed with Isabel. Even though they spoke with her, they were only aware of each other. Tristan's face was flushed with excitement, and he continually stole glances at D'anton when he was not looking.

D'anton seemed taken with Tristan as well, laughing at his jokes and teasing him. His eyes seemed to sparkle whenever he looked at Tristan, and on one occasion he pushed him flirtatiously.

At last, Isabel said to Sydnee, "Come, we must bring Christmas dinner back to these lazy boys." As they walked down the hall, she said, "It seems Tristan has received *his* gift from *Pere Noel* today," and they giggled.

Dinner was underway, and the aroma of turkey drifted out to them. They could hear guests talking and the tinkling of silver and crystal.

They turned into the serving room where the cooks made up plates for them. There was turtle soup, roast mutton and duck, turkey with oyster dressing, corn pudding and green beans with pecans. For dessert there was gingerbread and sweet potato pie. There was so much food, the cooks had to help them carry it into the library.

Sydnee had never seen such bounty. Margarite had not exaggerated when she described the wealth of the planters, in fact, it was more than she had ever imagined.

Even though the group had to balance their dinner plates on their laps, they were greatly relieved they did not have to attend the stuffy gathering in the dining room.

"Why did your family move here from Paris, D'anton?" Isabel asked before taking a bite of turkey.

"My father has business here. I will live in New Orleans only a short time and then return to Paris to complete my education and take the Grand Tour."

"You will be on your Grand Tour soon too," Isabel said to Tristan.

He nodded and shrugged. "It is expected." Suddenly, he looked up. "Has anyone taken dinner to Mortimer?"

"Sydnee and I will take him something," Isabel said. "I have a gift to give him anyway."

The boys went back to talking, and Isabel looked at Sydnee, rolling her eyes. "They have forgotten about us already. Let's go."

"Do you suppose the kitchen will have any leftovers for the dogs?" Sydnee asked, brushing off her skirt.

"Without a doubt. We will send a package home with you."

The girls took a plate of food down to Mortimer who was getting ready to return to *Saint-Denis*. "You cannot leave yet," Isabel said. She handed him a plate with a napkin over it. "We have dinner for you."

"Thank you," he said, stealing a look up at her through his hair. He took the plate and fork and sat down on some hay in a corner.

In spite of her fine gown, Isabel sat down next to him. Sydnee was unsure whether she should sit in the hay, but she followed Isabel's example.

"How is D'anton's mare?" Sydnee asked.

"She is unhurt, but I applied some liniment to her leg just in case."

"You must be hungry, the way you gobble your food," Isabel observed.

Mortimer nodded with his mouth full. He swallowed, picked up a turkey drumstick and asked, "Where is Tristan? I haven't seen him all day," asked Mortimer.

The girls looked at each other and laughed. "Oh, he is smitten with D'anton," Isabel said. "The boy who was thrown from his horse today. He is up at the house with him now."

Mortimer looked from one girl to the other and mumbled, "Oh."

He took a last bite, sighed and leaned back on the stable wall. He had cleaned his plate. "It was good."

"You're not done yet," Isabel said, reaching behind her back. She pulled out a brown paper package. "This is for you. *Joyeux Noel*"

Mortimer looked at the gift, and a smile flickered on his lips. Sydnee noticed his face flush.

"Open it," Isabel said.

He carefully unwrapped the package, held up a book and smiled. "*The Talisman.* You remembered that I like Scott. Thank you."

Isabel was beaming. "Now that you live near us, we can talk books together every day."

"Now it is my turn," Mortimer said, rising.

Isabel looked surprised. He walked over to his saddlebag, pulled out a battered leather notebook and handed it to her. "It is all I have to give."

Mortimer sat back down stiffly. He seemed nervous.

Isabel opened the notebook, read one of the pages, and her lips parted. She looked up for a moment at Mortimer then read another page. With tears in her eyes, she said, "It is your poetry."

Mortimer looked down. He was embarrassed and mumbled, "It isn't very good, but—but I mean what I say to you."

"To me?" Isabel's eyes grew wide.

Suddenly Sydnee felt uncomfortable. It was not right to be part of such an intimate moment. She stood up and announced, "Isabel, I am taking your dogs for a walk."

Isabel continued to stare at Mortimer, and he returned her gaze. They never heard Sydnee.

Calling the dogs, she walked swiftly out of the stable. As she walked along the river that Christmas afternoon, she considered the plight of her new friends. Sydnee could see that each one of them was walking a dangerous path to fulfill their dreams. They were sharing their most intimate and tender feelings with someone forbidden to them. She realized then that although they lived in a world of wealth and opulence, it came at a price.

Chapter 13

The festivities continued until Twelfth Night when friends and family gathered once more at the Trudeau plantation for farewell toasts and King Cake. This signaled the end of the Christmas season for everyone, and they now turned their attention back to work and business.

Tristan and D'anton had been inseparable during the holiday. In the landau on the way back to New Orleans, Tristan told Sydnee that he was in love.

"I am happy for you, but you must be careful," she warned. "Your parents return tonight."

"Yes, and they return months early. I will have to find a safe way to see him."

"Is his ankle improved?"

Tristan nodded. "It is almost completely healed. He returns to the city tomorrow."

Sydnee left the dogs at *Saint-Denis* to be safe. She took comfort in the knowledge that they had acres to run and that they adored Mortimer.

When they arrived at the town house on St. Louis Street, Monsieur and Madame Saint-Yves had already returned. Tristan went right in to greet them as Sydnee ducked out through the courtyard and into the schoolroom of the **garçonnière**. She peeked out at the house. The atmosphere was so much like mourning that she half expected to see a funeral crepe hanging on the door.

The next morning, Maxime resumed class, and in the evening, Tristan and Sydnee returned to Madame Picard's school. Everyone seemed to settle back into a routine, albeit an uneasy one. Sydnee missed Isabel and Mortimer desperately, and it seemed to her as if the carefree days of Christmas had been a long lost dream. Although she saw Tristan daily, he was distant from her too. He was so busy trying to please his parents and preoccupied with his thoughts of D'anton, that she felt quite alone.

Another disconcerting occurrence was the sudden attention Monsieur Saint-Yves was giving her. Several times when she was alone in the schoolroom he appeared with the excuse that he was looking for Maxime. Another time he brushed past her closely in the hall when she was going to bed. Each time he tried to catch and hold her eye. Memories of the men at The Devil's Backbone began to haunt her again, and she started having nightmares.

Things had certainly taken a turn for the worse in the new year.

*   *   *

"Tristan," said Monsieur Saint-Yves one night at supper. "It has come to my attention that you are acquainted with a young gentleman by the name of D'anton Delacroix."

Tristan almost dropped his spoon into the bisque. Putting his hands into his lap to steady them, he looked up at his father. Swallowing hard, he raised his chin and said, "Yes, we met at the fox hunt."

"His father is a business associate of mine, and they have moved here recently from Paris. Monsieur Delacroix would like his son to be introduced to other young men of good family in New Orleans. I have suggested the two of you attend one of the balls this evening."

"Very well, Father," said Tristan, trying to act nonchalant. He did not notice his mother purse her lips and raise an eyebrow.

Her look was not lost on Monsieur Saint-Yves though. He knew that his wife objected to these soirees. It was common knowledge that young women of mixed race would attend these balls where a suitable match may be made with white gentlemen of property. Contracts would sometimes be negotiated for a suitable long term sexual relationship. This is where Monsieur Saint-Yves had found his mistress.

"Odette," he said to the slave who was attending their supper. "Please pour some wine for your mistress. She needs to calm her nerves."

Augusta Saint-Yves looked up sharply. "What is this?"

"You are correct, Madame. I don't ordinarily allow you wine at supper, but tonight you seem somewhat—anxious."

Odette brought the decanter around to her mistress and poured her a glass. Madame Saint-Yves looked at her husband suspiciously as she tipped the crystal wine glass to her lips.

The rest of the meal was taken in silence. Monsieur watched his wife, as she refused food and consumed glass after glass of wine. When dinner was finished Odette had to help her up the stairs because she was so inebriated.

"Take her to Guy's room," Cuthbert Saint-Yves ordered, watching them climb the steps. "She is most comfortable there."

"What time does the carriage come around for me, Father?" Tristan asked, his face flushed with excitement.

"At half past the hour."

Tristan dashed upstairs to get dressed. When he was ready he knocked on the door of Sydnee's bed chamber. "How do I look?" he asked. He was dressed in his finest frock coat of dark green with black pantaloons and a gold waistcoat.

"Very nice," she said. "Where are you going?"

"To a Quadroon Ball. D'anton's father arranged it. I am guessing our fathers want us to look for mistresses."

Sydnee went to bed that night wondering about this new turn of events for Tristan. She was anxious to ask him more about it in the morning. She fell asleep quickly but was awakened with a knock on the door. Putting her wrap on, she stumbled across the room, opened the door, and there was Maxime. "Monsieur wants to see you in his bed chamber."

Sydnee stared at him. He gave her a look of mixed pity and apology, before dropping his eyes.

She nodded and closed the door. Sydnee knew that she could not refuse the master of the house. Reluctantly she pulled on her everyday gown, slipped on her shoes and stepped out of the room. Pausing a moment, she squeezed her eyes shut to try to steady herself. *So it is starting again.* As if it was yesterday, she could hear her father roaring for her to come to the cabin. She could feel the men groping her and smell their stinking breath.

As if she was going into battle, she took a deep breath and started down the hall. As she passed Guy's bed chamber, she hesitated. Someone inside was sobbing. It raised the hair on her arms to hear sounds coming from that room, and then she realized it was Madame Saint-Yves. She bit her lip and continued down the hall.

When she stepped up to the Master's bedroom, she squared her shoulders and knocked.

"Enter," was the reply.

Cuthbert Saint-Yves was standing by the mantel in a long burgundy dressing gown, smoking a cigar in the candlelight. His long face was white and his narrow eyes were cold. Putting out his cigar, he ordered, "Go stand by the bed."

Her heart hammering in her chest, Sydnee complied. When he walked over, he seemed to be seven feet tall. Suddenly, he reached up, grabbed a handful of hair and bent her over the bed, facedown. She cried out, terrified. With the violence of a madman he pushed her head into the bedclothes as he lifted her skirts. Sydnee squeezed her eyes shut trying to endure the pain and humiliation. *Give me strength. Please take me away.*

Gradually her petitions were answered, and she could hear the gentle tinkling of wind chimes and see the blue expanse of the Mississippi. There were birds soaring overhead.

"You filthy whore," a hoarse voice whispered. It was Saint-Yves mumbling obscenities in her ear. She listened to his vile language and squeezed her eyes shut. The man's violence was terrifying.

Just as she was struggling to escape to someplace peaceful once more, there was a shriek from another room. Saint-Yves pushed himself up off of Sydnee and ran from the room. Through the open door, Sydnee could see light flickering and heavy smoke rolling down the hall. Something was on fire.

She dashed down the hall to see Guy's room in a blaze. The vigil lamp was smashed on the floor, and the bed curtains were in flames. In the middle of the inferno, Monsieur and Madame Saint-Yves were struggling. She was in a long white nightgown, biting and kicking her husband savagely as he tried to choke her.

Sydnee stood on the threshold paralyzed at the macabre sight. They staggered from one end of the room to the other, locked in a deadly embrace. Madame was like a wildcat, clawing and screaming while Monsieur Saint-Yves looked down at her squeezing her neck. At last, they tumbled into the flaming curtains.

Sydnee sprang forward to stop them just as Madame Saint-Yves' gown started on fire. The flames crackled up her back jumping to the loose ends of her dark hair. She screamed in terror, wrenched herself free and lunged for the door, but her husband was too quick. He caught her by the wrist and threw her to the floor.

Sydnee dashed over and pulled a blanket from the linen press. Saint-Yves snapped back to reality and helped Sydnee roll the woman into the bedding.

The room was engulfed in flames. The drapes and the wardrobe were on fire as well as the carpet. Saint-Yves picked his wife up and carried her down the stairs in the blanket. Sydnee ran behind him. She ran for help, but it was too late. The house on St. Louis Street burned to the ground.

*   *   *

"My mother will recover with few scars," Tristan told Sydnee late the next day as they stood before the smoking ruins of the house. He ran his eyes over the charred remains. Only the chimneys were left standing with blackened rubble around them. One of the adjoining houses had been affected, but the fire had been extinguished before there had been extensive damage. The air was thick with the smell of burnt timber.

Tristan turned back toward the *garçonnière* which was unaffected. The carriage house and slave quarters were intact as well. "You and I will stay in the *garçonnière*," he said. "I told my father that I do not want to go to *Saint-Denis*. I will have a bed brought in, so we can make up a room for you in the classroom."

Sydnee looked at Tristan. The last few months he had changed, gaining confidence and maturity. Although he was getting ready to step into his role as a gentleman of means, it wasn't just the acquisition of manners and social graces that had changed him. It was something more fundamental. He stood taller and was more in charge. It was as if he had become a soldier readying himself for battle. Sydnee had not told him about the incidents that occurred the night the house burned, yet somehow she believed that he knew.

They settled into the *garçonnière* for the next few months. They slept, ate, and attended class while crews outside shoveled and carted away rubble and debris.

One afternoon, a slave came to the schoolroom interrupting Maxime's lesson. He informed Tristan that his father wanted him to attend supper at Victor's Restaurant on Bourbon Street that evening.

"My father is in town?" Tristan asked with surprise.

"Yes, sir."

"I thought he was in Natchez," he said with a sigh. "Very well. Please tell him I will meet him at eight, no earlier."

Sydnee's eyebrows shot up, and she looked at Maxime who was staring in wonder at Tristan. The hint of a smile played around his lips, and he nodded his head. She could tell he was pleased that his student was finding his voice at last.

That evening Tristan called for a carriage and went to Victor's Restaurant to dine with his father. It was an intimate eating establishment catering exclusively to the upper class of New Orleans. Its pristine interior had murals on the walls, crystal chandeliers and crisp white linen. Even though it was a busy night, Cuthbert Saint-Yves was seated at the best table in the house, drinking an aperitif. Through the window he could see Tristan step out of the family landaulet.

Cuthbert Saint-Yves narrowed his eyes as he puffed on his cigar and watched his son. The young man was fashionably dressed in a black evening coat and pantaloons and a white satin waistcoat and cravat. Heads turned as he walked into the restaurant. He checked his hat and gloves at the door and came over to the table. "Good evening, Father."

"Why is it necessary we dine at eight?" Cuthbert said, without greeting him.

"I had some matters of business to attend to," Tristan replied, flipping his coattails up and sitting down.

A hint of anger passed over his father's face. "I hope this time is convenient for you," he said sarcastically.

Ignoring the gibe Tristan replied, "Why yes, it suits me well, thank you. How is Mother?"

Monsieur Saint-Yves sat back and puffed on his cigar, studying his son. The young man seemed different to him. Tristan returned his gaze coolly.

"Your mother is almost completely recovered."

"That is good news. Send her my regards, will you?"

Saint-Yves continued to watch his son as a waiter came up to take the young man's order. "I will have sherry, and I believe that I would like the duck tonight."

"I have already ordered the roast chicken with bordelaise for you," his father announced.

Tristan handed the menu to the waiter and said, "Cancel that. I will have the duck.'

Monsieur Saint-Yves raised an eyebrow as the waiter bowed and left. He did not like his son's new found independence, but he ignored it and continued, "I summoned you here to inform you of several changes," he said, leaning forward and putting out his cigar. "First of all, you will not continue to live in the *garçonnière*. You will sail as soon as possible for Paris to complete your education and start your Grand Tour."

Tristan's heart jumped. Once again fate had looked favorably upon him. D'anton was leaving for Europe soon too.

"But that creature, who you have been keeping as a carnal tutor, must go."

Tristan set his jaw. He had been anticipating this moment for months, and he was ready. "Yes, father. I agree. It is not appropriate having her stay in the *garçonnière* any longer."

"Good, I am glad you are listening to reason."

"I will be taking her permanently as my *inamorata*," stated Tristan.

Cuthbert Saint-Yves slammed his hands on the table and barked, "You will not!"

Several customers looked over at them, but Tristan did not flinch or take his eyes from his father's face. "You are too late, Father. I have made arrangements for a town house on Dauphin Street."

"With *my* money?" his father said, his chest heaving.

"No, I have my own money from Grandfather. You know that."

The waiter approached with aperitifs, and the men fell silent.

"This is an outrage," his father hissed.

"*You* have a mistress, Father," Tristan said calmly, sipping his sherry. "Why is this an outrage?"

Cuthbert looked from side to side, afraid someone had heard. He lowered his voice and said, "Adelaide is a distinguished quadroon of refinement and breeding. Papers were drawn up--"

"Yes, I have everything in order too. That is my last word on it, Father."

At that moment, the waiter approached and set down the meals. "Oh look, here is our food. Very good," said Tristan to the server. "I have just what I want."

*   *   *

On her sixteenth birthday, Tristan presented Sydnee with her new townhome on Dauphin Street. It seemed as if all of her prayers were answered in one day. She would not have to leave Tristan. She would have her own home, and Vivian and the dogs could live with her permanently.

From the moment she laid eyes on it, Sydnee fell in love with her little house. It was a petite two-story stucco townhome in a good neighborhood. Although it was in need of paint, new shutters and minor repairs, the foundation was strong, and the structure was sturdy.

Sydnee walked through the parlor, her eyes glowing. "Oh, I love it! How can I ever thank you?"

"Thank Monsieur Girard for drawing up the papers but especially thank D'anton. He helped me pick it out," said Tristan, holding his hat in his gloved hand. "He seemed to know just what you would fancy. With a little care, it will be the most charming house in the neighborhood."

"Oh, D'anton was right, but where is he?"

Tristan's smiled dropped. "He is having another one of his spells."

"How many days?"

"Three days sleeping," said Tristan. "I wish he would wake up. He needs to get ready for his voyage to Paris. He leaves within the week."

"And when do you leave?" Sydnee asked, not wanting to hear an answer.

"Not for another month."

Tristan reached out and touched her arm, saying cheerfully, "Which will give us plenty of time to bring this house to life."

Sydnee laughed and looked around. "I am very happy."

"I'm glad."

They stepped through the French doors out into a small courtyard. It was overrun with weeds and vines, but Sydnee found a trellis and wrought-iron loveseat beneath the tangled overgrowth. She pulled back the brush and sat down. Tristan bent over, ducked in and sat down beside her. "With some raking and weeding, this too will be beautiful," he said. "And you will never have to leave me."

*   *   *

Every day when they were finished with their studies, Sydnee and Tristan would change into old clothes and go to the house on Dauphine Street to work. They swept the floors, knocked down cobwebs, weeded, and raked.

Madame Trudeau had shopping in New Orleans one day, so Isabel came to help too. Knowing that her mother would not approve of Sydnee's living arrangement, she told her that Sydnee was setting up housekeeping with her old aunt. Isabel knew that soon enough her mother would find out, but until that time, she chose to mislead her.

Isabel washed windows, planted flowers and dusted. Then a week later, when Mortimer came in town to pick up a new mare, he assisted in repairs to the roof and balconies. Gradually they transformed the little town house from a dirty rundown shack into a charming well-kept cottage.

One mild spring afternoon, Sydnee brushed the hair from her face and asked Tristan, "Do you think the house is ready for me to move in?"

"It better be ready. Isabel comes tomorrow to help us decide on furniture," was his reply.

"I have been talking to Madame Picard, and she told me to order modest furniture of good quality and to remember that classic styles are the best."

When they began ordering furnishings, Tristan marveled at Sydnee's sense of style. She had an instinct for colors and textures, fabrics and design that astounded him. Sydnee surprised herself too. She adored decorating, and by the time they were done, the house on Dauphin Street resembled an elegant doll house. The parlor was done in a pale green with cream and green *toiles peintes* drapes. The sofa, two chairs and carpet were upholstered in a light dusty rose. Overhead was a miniature crystal chandelier and hanging above the fireplace was a portrait of Tristan.

"I feel like a fool," he said, looking up at his likeness. He was mounted on a gelding dressed for the hunt.

Sydnee smiled a crooked smile. "If we are to convince the world that I am your *inamorata* we must have a portrait of you."

He rolled his eyes. "Well, turn it to the wall when there are no guests here."

They picked out a mahogany table with six chairs for the dining room and the master bedroom had an oak half-tester bed with blue and cream-colored curtains and spread. The other two bedrooms were also done in soft pastels.

"What time do we go to the plantation tomorrow?" Sydnee asked.

"First thing in the morning. But we will not stay long. I have so much to do before I sail in two days. Does Mortimer know we are bringing the dogs and Vivian back to live with you?"

"He does," Sydnee replied.

The next day they travelled to *Saint-Denis* so Tristan could say goodbye. Isabel was there, tears streaming down her face, and Mortimer disappeared deep into the stable when it was time to say goodbye. Tristan frowned and looked at Sydnee. "I want to go home. This is too hard."

Sydnee nodded and whistled to the dogs who jumped into the landau, and Vivian flew along behind the carriage. They were quiet on the way back, knowing that their lives were about to change.

*   *   *

The sky was fair the day of departure as Sydnee and Maxime stood on the landing waiting for Tristan to return from checking his trunk. The docks were teaming with activity as passengers boarded vessels and crews loaded cargo. It was noisy as draymen roared past, whistling and cracking whips and peddlers hawked their wares.

Sydnee ran her eyes over Tristan's ship. She had never been close to an ocean going vessel before. It was completely different from the square sturdy steamboats that lined the landing all around it. This craft was oblong with three poles standing upright in a row which Maxime called masts. Attached to these masts were sails which, she was told, caught the wind and propelled the craft. From her studies she learned that the oceans were even vaster than the mighty Mississippi River, and if this was true, this vessel seemed very small indeed. She tried hard not to think about the fate of Guy Saint-Yves on his voyage to Europe and that her friend may be at risk.

Tristan approached Maxime. "Everything is in order," he said. "They are ready to depart."

"Your father sends his regrets," Maxime said apologetically. "He is very busy today."

Tristan shrugged. "Those who matter to me are right here."

He took a breath and looked away, holding back tears. "How will I know what to say and do without my dear teacher?"

Maxime swallowed hard and tried to speak, but he could not. Instead he took Tristan's hand, squeezed it hard and walked away.

Then Tristan turned to Sydnee. They looked at each other a moment and then collapsed into an embrace. At last Tristan pushed her away and ran up the gang plank onto the deck stopping at the railing to look back at her.

Sydnee wiped her eyes and waved. The crew burst into action, getting ready to set sail. Some of them stayed on deck while others climbed aloft to loosen the rigging. "Let fall," she heard someone call, and the white sails dropped.

Passengers crowded around to shout good bye to loved ones on shore. Some were waving hankies and others were crying, but Sydnee did not notice them. She could only see Tristan.

Suddenly the sails bulged with harnessed energy, and the ship began to creak and move away from the landing. As the vessel moved downriver, the crowds gradually dispersed on the landing. Families crawled into carriages and others departed on horseback, but Sydnee did not move. She remained motionless determined to watch Tristan until the last.

He stayed where he was too, never taking his eyes from her. She looked so small and helpless standing there all alone, and suddenly he panicked. Had he left her enough money? Would she be safe? As the vessel rounded a bend and he lost sight of her, he took comfort in the fact that as tiny and as frail as his dear friend appeared, she had the heart of an Amazon.

Chapter 14

It took weeks for Sydnee to adjust to life without Tristan. He had become such an important part of her existence that she felt lost without him. Tears would fill her eyes unexpectedly throughout the day and at night she would lay awake worrying about his long voyage across the Atlantic. Many mornings it was hard to pull herself out of bed, but her loyal companions, Vivian, Atlantis, and Baloo reminded her that someone still needed her for their happiness.

In spite of her loneliness, Sydnee was grateful for her new life, thanking the spirits often. Her home on Dauphin Street was a satisfying distraction for her, and she worked long hours trimming and manicuring the shrubs and flowers at the front entrance and in the courtyard. On several occasions Isabel visited her, and together they planted hibiscus, Indian pink, bee balm, and bright blue iris.

Sydnee planted an herb garden by the back door where she could harvest plants for cooking and for medicines. She had memorized Margarite's recipes for gumbo, soups and *cassoulets* and began to hone her culinary skills. Sydnee also made Hoodoo powders and oils in her small stillroom off the courtyard in case of accidents or disease.

Tristan left Sydnee ample funds for living expenses at her new home and, with Maxime's help, she was learning to handle money. Although Tristan had been unable to arrange further academic instruction with Maxime, she was able to continue with Madame Picard's School of Etiquette. Maxime was occasionally at the house, and after class he would teach Sydnee about money management.

Even though Sydnee was no longer able to receive tutoring, she was determined to continue her education. Although Madame spent hours teaching her needlework, it was academics she craved. Madame Picard was keenly aware of her hungry mind, so she gave Sydnee complete access to her personal library and spent time with her after class helping her improve her French and English skills by discussing world events with her.

Sydnee read voraciously, studying everything from literature to politics. After only a few months, Isabel noticed the change in her. "My goodness, you know more than my father about the upheavals in Paris."

Sydnee shook her head. "I understand nothing. There is so much to learn."

"Say," Isabel said changing the subject. "*La dame blanche* is opening tonight at the Opera. My Aunt Beatrice is too feeble to attend anymore, but she enjoys watching everyone enter in their finery. We sit across the street in the carriage and watch the crowd. Would you like to come with us?"

Sydnee's eyes grew wide. "I would!"

"*La dame blanche* is based on Sir Walter Scott's work. We must find someone who attends the performance so we can give Mortimer a recounting. Scott is his favorite," Isabel said.

"How is Mortimer? I miss him."

"He is well. His skills as physician to animals only improves. Planters from all over the county consult with him now."

Sydnee smiled. "Someday he will have his own livery."

"He will if I have anything to say about it," said Isabel.

That evening Isabel returned for Sydnee in the family carriage with Aunt Beatrice, a good-natured voluminous woman of later years. "Oh, to be young again," she said as she fanned herself, looking at the girls. "Someday you two will be attending the opera."

The *Theatre d'Orleans* was a large two-story stucco building with a colonnade on Orleans Street. Greek and Roman statues lined the rooftop, lounging, reading scrolls or standing at attention.

The coachman parked the barouche across from the entrance so they could watch the promenade into the theater. Although many arrived in carriages, the majority of the patrons strolled up on foot, coming from dining establishments nearby.

Sydnee leaned forward wide-eyed. She never imagined such a grand sight. Everyone was in formal evening attire and sporting the latest fashion. The men were dressed in crisp coats with padded shoulders, cinched waists and dark trousers. Many of them had cloaks and carried canes. All of them wore tall hats and had curled their hair.

As dashing as the men appeared, it was the ladies who captivated the girls. "Look at the gowns," murmured Isabel in awe.

"Just look at the fabrics," echoed Sydnee.

The female patrons wore a dazzling array of colors. Their necklines were cut wide and low for the evening with sleeves that were dropped off the shoulder, short and puffed. To cover their arms, they wore long silken gloves and carried shawls. Waistlines were emphasized and made smaller by belts and large voluminous skirts, padded with multiple petticoats. They wore their hair in knots upon their heads and ringlets framed their faces.

"Someday I will come to the opera dressed as a fine lady," Sydnee said wistfully.

"Isabel, my dear," said Aunt Beatrice, "When you marry Tristan, you must ask him to bring you here."

The smile dropped from Isabel's face. She swallowed hard and said quietly, "I most certainly will."

On the way home Sydnee watched her friend. Isabel sat back in the shadows concealing the look of melancholy on her face. Sydnee did not try to draw her into conversation. Instead she turned and looked out the window at the streets of New Orleans. She worried about Isabel and her love for Mortimer. She was afraid it would destroy them both. Once more Sydnee felt gratitude for her quiet life with Vivian, Baloo and Atlantis.

*   *   *

The girls saw each other off and on all summer until one day a note arrived from Isabel saying that her mother would not allow her to come to the city anymore. She explained that there had been an outbreak of a disease called cholera in Paris and

New York, and several infected people had carried it to New Orleans.

"Have you heard about it?" Sydnee asked Madame Picard after class that evening.

"Indeed I have," she said, frowning as she put away chairs. "It is most troubling. We are just coming out of yellow fever season, and now we have this malady. They say it is most virulent."

"Are people dying?"

"Yes and very quickly, in a matter of days, sometimes hours."

Sydnee had a lump in her throat. She asked in a small voice, "This cholera was in Paris. Do you suppose Tristan has it?"

Madame Picard straightened up and rested her blue eyes on Sydnee. She reached out, touched her cheek and said, "Oh, little one, worry not. He is young and strong. Usually these things take the very old."

But Madame Picard was wrong. Cholera swept New Orleans that fall of 1832 like a hurricane. It took the young, the old, the rich, and particularly the poor. The city became a ghost town as people left for the country, fleeing the "miasmas" or infected air.

The first thing that Sydnee did was make Margarite's sickness tea. For as long as Sydnee could remember Margarite told her when there was contagion to drink only raspberry leaf tea with some black pepper and to eat nothing but bubbling hot gumbo. When asked why, Margarite would shrug and say that the spirits had advised it.

Business in the city came to a stand-still. Madame Picard cancelled class until further notice and people stayed indoors. Small bonfires were built at each intersection to purge the air and every half hour there was a deafening blast from a cannon to cleanse the atmosphere.

Sydnee found it unnerving. The heavy stench from the fires seeped into her home, and the cannons startled her every time they blasted. After a week of seclusion, Sydnee decided to go to market. She was in dire need of food. Planning to stock up so she wouldn't have to go out again, she strapped baskets on the backs of Atlantis and Baloo and stepped out into the street.

The usually busy thoroughfare was empty. The town was more deserted than it had been during yellow fever season. She noticed a fire smoldering near the curb, adding heat to the already sweltering temperature. There were smoke pots smoldering in front of houses giving the city a surreal landscape.

An elderly gentleman walked down Dauphin Street with a handkerchief tied around his nose and mouth. When he saw that Sydnee did not have her face covered, he crossed the street.

Looking around self-consciously, she reached into her drawstring purse and pulled out a hankie to hold over her nose and mouth as she walked.

The market was deserted as well. A few tenacious vendors turned out, standing with their carts, eager to make some kind of sale. Sydnee made her purchases and hurried home.

On Bourbon Street she passed a funeral, but there were only two mourners. The coffin was covered heavily with flowers to absorb the diseased air emanating from the remains.

Sydnee was grateful to be home, and she stayed inside for another week enduring the heat and the isolation. The days were gradually getting shorter and this pleased her. She did not want to see the funeral processions go past her front window or see the carts full of corpses. Darkness did not give her complete relief though, she could hear the gravediggers ring bells and call, "Bring out your dead!"

She worried constantly about Tristan and wondered if Isabel and Mortimer were safe residing in the country. She longed for news about the progression of the disease but did not dare go out to ask questions. The farthest she ventured would be into her courtyard and even then she had to come in at dusk because the night air was thought to be dangerous.

There was a restlessness in the spirit world too, akin to her experience in St. Louis Cemetery on All Soul's Day. She felt a darkness gathering like a thunderstorm, and it lessened only when she went into the sunlight of her garden. It disturbed her sleep as well, and one night in early October it jolted her awake several times. It was a vision that presented itself repeatedly. In the nightmare she was standing in front of the *garçonnière* which was shrouded in mist. She opened the door and walked inside the schoolroom. It was too dark to see anything, but there was a disturbing presence within the room. Then she would wake up.

The third time the vision occurred Sydnee sat up in bed and cried out. The dogs jumped up terrified. Sydnee clutched her head, gasping, and her gown was soaked in perspiration. When her breathing slowed she realized that she must go to the *garçonnière* and investigate or this nightmare would rob her of her sanity.

Swallowing hard, she threw the covers back, slid out of bed and dressed. The dogs watched her expectantly. "Come along," she said to them. "We must put an end to this thing."

Tying a hankie over her nose and mouth, Sydnee stepped out onto the street. The only movement she could see was from a lantern on a corpse cart a block away. She could hear the gravedigger ringing the bell and calling for bodies.

Vivian swooped down and landed on Sydnee's shoulder, startling her. She took a deep breath to calm herself and started walking with her lantern. Her shoes clattered loudly on the bricks as she hurried to the property on Rue St. Louis.

The bell in the cathedral tolled three. Baloo and Atlantis trotted behind Sydnee, blissfully unaware of the morbid atmosphere in the city. Sydnee walked several blocks, rounded the corner and saw the charred remains of the chimneys at the former Saint-Yves residence. It was so quiet that the hinges seemed to scream as she opened the gate to the courtyard. The *garçonnière* stood before her, sitting innocuously in the moonlight.

Still, Sydnee wanted to run home and hide in bed. Nevertheless, she took a deep breath and crossed the garden. The dogs were by her side, and Vivian was on her shoulder. Sydnee's mouth was dry, and her heart was hammering in her chest as she opened the front door. All was dark, and just like in the nightmare, she felt a presence in the room. The hair raised on her arms, and Atlantis started to growl.

Cautiously Sydnee stepped inside, holding up her lantern. Nothing looked out of the ordinary. Things were as they left them. She saw bookcases, desks and papers. Chairs were scattered around the room, and she saw the stairs up to Tristan's bedroom.

Nevertheless something was amiss. She could feel it. The dogs approached the corner where she used to sleep. Sydnee held up her lantern, and her heart jumped into her throat. Someone was on the bed.

It was Maxime.

"Oh, Mon Dieu!" she gasped.

He was on his back, and his mouth was open. His cheeks were sunken, and his clothes were covered with vomit. She had little doubt that it was cholera. When she touched his forehead, he opened his eyes. "Maxime, how is it you are here? I thought you were in the country."

He moved his cracked lips but no words came.

"I will get you help," she said quickly.

"They--" he murmured. "--brought me here."

Sydnee frowned. She knew what had happened. The moment they discovered Maxime was sick, Monsieur Saint-Yves had him dumped him here alone in the city to die.

"I must leave you for a few moments, but I will return with help. We will take care of you."

His eyes rolled back in his head, and he fell back into a swoon. Sydnee dashed out of the *garçonnière* with the dogs behind her. Vivian flew overhead. She raced through the streets not stopping until she reached Madame Picard's residence.

Banging on the door, she looked through the entry window anxiously. She saw candlelight move down the stairs, and then Madame Picard looked out the window with her servant standing behind her. Pulling the door open, she gasped, "Sydnee what—"

"Maxime is sick. He is alone in the Saint-Yves *garçonnière*."

Madame Picard stared at her a moment, absorbing the news. She was in her dressing gown and her servant, Clotilde was holding a candle in a glass shade.

"Come in," she said taking Sydnee's wrist and pulling her inside. "I will summon Frederick."

Sydnee, Madame Picard and her elderly black coachman, Frederick left to bring Maxime back to the house while Clotilde stayed behind preparing a room. Maxime tried to move his parched lips when he saw Ninon at the *garçonnière*, but she touched his lips and murmured, "Say nothing, my dear one. I am here now."

After moving him to her residence, Madame Picard stayed at Maxime's side throughout the day and well into the next night. He was in a small bed chamber next to her room. Clotilde and Sydnee answered requests, changing and boiling soiled sheets and blankets and keeping vigil while Madame Picard slept for a few hours.

Maxime awakened seldom. He was thin and frail. He did not look like the Maxime Sydnee had known, so haughty and elegant, capable and self-possessed.

Sydnee slept that night for a few hours and then took over for Madame Picard. She sat by the lamp reading but avoided looking at Maxime. He looked even more drawn and withered then when she first discovered him, and his skin looked like parchment.

Suddenly he opened his eyes and tried to speak. Sydnee set her book down and put her ear to his lips.

"I must tell," he whispered. "Ninon."

Sydnee looked into his face. His eyes were glassy. "Madame sleeps. It is Sydnee," she said.

He continued. "You must--you must help them."

At that moment, Madame Picard came from her bed chamber. She was rolling up her sleeves and said, "I am awake now. What is it, Sydnee?"

"He wants to tell you something."

Madame said quickly, "I will attend to him. You rest now."

Sydnee went to her room, fell into bed and slept heavily. When she awoke at dawn, she was surprised that Madame Picard had not come for her. She noticed that Clotilde was sleeping as well. Sydnee went to Maxime's room and gently pushed the door open. Madame was asleep in the chair, and Maxime was very still on the bed. The sunlight streaming through the sheer curtain illuminated his face. His head was back, and his mouth was open. He was dead.

"Oh, Maxime," Sydnee uttered, tears filling her eyes.

She dreaded telling Madame, but it must be done. "Madame, wake up," she said, lightly touching her arm. "Madame."

The woman's skin was cold and clammy, and like a bolt of lightning, it hit Sydnee. Madame was not sleeping, she was unconscious. "Clotilde!" she screamed. "Clotilde!"

The servant ran into the room. "Madame is sick now too."

Together they picked up Madame Picard and took her to her bed chamber. Frederick summoned the corpse cart, and Sydnee watched Frederick carry Maxime down the stairs. Tears were streaming down her face, and her hands were in fists. His body would be thrown into a mass grave with all the other slaves to be buried or burned. It seemed a sorry tribute to the life of a man who had given so much to this world.

Sydnee swallowed hard and returned to Madame Picard's side. She must attend to the living and be quick about it. Somehow she would keep this woman alive.

*   *   *

With the help of Margarite's remedies and Hoodoo potions, Sydnee managed to save Ninon Picard's life. Clotilde and Frederick were of great help as well, putting themselves at risk washing linen, emptying chamber pots and standing watch.

Sydnee lit many candles, invoked the power of the spirits and allowed Madame Picard to drink only Margarite's sickness tea. It took several days but gradually her color returned, and her eyes seemed to take on life again.

Sydnee did not have to tell Ninon about Maxime. She already knew, and the two women suffered in silence. Although Sydnee grieved for Maxime she knew her loss was nothing compared to the emptiness Madame experienced. Sydnee knew Madame Picard had lost the great love of her life, but the woman carried on, holding her head up high.

Over time they returned to their daily tasks, but things had changed. Ninon Picard coped with her loss of Maxime by filling her life with Sydnee. She mentored her and fostered her like a daughter, teaching her everything she knew about great literature, politics, art, and the ways of polite society in the South.

Sydnee was overjoyed with this turn of events and soaked up everything like a sponge. It took many months of mentoring, but by the time she was done, Madame Picard had sculpted a young woman ready to play her part with skill and grace in the aristocratic but deadly world of 19th Century New Orleans.

Chapter 15

New Orleans 1835

Tristan stepped off the ship in New Orleans and took a deep breath of home. There was the rich smell of crayfish boiling at a stand, the heady scent of flowers wafting up from Jackson Square and the aroma of chicory so thick he could taste it. He sent the carriage driver ahead with his trunk, informing him that he preferred to walk. He wanted to stroll the streets once more and immerse himself in the rich ambiance of this flamboyant city on the Mississippi.

Tristan returned to New Orleans a grown man. Although he was taller and his face was leaner, his hair remained as golden as sunshine and his eyes as blue as robin's eggs. He carried himself now as a gentleman, with an air of confidence and poise. The years he spent on the Continent, he learned self-reliance and determination to succeed.

He was also a man of means. Not only was he in line to inherit the Saint-Yves properties and holdings, but he had interests in several textile industries in Paris and London which were increasing his wealth daily. Shortly before his death, Maxime advised Tristan of three excellent opportunities in cotton which he seized immediately and turned to his benefit. Initially Tristan had devoted a huge amount of time to these ventures, but now the investments had become lucrative enough to hire business managers.

How Tristan missed Maxime. By the time Sydnee's letter had arrived in Venice, he had been dead for months, and when he read her account, he was devastated. Tristan loved Maxime like a father, and he felt empty and alone without him. D'anton tried to comfort him but without success. For weeks he distracted him with outings to fashionable cafés and salons, or

152

with tickets to the opera, but the passage of time seemed to be the only panacea for him. Eventually he started to smile again, and gradually he returned to his favorite pursuits. Nevertheless, his life was fundamentally changed.

Dressed in a charcoal-colored coat with a black cravat, tall hat, gray vest and pantaloons, Tristan was the picture of fashion strolling down the street. He washed and changed on the packet before going ashore, gladly shedding his dirty ship-board clothing.

It was curious to be walking on land again, and he was glad he had the use of his cane. Pedestrians stole looks at this attractive young gentleman taking in the sights of the city with a half-smile on his lips. In spite of his growth into manhood, Tristan still had the countenance of an angel. It gave onlookers pause when they beheld him.

The streets were busy today. It was late fall, and everyone had returned from the north to enjoy the cooler months in New Orleans. Market was in full swing and vendors called out to customers. Tristan lifted his hat to the ladies and greeted the gentlemen cordially as he passed. Turning onto Royal Street he came up behind two men strolling and discussing the gossip of the day.

"I have never been this close to her. I heard that she is most exceptional," said one of the gentleman, swinging his cane.

"Madame Picard has been hiding her all this time," said the older man. He dropped his voice and said discreetly, "He is foolish to leave her alone this long."

Tristan looked across the street at the young woman they were discussing. She was walking with a parasol on her shoulder, dressed in the latest Parisian fashion. Her gown was of soft gold silk, fitted on the upper arms, voluminous at the elbows and tight fitting at the cuffs. Her cinnamon-colored hair was swept up onto her head and tied loosely with ribbons, and she had a basket over her arm.

Tristan recognized Sydnee immediately by her large, mahogany colored eyes. Although now a young woman of nineteen, she still had the appearance of a waif. Although a voluptuous body was *de rigueur*, her chic, gamine look was the perfect frame for fashion, and she wore it well.

The two gentlemen watched in awe as Tristan dashed across the street, jumping from stepping stone to stepping stone, avoiding carriages and pedestrians. He jumped into her path, swept off his hat and bowed low.

Sydnee stopped, wide-eyed. When he straightened up, she cried out. Clutching his arms, she was about to embrace him but then remembered she was in public and kissed his cheeks instead.

"Tristan, Tristan!" she exclaimed. "I had not expected you for several days!"

"The winds were in our favor, and we arrived this morning," he said, looking into her eyes and holding her hands. "My dear friend," he murmured.

Becoming aware that they were blocking the sidewalk, Sydnee took his arm, hugged it, and started walking. "Where is your carriage?" she asked.

"I sent it on home. It was such a beautiful day, I thought I would walk."

"That is how I felt."

Suddenly there was a flapping of wings, and Vivian landed on Tristan's shoulder. "Vivian! You haven't forgotten me," he said, stroking her feathers.

"Ah, but she was angry with you for a long time."

"How is Isabel? Mortimer?"

"They are well. Is D'anton still returning at the end of the month?" she asked.

"Yes, he has completed his law studies at Harvard and is ready to start his practice. We have so much to talk about. Can you skip your marketing for today and return to the house?"

"I certainly cannot. This calls for a celebration. We need oysters, champagne--"

"I brought some champagne back from France," Tristan said.

"We will drink that."

After purchasing oysters, fish and fresh produce at market

they returned to Sydnee's townhome. They sat at a small café table in the courtyard and ate their supper in the half light of sunset. Vivian sat nearby, not letting Tristan out of her sight, and the dogs were at his feet, overjoyed at his return.

"It is wonderful to be back," he said, sipping his coffee and sitting back. "I have been homesick. It was too long."

"Are you going to see your parents?"

He sighed. "I don't want to see them, but to do business, I must see my father. You know that mother is raising Giselle's child in Natchez?"

"Yes, there is always talk when they visit *Saint-Denis*."

"They will press me to marry Isabel now that I have returned, you know."

Sydnee nodded.

Tristan continued, "It is a masquerade that is inevitable for all of us. At least Isabel knows and will not expect--or want anything from me."

He looked at Sydnee. "And you have changed, my dear friend. You are so poised and well spoken. It is apparent you have continued your education."

"I read and study with Madame Picard daily."

"You must realize that you are exquisite."

Sydnee blushed and shook her head. "Tristan, you embarrass me."

"Do you have beaux?"

"Hardly, I am being kept by a gentleman of property."

"Ah yes," Tristan said wistfully. "We are all trapped in this charade."

* * *

The wedding celebration was set for Christmas day at *Saint-Denis*. The ceremony would be at St. Louis Cathedral first and then guests would be invited to an intimate wedding breakfast at the house afterward. Madame Picard told Sydnee that weddings in Louisiana were quiet affairs and usually at the home of the bride's parents, but since Monsieur Trudeau's health had been poor lately, they decided to entertain at the groom's plantation. Later in the day Tristan and Isabel would return to New Orleans where they would reside. Tristan purchased a modest home for them in New Orleans on Chartres Street.

Sydnee had not spoken with Isabel since Tristan returned. The roles they played now as adults did not allow them to see each other publicly. The mistress and the wife would never meet socially. These same constraints made it difficult for her to see Mortimer as well, although on several occasions, when he was in the city to minister to sick horses, he called on Sydnee.

He would come to the door holding his hat in his hand, but never step inside the door. Mortimer was not comfortable indoors, and Sydnee understood this, so she would call the dogs, and they would walk along the river together.

Mortimer continued to amaze her with his boundless intellect which encompassed so many subjects. He could speak articulately on everything from world history to folk remedies. His personal feelings were more difficult for him to express though. They had never spoken of Isabel's marriage to Tristan, but Sydnee knew that it caused him great pain. They would speak instead of books, music or their favorite topic, Hoodoo remedies.

As her education progressed with Madame Picard, Sydnee's world became larger too. She had a deeper understanding of politics, philosophy and culture. She loved hearing Madame speak of the famous women of the Parisian salons who hosted gatherings of the greatest minds in all of Europe. She learned that these women had played an integral role in planting the seeds of The Grand Enlightenment which later gave birth to the United States.

The day of the wedding Sydnee awakened early, well before the sun rose. She made herself some chicory coffee and paced. She was worried about Mortimer and D'anton. The dogs watched her walk back and forth, rubbing her forehead. At last she stopped, looked at them and said, "I have decided. Since none of us are welcome at the wedding, I shall keep Mortimer and D'anton company today."

Atlantis and Baloo wagged their tails in acknowledgement.

Tristan bought Sydnee her own landaulet with instructions to hire Frederick, Madame Picard's coachman, as needed, so at sunrise Sydnee called on her to ask if she could borrow Frederick, for the day. A few hours later Sydnee was on her way to the wedding celebration at *Saint-Denis* to be with Mortimer. She stopped for D'anton along the way, but his servant said that he was not receiving anyone today.

Wearing a plaid gown with a hooded blue cape, Sydnee looked out of the carriage at the rain splashing on the street. The weather seemed to suit the occasion. She had given Frederick instructions to drive around to the back of the house to the stables. When they turned in the driveway, carriages were arriving for the celebration.

Sydnee pulled up her hood to conceal her face and looked out the window.

The balconies and doors of the plantation were decorated with evergreen boughs and wreaths but instead of red accents for Christmas, the ribbons, flowers and berries were white for the wedding. Sydnee sat back in her seat and sighed. She was glad that she did not have to witness this wedding. Although Isabel's gown would be grand and Tristan would look dashing in his suit, she knew their hearts would not be in their vows. It would be for them a sad occasion.

Mortimer was unhitching horses when she arrived. With her hood up, she dashed into the stable. He walked in after her, carrying a saddle. Sydnee pulled off her hood, and his jaw dropped. Mortimer looked at the young stable hand standing next to him and then back at Sydnee, saying formally so he did not give her identity away, "How may I help you?"

Sydnee hesitated a moment, looking at the boy. The young man walked away to leave them alone.

"I thought I would pay you a visit today since we are in similar situations," Sydnee murmured.

Mortimer swallowed hard and dropped his eyes, not replying. When Sydnee walked over to sit on a bale of hay, he barked, "No!" and dashed into his quarters, returning with a desk chair. "You are a lady now."

Sydnee sat down. "I am still the same old Sydnee to you."

He nodded, took a brush off the wall and started to groom one of the horses.

She untied her cape and let it drop back onto the chair. "I stopped by to see D'anton, but he was still in bed."

"He will be in bed all day, I suspect," he added.

Sydnee nodded and looked around the dark stable. "I see you have unhitched some of the teams. Are there overnight guests?"

"Yes," he replied, offering no more information.

After a long silence, Mortimer stopped brushing the mare and looked at her. "Don't you think you should keep your hood up in case someone recognizes you?"

Sydnee looked perplexed. "There are only a handful of people who know who I am."

"You are wrong. Everyone knows who Mademoiselle Sauveterre is."

Reluctantly, she drew up the hood over her head.

They spent the rest of the morning discussing everything except the wedding. He updated her on all the animals in his care, and she told him how Vivian had injured her wing recently and how well it had healed. He showed her the books he was reading, and she shared recent news from Europe.

Their conversation helped pass the time, and at last it was time for guests to leave. The cold drizzle soaked Mortimer to the skin as he prepared the horses and carriages for departure, adding to his already miserable state of mind. The worst task was preparing the wedding carriage. Tristan and Isabel would be leaving in a few moments for their first night together in their home in New Orleans.

Like the big house, the wedding carriage was decorated in evergreen boughs, white flowers and ribbons. Nevertheless it too looked miserable. The flowers drooped in the rain and the ribbons sagged to the ground as the driver pulled up to the front door of the big house. Mortimer and Sydnee could hear cheers as the newlyweds left for their new home.

It was early in the evening when the last of the guests departed. Sydnee sighed. "I am glad this day is over. I shall be leaving now too."

"Wait," said Mortimer, looking up at her through his stringy hair. "Stay and eat something with me."

Sydnee knew that he was feeling lonely, and she too felt a nagging emptiness that wasn't just hunger. Mortimer took her back to his quarters. Sydnee looked around as she pulled off her gloves. His rooms were comfortable, spacious and warm. Although he was not supposed to have female guests, they both knew that the family would have no reason to come to the stable tonight. Mortimer bustled around the fire making them gumbo and fresh biscuits.

Just as they were finishing their meal, they heard a carriage pull up. Mortimer grabbed Sydnee's wrist, and they dashed out of his quarters. She ducked into a corner behind one of the horses as he went to the stable door.

She heard voices and then Tristan called, "Sydnee, I know you are in here! I see the landaulet."

She stepped out of the shadows. He was standing by the wedding carriage dressed in his finest blue suit, and Isabel was leaning out the window. She was dressed in a voluminous white gown, and on her head was a wreath of flowers. A white veil was attached to the back of the wreath, and it draped down her back. "Well, hurry up. Get in!" she called to them.

Blinking in disbelief, Sydnee approached the carriage. Isabel laughed and started pulling the muddy ribbons and flowers off the side of coach. "Foolishness!" she said.

Suddenly, everything was different. Joy and laughter had returned.

"Look! We have picked up D'anton," Tristan announced. The young man leaned forward and waved to them with a huge smile.

"You are done for the night, are you not, Mortimer?" Isabel asked.

"I am," he mumbled, stealing a quick look at her.

Tristan explained, "Isabel and I went to our new house on

Chartres Street, had a glass of champagne and realized we were lonely. We discussed things and decided that nothing has to change. We are all still best friends, are we not?"

Sydnee and Mortimer nodded.

"Well, then we carry on as before," Tristan stated.

"Get in!" Isabel demanded.

Standing up straight and holding the door as if he was a footman, Tristan demanded, "We shall go to Sydnee's town house for a celebration of friendship."

With a shy smile, Mortimer stepped over to the other side of the door and held out his hand for Sydnee to step into the carriage. She stepped up into the coach followed by Tristan.

Mortimer shut the door behind them, pulled up his collar and climbed up beside the driver.

Tristan leaned toward the window to tell him to ride inside.

"No," laughed Isabel. "He is happiest out there."

*   *   *

A few months later, Sydnee sat in the open carriage on her way to the opera with Madame Picard. She felt like a queen dressed in her finest gown, white silk with lavender stripes and short puffed sleeves. The low neckline was bordered in lace and draped over her bare shoulders was a delicate white lace shawl. Her hair was dressed high upon her head and a string of faux pearls was woven through her coiffure.

Madame Picard sat next to her, her back straight and her head held high. She was dressed in a burgundy evening gown and around her neck was a string of garnets. Even Frederick was dressed for the occasion, in his finest livery trimmed with gold braid.

The opera was *Robert le diable* and at last Sydnee was attending the performance, not watching from afar.

"When Georges died, he left me his private box," Madame Picard informed her. "Even so we will go to the opera house early, before everyone else arrives."

When Sydnee asked why, Madame's reply was, "Although they endure us, polite society does not want to mix publicly with the *inamorata*."

Arriving early gave Sydnee a chance to admire the elaborate interior of the *Theatre d'Orleans*. It was the grandest building she had ever seen. The ceiling of the lobby was covered with colorful murals depicting classical mythology and stories from the Bible. There were angels doing battle with demons, beautiful goddesses lounging on divans and handsome Greek warriors brandishing swords astride muscular horses. All of the pictorials were bordered with intricately carved flourishes painted in gold. Marble pillars and chandeliers lined the hall, and at either end of the lobby were circular divans upholstered in red velvet.

Madame Picard swept across the granite floor like a queen. "Good evening, Sebastien," she said to a tall dignified man in a white jacket standing behind the counter. He was polishing a silver spoon. "How is your wife?"

"She is well, Madame Picard. Thank you."

"Mademoiselle and I will have absinthe if you please, lightly prepared."

He nodded and Sydnee watched the man pour an emerald green liquid into a glass and rest a perforated spoon over the rim. With a pair of tongs he placed a cube of sugar onto the spoon and put the goblet under the spout of an elaborate glass fountain with a silver spigot. Sydnee noticed that the base of the fountain was a slim silver fairy holding a glass tower filled with ice water. The man turned the spigot slightly, allowing the water to drip through the sugar cube into the green liquid below. Gradually the drink was transformed into a light green cloud.

With their drinks, Madame Picard and Sydnee sat down on one of the divans. "This is a special occasion," Madame said. "Tonight is your graduation."

Sydnee stared at her a moment. She had felt this coming for some time. Her conversations with Madame Picard had been changing lately. They had become less tutorial and more of a thoughtful exchange between two adults. The spirits had been restless the past weeks as well. Sydnee knew that she was at a turning point in her life, but instead of being excited, she felt unsettled.

"There will be no more school with you?" she asked

uncertainly.

Madame Picard sipped her drink and shook her head. "No more formal schooling, but I will always be at your side. You are ready to take your place in society. There is no question now that you are suitable to be Monsieur Tristan's courtesan. But more than that, I wanted to educate you so you could survive in this world if something unexpected happens. Planning for the future is why I am secure today."

Sydnee nodded her head. "But, Madame—is this all there is? Just being someone's *inamorata?*"

Madame Picard was about to take a sip of her absinthe but stopped midway, lowering her goblet. She turned and studied Sydnee for a moment and then a smile flickered on her lips. She looked pleased. There can be more, but it will be revealed to you by the good Lord in his own time."

Chapter 16
New Orleans
1838

The next three years flew by quickly for Sydnee. Tristan and D'anton visited her frequently, introducing her to many of their business associates and friends. They were all young, ambitious members of the New Orleans and Natchez aristocracy who were interested in animated discussions about art, politics and philosophy.

Although many people sought their company, the three friends were careful who they befriended. Tristan, D'anton and Sydnee wanted men and women who were not just witty and charming but interested in looking at the world in different ways and with open minds.

They discussed the coronation of Victoria, studied Victor Hugo's works and dissected the relationship of George Sand and Frederic Chopin. They revisited the philosophies of Kant and Rousseau, argued about the policies of Van Buren and speculated on a new invention called a telegraph. The world was changing quickly, and they were glad to be a part of it.

Over time, the town house on Dauphin Street became known throughout the South as a great salon of enlightenment, rivaling that of Paris and London, and Sydnee Sauveterre was at the very heart of it. She was a gracious and dignified hostess, encouraging all perspectives and ideas, creating a setting ripe for discourse. If anyone scoffed or indulged in snobbery, she never invited them again. Even though Madame Picard's influence was apparent, the success of the salon could be attributed to Sydnee's generous nature and respect for others.

Sydnee had come a long way since the Natchez Trace. Over the years she had evolved from a homeless waif to the toast of

New Orleans. Her fashion and style were emulated throughout city, her hospitality and grace known across the South. Over time she surpassed the fame of even Madame Picard, who was Sydnee's greatest devotee. She was proud of her student and overjoyed at her success.

Tristan was ever her loyal companion and always Sydnee's generous sponsor. He never forgot that she was integral to the illusion that gave him complete freedom to pursue his relationship with D'anton.

In spite of this new life filled with adulation, Sydnee never forgot her roots, her life with Margarite, the kindness of Maxime, or the guidance of the spirits. They were with her always, whispering in her ear, guiding her course. Tristan offered to purchase slaves for her service but Sydnee politely declined, suggesting servants instead.

Several nights a week, Sydnee held soirees. They would dine on oysters or sip aperitifs in the courtyard and discuss events of the day. The salon guests were all pleasant, well-mannered acquaintances, witty and intellectual, but none of them knew intimate details about Sydnee, Tristan and D'anton's personal lives. The three friends made sure to keep them at arm's length, telling them nothing of their arrangement. Everyone speculated about their relationships, and many longed to be closer, but no one was admitted into their private circle.

Ironically, Sydnee found a certain freedom in masquerading as Tristan's mistress. Her lifestyle was already considered unconventional, so she did not have to hide the fact that she came from humble origins.

Isabel and Sydnee had to meet in secret though. The young women would include Mortimer when he was in town, but never were they seen publicly, and never did the entire group of friends gather as a group anymore.

Frequently Sydnee would meet Isabel in the courtyard of Madame Picard's home, where they would visit for hours, laughing and sharing all the latest news. Isabel told Sydnee that she was happy with Tristan. Although their relationship was platonic, the bond of friendship and love between them was unbreakable.

The young women would arrive after dark in covered carriages for their rendezvous at Madame Picard's home, but the past two weeks Isabel had been ill. Tristan told Sydnee that it was a malady of unknown origin, but at last Isabel started to improve. When she finally came to Madame Picard's home again, Sydnee was shocked to see how thin she had grown. Her face was drawn, and her blue eyes looked pale.

"What was your illness, Isabel?" Sydnee asked, drawing her down into a seat under the arbor. Isabel's hands felt as cold as ice. "Was it the fever?"

Isabel shook her head and dropped her eyes. "It was not yellow jack."

"What was it?"

Isabel murmured, "I lost a child."

Sydnee's jaw dropped.

"I didn't tell Mortimer this time. He worries so."

Sydnee looked at Isabel, blinking. "There have been other times?"

"Yes, I lost one several months back. I was not far along."

"Does Tristan know?"

"No," said Isabel. "He would not object though if I had a baby, so I must keep trying."

Sydnee's eyes grew large. She was flabbergasted considering the implications, Tristan raising Mortimer's child, Mortimer watching from afar, and Isabel playing the part of dutiful wife and mother, to say nothing of the ramifications of inheritance. It all seemed so fantastic.

Sydnee stood up and walked to the fountain, rubbing her forehead. She turned and looked at Isabel who seemed so small and frail. "So—so you will try this again?"

Isabel looked at her with surprise. "Why, of course, Sydnee." In the half-light coming from the house, her eyes looked feverish and wild.

"Oh, Isabel," Sydnee gasped. "So much can go wrong!"

Isabel jumped up and snapped. "What would you have me do, Sydnee?"

"There must be another—"

"Another way? And what would that be?" Isabel interrupted. "You are quite happy with your salon and all of your friends while I remain home alone and lonely."

Isabel picked up her drawstring bag and started down the walkway out of the garden. When she opened the gate, she stopped walking. There were tears rolling down her cheeks. Taking a deep breath, she turned and ran back to Sydnee throwing her arms around her. "Oh, my friend I am so sorry," she sobbed.

"I am so sorry too for not understanding," Sydnee said, her words muffled in Isabel's voluminous hair, but she was still uncertain. "We will see this through together."

*   *   *

For years, Sydnee had seen the way Isabel and Mortimer looked at each other. She had witnessed the love between Tristan and D'anton, and sometimes she wondered why she did not have an intimate relationship herself. When she was young, the thought disgusted her, but with time and adulthood she found herself wanting to find love as well.

So far the gentlemen who frequented the town house bored her. Although they were handsome and intelligent, they seemed predictable and lackluster to her. They sensed her indifference toward them and this inflamed their ardor. The gentlemen flirted outrageously with Sydnee, competing for her attention, bringing her gifts, or flattering her. But again and again, she rebuffed them.

For a brief time in the spring a dashing French emissary had awakened a flood of passion in her, and she indulged herself for several months, but when he became hungry for more intimacy, she refused. She used the excuse that her heart belonged to Tristan.

Last month there had been a planter from Natchez that caught her eye, but she stopped that too, telling herself that she must be cautious and appear as if she belonged to Tristan.

Years ago, she asked Madame Picard if being an *inamorata* was all there was for her in life, and she told Sydnee to wait for the spirits to show her more. Since that time she had been waiting and waiting for a path to be revealed to her, but nothing happened.

"Allenger will be disappointed if you are not here tonight, Sydnee," said D'anton one evening at her townhome. He was smoking a cigar in the parlor waiting for the guests to arrive for supper. He looked dashing, dressed in a black suit with a red vest and black cravat. He had his arm slung over the back of a chair.

Sydnee wrinkled her nose. "Foolishness."

"The man adores you," D'anton teased, as he bent down to pet Atlantis.

Sydnee shook her head and swept across the room in her royal blue gown. It was the latest fashion, closely fitted around the upper arms, full at the elbows and tight at the cuffs. It was trimmed in military fashion with gold braid. She adjusted her hair a moment in the mirror and then checked the humidor for cigars.

Suddenly she turned to D'anton and said, "I am so weary, D'anton. I am tired of all the witty conversation, flippant attitudes and--"

His eyebrows shot up. "So you are serious. Say no more, my dear. You are entitled to a night of peace and quiet."

Sydnee sighed, walked over and kissed his head. "Thank you for understanding."

He chuckled. "God knows, I understand. I take breaks for *days* at a time."

"That is different, and you know it."

He shook his head slightly and murmured, "Not really."

Sweeping his arm, he commanded, "Now go! Your little Marie will serve supper, and Tristan will handle the entertaining." He took a puff of his cigar. "Tonight Madame Girard is bringing the latest Dickens novel. I plan to be the first to read it."

"Something Twist, isn't?" Sydnee asked as she draped a shawl over her shoulders.

"Yes something like that. Love you darling," he said kissing the air in her direction.

"You too," she said, closing the door behind her. She ducked out into her carriage before the guests arrived and set off for Madame Picard's house.

The women dined on capon and new potatoes that evening, ending with a rich éclair and coffee. It was good for Sydnee to be near her dear friend once more. Madame had been away for months visiting friends near St. Louis, and Sydnee missed her terribly. It seemed as if she was spending more and more time away from home lately.

"Are your St. Louis friends well?" Sydnee asked.

"Yes they are. I also visited Maxime's sister. She has recently purchased her freedom. She is setting up housekeeping just outside of town."

"I didn't know that he had a sister," Sydnee said, about to take a bite of dessert.

"Yes, he would be proud to know that his sister is free. He never could afford his own papers. He was too brilliant and valuable for his own good."

Sydnee looked down at her plate. "I still miss him."

Madame Picard nodded. "I do too. More than you can imagine."

The rest of the night the women talked by the fire and when the hour grew late, Madame told Sydnee to take one of the guest rooms. She was tired and complied willingly. Unsure how late the soiree would last, she did not want to return to a house full of guests.

Sydnee set down the lamp and looked around the guest room. It had not changed since Maxime had died. The sheer curtains were still on the window, the plush Turkish carpet was on the hardwood floor, and the light blue duvet was on the bed.

She undressed to her chemise and slid under the covers. It was difficult pushing back the memories, but eventually she fell into a dreamless sleep. She slept for several hours and then was awakened suddenly by someone banging on the door downstairs. Sydnee sat up, her heart hammering. When she heard Madame Picard start down the stairs, she grabbed a dressing gown and rushed down after her. When she reached the landing, Madame Picard was just putting the lamp down on the entry table. When she opened the door an elderly white man with a gray beard was standing on the step. He had a huge build and was dressed like a farmer.

"Thou must flee," he said breathlessly. "They know."

He looked at Sydnee, suspiciously.

"She is a friend," Madame Picard explained. "How much time?"

"Ten minutes."

"My bag is ready," she replied.

The man returned to his wagon.

Madame shut the door, picked up the lamp and glided quickly up the stairs with Sydnee behind her. "What is that man talking about, Madame?"

Ninon Picard calmly walked into her room, opened the wardrobe and pulled out a gripsack which was already packed. "Sydnee, that man is a Quaker and my friend. I must flee with him tonight. And you--" she pulled a brown woolen traveling gown over her head. "You must go home, right now."

Sydnee stood in the room shaking. She was in her bare feet with her arms folded across her chest. "What is happening? Why are you in danger?"

Ninon stopped buttoning her gown and looked at her. "Sydnee, I help slaves escape to freedom. I have been doing this for many years."

Opening her jewelry box, Madame Picard emptied the contents into her bag along with a wad of notes she pulled out of the back of a book. She looked around the room one last time, took Sydnee by the wrist and pulled her down the stairs behind her. When they reached the landing she faced her. "My little one, do you remember Maxime's words before he died?"

Sydnee's lips parted and she nodded, wide eyed. "He said I must help them."

Madame Picard nodded. "He said it again to me just before he died. He said, 'Sydnee must help them.' So I taught you everything I know so you too have the power to change lives."

"I must help slaves escape?" Sydnee asked desperately.

"Only you can answer that question."

For a moment Sydnee thought she was looking into Margarite's eyes.

Madame Picard brushed the hair from Sydnee's eyes and said gently. "Listen to your spirits. They will help you find your way."

Opening the door, she looked both ways and then rushed down the walk. Sydnee followed her. The farmer was waiting by the wagon. There was no moonlight, and the street was dark. He had cleared a spot in the middle of the wagon for Ninon to hide among the produce.

She stopped, turned around and put her hand on Sydnee's cheek. "How I have loved you, my little one."

Tears filled Sydnee's eyes. She shook her head and gasped, "But—but this is too fast. This cannot be happening."

The farmer stepped forward and held out his hand to help Madame Picard onto the back of the wagon. She stepped up onto the flatbed, laid down, and he pulled the canvas over her. Jumping into the driver's seat, he snapped the reins, and they were off.

Sydnee walked out into the middle of the street watching the wagon disappear into the darkness. In a matter of moments, in a whirlwind of panic and despair, her world had changed forever.

Chapter 17

New Orleans 1839

It was difficult coping with the loss of Madame Picard, but Sydnee continued with the salon and her role as a consummate hostess. She carefully concealed the emptiness she felt inside, confiding with only Mortimer about Madame's secret life, since Tristan and Isabel came from slave-holding families. Initially Sydnee was questioned by the authorities about Madame Picard's organization, but she had nothing to hide. She had been completely ignorant of the clandestine activities. For several weeks they pressured her until she asked D'anton to put a stop to it.

Time passed, and as Sydnee's fame grew with the salon, so too did Mortimer's reputation as a healer of animals. Planters all over Louisiana and Mississippi badgered Monsieur Saint-Yves for time with the young man, and eventually he tired of these petitions and encouraged Mortimer to strike out on his own.

Isabel and Tristan provided Mortimer with the capital to buy out Carl Schinden, whose livery was bankrupt, and in less than a year, Mortimer had a successful business housing and treating animals. He was able to return the principal to the Saint-Yveses in no time and with generous interest.

Mortimer had never been happier. With diligence and love, his dream was at last fulfilled. Gish Livery was more like a hospital than a stable. It was immaculate, efficiently run, and a clearinghouse for all the latest information and techniques on animal welfare. He employed three assistants, and they treated animals, particularly equines, from as far upriver as Memphis. Race horses seemed to be evolving as his specialty, but Mortimer loved all creatures and worked around the clock on everything from horses to cats to parrots. Sydnee would visit him frequently at his new livery, and now that she could no longer rendezvous at Madame Picard's home with Isabel, the women would meet her there too.

One rainy afternoon in November, Tristan paid Sydnee a visit at her townhome. "Well, you are early for the supper tonight," she said smiling, as she escorted him into the parlor. She had recently redecorated the room with freshly painted jalousies, silver-colored draperies and upholstery. On the floor was a gray and burgundy Turkish carpet.

The moment Tristan sat down, Sydnee knew something was wrong.

"We must cancel the supper this evening," he said with an anxious look on his face.

Sydnee stared at him. The rain beat on the window panes.

"Monsieur Trudeau caught Isabel with Mortimer in his quarters at the livery."

Her jaw dropped. "Were they--?"

Tristan nodded and dropped his eyes. "There was a terrible scene."

Sydnee gasped. "What happened?"

"He attacked Mortimer, but Mortimer refused to defend himself against a man of his years. In the end, Isabel pulled Monsieur Trudeau into his carriage, and they left."

"Where is Isabel now?"

"At home and extremely distraught."

Sydnee stood up and began to pace in front of the fireplace. Thunder rumbled.

"Who told you?" she asked.

"Isabel. Her father threatened to tell me, but she assured him that she would confess everything to me immediately." Tristan grimaced. "Oh, Sydnee, the hideous names he called her, and the words he used for Mortimer were--I cannot repeat them. The worst of it is that he wants Mortimer expelled from the community."

"Oh, Tristan," Sydnee moaned.

He bit his lip and nodded.

She sat down on the edge of a chair and asked, "So what

happens now?"

He shrugged. "There is little we can do. Our grand charade is beginning to unravel."

*   *   *

Sydnee did not sleep that night. She did not need to consult the spirits to know that things were changing for the worse. When she walked the dogs past Gish Livery in the morning, Mortimer would not speak with her. Every day for a week she asked to meet with him but was met with refusal.

D'anton stopped by that evening and told her that Monsieur Trudeau had taken ill, and that it seemed to be quite serious. He was having trouble speaking, and his walking had become palsied. "The doctors believe that he has suffered an apoplectic fit," he said.

Frantic with worry, Sydnee tried to see Isabel, but she too was refusing visitors. Tristan told Sydnee that she would not rise from her bed and would not eat. He assured her that he was staying by Isabel's side and that she would recover soon, but Sydnee could see the doubt in his eyes.

Sydnee felt so helpless. All she could do is appeal to the saints and light candles for them all. Then early one morning, a boy brought a message from Mortimer. The note said that he had closed the livery permanently, and left for Memphis. Mortimer enclosed a letter for Tristan and one for Isabel which he asked Sydnee to deliver.

She sat down on the front step and hugged Baloo's neck, her eyes filling with tears. "Our dear old friend is gone, Baloo. Our world seems to be getting smaller and smaller."

*   *   *

Gradually over a period of months, Isabel recovered but her father did not. He died the following March, and Isabel blamed herself for his demise. Madame Trudeau having a kind and forgiving nature, reached out to her daughter, but Isabel withdrew from the world never leaving her bed chamber. She grew pale and fragile, yet when Sydnee saw her, she seemed more beautiful than ever. Tragedy had etched character into her face and added depth to her azure eyes. But there was little

173

solace in her beauty; she was desperately unhappy.

One day Sydnee had an idea which she decided to present to Isabel. She had Tristan sneak her into the house late one night to speak with her. He ushered her to a small sitting room off Isabel's bed chamber and left the two women alone. The room was draped in heavy fabrics of burgundy and gold and had been shut up for so long, it smelled of stale rosewater and dead flowers.

Isabel sat down on the edge of a chair. She was dressed in a light green dressing gown with her hair tied back, several wisps framing her face.

"Isabel," Sydnee said, pulling her gloves off and sitting down on a divan. "I want you to take a moment to consider what I am about to say before casting my idea aside." Sydnee swallowed hard. "I think--I think you should adopt a child."

Isabel stared at her a moment and then looked down at the carpet. "I am in no condition to care for a child. You know that."

"You can hire a nanny," Sydnee countered eagerly. "It would give you someone to love and turn your attention away from your troubles and loneliness. You have the means to provide a home and food for a little one."

"No, Sydnee. Too many of these children come from questionable--"

"Remember," Sydnee interrupted. "Tristan was adopted."

Isabel pushed herself up from the chair and said, "Thank you for coming and for thinking of me, Sydnee, but I don't feel well. I must return to bed."

Holding her drawstring bag tightly, Sydnee stood up, ready for the final assault. Her voice was gentle and soft, but her words were like cold steel. "Isabel wait," she demanded. "Have you ever considered what Tristan may want? He has been ever patient and kind, taking care of you for months now. Perhaps *he* would like a family. I believe you are being selfish, and you forget that he too is a victim here."

Isabel was thunderstruck. She stared at Sydnee with her mouth open, blinking at her audacity. "How dare you!" she gasped.

Sydnee looked her in the eye. She was not about to back down. "If you care for him at all, ask him what *he* wants for a change."

*   *   *

Sydnee knew she would win. Tristan, of course, embraced the idea of a child and several weeks later, Sydnee and Isabel were headed for the Ursuline Convent to inquire about adoption. Tristan had to leave town on business for a month, but he encouraged Isabel to speak with the nuns, and when he returned, he would be a part of the final decision.

The day of the appointment, the women dressed in modest attire and wore hats with dark veils to cover their faces. They must not be seen together in public, and they definitely did not want anyone to suspect their errand.

The Ursuline Convent was a sprawling complex of buildings by the river housing an orphanage, a hospital, school and chapel. Two stories high and lined with large shuttered windows and gardens, the structure was imposing.

Sydnee and Isabel stepped out of the carriage and swept through the front door, lifting their veils as they stepped into the dark entryway. They were greeted immediately by a novice who escorted them to the office of Mother Baptista. It was an austere room with an oak desk, two chairs and a crucifix. The plaster walls were painted a dreary beige.

Mother Baptista stood up to greet them. She was a humorless woman of middle years who looked stern and imposing in her long black habit. She mustered a smile and invited them to sit down. Taking a chair behind her desk, Mother Baptista picked up Isabel's letter and ran her eyes over the page. "You and your husband are unable to have children?"

"That is correct, Mother," Isabel replied, her cheeks flushing slightly.

"And where is your husband today?" the woman asked.

"Away on business, but he will join me next time. He was a foundling here himself long ago."

Mother Baptista raised her eyebrows. "Indeed?"

"Yes, with his older brother." Isabel shifted nervously in

her chair. "Do you have children right now, Mother Baptista?"

"We always have children, Madame Saint-Yves."

"Would you," Isabel hesitated, not wanting to sound too bossy. "Would you mind telling me a little about them, Mother?"

"Well," the nun said, putting Isabel's letter down and resting back in her chair. "They are all ages. Some of our foundlings are products of unfortunate liaisons, some of them come from houses of ill repute and many, particularly in the summer months, come to us as orphans of disease. Some children are surrendered to us by mothers incapable of feeding and clothing them or who are afraid for their lives."

The nun sighed. "Unfortunately most of the foundlings we have now are sick. We wish we could house them all but we can minister only to those in dire need. We would love to take in all the orphans we see on the streets but it is beyond us at this point. We know some of these children are being used for unthinkable purposes."

Sydnee swallowed hard and looked down at the floor. She knew what Mother Baptista was alluding to and dark memories began to stir. She heard her father calling her to come up to the cabin. She could hear men laughing, and she could feel their rough hands upon her body. She could smell their sweat and the stink of alcohol on their breath.

Noticing that Sydnee had turned pale, Mother Baptista asked, "Would you care for a glass of water?"

Startled back to reality, Sydnee murmured, "Yes, thank you."

Scrutinizing her, the nun handed her a mug of water.

At last Mother Baptista turned to Isabel and said, "Shall we meet the children?"

"Yes, I would like that," Isabel replied, standing up.

Sydnee stayed seated.

"Are you coming?"

"No, thank you. If you don't mind I will stay here," Sydnee said. She was feeling a bit unsteady.

"Very well," said Isabel reluctantly. She looked over her shoulder at Sydnee as she left the room.

Sydnee stayed in her chair for a long time, staring straight ahead, trying to make sense of the visions and voices swirling around her. Something was moving inside her world. Something was changing, and it scared her. She could hear Margarite's voice repeating, "The name Sauveterre, did I never tell you, child? *En français*, it means safe haven."

Sydnee rubbed her temples, stood up and started to pace.

"Did I never tell you child? *En français*, it means safe haven," Margarite's voice said again.

Next it was Madame Picard she heard. "There can be more, but it will be revealed to you by the good Lord in his own time."

Sydnee squeezed her eyes shut.

"It will be revealed to you, revealed to you, revealed to you," Madame Picard's voice echoed in her ears.

"You must help them, help them," she heard Maxime murmur.

Feeling light-headed, Sydnee stepped out into the hallway. She took a deep breath and put her hand against the wall to steady herself. A girl of about seventeen was down on her knees, scrubbing the floor. When she looked up, Sydnee was startled. The girl's face was purple with bruises, and her eyes were black. Blinking and staring for a moment, Sydnee murmured a greeting and turned away.

Still breathing hard, she walked down the hall to the entry. She had to get outside for fresh air. Just as she was about to take the handle, a small door cut in the wall caught her attention. Attached to the base of the door was a large revolving tray, half of it inside the building, half outside. The tray was on a hinge so it could rotate.

"Infants are frequently left to us on that device," someone said behind her.

Sydnee jumped. It was Mother Baptista with Isabel. "The child is placed on the tray on the outside and swung around to the interior for us to find. Sometimes they ring the bell to alert us."

"I see," murmured Sydnee.

The nun turned, and they followed her back to the office

to discuss more adoption details. Sydnee tried to listen but was too distracted. Before they left, she deliberately dropped her drawstring bag on the floor by her chair.

"Thank you for your help today, Mother Baptista," Isabel said with a smile.

"God bless you until we meet again," the nun replied formally, walking them to the door.

Isabel and Sydnee dropped their veils back over their faces and started for the carriage. The moment Isabel stepped into the vehicle, Sydnee feigned surprise and said, "Oh! I have forgotten my bag."

Turning, she rushed back into Mother Baptista's office. "I beg your pardon, Mother. I have forgotten my bag," she explained. After retrieving it, Sydnee lifted her veil and said, "I have a question, if you please, Mother Baptista."

"Yes?"

"What happens to the mothers of the foundlings?"

Mother Baptista shrugged. "Most we never see. If they do need sanctuary, we can provide it for them but only for one night. Women come to us for many reasons, not just motherhood. Sometimes they are in grave danger, trying to escape from violence. Many are young girls, fourteen, maybe fifteen years of age."

"Where do they go after they leave here?"

"I would like to think they escape to a safe haven, but alas, I believe most return to the same situation."

"I see," said Sydnee thoughtfully. "Thank you, Mother Baptista."

As she walked out of the convent, she stopped and gave the young woman washing the floor all the coins she had in her purse.

Chapter 18

Everything changed for Sydnee after that day. Her world no longer seemed empty and meaningless. At last the spirits revealed the way. She knew now that she must help women and girls find a safe haven away from lives of bondage and violence. How she would help them break free remained a mystery, but she knew that she would find a way. She managed to escape her own misery, and now she was determined to help others break free as well.

Sydnee was committed to this mission, but she was not naive about the danger it posed. The memories of her own rapes and beatings would haunt her forever, so she knew that caution and vigilance would be of the utmost importance.

For days she took the dogs on long walks trying to gather her thoughts and make plans. Gentlemen and ladies on the street wondered why New Orleans' premier hostess seemed so distracted. Sydnee would respond to their greetings politely, but she was distant and aloof. In reality, she was looking at the homeless and destitute people all around her. For the first time in years, she noticed the impoverished prostitutes leaning in doorways and waifs begging on the street. She listened to babies crying and heard the raucous laughter in taverns on the wharf. She smelled stale spirits and vomit and noticed the lurid stares of dock workers and sailors. The degradation and the suffering was everywhere, and now it was part of her life again. For a long time she tried to forget this world, but now it was back again.

One sunny afternoon in May, she decided to stop at the Ursuline Convent to speak with Mother Baptista. She knew that she needed the nuns to help her find those in need. Sydnee felt nervous, but she was not about to be deterred.

"Stay," she said sternly to Vivian and the dogs. Vivian obediently coasted up into a tree, and the dogs sat down at attention by the entry. "I will be back soon," she assured them.

She collapsed her parasol and pulled the bell cord of the front door. The same novice answered and took her to Mother Baptista's office.

"Good afternoon, Mother," Sydnee said shyly. "I am sorry to come without an appointment, but may I speak with you a moment?"

"Of course, Mademoiselle Sauveterre."

The nun motioned for her to sit down, and Sydnee swept her skirt to the side sitting on the edge of a chair. The nun ran her eyes over the fashionable gown, the perfectly coifed hair, and the soft brown eyes.

"Mother Baptista," Sydnee said, swallowing hard. "Ever since I visited here several weeks ago, I have been thinking about the fate of the women who come here seeking help."

"Yes?"

"I would like to help."

The nun nodded her head. "We are always grateful for donations."

"No, Mother. I want to help in another way. I want to help them to safety."

The nun frowned. "To safety? How?"

Sydnee had rehearsed her words. "I want to provide a means of transportation and a network of homes to help women and girls escape to safety and start new lives elsewhere."

Mother Baptista stared at Sydnee, thunderstruck. It took a moment, but at last she believed she understood. *Here is another spoiled young woman who needs a diversion.*

She chuckled. "I see. You have been moved by the misfortune of others, but you really do not understand, Mademoiselle--"

"Oh yes, I do," Sydnee interrupted, her eyes growing hard. "I understand much more than you realize."

"I am very busy today," Mother Baptista said, standing up. "Please know that you are a nice girl, and your offer is appreciated."

Sydnee rose too, and although she was shorter than the

nun, she looked her in the eye and said firmly, "If you think this is a passing fancy for me, Mother Baptista, you are mistaken."

The nun's eyebrows shot up at her audacity. Suddenly she remembered how pale Sydnee had grown in her office several weeks earlier when she spoke of children being used for unspeakable purposes.

They locked eyes until Mother Baptista said, "This is against my better judgment but please sit down."

When Sydnee was seated, the woman said, "You must understand, we will never interfere with the sacred bonds of matrimony. A wife should always be at her husband's side."

Sydnee did not like it, but she knew the church would hold firm on this matter.

"Most of the women who come to us are married, most return home gladly, but we do see a great many prostitutes who may benefit from help. Also some of the girls are apprentices or servants being beaten by employers. These females we could refer to you, but sometimes there are girls who have run away from their parents. Those girls must return home. We cannot interfere with family matters or bonds of legal ownership. Each situation is different and dangerous. You must understand; escape is a highly unusual idea. I have not given my consent but," and she hesitated. "If I send women to you, where do you propose to house them?"

"At my town house."

"Out of the question. It is too dangerous. They are frequently followed. You need a neutral location that is private."

Sydnee stared at her. She had not considered this possibility.

"I will make arrangements," Sydnee assured her.

"Will you take mothers with children?"

"Yes," Sydnee replied.

"Where will you take these women and children? You must have housing for them in their new location. You cannot dump them on the street of a new city."

"I have considered that, and I will be making trips in the next few weeks for that purpose. I did not want to make any arrangements until I had spoken with you."

"And what transportation will you provide from the convent to their sanctuary in the city here?"

This was another problem that Sydnee had not considered. She lifted her chin and said, "I will have that addressed along with your other concerns before we meet again."

The nun sighed and shook her head. "You have many obstacles to overcome before you start. I will give it some thought, but I have strong reservations. We can give you no help beyond notification of women in need that qualify." Mother Baptista studied Sydnee for a moment. She had misjudged this young woman. She knew now that something motivated her beyond mere whim. Something must have occurred in her past to give her this firm resolve.

Sydnee stood up. "Thank you, Mother Baptista."

"One moment," the nun said. "At some point you will have to defend yourself, Mademoiselle Sauveterre. Are you prepared for this?"

Sydnee looked out the window at her friends waiting for her outside and said, "That is not a concern, Mother. I have three weapons with me at all times."

*   *   *

It did not take long for Sydnee to realize that Gish Livery was the perfect location to house the women and children before they started their escape to new cities and towns.

"What on earth do you want with a stable, Sydnee?" D'anton asked. They were sitting at his desk in his elegant office on Jackson Square.

"It helps Mortimer to receive a little income, and it helps me," Sydnee said, offering no more information.

D'anton was making final arrangements for a trip with Tristan to Saratoga when she arrived that afternoon. As an attorney, he had been appointed by Mortimer to lease the livery. There had been little interest in the property until today, and it surprised D'anton that it would be Sydnee who would want to rent the building. He handed her a pen to sign the papers. Thinking that she was merely being a solicitous friend, D'anton shrugged and gave her the keys.

She left the square feeling satisfied and almost ready to approach Mother Baptista once more. As she walked through the streets with the dogs, she noticed New Orleans was emptying out. The searing days of summer were on the way, and the months for illness were looming on the horizon. She knew that many women would be widowed after the summer epidemics, and there would be many new orphans.

Sydnee remembered suddenly that today Isabel was taking Tristan to the convent to meet the three-year-old orphan she wished to adopt. Although the little girl had been malnourished and neglected, she was starting to thrive under the loving care of the Ursulines. Like Isabel and Tristan, the little girl had blue eyes and blonde hair. Tristan had delayed his trip to Saratoga for several weeks to spend time with the infant. They were both very excited. Sydnee smiled. She was happy for them.

She unlocked the service door in the back of the livery and stepped inside the empty stable, followed by the dogs. The livery was dark and smelled of hay. Mice scampered into the corners as they walked. Gradually her eyes adjusted to the low light, and she looked around. Mortimer had left it clean and in good repair. The stalls had been swept, and all the tack and medical supplies had been removed. Aside from the two hearses left by Schinden in the back of the building, the livery was empty.

Sydnee walked into Mortimer's personal quarters. All the furniture had been removed leaving the room hollow and lifeless. Her heels clicked loudly on the bare hardwood floor. She walked over to the fireplace wistfully remembering the evenings she dined here with him, discussing sick animals and exchanging remedies. Frequently Isabel joined them, and they would speak of their hopes and dreams, exchanging confidences meant only for friends. When the fire burned low, Sydnee would say goodnight and leave the two of them alone.

She pressed her eyes shut a moment longer, trying to savor the memories before harsh reality returned. She sighed and looked around. She must attend to the present. She would have to make these rooms comfortable for others. A table and chairs would be needed as well as a bed, a cradle and perhaps a trundle bed for an older child. There must be wood on hand for a fire and a few cooking utensils. Bedding and even some clothing must be obtained. Although she planned to house the runaways for only a few nights, they must have ample supplies because they could not leave the livery.

Everything seemed to be falling into place. Yesterday Sydnee booked passage for Memphis to visit Mortimer to enlist his help. She was eager to see her old friend once more, but her visit to him was not just social. She was going to approach him about finding places of employment and housing for refugees.

He too had been abandoned as a child, and she knew the beatings he endured from Schinden had scarred him for life physically and emotionally. She believed that he would be sympathetic to her cause and offer assistance.

D'anton had given her Mortimer's address and told her that he had opened a small livery in the center of town. He said that he was already making a success of himself. Sydnee was not surprised. She knew that before he left he already had many customers in Tennessee and that his skills were renowned throughout the South.

Memphis was just one place she planned on taking women in need, and she was also considering the Natchez Trace as an escape route up to Nashville. She knew that every few miles there were abandoned stands, and these would be perfect hiding places for a journey to the North. Her biggest problem was finding a trustworthy escort.

The last problem for her to solve before returning to Mother Baptista was transportation within the city. Sydnee rubbed her forehead. She knew that she could not use her carriage. Riding horseback did not provide enough cover, and walking was too dangerous. She considered purchasing a wagon, but too many people would recognize her dogs riding in the back. Putting her fist to her lips, she walked out into the stable, trying to think. Suddenly her eyes rested on the hearses in the corner. Of course, she thought. They were private, enclosed with curtains and the community was used to seeing hearses going in and out of this building. They would assume a new undertaker was housing his vehicles here.

Sydnee nodded her head. This could work. The dogs would ride in back with those trying to escape, and she could drive the coach dressed as a professional mourner. She knew her waif-like figure would serve her well for her disguise as a boy.

"That's it. I'm ready," she said. Atlantis and Baloo looked up at her with surprise. "Let's go speak with Mother Baptista."

*   *   *

Reluctantly Mother Baptista gave her consent to Sydnee's plan and within days she was on her way to Memphis to see Mortimer. She leaned against the railing of the paddle wheeler and smiled. At last she was riding a riverboat as a lady. Dressed in a cream-colored gown with light green stripes and tiny pink flowers, Sydnee looked crisp and fresh, standing on the upper deck with a white lace parasol resting on her shoulder. She knew that convention dictated she wear a bonnet, but she didn't care. She liked feeling the wind in her hair. So many bonnets looked dowdy, and they always seemed to make her head ache.

She ran her eyes over the steamboat. *The Jonas Riley* was a beautiful stern-wheeler just recently constructed in Vicksburg and on its second voyage up the Mississippi. It was painted white with a bright red paddle wheel and two tall, black smoke stacks. Sydnee remembered the first time she had seen a steamboat near Natchez years ago. She thought it looked like a huge, white frosted cake, and she still thought it looked like a fancy confection.

"Cast off the bow line!" the captain called and the whistle shrieked overhead. Passengers started to wave and call to loved-ones on shore as the big red wheel began to turn and splash. The *Jonas Riley* was filled to capacity, stuffed with passengers and supplies bound for the North Country and cooler temperatures.

Sydnee's stomach jumped. Soon, in less than two weeks, she would be knocking on Mortimer Gish's door. She had missed him terribly but nothing in comparison to Isabel's yearning. She was glad that Isabel had the child to distract her, but Sydnee could still see the sorrow in her eyes. Isabel asked

185

her to deliver a letter to Mortimer, but nothing else was said about their separation.

Sydnee looked back at New Orleans as it faded in the distance. This was the first time she had left the city since she had arrived nine years earlier with Maxime. Dear Maxime, she thought, he had changed the world for her, and now with nothing left but his spirit to guide her, she would change the world for someone else.

A bird soaring overhead caught her eye and startled her. For a moment she thought Vivian had escaped. Marie, Sydnee's housekeeper, was watching her friends for her while she was away. A young, free woman of color, Marie was efficient and dependable, but it would be no easy task to keep Vivian confined. Although the girl was trustworthy, Sydnee knew Vivian would try to be bossy and overbearing with her.

Sydnee turned around and stepped through the louvered door into her stateroom. A smile flickered on her lips as she looked around. It was a lovely room paneled in white with a maple wardrobe and a small four poster bed to match. There were mullioned windows with shutters and resting on a nightstand was a large copper urn filled with water for ablutions. In one corner, there was a tiny dressing table with a glass lamp next to a floor mirror on legs. By the bed was an ornately carved chair with blue flowers embroidered on the seat cushion and back.

Sydnee sat down on the evergreen duvet, running her hands over the fine fabric and smiled. Never forgetting how difficult life had once been, she was forever grateful for the blessings she received.

Sydnee reveled in these sumptuous surroundings. Traveling on a riverboat was elegant beyond her imagination. She spent most of that first day on the promenade deck watching the river, but when the gong sounded for supper she walked down the grand staircase to the dining room. She ran her hand along the ornately carved railing, admiring the workmanship and looked up over her head at the sun streaming through the stained glass ceiling.

She was seated with several couples at supper, all residents of Natchez and New Orleans. They knew her by name even before she was seated and bored her with endless accounts of their wealth and social standing. Sydnee knew that they were fishing for invitations to the salon, and the more they boasted, the more she was determined not to invite them.

She smiled graciously, pretending to listen, but she was actually savoring the delectable veal with dumplings, figs and lemon bars. A quartet played waltzes during supper and when the women adjourned to the lady's drawing room, they were serenaded by a musician at the grand piano. Boys with silver trays walked around the room offering beverages and coffee to the ladies while they relaxed and visited on plush divans and upholstered-back armchairs.

Most of the week, Sydnee spent reading on deck and watching the river. She noted the landscape change from cypress and swamp grasses, sycamores and Spanish moss to the darker greens of pine trees, standing out against the paper-white bark of the birch. The air seemed clearer in the north and stars seemed brighter. On several occasions, passengers pestering her with pretensions, drove her back into her stateroom, but on those nights she would wait until they retired and steal back out onto deck to enjoy the stars.

She liked to watch the activity when the *Jonas Riley* made stops to unload supplies at plantations and towns along the river or when passengers needed to go ashore late at night. She loved the lights and was fascinated when the crew brought the massive boat over to a landing. She marveled at their skill navigating the unpredictable river littered with submerged trees and debris.

When they finally reached Memphis, Sydnee was beside herself with excitement to see Mortimer. She looked around, overwhelmed by the activity on the landing. Memphis was indeed a busy river town. There were rows and rows of keelboats and paddle wheelers being loaded with timber and cut lumber, and she could hear saw mills buzzing in the distance. A large slave auction block dominated the landing, but at the moment, no sales were taking place.

The first thing she did was check her bag at the Chancellor Hotel, pick up her skirts and start to navigate the muddy street named Beale. She had Mortimer's address in her hand, and in no time she found Gish Livery.

Sydnee stood across the street at first to observe. There was no question Mortimer's Livery here in Memphis was smaller and more modest than his New Orleans' establishment, but it was still bustling with activity. Two boys were out front helping customers, and at last when they took the horses inside the stable, Sydnee could see Mortimer. He was consulting with an elderly gentleman about a thoroughbred.

When their conversation ended, Sydnee walked up. Mortimer glanced at her and then looked again with surprise.

She started to giggle with excitement.

"Mademoiselle Sydnee," he said in his monotone voice. "Why are you here? Is Isabel--"

"Oh, Mortimer!" she cried. "Isabel is well! Are you not happy to see *me*?"

"Oh, yes, yes, yes," he mumbled, all flustered. "I didn't mean--"

Sydnee took his hand. "I am teasing, my old friend. I am here for a short visit, but I don't want to interrupt your work."

"No, this is why I have help."

Mortimer turned and addressed the boys. "I will be back shortly. Mind Methuselah. She needs her ointment."

"Yes, Mr. Gish," they all replied.

Mortimer took his hat and coat from a peg on the wall, offered Sydnee his arm, and they walked down to the river. It was a warm sunny day, but it felt cool under the umbrella of the trees. It smelled of evergreens, sweet grass and the moist mud of the Mississippi.

"Why did you come?" Mortimer asked once they left the noise and bustle of town.

"I have several things to discuss with you, and I wanted to see how you fare."

He stole a glance at her up through his hair.

Sydnee's face softened into a smile. "Isabel has adopted a

child."

Mortimer stopped walking and looked at her.

Sydnee nodded. "Indeed."

They resumed walking, and she added, "Her decline was steady after you left. I feared—we all feared for her life. But now she has someone to live for again, a little three-year-old girl. She even looks like her."

Sydnee could see him smile through the strings of his hair. She reached into her bag and drew out the letter. "She sent this for you."

He stopped and stared at the letter as if it were something sacred. Carefully he took it, his hand shaking and slid it into his breast pocket.

They spoke at length of his business and the new life he was creating for himself in Memphis. "The livery is so small, nothing like the one in New Orleans. I hope to someday purchase something bigger."

"Well, I come with news on that subject too," Sydnee said, reaching in her purse again. "D'anton has sent a check for rent on your building in New Orleans."

Again Mortimer stopped, thunderstruck. "Someone is leasing it?"

"I am."

"*You* are?"

"Yes."

He frowned.

"What's wrong, Mortimer?"

"I cannot take your charity."

"Mortimer, this is not charity for you, but *it is* charity for others. I need your help," and she explained everything.

That afternoon, Mortimer returned only briefly to the livery. They talked long into the night in his rooms above the stable. Over the next week, he introduced Sydnee to several trusted friends, two of whom were Quakers. They were willing to provide temporary food and housing for the women and children when they came to Memphis. They had many options for employment too, domestic situations, farm labor and shop keepers. The Quakers informed Sydnee that Memphis was a growing community and opportunities for advancement were everywhere. Sydnee suspected these people were also involved someway in housing runaway slaves, but she would never compromise their safety by asking them directly. She wondered if they knew of Madame Picard.

The time spent with Mortimer was too short, and before she knew it, she was back on the paddle wheeler heading for home. The spirits seemed to be hurrying her and urging her forward to complete her plans. Sydnee also had the nagging feeling that something more was about to happen to her, more than just smuggling women and children out of New Orleans. This intuition gave her great anxiety.

Chapter 19

There were fewer passengers on the return trip to New Orleans. No one wanted to venture into the suffocating heat and disease of that city in the summer. The shortage of travelers suited Sydnee completely. She could sit on deck unmolested, watching the shoreline or reading. Occasionally there would be a greeting from a lady, or a gentleman might tip his hat, but few people stopped to visit.

Suppers were relaxed and leisurely in the main dining room, and the ladies in the drawing room were cordial. They did not try to dominate Sydnee's attention. All in all her first journey on a riverboat as a lady had exceeded her expectations.

The last day on the Mississippi, they stopped in Natchez, and Sydnee watched from the deck as a handful of men and women boarded. She looked at the rundown flop-houses and taverns along the waterfront then looked up at the bluff lined with grand homes and plantation houses. She found the contrast disturbing. She could just make out the steps of the whore house where she met Maxime so long ago. She sighed. So much time had passed and everything had changed.

Everyone agreed to dress for supper their last evening on the riverboat, so at eight, Sydney emerged from her stateroom in a copper-colored satin evening gown. It had short sleeves and a deeply cut neckline which highlighted her long graceful neck. The color complemented her hair which she swept high onto her head with several amber bejeweled hair combs. Sydnee adored fashion and stayed abreast of all the Parisian trends. Dangling amber bobs decorated her ears.

She looked up as thunder rumbled. Knowing that storms in the evening with this heat could turn violent quickly, she started to walk briskly along the deck toward the dining room. All of a sudden she heard a girl shriek from the deck below,

"Keep your hands off me!"

"I'll teach you!" a man said.

Sydnee heard a slap and then another.

"Go to hell!" the girl screamed. There was thumping on the deck as if there was a struggle, and then the man roared as if in sudden pain.

Alarmed Sydnee bent over the railing but could see nothing. Next there was the sound of feet pounding up the stairs. A girl about the age of thirteen with dirty blonde hair, tattered clothing and bare feet jumped onto the deck and started running toward Sydnee, followed by a burly crew member with a bald head and blood streaming from his ear. The girl raced past Sydnee with the man behind her.

"No!" Sydnee cried jumping in front of the man. He slammed into her with such momentum, that she almost toppled over the railing. Blinded by rage and bent on catching the girl, he ran on and caught the girl by the collar, throwing her down onto to the deck.

"You little bitch!" he snarled straddling her. He back handed her once and then again.

"No!" screamed Sydnee lunging for him, but before she could reach him someone picked him up and pushed him to the wall.

A tall gentleman with shaggy dark hair, pinned the crew member against the wall with such force that his eyes bulged. "You're finished here," the gentleman snapped in a British accent.

Panting, the crew member nodded. The gentleman let him go, and the crew member staggered. "That hellcat is a stowaway," he barked, clutching his ear. "And she bit me."

Frowning, the gentleman looked over at the girl as Sydnee helped her up. The waif was dirty and bleeding. "I'll take that up with the captain," said the gentleman. "Now go," he demanded of the crew member, jerking his head toward the stairs.

The man lumbered off, holding his ear.

There was more thunder, and it started to pour. The gentleman turned to the girl and shouted over the wind and the rain, "Is this true?"

"Yes," she snapped, brushing blood from her lip.

The gentleman pushed his hand through his thick mane of wet hair impatiently. He looked at Sydnee and demanded, "Who are you?"

The rain drumming on the deck was deafening. "I was here when they came up on deck," Sydnee shouted over the din. Her hair stuck to her forehead and rain soaked her gown.

"Come along," he said, taking the girl's arm. "We are going to see the captain."

"Keep your goddamn hands off me!" the girl barked, jerking her arm free.

Sydnee saw the man's eyes flash, but he did not try to restrain her. "Go then!" he roared, flinging his arm.

The three ran up to the pilot house. The crew member who assaulted the stowaway was just leaving the bridge and pushed past them with a surly look.

Captain Petosky was leaning over a desk when they stepped inside. He was a leathery-skinned man in his middle years with graying hair. "I am sorry but I must have you wait a moment. You understand with this weather--" he said apologetically.

The pilot handed them some towels and rejoined the captain to look at some charts.

They began to dry themselves. The girl was soaked to the skin. Her face was bruised, and her lip was bleeding.

Sydnee watched the gentleman as he peeled off his wet suit coat. He was probably in his early thirties, tall, broad shouldered, and well dressed in fine evening attire. He wore a white dress shirt with a cravat and a dark vest. He had long unkempt dark hair, very light skin and frown lines on his face.

Feeling her studying him, he turned and glared at her as if she was being rude. Sydnee looked away quickly.

She noticed the girl was shivering, and she wrapped a towel around her shoulders. With her head down, the waif watched everyone, her eyes darting from one to the other, like a cornered animal.

At last Captain Petosky looked up. "Good evening

Mademoiselle Sauveterre. I am sorry about this altercation on your last night with us. These things happen, but the crew is supposed to keep these problems on the lower decks."

Sydnee shrugged, dismissing it.

"Dr. Locke, I am sorry that you have been involved in this too."

"If there is some problem, I will pay her fare," Dr. Locke offered, reaching into his pocket.

"That won't be necessary," Captain Petosky assured him. "She will be dealt with when we reach New Orleans."

Sydnee's stomach lurched. After what she had seen on deck, she shuddered to think what punishment awaited the girl ashore. She noticed the look of concern on Dr. Locke's face as well, and he said, "No, Captain Petosky. There has been a misunderstanding. She is--this is my servant girl."

"*Your* servant girl? I did not see her board with you earlier," the captain said suspiciously.

"I, ah--I had my brother purchase her ticket up north." He turned and asked the girl, "Did you not receive it?"

The girl darted a look around at the men, and then shook her head.

"There you have it, Captain. My apologies," said Dr. Locke cheerfully.

Captain Petosky knew that he was lying, but did not press it further. He sighed and said to the girl, "Very well. Where did you board?"

"Hannibal."

"Hannibal!" Dr. Locke exclaimed. Covering his mistake, he said quickly. "Y-yes, my brother has a farm up there."

Captain Petosky told him the cost of the fare, and he reached into his pocket, starting to count his bills. "I believe I am short. Would you take a sight draft, Captain?"

Sydnee jumped in. "What is the remainder, if you please? Dr. Locke and I are old friends. It would be my pleasure to be of assistance."

"I will gratefully return your money when we arrive in New Orleans," Locke said to her and Sydnee gave a little shrug, opening her bag.

Paying the remainder of the fare, Sydnee followed them out of the pilot house. Locke reached out quickly and grabbed the stowaway as she tried to bolt down the stairs. "Not so fast, young lady. You have a debt to repay. Charity hospital needs help, and you will do nicely."

"I'm not working at any goddamned hospital emptying piss pots."

"You are indeed charming," he said sarcastically and then looked at her lip. "I must attend to that."

"You may use my stateroom, if you wish," Sydnee offered.

"I will get my bag and be right there."

"Room 27A," she said.

When they arrived at her stateroom, Sydnee had the girl change out of her wet clothes into a dressing gown behind a lacquered screen. Sydnee sat down at her dressing table and pulled the pins out of her hair. She ran a brush through her wet tresses and in no time she rearranged her hair and pinned it back up again.

"You're rich," the girl observed as she sat down on a footstool. Sydnee walked behind the screen to step into a fresh gown.

"What's your name?" she asked the girl.

"Ruth Barstow."

"I am Sydnee Sauveterre."

There was knock on the door, and Dr. Locke stepped in holding a black medical bag. He looked around the luxurious stateroom and then ran his eyes over Sydnee's change of clothing. She suddenly felt spoiled and overdressed.

"I apologize for my tardiness," he said. "I had to attend to that crew member whose ear you bit," he said, looking at Ruth.

"Why did you help *him*?" she said with a frown.

"I am a doctor. I cannot pick and choose who to help."

He knelt down on one knee and took Ruth's chin, turning her face from side to side, examining her split lip. He opened his bag and rummaged through it mumbling, "Where is my ointment?"

"I have some Balm of Gilead that should help," Sydnee offered, stepping over to her dressing table.

Dr. Locke looked at her sharply. "There will be no African remedies used on my patients."

"But it is most effective and from the cottonwood poplar—"

"Folklore nonsense," he stated and turned back to Ruth.

Sydnee did not like this man. He was officious, bossy and had a high opinion of himself.

Opening a bottle, he soaked a cloth with tincture. When he dabbed it on Ruth's lip, she jumped and swore at him.

He snapped his bag shut, stood up and asked the girl, "Why did you stowaway?"

"The old man was beating me back in Hannibal."

"Your father?"

"No," she said, as if he was stupid. "He's dead. So's my ma. I grew up in St. Louis. I was taken by a thug who sold me to a farmer up north. The bastard worked me to death."

"Well, when we get to New Orleans, you must work too, but we will pay you wages. I won't force you to stay, but if you want a roof over your head, you must work."

Ruth looked at him suspiciously and then started digging in her pocket.

Dr. Locke turned to Sydnee. "I would be most grateful if you could put her up for the night. She could sleep-" and he looked around. "On the floor or something."

Sydnee nodded, just wishing he would leave. Suddenly she smelled something and looked at Ruth. She had lit a cigar.

Dr. Locke barked, "What is wrong with you!" He yanked the cigar from her mouth, opened the door and pitched the tobacco in the river.

"Hey!" Ruth bellowed.

"Where did you get that?" he demanded.

"From your pocket."

Locke's eyes grew wide, and he looked at Sydnee. "I must say, I am *most* grateful to you for taking her tonight," and he walked out.

*　　　　　*　　　　　*

After getting Ruth something to eat, and making up a bed for her, the night passed without incident. Sydnee slept little, ruminating about what to do with the girl. Things had happened faster than she had planned. The spirits had been right to hurry her. She found it ironic that she had everything organized to smuggle women and children *out* of New Orleans, and now she was scrambling to bring someone *into* the city.

Initially she thought Ruth could stay in the livery, but she realized that she did not want anyone residing in the city to know of the hiding place. Ruth would have to stay at the town house until accommodations could be arranged. Sydnee also laid awake worrying about Ruth's reports of kidnappings. It was the start of yellow jack season, and these abductors would be flooding the city soon.

The following morning when they docked in New Orleans, Dr. Locke accompanied them off the boat. He was dressed more casually this time in a white shirt, vest and a Panama hat cocked to the side. He had slung his frock coat over his shoulder because of the heat. Again he ran his eyes over Sydnee's gown. It was saffron yellow, with short capped sleeves and cut low over the shoulders. She wore a smart black belt around her waist and carried a pale yellow parasol. Although it was daywear, it was of the latest fashion. Again she felt as if she should apologize for her appearance.

Next he looked at Ruth. Sydnee had given her a dress to wear, but the fit was poor. He scowled. "I see you found some shoes, but couldn't you have given the girl a proper dress?"

"I will look again," Sydnee said, her face flushing with anger. "I'm sure there's something in my *vast* wardrobe that would suit your tastes."

Uncertain about whether she was being sarcastic, he darted a look at her and then continued to walk down the landing stage.

"We will go to Charity Hospital first," Locke said to Ruth. "And you can meet the nuns."

"Nuns?" Ruth said, curling her lip.

"Yes, nuns and plenty of them. At least I think so." He

scanned Jackson Square, busy with vendors and foot traffic.

"You don't live here?" Sydnee asked.

"What?" he replied absent-mindedly. "No, I accepted a position at the hospital and the Ursuline Orphanage. I like working with children."

"So you live in Natchez?"

"Yes, I recently inherited a home from my uncle up there, but I was raised in Gloucestershire."

At that moment Frederick pulled up in the open landau with the dogs in the back. Atlantis and Baloo jumped out and bound up to Sydnee, wagging their entire bodies. She squatted down, hugged them and said to Locke, "Allow me to give you a lift to the hospital. You don't know the city, and it is far too warm to walk."

"Thank you." Dr. Locke helped Frederick with the bags and then sat opposite Sydnee and Ruth. Frederick snapped the whip and they were off, trotting through the streets of New Orleans.

Ruth said little, but her eyes were like saucers. Sydnee knew that everything was new to her, from the magnolias and Spanish moss to the people on the street from every race and walk of life.

Dr. Locke seemed to be enjoying the ride as well. He took his hat off running his hands through his thick hair. Sydnee actually saw him smile at the dogs loping along behind the carriage. Even though this man is attractive, Sydnee thought, his arrogance ruins him. *Such a pity,* and she turned away.

The Sisters of Charity Hospital in Faubourg St. Marie was a large stucco building similar in appearance to the Ursuline Convent. When they arrived Dr. Locke helped Ruth out and said to Sydnee, "My thanks. I will make inquiries today about a residence for Ruth, but if nothing is found may I bring her to you for one more night?"

Sydnee looked at Ruth. The girl was picking at her nails, trying to act bored, but Sydnee knew it was a ruse to cover her fear. "Of course, I planned on it," and she handed him her calling card.

As expected, late that evening there was a knock at the door of Sydnee's town house. Marie showed Ruth and Dr. Locke into the parlor. Ruth gawked at the tall windows dressed in silver drapes, the richly upholstery furniture and crystal wall sconces. Dr. Locke was less impressed. Instead he looked up at the portrait of Tristan.

"Welcome, please sit down," Sydnee said, sweeping into the room.

"I am sorry to call so late, but the dormitories were locked when we finally finished for the night."

She offered Locke a glass of sherry as Marie took Ruth upstairs to bathe.

Dr. Locke eyed Sydnee. He was interested in this woman and her relationship with this man in the painting. Seeing no ring on her left hand, he asked, "Is your husband at home? I should like to meet him."

Sydnee stopped pouring the sherry and looked at him. "Dr. Locke, as you have probably already guessed, I am not married. The portrait over the mantel is of a dear friend, Tristan Saint-Yves. Our relationship is no secret here in New Orleans. Would you care to explore the details further?"

They locked eyes a moment and then he said, "Not interested."

After sipping his sherry, he put his glass on the end table and stated, "It has been a long day. I appreciate your hospitality, but I must be going."

Shaking with anger, Sydnee walked him to the entry. The man was rude and presumptuous. It was all she could do to restrain herself from slamming the door after him.

*   *   *

The next morning when Sydnee woke up, Ruth was gone. It appeared as if she had slept only a few hours than left the house. Sydnee sent a note to the hospital, but Dr. Locke had not seen her. Sydnee noticed that her liquor and cigars were gone and someone had tried to force the lock on her silver cabinet. She believed that as the day wore on she would find other objects of value stolen too. Mother Baptista had been right.

Using her house as a refuge was not a good option.

Sydnee decided to focus on something happier. Today she was going to meet Isabel and Tristan's new child, and she was very excited. She put on a hat with a dark veil and had Frederick drop her off at the cathedral. After Mass she walked to their home with her face covered.

She was delighted to meet Delphine. She was a good-natured child with curly white hair and blue eyes. The three-year-old girl was frail but extremely alert and quick to smile.

"She is beautiful," Sydnee said. "And I am sure she is brilliant as well."

"Oh, she is," agreed Tristan. He held Delphine as she rode a rocking horse. He adored the little girl, and his eyes sparkled whenever he looked at her.

Isabel sat nearby, watching serenely with her hands folded in her lap. The color had returned to her face, and she was starting to fill out again. She had taken to motherhood instantly and was in constant communication with her mother on everything from discipline to baby bonnets.

Tristan was miserable that he had to leave for Saratoga so soon. D'anton, finding he too was taken with the child suggested they cancel their trip, but Tristan was meeting with several cotton manufacturers, and it could not wait.

Sydnee left the house that afternoon feeling grateful to a thin, little wisp of a girl for healing so many broken hearts.

*   *   *

Months passed and no word came from the convent on women and children in need of transport. Everything was ready in the livery, Sydnee had obtained the uniform of a mourner, and she had even found a suitable escort to take refugees up The Trace if the need arose. All she needed now were women and children to help escape.

September came and Sydnee was starting to grow restless. When she checked at the convent, Mother Baptista said that there had been several potential candidates who were prostitutes, but in the end they decided to return to their former lives. "In my experience," the nun said with authority. "Few of these women are interested in true reform."

Sydnee clenched her teeth. She wanted to say more to the nun but respect for the church stopped her. She stepped out into the hall feeling angry and frustrated. It was apparent now that Mother Baptista was not going to refer anyone to her. She pulled open the heavy front door and stepped out into the sunlight and stifling heat. Atlantis jumped up from the shade and stood by her side. Baloo elected to remain home. He was getting up in years and sleeping more and more lately. The heat and humidity bothered him.

As she started down the walk she noticed the girl who had been scrubbing floors the first time she had come to the convent was outside washing windows. The bruises were gone from her face and she looked healthier.

"Are you going to wash all of these windows?" Sydnee asked, running her eyes over the huge building.

"I am," the girl said with a smile. "It will take weeks, but it is worth it to see the sun stream through so bright and strong."

*   *   *

That evening at supper Sydnee's demeanor was lackluster, and it took great effort to make conversation. She had invited a small group to dine with her and to play cards. Most of her gatherings were small this time of year, and during a round of whist, Madame Cardona, a Creole from an old New Orleans family, observed, "You are pale, my darling child. What is it?"

Sydnee smiled weakly and said, "Thank you, but it is nothing."

"Do you miss our dear Tristan?"

"Indeed I do," Sydnee said.

The elderly woman recommended, "Drink some of your friend Margarite's sickness tea. That will help."

"I will. Thank you, Madame Cardona."

Hoping the tea and a good night's sleep would cure her, Sydnee went to bed early, but instead, she tossed and turned. Feelings of disappointment nagged her, and she felt utterly discouraged. Her plans to help women and children had failed. She felt as if she had been foolish and misguided to even consider the undertaking. She could still see the look in Mother Baptista's eyes when she first proposed it. That same look was on Dr. Locke's face on the riverboat. They thought she was shallow and spoiled. Sydnee sat up in bed and covered her face. "Maybe I am," she said, tears filling her eyes.

Baloo, who was sleeping by her bed, looked up, his tail thumping. Sydnee turned back the covers and slid down on the floor, hugging his neck. "You know me better than anyone, old friend. Is that what I have become?"

He thumped his tail and leaned against her.

In her bare feet, she walked downstairs to make more of Margarite's sickness tea. Taking the tea outside, she sat on the steps of the courtyard, sipping it. The bugs had cleared for the night, and she watched the moon, seeking guidance from the spirits.

She thought of the girl washing windows. It was good to see that she had found *her* safe haven. Taking another sip of tea she looked up at the stars, pleading with the spirits to speak to her. She listened, but they were quiet.

Draining her cup, she stood up and saw the reflection of the moon in the kitchen window. She remembered that girl again and what she said about the sun shining brighter through the windows if they were clean.

She smiled and walked into the house. Putting her cup down, she started up the stairs and then stopped. The image of the girl came into her mind again, but this time there was something more. Sydnee's lips parted. Now she understood. The spirits had been speaking to her all along, she hadn't been listening.

Chapter 20

The next day, Sydnee took the dogs on a walk past the convent. The girl was out again washing windows, and Sydnee waved to her. Every day for a week after that, Sydnee would walk past the convent with a basket on her arm as if she was going to market, trying to become acquainted with the girl. Sometimes she would stop and make small talk, sometimes she would just wave.

Eventually they exchanged names, and Sydnee shared some beignets with her. A few days later, she brought lunch. Sydnee kept their encounters short, hoping Mother Baptista would not see them together.

The girl's name was Liesl Schiffman. She was seventeen, originally from Prussia, and had been a seamstress apprentice before coming to work for the Ursulines. Just like Mortimer, she had been beaten regularly by her employer.

By the middle of October, Sydnee and Liesl had become confidantes, and Sydnee at last explained to the girl her plans of helping women and children escape to new lives.

"I have seen many ladies come here," she said to Sydnee in her thick accent. "Many have children. They stay one night only and then they must leave. Usually their men come for them. Some are happy to go back. But sometimes—sometimes these women--they are scared and return home because they have nowhere else to go."

Sydnee nodded. It was as she had expected.

Even though Sydnee was paying Liesl handsomely, the girl was reluctant to refer women to her, fearing for her job. Sydnee assured her that with her connections, there would always be employment waiting for her elsewhere if she was caught.

The plan they devised was quite simple. Every evening at nine, Frederick would drive past the convent in the carriage to watch for a signal. If there was someone in need, Liesl would put a candle in her bedroom window. Since the majority of the nuns retired after Vespers and rose before dawn, it was agreed that three in the morning would be a safe rendezvous time. Sydnee would make sure salon guests were gone from her home by two, leaving her enough time to change, fetch the hearse and pull up to the infirmary door of the convent. Liesl would usher the women and children into the back of the vehicle, and Sydnee would transport them to the livery where they could stay until traveling plans were made. Liesl would receive her pay after each successful rendezvous.

It only took a few days for a light to appear in Liesl's window. Frederick sent a note to Sydnee that night at the theater. Tristan and D'anton had returned home from Saratoga, and they were all attending the opera. It was difficult going to the late night supper afterward. Sydnee wanted to dash home, but she knew she must not deviate from her normal routine.

At about two, she said good night and returned home. She raced upstairs and put on dark breeches, boots and a mourner's suit coat. Next she wrapped her long hair tightly around her head. Calling for the dogs, she climbed into the back of the carriage and had Frederick take her to the livery where he hitched the horse to a hearse.

Sydnee's hands were shaking, and her knees were weak as she checked one last time to make sure everything was ready in the groom's quarters for overnight guests. When Frederick had the hearse ready, she put on the undertaker's top hat and climbed up into the driver's seat.

Old Frederick looked worried but said nothing to her as she drove out of the livery. The streets were deserted except for an occasional dog or cat foraging for food in the garbage cans. The horse's hooves clattered loudly on the cobblestone streets and every shadow made Sydnee jump. Her mouth was dry, and she wished the dogs were sitting up in front with her rather than in back behind the curtains.

Rather than going past the front of the convent, Sydnee turned down a dark street, which looked like an alley. Driving slowly, she looked for the proper door. At last, she found the infirmary door. It was between a necessary and several trash cans that were piled high with rubbish.

After scanning for pedestrians, Sydnee jumped down. She opened the door of the hearse, let the dogs out and knocked twice. Liesl swung the door open and came out, carrying a carpet bag. She was followed by a tall young woman who was heavy with child. The woman looked around furtively and ducked into the hearse at Sydnee's direction. Liesl pushed the bag in after her.

"These dogs will ride with you and protect you," Sydnee whispered to the woman as the animals jumped in behind her. After shutting the door and stuffing some bills into Liesl's hand, Sydnee climbed into the driver's seat and snapped the reins. It was all she could do to restrain herself from rushing madly through the streets, but she drove slowly, and they arrived at the livery without incident.

Once inside the stable, Frederick hitched the horse back up to the carriage, and Sydnee took the woman into the living quarters. "You will be quite safe here," she said, taking her hat off and shaking her hair out. The woman smiled weakly when she saw her transform from a boy to a young woman. Sydnee offered her a seat while she explained where to find everything in the quarters.

Dressed shabbily, the woman had brown hair, freckles and was about the age of twenty. She was wearing a modest wedding band on her finger. She had no scars or apparent bruises on her body, but she held her belly, as if she was protecting it.

"Are you feeling well?" Sydnee asked.

A look of concern passed over the young woman's face as she rubbed her stomach. "I think so. I just felt the baby move. I'm glad. He punched me in the stomach two times tonight and told me when the baby is born, he will kill it." She lowered her eyes. "He is worried about feeding a child which I understand but--"

"Say no more," Sydnee interrupted, swallowing hard. She remembered the fate of her own babes. "Saving your child is the most important thing."

"If it was just me, I would stay," she said, apologetically.

"You have made the right decision. I will leave Atlantis with you tonight. She will keep watch over you."

The woman reached down and touched the dog's head. Baloo followed Sydnee to the door. When she looked in the stable, Frederick had the carriage ready. Turning back to the woman she said, "I will be back in the morning, and we will put you on the first stern-wheeler for Memphis."

The young woman nodded, but she looked terrified. Sydnee remembered her own boundless fear when she was starting her new life. Suddenly, she was flooded with doubt about her mission. *What am I doing? What is this madness! My poor judgment could get this woman killed.*

She rubbed her head a moment, asking the spirits for some sign that she was doing the right thing. As she was about to leave, she asked, "What is your name?"

The woman looked up from petting Atlantis and said, "Margarite."

*　　　*　　　*

Sydnee did not sleep at all that night. She lay rigidly on her bed, staring at the ceiling. At the crack of dawn she jumped up, dressed and rushed out to purchase tickets at the landing. When she returned home she sat down at her desk and wrote a letter of introduction for the woman to give to Mortimer.

Sydnee could not relax until she saw the woman's riverboat disappear around a bend in the Mississippi River. Flooded with relief that she had smuggled her first victim safely out of New Orleans, she slept most of the day.

Sydnee indeed needed her rest because the candles began to appear with great frequency from that day forward. Instantly, she began to lead a double life. By day, she was the great lady of New Orleans' society and by night a shadowy figure of the underworld.

In one month she helped nine women and four children to safety. She had refined her rescue routine down to minutes, and she became calmer with each escape. Liesl was a great help to her as well, proving to be a reliable and trustworthy source inside the convent.

Everything seemed to be going smoothly until the beginning of November when a note from Liesl arrived. Her writing was poor, but she managed to scrawl out,

Meet me at noon.

Worried, Sydnee slung a basket over her arm and walked to the convent. Liesl was outside sweeping the walkway. Sydnee approached her casually, and they expressed pleasantries loud enough so the nuns tending the gardens would suspect nothing.

Liesl dropped her voice at last and said, "You must come before the sun sets today. There is a woman in grave danger." The girl's eyes darted around the gardens. "She is deathly sick. Last night her husband broke into the convent to try to take her home. He was caught, but tonight I think he will succeed."

Sydnee's heart started to pound. She had to consider all aspects of a daytime escape, and do it quickly. *Vespers is too late. The afternoon is not practical because there are too many people.* "What time is the evening meal in the refectory?" she asked.

"Five," Liesl replied.

"That might work. There will be fewer people around."

"Shall I say I am helping her to the necessary but instead bring her to the hearse?" Liesl asked.

Sydnee nodded. "Yes, but you must keep yourself safe as well."

"I will. See you at five," Liesl murmured and then turned away with her broom.

"It was very nice seeing you again," Sydnee called to her and started home.

Frederick's gray eyebrows shot up when she told him of the daytime rescue, but as usual, he asked no questions. Sydnee felt that the less he knew, the better.

She decided it would be safer during daylight hours to change at the livery, so she stuffed her disguise into a bag, tethered Vivian in the courtyard and climbed into the carriage with the dogs. Once she was at the livery and dressed, she took extra care wrapping her hair. There would be many more people that could scrutinize her in the light of day.

Setting out in broad daylight was unnerving, but Sydnee took a deep breath and snapped the reins. It was difficult navigating around the scores of pedestrians, carts and street vendors. She drove slowly, picking her way through the throng, perspiration running down her back. She noticed immediately that no one would look at her. Their natural aversion to undertakers and death kept her hidden and anonymous. For this she was grateful.

It was loud and confusing on the streets, and when she turned down the convent alley she breathed a sigh of relief. She jumped down from the driver's seat, and just as she was about to knock, the door opened. It was a nun. She was carrying a pail of slops to the necessary.

The woman frowned. "Why are you here? Have we had a death?"

Sydnee was struck dumb. She stared at the nun a moment, dropped her eyes and nodded.

"Wait here," the woman said. She walked down to the outhouse and dumped the bucket.

Sydnee's heart was hammering so hard, she was afraid the nun would hear it. The woman pulled open the infirmary door and signaled for Sydnee to follow. The infirmary was large and filled with long rows of beds. The room was dark and smelled of urine and camphor. Most of the patients were children, but a few were adults.

"Why has the undertaker been sent for?" Sydnee heard the nun ask a novice.

Sydnee scanned the room for Liesl. There were nuns and novices everywhere bending over patients, making beds, and carrying trays. The room was alive with activity, but at last she saw her in a corner, standing with folded linen in her arms. She was staring at Sydnee, and her eyes were like saucers.

"No," the nun announced walking back to Sydnee. "There has been a mistake. You are not needed."

Sydnee nodded and walked out the door. Breathless with anxiety, she stopped outside, trying to gather her thoughts.

Suddenly the door opened again. This time it was Liesl.

"What do we do now?" the girl asked frantically.

Sydnee licked her lips. "We--" she said, looking around and trying to think. "We will—um—I want you to bring her to the front entrance in one hour."

"What?" Liesl gasped. "He is always out there."

"I will find a way."

The girl opened her mouth to protest and then stopped. She nodded uncertainly and went back inside.

An hour later Sydnee was back at the convent, this time in her carriage. She had changed into an everyday gown with a hat and veil. Frederick was driving, and the dogs were riding in the cab with her. Sydnee looked out the window, scanning the grounds for the husband. She could not see him, but she knew he was in the courtyard somewhere.

She lowered her veil and stepped out of the carriage. Not wanting to summon a novice by ringing the bell, Sydnee slipped inside quietly and shut the door. Blinded by the darkness, she heard Liesl say, "We are ready."

Sydnee squeezed her eyes shut and then opened them again, trying to adjust to the low light. In front of her, in a Bath wheelchair, was a woman in her early thirties with dark hair. She was thin and pale, and she was resting her head on the back of the chair. Sydnee could see that, at one time, she had been a beautiful woman, but now her face was gaunt and covered with red bumps. A smile flickered on her lips when Sydnee said hello. Liesl was standing behind her, holding the chair.

"Can you walk a short distance?" Sydnee asked.

The woman nodded.

"Quickly then, we must find a room to change."

They found a storage room, and Sydnee started to undress, saying, "You will leave here disguised as me. You will wear my clothing and take my carriage. My driver knows what to do, and he will take you to a safe place."

"Thank you," the woman murmured. Liesl helped her exchange clothes with Sydnee and then wheeled the woman out to the front door. They helped her to her feet and opened the front door. Sydnee stepped back out of sight.

With the veil over her face, the woman took a deep breath and started down the walk. She walked slowly, shuffling. At one point, she staggered and then steadied herself and carried on. Frederick saw her coming and jumped down to assist her the rest of the way.

Liesl and Sydnee breathed a sigh of relief when the carriage finally pulled away. They ducked once more into the empty room.

"Was he out there?" Sydnee asked.

"I didn't see him," was Liesl's reply. "But what if he *is* out there? How will you get out? He will know the clothing and think you are his wife."

"Do you have any clothes for me?"

"I do," Liesl said and dashed from the room.

With her hands in fists, Sydnee paced the tiny room, anxious to get to the livery to help the woman. After a few moments the door opened, but it was not Liesl. It was a novice. "Oh!" the girl exclaimed.

Sydnee blurted, "I thought this is where Mother Baptista's office was," and pushed past her.

Looking confused, the novice called, "N-No, it is down the hall."

"Thank you," said Sydnee.

Once out in the hall, she slipped out the front door and started down the shadowy walkway towards the street. It was dusk, and there was no sign of the husband. Sydnee was concerned about getting to the livery as soon as possible in case the man had followed the carriage.

Shops were closing for the evening, and the taverns and exchanges were beginning to fill with revelers. She turned onto the street, walking briskly. She wore a threadbare gown and clutched a shawl over her head. Just as she was passing an alley, someone hooked an arm around her neck and yanked her backward, dragging her. Terrified, she squirmed and tried to cry out, but the grip was so tight that she was mute. She clawed at the man's massive arm and struggled to free herself, but he dragged her so quickly down the alley no one noticed.

"Where the hell do you think you're going?" he said to her.

Sydnee struggled again, and he tightened his grip. "You bitch," he snarled. "The only way you'll leave me is feet first."

Sydnee started to feel light-headed and began to gasp for air. The man loosened his arm, and she dropped to her knees coughing. Taking her by the hair, he jerked her up violently, looked into her face and growled, "Now you listen--" He stopped mid-sentence staring at her. Even in the semi-darkness he could tell that she was not his wife.

His jaw dropped, and he stared at her dumbfounded. "Jesus-" he gasped and let go. He backed up several paces and then bolted away into the darkness.

Holding onto the wall, Sydnee staggered out into the street and stood under a light to gather her breath and her strength. She knew that it was not safe continuing on the street alone. The man may return. The Allard House and Restaurant was across the street, and she staggered over to the ladies entrance between two huge pillars. It was imperative she stay around people, so she straightened her clothing, dropped the shawl off her head and stepped inside. Sydnee had not been to this establishment in many months. Although it was not fancy, it had a good reputation with a respectable clientele. The ladies entrance bypassed the bar and opened directly into one of the more intimate dining rooms. It was busy, filled with customers dining at tables with white linen.

The *maître d'hôtel* stepped up to her and ran his eyes over her disheveled appearance. "May I be of assistance?"

Sydnee asked breathlessly, "May I wait here a moment?"

The man raised his eyebrows and said reluctantly, "Well, yes, but not for long, madam."

Clearly they did not want unescorted women lingering in the doorway. Sydnee looked around for a boy to deliver a message to Frederick. A group of men came from the bar into the dining room to be seated for supper. As they passed, one of them stopped and looked at Sydnee, blinking. It was Dr. Locke. Although he recognized her face, the clothing confused him, and he could not place her. He continued to stare at her, baffled.

"May I help you, monsieur?" the *maître d'hôtel* said.

Dr. Locke ignored him and stepped forward, "Mademoiselle, Mademoiselle Sauveterre, is that you?"

Sydnee turned with a look of surprise.

"Why?" he blurted, running his eyes over her. "Why are--"

"I am meeting a friend, Dr. Locke," she interrupted.

He looked confused and then recognition spread over his face. "Ah ha," he said slowly. He assumed she was out to meet a lover. He raised his eyebrows and chuckled. "Of course, I understand now."

Sydnee did not like his tone but had to make the best of it. "Yes," she snapped.

"Frolicking with the pedestrian element for a change?"

Sydnee's eyes narrowed. Oh, how she itched to slap this man, but then she remembered the woman in danger at the livery. She must remain prudent and hurry. Swallowing hard, she turned toward the *maître d'hôtel* and asked, "Would you hail a cab for me please?"

"Nonsense," Locke interrupted. "I will see her home."

Sydnee did not want to be escorted home by this insolent Englishman. "Thank you but you were about to dine," she countered.

"I can join them later," he said, stepping out the door to hail a cab.

There was a hackney carriage nearby, and they ducked in just as it was starting to rain. Sydnee settled into her seat, refusing to look at Locke. She stared out the window instead.

He did just the opposite, watching her with his arms crossed over his chest, a smirk on his face. "Spurned?" he asked.

"I beg your pardon?" Sydnee asked curtly.

"I say, did he spurn you?"

"Dr. Locke, if I am required to discuss my personal life as payment for this cab, let me out now."

"No, no," He said, putting his hands up in mock protest. He turned away to look out the window, still smirking.

Sydnee stole at look at him. He cut a fine figure in his

evening attire. He was wearing a close fitting dark cutaway and trousers, and a white shirt with a loosely tied plum-colored cravat. She suspected he was used to fine clothing and was of the English aristocracy.

Sydnee had heard many unflattering accounts of the conceit of the British landed gentry, and so far Dr. Locke fit this description perfectly. Yet, something confused her. It seemed inconsistent that he would be interested in helping children and victims of yellow fever. Sydnee shook her head and went back to looking out the window.

Suddenly it dawned on her that maybe Locke could help her runaway at the livery. Although she did not know what the woman's ailment was, there was no question she was too weak to travel right now and needed help. The rest of the way home she wrestled with the idea, weighing all the pros and cons. When they arrived at her townhome, she decided not to compromise the anonymity of the mission, and would contact Locke later if she needed him.

The driver opened the door, and Dr. Locke stepped out with Sydnee walking her to the front door. The rain had stopped.

"Thank you," she said.

He bowed as she went inside and shut the door.

Lighting a cigar, Locke took his time walking back to the hackney. He had to admit, this courtesan fascinated him. The Louisiana French were indeed unusual. He strolled down the flower-lined walkway puffing his cigar and considering their lifestyles. Without a doubt, their morals were questionable, but he had to admit, the English were not much better. They were just more discreet.

Before getting into the cab, he turned one more time and looked up at the house. He saw candlelight appear in the upstairs window. Her bed chamber, he thought. He speculated a moment on what activities might go on in that room. Puffing of his cigar, he blew out the smoke thoughtfully. This Sauveterre woman was undoubtedly attractive and certainly an enigma. She appeared to be every inch a lady, but there was something else, something that went beyond the apparent breeding and refinement, but he could not identify it. He shrugged and threw his cigar into the wet gutter. Stepping into the cab, he sat down and rapped on the ceiling. The driver snapped the reins, and they disappeared down the street.

Chapter 21

Sydnee summoned Frederick and went to the livery immediately. When they pulled into the stables and closed the doors, she approached him. "Frederick," she said. "Something happened this evening that has led me to reconsider having you drive for me."

The old gentleman looked at her with surprise.

She sighed and shook her head. "I cannot allow you to continue. Forgive me for saying this but not at your age. It is far too dangerous, and I have never discussed fully with you what I am doing or the risks involved. I am sorry but thank you for your loyal service."

He frowned, and replied in his thin voice. "Mademoiselle, I am a free man of color and make my own choices. I have understood from the beginning what you are trying to accomplish and the risks involved."

Sydnee studied his gaunt, heavily creased face and kind brown eyes. "Do you realize that you could lose your life?" she asked.

"I do."

She nodded hesitantly. "Very well," she said and then turned away, but he stopped her.

"Mademoiselle?"

"Yes?"

"There are things that I have not explained to you either," and he hesitated. "My--my daughter was beaten to death by her husband ten years ago. That is why I am here."

Sydnee's jaw dropped.

He swallowed hard, lifted his chin and straightened up as if at attention and said, "I am at your service."

She searched his eyes. Behind the wrinkled face and frail exterior, she saw a man of strength and determination who grieved deeply for his daughter. Sydnee did not want him to see her cry, so she patted him on the arm and walked to the groom's quarters.

A lamp was lit on the nightstand shedding a dim golden light on the bed. The woman was still fully dressed in Sydnee's clothing and stretched out on top of the bed. Shoes were still on her feet.

"Madame," Sydnee murmured.

Her eyes fluttered and opened.

"I will help you into some night clothes. You will be more comfortable."

She sat up, and Sydnee helped her change. It was obvious the Ursulines had taken excellent care of her. She was clean and there were fresh bandages on her injuries which were minor. There was a laceration on her leg and one on her hand. Multiple scratches covered her ankles, but what was alarming was that she covered with hundreds of red bumps and sores everywhere on her body.

"Did the nurses tell you what ails you?" Sydnee asked.

The woman licked her dry lips and said, "Hunger, fatigue," and she pointed to the red sores. "These are mosquito bites."

"*Mais non!* You were left outside?"

She nodded. Sydnee helped ease her back down onto the bed and then covered her with a blanket. "I will feed you and make a tea for you that will help fight the venom. When you are well enough, we will set you up with a new life elsewhere. Well away from the person that did this to you."

A smile flickered on the woman's lips.

Sydnee built a fire and hung a tea kettle to boil. She also arranged a spider trivet over the coals so she could fry some salt pork and eggs. When the meal was ready, Sydnee pushed pillows up behind the woman's back and gave her the tray of food and tea.

"Thank you. This looks delicious," the woman said. After eating, she seemed stronger and began to explain to Sydnee what had happened.

"That is not necessary right now," Sydnee said. "You must

rest."

"No," the woman said, reaching out. "I must tell someone."

Sydnee was reluctant but sat down to listen.

"We were very happy when we were first married. I could not have asked for a better husband. But as the years passed, something happened to him. He started staying out late. When I asked him where he was or what he was doing, he would tell me to shut up and slap me. Each time, he would hit me a little harder."

The woman stopped, trying to catch her breath.

"A few days ago we had a terrible argument, and somehow I knew that he was done with me. He tied me to a wagon and took me deep into the country, far out into the bayou and left me there. He said if I tried to follow him, he would kill me."

She looked at Sydnee and smiled weakly. "I don't know how long I wandered there, but an Indian found me and brought me to the edge of town."

"How does he know you are still alive?"

"With the last ounce of strength I had, I went back to the house to get money so I could leave him forever, but that was a mistake. I collapsed a few blocks from home, and someone brought me to the Ursuline hospital. Once he discovered the money was missing, it was easy for him to find me."

*   *   *

It took many days before the woman was strong enough to make her journey out of New Orleans. During that time, a mother with two children needed shelter in the livery as well, but they did not stay for long. The mother decided to return home and reconcile with her husband.

Sydnee was used to this outcome. Women would frequently forgive the beatings and return home. The idea of starting a new life was daunting, but unfortunately, it was only a matter of time before Sydnee saw them again.

At long last, when the bites and injuries healed and the woman's strength returned, she boarded a paddle wheeler for Memphis. Sydnee was especially grateful for this escape since she experienced first-hand the brutality of this woman's husband. She was glad to finally put it to rest.

By the spring of 1841, Sydnee's escape organization had expanded and was growing, but her role as the first lady of New Orleans' society had changed little. She continued to give soirees and suppers, attend operas and make secret visits to see Delphine.

Sydnee loved watching the little girl grow. The child was thriving and healthy, and she cherished each visit, cuddling her and playing with her. Sometimes grief for her own departed children would flood Sydnee, but she buried her despair and savored each moment with Delphine instead.

She knew that it was only a matter of time before she would have to stop seeing the child. Delphine would start to recognize her, and if she saw Sydnee in public, it would be difficult to explain how the little girl knew her father's mistress.

"Sydnee, come with me tonight to Antoine's," D'anton said one evening in April. "You look tired. You have been entertaining too much. It's time someone entertained you."

"Oh, D'anton, I don't know," she replied. She had been looking forward to a quiet night at home.

"Please?" he whined.

"Oh, very well," she said wearily. Sydnee could never refuse D'anton. He grew more charming and handsome every day. He was tall and thin, always dressed in the latest fashion and had sparkling green eyes. When Sydnee looked at him, she found it hard to believe that when his "spells" were upon him, he would take to his bed and not eat or bathe for days at a time. When he was lucid though, D'anton was unmatched in Louisiana for his wit, charm and appeal.

Even though she was fatigued, Sydnee was glad to be going to Antoine's Restaurant again. It had opened only a year ago and was already considered the finest restaurant in all of New Orleans. It had the light airiness of an outdoor Parisian cafe with crisp white curtains in the front windows, pastel décor and the finest cuisine in the city.

What Sydnee did not know, was that Fletcher Locke was

among the party that was gathering with D'anton at Antoine's that evening. D'anton met him less than a month ago when Locke hired him as an attorney, and they had become fast friends.

Locke arrived earlier with several other couples. They were sitting in the back of the main dining room, sipping aperitifs waiting for everyone to arrive. Tonight he was escorting Renata Olmos, the lusty widow of a wealthy Creole cotton broker. He had been seeing the woman for several months now, but for all of her dark beauty and fire, he was bored and disinterested.

Fletcher was angry with himself. When he left England he was sick of all the pretentious snobbery, but here he was immersed in it again in Louisiana. He tried escaping it over the Christmas season, traveling to his grand home on the bluff in Natchez, but there he was pursued too, especially by mothers eager to make good matches for their daughters.

He sat back and sipped his drink.

"You seem out of sorts tonight, darling," murmured Madame Olmos. When she was done speaking, the dark skinned brunette blew seductively into his ear. He moved his head away irritably and puffed on his cigar.

The other couples were engaged in a discussion about the woman D'anton was bringing to supper, but Fletcher was not listening. He wanted no part of it, but they continued to drag him into the gossip. "Fletcher, I cannot believe you have not heard of her. Her salon is known throughout Europe."

He shrugged.

A woman chimed in saying, "And her style is emulated throughout the South. You would never know her beginnings were humble--"

Suddenly something caught Fletcher's eye. Madame Olmos turned to see what had interested him, and the smile dropped from her face. It was Mademoiselle Sauveterre on the arm of D'anton Delacroix.

"There she is," one of the men said at the table.

Sydnee looked stunning, dressed in a gown of yellow brocade silk with short lace sleeves draping delicately onto her arms. Her hair was swept up in simple knot encircled by an intricate braid. Wispy bangs framed her face, enhancing her large dark eyes. D'anton was the picture of fashion as well, in a dark cutaway suit with a gold double-breasted vest.

Their progress toward the table was slow because they were being greeted by acquaintances and friends. Locke's eyes narrowed as he watched Sydnee smile and converse. Men would jump to their feet and bow low over her white gloved hand trying to dominate her attention.

He chuckled and shook his head. "Well, well," he mumbled.

"What is it?" Madame Olmos asked.

"Nothing, my dear," he said, never taking his eyes from Sydnee. "Nothing of consequence."

She scowled, tossing her head.

He sat back and blew out cigar smoke, waiting for Sydnee's reaction when she saw him.

When D'anton and Sydnee reached the table, the men stood up, and the ladies smiled.

"Good evening," said Sydnee running eyes over the group. When she saw Locke, she held her hand out and said smoothly, "Dr. Locke, how nice to see you again."

He smirked and bowed low over her gloved hand. Her dislike for him was apparent to no one, and Fletcher found it disappointing. He would have enjoyed a response of some kind, instead she acted as if she barely knew him.

"So the two of you have already met?" asked D'anton.

"Yes," Sydnee said, taking her seat. "On the packet from Memphis."

"And we met on one more occasion when Mademoiselle Sauveterre was in disguise."

D'anton's eyebrow's shot up. "At Carnival?"

Sydnee took a sip of her aperitif and shook her head.

"A ball I was not invited to?" D'anton said, throwing his hands into the air. "Fletcher, I don't understand. You told me that you don't dance, and the only exception will be when you marry."

"No, it was not a ball," Locke said, looking at Sydnee. "But she *was* incognito."

Sydnee did not flinch, instead she smiled and turned to visit with the woman seated next to her.

Fletcher suddenly found this game amusing. The night was not so boring after all. He continued to watch Sydnee steadily, impressed and fascinated with her aplomb. This is not the first time this woman has buried her dislike under a façade of smooth self-assurance. *I wonder if I can crack that poised exterior.*

Sydnee could feel Locke's eyes upon her. She could feel his challenge, and she was not going let him rattle her. This man despised her and the life she led, and she was not about to let him publicly embarrass her.

Locke's opportunity came over coffee. It was understood by everyone that they would adjourn to Sydnee's townhome for drinks, but no one was sure if Dr. Locke would be invited. Everyone had noticed how rude he had been to her throughout supper. It was common knowledge that Sydnee was very selective about who she invited to the salon, and if you were included it was a great honor.

"Thank you everyone for an enjoyable evening," D'anton said. Then he looked at Sydnee, expecting her to invite Dr. Locke and Madame Olmos to the town house.

Smiling, Sydnee turned and started talking to one of the gentleman across the table. She was not about to have that self-righteous bore to her home.

D'anton looked confused. He had indulged in a little too much wine and could not understand why Sydnee had not invited Locke. He liked Fletcher and thought he would be a refreshing addition to the salon. "Sydnee, would you consider inviting Madame Olmos and Dr. Locke to the house tonight?"

The table fell silent.

Sydnee hesitated and then said stiffly, "Most certainly, I have been remiss. Would you please join us?"

Madame Olmos' face lit up. She had been waiting months for an invitation to the salon, and she smiled broadly.

"No thank you," Fletcher said. "I need to wake up early

tomorrow and make a difference in the world."

Sydnee locked eyes with him.

Madame Olmos' smile dropped, her hopes of an invitation dashed. The only one who laughed was D'anton.

When everyone stood up to leave, Madame Olmos swept out the door, leaving Dr. Locke behind.

Again D'anton looked confused and asked Fletcher, "Is she ill?"

Locke shrugged. "The only thing I know for certain is that she will never want to see *me* again."

*   *   *

Sydnee found it hard to keep up with all the demands on her time. Arrangements had to be made for transporting the women and children; the living quarters had to be stocked regularly with food, and disguises had to be obtained for the runaways.

The salon alone was a full-time job, even with Marie's help. There was menu planning to be done and daily trips to the market. Sydnee had to coordinate housekeeping and provide entertainment for her guests. She had to stay abreast in politics, world events and books so she could to contribute to conversation, and it made her head spin the way Parisian fashions were always changing.

"Marie," Sydnee called down the hall late one afternoon. "I am off for my fitting."

"Yes, Mademoiselle Sydnee."

Taking her parasol, she set out for Tustin Dressmaking, a small boutique with only a few select clientele. Tustin's made only the finest gowns of the best fabrics, reflecting the latest fashions from Paris. The shop was expensive and exclusive. The only way to do business with them was by introduction. Madame Picard had made arrangements for Sydnee to be fitted there years ago.

The bell tinkled when Sydnee walked in. The shop was an explosion of color with bolts of fabric in stripes and prints, pastels and rich solids. There were ribbons hanging out of drawers and faux flowers in boxes, huge spools of thread, and dressmaker mannequins everywhere.

"*Bon jour*, Mimi."

"*Bon jour*, Mademoiselle Sauveterre," said a young woman sitting at a table, sewing.

Mimi Gruenwald was the heart and soul of Tustin Dressmaking. Her talents as a seamstress were known from New Orleans to Baton Rouge to Natchez. She was a free woman of color and had been working for Madame Tustin for the past fifteen years. Everyone knew that without her, Tustin's would be nothing. She was a quiet young woman, extremely overweight with a pock-marked face. She was not a beauty, but her kind demeanor and gentle nature made her one of the most beloved people in the city.

"Hello, Edith," said Sydnee to another young woman.

"Lo," Edith said loudly to Sydnee and then slurped her saliva. Edith was Mimi's younger sister. The victim of a troubled birth, Edith was mentally slow and had a pronounced limp. She was easy-going and always eager to please.

"Thank you," Mimi said to her sister, taking the tape measure she brought over.

"No Madame Tustin today?" Sydnee asked.

Mimi stared at Sydnee a moment as if she was going to say something and then replied, "No, she is gone for the evening."

Madame Tustin was the proprietor of the shop. She was a shrewd businesswoman who knew how to pander to the rich. She had one son, an overbearing twenty-year-old, who would strut through the shop regularly, helping himself to money from the till.

"Shall we begin?" Mimi asked, and Sydnee nodded.

They looked at dressmaker's dolls displaying the latest fashions from Paris as Edith fetched supplies and awaited instructions. Mimi measured and pinned, wrote down measurements and consulted with Sydnee on orders.

By the time they had finished, the sun had set. "Thank you, Mimi," Sydnee said, starting for the door. "You will send someone around when the gown is ready?"

"Yes—um, Mademoiselle Sauveterre would you please

wait a moment?"

Sydnee turned around. Mimi reached around her, locked the door, and dropped the curtains over the windows.

Sydnee looked at her with surprise.

"May I speak privately with you?" Mimi asked.

"Of course."

Turning to Edith, Mimi said, "Edith please go in the back and have a slice of cake and look at your picture book."

Edith nodded and shuffled off into the back of the shop where they lived. Madame Tustin and her son lived upstairs.

Mimi swallowed hard and motioned for Sydnee to take a seat. "I hardly know where to begin," she murmured. "But I must make haste. You may know that I am friends with Liesl Schiffman. I need your help, Mademoiselle Sauveterre."

Mimi unbuttoned her dress and lowered the shoulders on her shift. Along her chest and upper arms were dark bruises. She bent down and lifted the skirt of her gown and rolled down her stockings. More dark bruises ran along her shins where she had been kicked.

Sydnee's eyes narrowed. "Madame Tustin?"

Mimi nodded. "And her son. They do their work where no one can see it."

"Yes, indeed," said Sydnee. "They have a reputation to uphold."

Mimi pulled her gown back up and said, "I have endured it for many years but--"and she hesitated. "Now the son is going after Edith."

"He hits her as well?"

"Not that," Mimi said and looked into Sydnee's eyes.

Sydnee understood what she implied. Knowing there was not a moment to lose, she put her fist to her lips. She said finally, "What time do you expect them to return tonight?"

"Soon."

"Very well, when you are certain they are asleep come here," and she scrawled the address of the livery on a piece of paper. Mimi looked at it and handed it back to her. "Take it with you, Mademoiselle Sauveterre. I have memorized it. If they were to find out I was trying to leave, they would threaten Edith's life just to keep me here. I did not write your name in the appointment book either, just in case."

"Good, you are very thorough," said Sydnee, putting the paper in her purse. "I will be waiting for you."

Late that night Mimi and Edith arrived at the livery in traveling clothes. "Any chance you have been followed?" Sydnee asked.

Mimi shook her head.

"Good, come in."

Sydnee showed them around, and when Edith was finally asleep, the two women sat down to talk. It was a warm night, and they sat by an open window in the moonlight. Atlantis was at Sydnee's feet.

"I don't think it is safe for you to take a riverboat," whispered Sydnee. "I usually provide my runaways with disguises for the landing, but there is no way to hide Edith's limp. Even if you were to escape on a paddle wheeler, I believe they will search for you in river towns up and down the Mississippi. You are like gold for them. We must smuggle you to freedom elsewhere."

"If we don't take a riverboat, how will we go?"

"Up the Natchez Trace."

"That old road up to Nashville?" Mimi whispered.

"The very one. You will go in a cart up to Natchez, and I have a contact there who will escort you the rest of the way."

"But we cannot walk. Edith's leg--"

"No, they drive wagons. Nevertheless, it will be a very long and strenuous journey. You will stay in abandoned stands along the way."

"I will do anything to get Edith away from them."

"You must rest now," Sydnee said, standing up. "Atlantis will watch over you. Good night."

*   *   *

Sydnee had to wait full a day until her contact in New Orleans was ready to leave. Her name was Eileen O'Bannon, a large raw-boned Irish woman who had spent many years as a drayman delivering goods between New Orleans and Natchez. Her sister had the same business only she delivered goods between Natchez and Nashville on The Trace. Not everyone could afford to ship goods on the paddle wheelers so there was still demand for overland travel.

Sydnee had met these women several times when she was growing up, and although they were rough and ready, dirty and sometimes dangerous, they had good hearts and would be able to assure Mimi and Edith a safe journey with job prospects in Nashville.

It was extremely perilous smuggling the sisters out of New Orleans. Madame Tustin had the entire city searching for them. The woman labeled it a "kidnapping" and feigned despair at the loss of her loved ones. In reality she was only devastated at her loss of income.

Nevertheless, Sydnee was successful and smuggled them out safely. The clamor for justice was short lived, and after a few days, it was all over. The upper classes liked their fashion, and they soon found a new shop to patronize. Madame Tustin was ruined.

The year came to a close, finding Sydnee overjoyed at the success of her operation. With the help of her agents throughout the South, she successfully smuggled out almost eighty women and children. As she was getting ready to leave for a soiree on New Year's Day, she drank a champagne toast to the spirits, thanking them for all of her blessings. She had no way of knowing that the new year would bring a very dark turn of events.

Chapter 22
1842

Isabel adored being a mother. She was fulfilled in so many ways, and for several months she was content, but as time passed Sydnee noticed her grow thin and frail again, and the dark rings returned under her eyes. She knew that Isabel was lost without Mortimer. He was the great love of her life, and no amount of distance or time could ever change the devotion. Yet Isabel's commitment to Delphine never wavered either. She was a good mother and attended to the child's every need, but it was imperative that she see Mortimer, if only for a short time.

A boy brought a note one afternoon to Sydnee saying that Isabel was coming to see her after the opera that night. Marie put the letter on the entry table, but Sydnee never saw it. When Isabel arrived just before three in the morning in a hackney coach, Sydnee was leaving for a rescue. She opened the door ready to leave, and there stood Isabel.

Sydnee was thunderstruck. "What's wrong?"

Isabel looked her up and down and said, "Nothing is wrong, but why are you dressed like that?"

A thousand excuses ran through Sydnee's head, but they all seemed foolish and transparent. When she didn't answer, Isabel asked, "Didn't you get my note?"

Sydnee shook her head, confused.

"Well, it is nothing pressing, but I did want to see you. I was wondering if you had any news from Mortimer."

"No, I have heard nothing from him," said Sydnee. "I think you should go and see him."

"Oh, Sydnee, you know that's impossible."

At that moment, Frederick pulled up with the carriage, and Sydnee rubbed her forehead. "Can you wait for me? I know the hour is late, but I will return shortly and we can talk, even about my disguise."

Isabel chuckled and stepped inside, pulling her gloves off and untying her bonnet. "With all this mystery, there would be no sleep for me tonight anyway. I'll be in the parlor."

The runaway was a young prostitute with an infant. She was probably only fourteen years old. Her arm was broken and her front teeth were knocked out. Sydnee carried the baby into the livery, thinking to herself that she must devise some sort of a sling for the girl to carry the baby to free up her good arm. Sydnee explained everything to the girl in a hurry. She was preoccupied with Isabel being back at the town house. After settling them in for the night, she returned home.

Sydnee walked into the parlor still wearing her disguise.

Isabel put her book down and raised her eyebrows at Sydnee as if she had been a naughty child. "I suggest you start at the very beginning."

Sydnee took a deep breath and explained everything, from her epiphany at the convent to her most recent undertaking that evening. She explained how her own background on The Trace had influenced her decision to help women and children and how the spirits, Madame Picard, and Maxime had guided her. She talked at length about Mortimer's role in Memphis as well.

Isabel listened with her mouth open. She had been completely ignorant of everything. "Does Tristan know or D'anton?"

Sydnee shook her head. "No, the less people involved the better."

"I understand," Isabel said. "But this is a deadly undertaking, Sydnee. I worry for your safety."

"Indeed it is," she agreed, reaching down to pet Atlantis. "I have--" Suddenly, like a bolt of lightning, it hit her. She had forgotten to take Atlantis to the livery.

"Isabel!" she cried, jumping to her feet. "I forgot to leave the dog with the woman!"

Before Isabel could say another word, Sydnee dashed out of the room and down the front walk with Atlantis behind her.

There was no time to saddle a horse, the only option was to run through the streets in a mad attempt to get to the girl.

Up one street and down the other she raced, her mouth so dry and her heart hammering so hard she thought she would drop in her tracks, but somehow she found the strength to continue running. At last she arrived at the livery and with shaking hands, she took out her key and unlocked the door. Dashing into the living quarters, she ran through the front room and into the bedroom, but the room was empty. Sydnee looked down. A window was broken, and there was blood on the sill. A chair was overturned and a plate of food was face down on the floor.

Sydnee's heart dropped. She stood and stared at the glass scattered everywhere. Because she had been negligent, this woman's safety had been compromised. If Atlantis had been here, the attacker may not have dared to enter the room and drag the woman and child away.

Shattered and overcome with remorse, Sydnee put her face in her hands and began to sob.

*   *   *

It took months for her to forgive herself. No matter how many successful escapes she orchestrated after that night, she would remember the mother and child who were yanked back to lives of misery, and she would chastise herself.

Sydnee's sleep was disturbed as well, and for a while, she ate very little. But slowly, with the spirits whispering in her ear, she regained her strength. Gradually she returned to appreciating life and her own contributions to it.

It helped her to watch Isabel prepare for her journey to see Mortimer. She was so excited. Isabel initially refused to leave Delphine, so Sydnee enlisted Tristan's help. Immediately he suggested they go as a family, and together they could introduce the baby to Mortimer. They would travel during the heat and disease of summer, and he could leave Isabel in Memphis while he conducted business in the north. If they took the nanny along, Isabel and Mortimer could find time to be alone.

Listening to Isabel make travel plans and chatter endlessly

about Mortimer made Sydnee long for a great love too. She wondered why it had never happened to her, and she reproached herself for being so selective about men. Sometimes she thought it was because Tristan and D'anton were so good to her, showering her with affection and love constantly, but she knew that they were not responsible. She yearned for something more, an intimacy of the body *and* of the soul.

Shaking her head, she dismissed the idea of finding love. She was overwhelmed by all the blessings she received, and that was enough. Sydnee turned her attention back to the rescue of others, not realizing that she was the one in need of a lifeboat.

*   *   *

Summer came and so did yellow jack. Tristan and Isabel were gone to Memphis, and D'anton left for Saratoga where he would meet Tristan in August. Sydnee hated this time of year. The streets were empty and everything smelled of death. Fewer paddle wheelers made trips on the river which meant she had many more nights to have to hide escapees at the livery. Everything had gone smoothly since that fateful night when the mother and child were abducted though. There had been many successful escapes, and at last Sydnee was starting to feel confident again.

One night in July, she escorted a young Irish woman and her five-year-old twin boys to the livery. The girl looked so young that Sydnee thought there were siblings. The boys were thin with dark hair and rosy cheeks. They were shy, standing behind their mother's skirts staring at Sydnee and Atlantis. They had just arrived from Cork, and the girl saw America as her opportunity to break free from her husband. She had recently escaped to the convent.

"There is work here in America," Roisin O'Malley said in her thick brogue. "There was nothin' in Ireland. Here I can take care of my wee ones by myself. We don't have to put up with the beatins' any longer."

Sydnee marveled at the girl's strength and determination at such a young age. She had no doubt that she would be a success.

The family stayed in the livery two nights waiting for a

riverboat out of town, but the second night when Sydnee came around to check on them, she found the mother distraught. Her boys were sick and feverish with chills.

Mrs. O'Malley watched Sydnee anxiously as she examined her children. It was obvious they needed help quickly. Even though taking them to a hospital would compromise their safety, it was necessary, and Sydnee was ready to move them. Suddenly she thought of Dr. Locke. He had told her once that he worked with children. "Wait here. I have another idea. I am going for a doctor instead," Sydnee said.

"Oh, for the love of God, please hurry," Mrs. O'Malley pleaded.

Sydnee had Frederick take her to the hospital first. They told her that Dr. Locke had left for the day, but they gave her his address. Moments later Sydnee was running up the walk to his house. It was a charming home, painted a pale salmon color with balconies dripping with vines.

Sydnee's hair, damp with perspiration, clung to her forehead. Please let him be at home, she prayed as she banged on the door and waited, wringing her hands. At last a servant answered and went to find Dr. Locke.

"What is all this banging?" he said, coming around the corner. His shirt sleeves were rolled up, and he was wiping his hands on a towel. It appeared as if he had been cooking.

"Dr. Locke, I have been taking care of a mother and her two twins. The boys are extremely ill."

He was immediately all business. "How old?" he asked, rolling his sleeves down and buttoning the cuffs."

"Five."

"What is the problem?"

"Fever and vomiting," she replied.

"Malaise?"

"Yes."

"Very well, I will get my bag," he said, stepping into a room off the entry. He returned with his coat and black medical bag.

Frederick rushed them to the livery, and when Dr. Locke stepped out of the carriage he looked confused. The street was dark and abandoned, and he frowned as Sydnee unlocked the door. "I don't understand. Why are we here?"

"I will explain later," she said.

They walked quickly through the stable into the living quarters. In the bedroom they found one boy in bed and the other child on a trundle nearby. Atlantis was at their feet. The boys were in night shirts and covered with a light sheets. Their sunken eyes grew large when they saw Locke. They were afraid of him.

"Good evening, I am Dr. Locke," he said to the mother.

Roisin O'Malley was wringing her hands, and she stood up, with tears in her eyes. "Thank you for coming, doctor."

Looking at the twins, he said, "Hello boys." There was no response. Turning to Atlantis he bellowed, "I understand this dog is feeling poorly."

Out of the side of his mouth Fletcher murmured to Sydnee, "Dog's name?"

"Atlantis," she whispered.

"Atlantis sent me a note today and told me to come and take a look at him."

"Her," Sydnee corrected quietly.

"Her," he echoed.

"May I, Atlantis?" Walking over, he squatted down by the dog.

The boys were watching carefully.

Atlantis looked at Sydnee, nervously. "Yes, Atlantis. You will be all right," she said.

The dog sat very still while Dr. Locke petted her, lifted her paw, gently poked her in the ribs and put a wooden tube to her chest to listen to her heart. Fletcher even opened her mouth and looked inside.

"I beg your pardon?" he said putting his ear to the dog's mouth. Weak smiles passed over the boy's faces. "Yes, yes, very well. I will ask them."

Dr. Locke stood up. "Atlantis said that it might be a good idea if I took a look at you two as well."

The boys did not protest when he sat down on the bed.

"Can you tell me your name?" he asked the child in the big bed. There was no reply. His mother said, "Killian, and the other is Kyle."

"I will do the same things to you that I did to your friend, Atlantis. Is that all right?"

Killian nodded. Fletcher examined both the boys thoroughly and then stood up. "Well, I have good news for you all, including Atlantis. Everyone will feel much better if they drink lots and lots of water and eat rice and crackers."

He rumpled Kyle's hair and said, "Now, time to rest. That goes for you too, Atlantis."

The dog looked at him with her ears perked.

Dr. Locke took the women into the front room and murmured, "Well, this is not yellow fever but it *is* dysentery. I imagine they contracted it on the ship. This disease can be deadly for children if they do not drink enough fluids. Boil all their water first, allow it to cool and give them as much as you can manage, also bland food. They are not in danger yet, but they will be if they do not drink. I cannot stress this enough."

He ran his hand through his thick mop of hair and said, "Good God, it's hot."

As he started for the door, Mrs. O'Malley said, "Thank you, Dr. Locke. I have nothing to pay you but--"

"Say no more," he said. Jerking his head toward Sydnee, he declared, "I will take payment from this woman. Send for me if anything changes for the worse."

Sydnee walked out with Fletcher and locked the door. He watched her and frowned.

Frederick stepped up, "Where to, Mademoiselle?"

"To Mademoiselle's house," Locke replied, before Sydnee could speak. "She owes me a meal and an explanation."

When they climbed in the carriage, Sydnee said with relief, "I am very grateful to you, Dr. Locke. Thank you so very much." She reached into her drawstring bag to pay him, and he stopped her.

"I meant what I said. You owe me a meal and an explanation."

233

Sydnee looked dismayed.

"If you are worried about what people may say if they see a man enter your home after midnight, you are too late."

Sydnee started to laugh and so did Locke.

"You have a caustic wit, Fletcher Locke," Sydnee said.

"So I have been told," he replied.

He sat back and looked out the window. Something stirred in him a moment ago when Sydnee had used his given name. But he dismissed it as another curiosity about the evening.

When they arrived at Sydnee's town house, Fletcher told Frederick he would walk home and that it was not necessary he wait up.

"*Tres bien, Monsieur*," Frederick said with a bow.

Sydnee stopped in the front entry and lit a candle. Locke followed her down the hall to the kitchen. He glanced quickly in the parlor. He remembered seeing Saint-Yves' portrait hanging over the mantel. He met the man on one occasion and found him good looking and charming.

"Didn't you have two dogs before?" he asked looking around.

"I do, but Baloo suffers so in this heat. He sleeps out in the courtyard where it is cooler."

Sydnee lit a few more lamps in the kitchen. "Marie has retired for the night, but I will see what she has left us," she said, walking into the pantry.

Fletcher sat down on a tall stool by the work table.

"There is some leftover meat pie. Does that sound good?" she called.

"Yes, that will do nicely."

Sydnee brought the tin out and set it on the table with two plates and forks. She went to the cupboard, took two glasses down and poured them some wine.

As she was cutting a slice of pie, he said, "I was making a steak and kidney pie when you called tonight."

Sydnee looked across the table at him. "No, that is not possible."

"Why?"

"Because the English cannot cook," she said with a smirk.

"This Englishman can," he said proudly.

He took a bite, wiped his mouth and said, "Now suppose you tell me what is going on down at that livery."

Even in the candlelight, Sydnee could see the intensity in his eyes. He was not about to be put off any longer. Sydnee did not want to tell him. Locke was the kind of man who would try to shut her operation down. A moment ago she was actually amused by him, but now she remembered how pompous and self-righteous he could be.

"I want the truth. I know you have been concocting a story all night."

She put her fork down and said, "You are reading into things, Dr. Locke. Rosin O'Malley is staying at the livery until her room is ready here. She is my new house--"

"Don't waste my time!" he barked, tossing his napkin on the table and standing up. "The authorities will be more persuasive. I assure you."

Sydnee blanched. This was just what she feared. If she didn't tell him, he most certainly would expose her. Now all she could do is tell him the truth and hope for his silence.

"Please sit down," she said.

Locke was pleased. His bluff worked. He sat back down on the chair and took another bite, staring at her.

She pressed her eyes shut a moment, gathering her thoughts. "I help women and children who are being beaten escape to new lives elsewhere."

He stopped chewing. This was more than he imagined. "What?"

"Women come to me, and I put them in hiding at the livery until I can ship them away. Each situation is different. Most are wives being beaten by their husbands but some are servants or apprentices being beaten by their masters. Some are prostitutes being forced to solicit. Many have children who are being beaten too."

"How do you find them?"

"I have a contact."

"Have you been successful? That is to say, how many times have you done this?"

Sydnee had to think. She said at last, "Eighty, perhaps ninety times."

"What!" he roared, standing up again. This was unthinkable. This elegant New Orleans' courtesan was leading two lives: one as a prominent socialite, and one as a smuggler. All this time he believed she was shallow and self-absorbed.

He began to pace the kitchen while Sydnee watched him, her hands in fists in her lap. "Outrageous," he mumbled. Turning suddenly, he said, "Dangerous, extremely dangerous. What of the men?"

"There have been incidents, but we have been lucky so far."

"Yes, so far." He looked at her as if she was daft. "I have heard of this for slaves but--"

Sydnee swallowed hard and asked, "Are you going to report us?"

Locke did not answer. He was too preoccupied.

"Dr. Locke?" Sydnee said firmly.

"Yes?'

"Will you report us?"

"Oh, of course not," he said.

Sydnee put her head back and gasped.

"You aren't breaking any laws. Even if you were I--" and his voice trailed off. He was lost in his thoughts.

Running his hand through his hair, Locke mumbled, "I'm-I'm really not hungry anymore."

He picked up his coat and went home.

Chapter 23

Fletcher Locke did not sleep well that night. His mind was racing with the information he had just received. It all seemed so fantastic. This petite young woman was goading the leviathan *and* tempting fate at the same time. There was no doubt that it would end badly, but there she stood before him, her spirit undaunted.

He turned over in bed, exasperated and feeling guilty. How many times had he railed at the injustices he had seen in the hospitals? How many wounds had he bandaged or bones had he set after a woman had been stabbed or a child beaten? And what had he done? Nothing. He had passively accepted all of it as a fact of life. But this woman, this wisp of female, had found the courage to make a difference. Again he tossed over in bed, punching his pillow. It was going to be a long night.

* * *

Sydnee too was having difficulty sleeping. She was no longer worried about Locke reporting her to the authorities, but something different nagged her. It was something far more personal. Tonight she had seen Fletcher Locke at home in his world. She had seen an esteemed and talented physician drop all of his lofty pretensions and take great pains to gain the trust of two fearful children. She had witnessed patience and tenderness in him even when he approached a wary canine. She could not understand it. How could one person have two so very different sides to his character?

These new impressions disturbed her, and she wished this had never happened. It was much more comfortable disliking the man. At least she had been able to sleep.

The next morning Sydnee was stiff and tired. She had managed to rest for only a few hours. The house was quiet. Marie had gone to market, so Sydnee took some coffee and went out into the courtyard to sit and think about what had transpired last night. She decided to consult with her ever-faithful confidant, Baloo about this new turn of events. She found Vivian first, sitting in the magnolia tree.

"Good morning, Vivian," she said, walking over to the bird.

She held up her arm for her to come and perch, but Vivian did not move. She just stared at Sydnee. "What's wrong?" she asked, perplexed. She could feel that something was wrong. She squeezed her eyes shut for a moment, and then looked down. There was Baloo curled up under the tree, sleeping peacefully. His nose was tucked under one paw, and his head was on his leg. Sometime during the night, her old friend had fallen asleep and never woke up again.

*   *   *

She buried Baloo where he died, in the shade of the magnolia tree. She knew that it would be cooler for him there. From that day on, Vivian would sleep every night on the branch above his last resting place. Sydnee marveled at the old crow. *She may be a nag, but she is a good mother.*

Sydnee grieved terribly for Baloo. He had been her rock and her oldest friend. He was from the old days on The Trace when she had been a child, and he had protected her like a father. Time would be a soothing balm, but the scar would never fully heal.

In late September, Tristan, Isabel and Delphine returned home. It was a welcome diversion for Sydnee to listen to news about their travels. Isabel chattered endlessly about Mortimer and delivered news that some of the families Sydnee smuggled up the Mississippi were thriving and happy. Most of them Mortimer never heard from again but a few stayed in touch, stopping by his livery to visit.

"I am so grateful to have had the summer with him," Isabel said. "But it was excruciating to leave. Oh, how I wish I was born in another time and place, Sydnee," she said wistfully. "How I detest the confines here in the South. Just look at all of us, laced so tightly in these corsets of convention that we are suffocating to death."

With Tristan back, the salon season began again. Business had been difficult for him lately. Although his enterprises were thriving, he was spending a great deal of time helping his father sort through financial difficulties. Cuthbert Saint-Yves had speculated poorly and lost a great deal of money over the past few months. He resented help from his son but needed him if he was going to continue his lavish lifestyle in Natchez and at *Saint-Denis*.

Many nights, Tristan sought refuge at the town house with Sydnee, and it was good for her to have him around once more, but D'anton's visits in the evening had stopped. He had taken a wife, a woman his parents had introduced to him when he was in Saratoga over the summer. Like Tristan, his marriage had been arranged, but he had not been as lucky. Paula Delacroix was from New York, not familiar with the ways of the Creole and certainly not as understanding a wife as Isabel. She jealously guarded D'anton's affection and would never abide him taking a lover.

Paula Delacroix was completely unaware of her husband's devotion to Tristan, believing the two men were merely business associates. D'anton and Tristan had to meet at Sydnee's townhome in the afternoon to be alone when Paula believed D'anton was at the office. At those times, Sydnee would give them the entire house, and she would go to market or call on friends. This was the understanding she had with Tristan from the start, that they would protect each other.

Paula Delacroix was aware of Sydnee's salon, but she did not acknowledge that it existed. In her eyes it was just one more decadent gentleman's club in New Orleans, nothing more than a chic whore house. She was not sure if D'anton ever attended a supper there, but she did not ask.

With summer ending and salon season resuming, Sydnee was busier than ever. Several evenings in October she had musicians perform for her guests. Sydnee liked to introduce these young virtuosos to potential patrons and *après* supper performances were the perfect setting.

It was during one of these performances that Frederick delivered a disturbing note to her. It was regarding a woman who wanted to be smuggled out that night. Liesl had been instructed never to write down the name of a woman in crisis, but this woman was the wife of one of the wealthiest planters in Louisiana, and Liesl wanted Sydnee to be aware of the danger.

"Thank you, Frederick," Sydnee murmured. "I will be there."

Sydnee told herself that this escape was no different than any of the others, but she felt uneasy. She knew that tonight more than any other night, her anonymity was in jeopardy. Although she did not know Charisse Archambeau personally, there was a good chance that even in her disguise this woman might recognize her. She would have to drop her at the livery, and have Frederick takeover from there. Sydnee had met the husband, Royden Archambeau, on one occasion and found him to be pompous and ineffectual. She was not surprised when she learned that he had merely inherited the successful plantation, not built it.

Immediately when Sydnee arrived home she burned the note from Liesl. She would take no chances tonight. Changing quickly into her disguise, she headed to the livery with Frederick.

It was raining and the streets were deserted when she left with the hearse. She pulled up her collar, adjusted her mourner hat so the water would not run down her back and snapped the reins. She wound through the city, listening to the rain splash on the cobblestones. It was a lonely sound.

When she arrived at the convent, she waited only moments before the infirmary door opened, and Liesl stepped out with Madame Archambeau. She was an attractive young woman with dark hair, wearing a travelling cloak and carrying a leather bag. Sydnee stayed in the driver's seat to protect her identity.

When the woman was safely inside the back of the hearse with Atlantis, Liesl came around and said to Sydnee, "In the past when women have escaped, the nuns have always assumed they went home during the night, but with this one there will be questions. What shall I say, Mademoiselle?"

Just as Sydnee was about to reply she heard a man's voice from the back of the hearse. With her heart in her throat, she jumped down to see what was happening.

They found Madame Archambeau standing in the pouring rain with her head down and her arms crossed over her chest. A well-dressed man in a cutaway stood in front of her, his wet hair plastered to his forehead. Sydnee knew him immediately as Royden Archambeau. Rain and tears streamed down his face.

"How could you do this to me?" he whined. "I have always loved you."

"Please, Royden," Charisse Archambeau pleaded. "Just let me go."

He looked at Sydnee and Liesl. "Who are they?"

Charisse did not reply.

He wiped his nose and snuffed. "This is none of your affair," he said in a shrill voice. Turning back to his wife, he appealed once more. "I have been under a lot of strain lately. It won't happen again."

"Please, I just need some time--"

"No!" he screeched.

Sydnee jumped.

Realizing Atlantis was still locked in the back of the hearse, she moved to unlatch the door, but someone stepped up from the shadows, and she stopped. It was an older woman, impeccably dressed with white hair.

"Mother!" Charisse cried.

"My darling," the woman said, rushing up and taking her daughter's hand. "I know this is difficult, but listen to Royden. Your place is with your husband."

Charisse stared at her mother, dumbfounded. "So you were the one who told him where I was tonight. That note was meant only for you."

"But dearest--" her mother said.

Archambeau stepped forward and took Charisse's arm. "We are going home now." He looked at Sydnee and warned, "And you stay away from her."

Charisse jerked her arm free and started to back up.

"Come," he said, flicking his fingers at her as if he was calling his dog. "Come now," he demanded.

Tears streamed down Charisse's face, and she shook her head.

"Why are you doing this? Why, why, why?" he whined.

"I mean what I say, Royden. I have to go," she said with conviction.

He blinked and then stared at his wife as if he finally believed what she was saying. Suddenly he reached into his breast pocket and pulled out a pistol. "Goddamn it, you'll never leave me!" he screeched. Stepping back, he aimed and shot her in the chest.

The blast sent the woman into a spin, and she tumbled backward, slamming against the hearse and then down onto the wet pavement, blood soaking her bodice. Her mother screamed and dropped to her knees beside her daughter as she lay gasping for air.

Sydnee lunged to let Atlantis out, but it was too late. Archambeau had reloaded his pistol and ordered, "Stop!"

She froze, staring at him.

Royden's red-rimmed eyes were on her, and Sydnee knew he meant to kill her too. Suddenly he staggered forward and dropped face down in the mud. Standing over Archambeau with a cudgel was Frederick.

It was like the world stood still. No one moved. The rain was splashing on the pavement and Charisse's mother was sobbing. A river of blood was running between the cobblestones. Her daughter was dead.

Panting, Sydnee swallowed hard and said to Frederick, "You must go before he wakes up."

Frederick didn't hear her.

Sydnee took the old man by the shoulders and pushed him toward the hearse. "Get in!" she ordered. "You too!" she said to Liesl. "We can't stay here."

Slamming the door, Sydnee scrambled up into the driver's seat and snapped the reins. Grateful for the pouring rain, she drove the hearse madly through the streets. Haste would not seem unusual in weather this foul. Sydnee's mind was racing too as she tried to formulate an escape plan for them.

When they arrived at the livery, she opened the stable door and quickly pulled the hearse inside. Frederick and Liesl jumped out.

"Change clothes," Sydnee ordered. "I have work clothes for you in the trunk, Frederick, and Liesl put on the gown I wore here tonight. I will explain later."

While they changed, she built a fire. She stood, staring into the flames, clutching herself and shaking. Liesl would be easy to smuggle out of New Orleans. She could join the O'Bannon sisters on their next run to the North. It was Frederick she worried about. Assaulting a white man in the South would mean a lynching. As perilous as it was smuggling slaves out of Louisiana, helping a black man escape who was wanted for assaulting a white was next to impossible.

Sydnee told herself, no matter what happened, she would find a way to save him. He had saved her life.

"You should change out of those wet clothes, Mademoiselle Sauveterre," Liesl said.

As if waking from a dream, Sydnee blinked and then murmured. "No, I will be driving you to my townhome in the carriage. You will be masquerading as me. That is why you are in my gown. It's dark and without my mourner's hat I will simply look like a carriage driver."

Sydnee turned to Frederick and said, "I must speak with you alone."

Nodding, he followed her out into the stable. He was dressed in a tattered shirt and vest, and wearing threadbare trousers.

She looked up into his wrinkled, care-worn face. "You saved my life. How can I ever thank you?"

He nodded slowly and said, "At least I could save *you*."

Sydnee knew that he was remembering his daughter. She started shaking again. The weather and the night had thoroughly chilled her. "I will get you to safety in the North, but I must ask if you know of anyone that participates in the Underground

Railroad."

"I know someone, and so do you," he replied. "Do you remember Madame Picard's Clotilde?"

"Yes."

"She picked up where Madame left off."

Sydnee raised her eyebrows. "I'm glad. Do you know where I can find her?"

"She lives above the carriage house at 41 Rue Saint Lazare."

Sydnee thought a moment and then frowned. That was only one block from the convent. It would be crawling with constables after the shootings. Nevertheless, she knew she must go. "I will find her right away. We must get you out of the city before they can organize a search."

As she was leaving, she thought of something and asked, "Frederick, how is it you were at the convent tonight?"

He smiled weakly. "You don't think I'd let my girl go out alone? I followed you on foot every time you went out on a run."

Sydnee gasped and then said, "I am most grateful."

She told Liesl to bring her own clothing and get into the carriage. Locking Frederick and Atlantis in the livery, she drove the carriage back to the town house. After showing Liesl to her room, Sydnee changed into the girl's faded print gown. It was too big for her, but it would be adequate for a night time journey. She stepped out into the courtyard. It had stopped raining, and the clouds were giving way to fragments of moonlight. Sydnee walked quickly toward the magnolia tree where she could see the figure of Vivian sitting on her branch, keeping vigil over Baloo. She ruffled her wings, side stepped a bit, and settled back down. Cold fear started to creep up Sydnee's spine, and she was suddenly flooded with doubt. A young woman was dead tonight, quite possibly because of her.

"No," she said, putting her face into her hands. "No, I won't do this again. It is not my fault. Please give me strength. Please give me strength to save two more."

The wind chimes tinkled by the kitchen door. Hearing their sweet sound, Sydnee squared her shoulders and walked out the courtyard door.

It was well after three in the morning as she rushed through the streets of the city. All was quiet until she came near the Ursuline Convent. Two constables were knocking on doors, waking the neighborhood. Sydnee knew they were looking for information about the shooting and the assault on Archambeau. Just as she was about to duck down an alley one called, "You there!"

Sydnee froze, her heart pounding. She wondered if she should run, but instead she quickly unbuttoned the top buttons of her bodice. Walking up to them, she cocked her head to the side coquettishly and said in her French patois. "Would you like some company?"

The constables were dressed in gray uniforms, wore wide belts and carried nightsticks.

"Did you hear a gunshot earlier?" one asked.

Sydnee's heart was hammering so hard she was afraid they could see it as they ran their eyes over her breasts. "Monsieur, this is New Orleans. There are always gun shots."

"No," he barked and pointed. "Over there by the convent."

She shrugged. "No. It has been a busy night."

"Did you see a hearse?" the other asked.

Sydnee smiled and raised her eyebrows. "No, I am sure I was pleasing a customer at the time."

"Worthless whore," he mumbled and walked away. The other constable ran his eyes over her and then walked away too.

Dodging down an alley, Sydnee arrived moments later at 41 Rue Saint Lazare. Praying that there were no dogs in the courtyard, she quietly opened the gate and tip-toed across the garden. She picked up a stick and climbed the stairs to the quarters above the stable. Running it along the shutters, she whispered, "Clotilde, Clotilde, I must speak with you."

After a few moments, Clotilde unlatched the shutter and looked out. "Who's there?" she said. She was wearing a shift and a night cap, and she was in her bare feet. She did not recognize Sydnee. "Heaven's above what is going on?" she said.

"Clotilde, it is Sydnee Sauveterre, Madame Picard's

student. Do you remember me? Frederick needs help."

The woman was groggy and stared at Sydnee. She did not expect to see her in such shabby clothing.

Sydnee looked over her shoulder. She was afraid someone would see her. "Frederick told me to find you. We must speak privately."

Clotilde let her in and lit a candle. The room was small and sparsely furnished with only a bed, a small rocker and a rickety wash stand.

"Frederick told me you are a conductor. He needs to escape to the north tonight."

Clotilde was mute.

"Please trust me, Clotilde. Remember, I said nothing to the authorities about Madame Picard's escape. Please, for the sake of Frederick."

Clotilde sat down heavily on the bed. "What has happened?"

"He knocked a white man unconscious with a cudgel. He saved my life. For months now we have been smuggling women and children out of New Orleans, women and children who are being beaten. Tonight a prominent citizen tried to escape, and her husband killed her. Then he turned his gun on me, and Frederick knocked him unconscious."

Clotilde rubbed her forehead and gasped. "*Zut alors!* We must act quickly. Where is he?"

"The old Gish Livery. Do you remember it?"

"I do."

"I will go there and wait," Sydnee said. "But be forewarned. I will not open the livery to anyone unless a note is passed to me first."

"A Quaker will be there with a produce cart before sunrise," Clotilde said.

"Have him come to the stable doors, and he can pull inside the building to get Frederick. How can I ever repay you, Clotilde?"

"I assure you, someday you will return the favor," the woman said.

*   *   *

Frederick jumped to his feet when Sydnee walked in.

"Someone is coming for you before sunrise," she said.

"Who?"

"I believe it may be the same man who came for Madame Picard, a Quaker farmer. He will bring a cart filled with produce and hide you under a tarp. Then the Railroad will get you to the North."

Sydnee brought the fire up, pulled out a spider trivet and began to make johnnycakes. "You will need some breakfast. Hard telling how long until your next hot meal."

Frederick poured a cup of tea for Sydnee. "Drink this. You are still shivering," he said and then sat down rigidly in the rocking chair.

Sydnee finished making the johnnycakes, handed him his breakfast and then took a sip of tea. It seemed to warm her right to her toes. "If you see Ninon Picard, please tell her--please tell her that I miss her terribly."

Frederick nodded and ate his breakfast. There was a knock on the door, and they both jumped up. "Stay here, just in case," she said. Sydnee dashed out into the stable and picked up the note that had been pushed under the door. It stated simply,

Here for pick up.

As she started to unbolt the door, she heard the Quaker call to someone, "I stopped here because I thought the horse was lame but, praise God, it was just a stone!"

Sydnee leaned against the door, listening. She heard men's voices mumbling in reply. Then the Quaker said, "No, I've seen no hearse."

Her stomach lurched. She looked down and saw tracks from the hearse leading into the stable. The wheels on it were still wet and muddy, evidence that it had been out recently. Picking up her skirt, she raced into the front room. "The constables!" she said to Frederick.

"Is there a back door?"

"No," Sydnee said. "Help me pull the wood off this window." They dashed over to the window that had been broken several months back.

The constables were banging on the stable door. "Open up!"

Sydnee and Frederick struggled madly to loosen the wood, but the fit was too tight.

The banging grew louder. "Open up!" Some of the men came to the service door and were trying to kick it in.

Frederick dashed to the hearth, grabbed a poker and pried the wood as Sydnee pulled. At last it came off with a crack, and Sydnee tumbled onto the floor. Frederick pulled her to her feet, just as the constables broke through the service door. With Frederick's help, she scrambled through the window and then helped him through as well. They ran down the alley where the Quaker was waiting anxiously with his cart. Flipping back the tarp, he helped Frederick onto the wagon bed quickly.

"God's speed," Sydnee said, as they bolted off.

Straightening her gown, she took a deep breath and tried to walk down the street slowly. In spite of the blood pounding in her ears, she did not run. She could hear men shouting, whistles blowing, and banging on doors, but by the grace of God, no one bothered her.

When she arrived at home her legs felt like butter. She collapsed onto a stone bench in the courtyard and sighed. Her heart gradually slowed as she looked at the sky brightening in the east. She still had to get Liesl to safety, but that would not be a problem.

"I'm afraid our mission helping women and children is over, old girl," she said to Vivian, who was sitting overhead. Sydnee knew that it was over. There would be no more escapes for women and children. It was far too dangerous now, and the Ursulines would lock down the convent tightly after this incident.

Pushing herself up, Sydnee started into the house. She was weary and filled with despair. In one night everything she had worked for was over.

Chapter 24

Dr. Locke heard about the shooting the next day. He knew exactly what had happened, and he knew Sydnee had been a witness to it all. He listened to the rumors and gossip and pored over every article he could find in the newspapers.

The authorities approached D'anton about the incident, since he was the legal representative for the livery, but of course, he knew nothing. They attempted to pin the blame on a free man of color named Artemis Perry, but too many whites testified seeing him at Pascal's Tavern by the landing that night. The outrage and lust for blood continued for weeks and did not subside until the Archambeau family moved to Natchez and Charisse's mother left for Raleigh. Monsieur Archambeau bought a speedy acquittal from a murder charge and left town as well.

During this time, Locke listened for news of Sydnee, but she was never implicated in any way. Liesl was never heard from again either, and by Christmas Day, it was all over.

*   *   *

It was a grueling fall at the hospital for Fletcher Locke. It had been a particularly virulent year for yellow fever, and it had left him exhausted. His days were full from beginning to end and most nights he arrived home late, ate a cold supper left by his housekeeper, and fell into bed.

Initially he had seen many children orphaned as a result of the fever, brought in off the street for malnutrition, injuries, and disease, but as autumn progressed their numbers were fewer. It was not until he took a few days off near Christmas that he began to wonder where they had gone. He was not naïve. He knew that they were not miraculously adopted into happy homes, so one afternoon after his rounds at the convent, he approached Mother Baptista.

"Indeed their numbers are fewer, Dr. Locke. Of course you know many children are orphaned each year after the epidemics, but this year gangs have been combing the streets for them. We believe they are kidnapping the children and selling them in the north for labor or for--" and she hesitated, pursing her lips. "For other reasons."

He had a vague recollection of the stowaway on the paddle wheeler mentioning she had been kidnapped in St. Louis and taken north to work on a farm, and he nodded. He realized that they were starting the abductions down here as well.

Locke was bothered by this information, and every day that passed he grew increasingly disturbed. He couldn't sleep, and his stomach was tied up in knots day in and day out. He knew he had to stop these abductions, but where to start was beyond him. One thing he knew for sure, he was going to approach that Sauveterre woman for help.

*   *   *

For months after the shooting, Sydnee was beside herself with remorse. She was eating little and nothing seemed to interest her. She tried not to blame herself, but there was always the nagging doubt regarding her responsibility in orchestrating the dangerous affair. Her role in saving scores of women and children in the past two years never occurred to her. All of the beatings and possible deaths she prevented never entered her head. Instead she chastised herself continually, scanning her conscience for mistakes that night.

"It isn't like you to be brooding, Sydnee," Tristan said one afternoon at the town house. D'anton had just left and they were having an early supper. "You are the only person I have in my life on a balanced course. Between D'anton and his spells and Isabel pining over Mortimer, you are the only steady person I know."

She sighed, picking at her chicken. "I never thought of it that way, Tristan. I'm sorry."

"So what is it? Are you ill? Bored? Do you need to take a lover?"

Sydnee chuckled, "Certainly not a lover. That would be one

more problem. Perhaps I need a diversion until the ennui passes," she said with a weak smile.

Tristan leaned across the highly polished mahogany table and poured her more wine. "What about a ball?"

"A Christmas ball?"

"I think Twelfth Night would be more fun," he said. "You and I will plan it together, and we will spare no expense."

"It sounds like a lot of work."

"Sydnee, stop it! I need my friend back," he said slapping the table.

Sydnee looked at him, wide eyed. It was the first time Tristan had ever scolded her. "Well, I have not danced in a long time," she conceded. Then she added, "Remember the old days when we would practice after Madame Picard's classes?"

"I remember. You were a terrible dancer," he said, lighting a cigar with a twinkle in his eye.

"You were not much better, taking Baloo's paws and forcing him to waltz with you," Sydnee countered.

"Perhaps," and then he said suddenly, "Say, this would be the perfect occasion for you to meet Charles."

"I *don't* want a beau, Tristan," Sydnee said firmly.

"No, my little nephew, Charles. Although, he is not so little any more. I believe he is eleven or twelve."

Sydnee's eye's widened. "You mean Giselle's--"

"The very one," Tristan said, puffing on his cigar. "My mother keeps such a tight rein on him that he is very backward. He needs to work on his social graces."

"Oh, Tristan, he is too young for a ball and besides every child is gauche at that age."

"I wasn't," Tristan said, straightening up.

"Oh, of course not," Sydnee said, sarcastically. "Your mother will never allow it, you realize."

"She will never know. I'll invite him for the entire week, and he can attend the ball for an hour or so. It will be good for him."

Sydnee wondered about the boy. She hoped he had not witnessed the kind of violence she had seen in the Saint-Yves household.

"What about Isabel?" she asked. "She will be left out again."

Tristan sighed. "Yes indeed," he said, drumming his fingers on the table. "I know! We will make it a masquerade. No one will know it is her."

"That might work."

"And if she is unmasked for any reason, we can say she was spying on her husband and his mistress, the most natural thing in the world, and it will all be forgotten in a day."

"Very well," said Sydnee. "A masked ball will cost a great deal of money, but you are the one with the pocketbook. I will have all the fun planning."

"That's what I want to hear." Holding up his wine glass Tristan said, "Let's drink to the social event of the season."

*   *   *

"I suppose you are going to Mademoiselle Sauveterre's ball?" D'anton asked Fletcher one morning in late December at his office. They were discussing Locke's properties and holdings in England.

"What ball?"

"Oh, can it be true? You fill me with delight," said D'anton. "I thought I was the only one not going. She is hosting a Twelfth Night Masque, and Madame Delacroix will have none of it. She thinks Sydnee and Tristan are nothing more than decadent Creoles. I may be able to arrange an invitation for you though."

Locke chuckled, "No, thank you."

"Ah yes, you don't dance," D'anton laughed. "You are saving yourself for marriage."

*   *   *

A diversion is just what Sydnee needed to sweep away her cobwebs of melancholy. She rented out the luxurious Orleans Ballroom, mailed invitations, and after planning the menu, she began the design of her costume.

Tristan and Isabel were positively ecstatic and chattered endlessly about the masquerade. Even D'anton, determined not to be left out, was formulating a plan so he could attend the event without Paula's knowledge.

The night of the ball, to make it appear Isabel knew nothing of the affair, Tristan came to the town house with Charles to dress. Charles was a gangly, tawny-skinned boy with blue eyes and brown curly hair. Sydnee noticed Giselle immediately in his face. He had her high cheekbones and full lips.

"Welcome Charles," Sydnee said. "You have your own room in which to change. Marie will take your costume and show you upstairs."

The boy stared at Sydnee until Tristan gave him a nudge. When he disappeared upstairs, Tristan said, "I think you have a new admirer."

"Nonsense, I am probably the first woman he has ever met socially."

"Oh, I'm sure that's it," Tristan said, smirking.

"Well, do stay by his side tonight, Tristan. He will be uncomfortable at the ball."

"I will. It will only be for an hour. This should be interesting. He told me that he is learning to dance."

"Mademoiselle," Marie interrupted, from the top of the stairs. "It is time."

"Yes, thank you, Marie."

Picking up her skirts, Sydnee started upstairs to her bed chamber which was flooded with candlelight. The first thing Marie did was fasten Sydnee into her corset and petticoats. Then she stepped into her gown. It was a voluminous garment of black satin, with a close fitting bodice, dropped shoulders, and three quarter length sleeves.

Marie fastened large black plumed wings to her shoulders. Next she covered Sydnee's head with a hat of shiny black feathers which were slightly ruffled and combed back.

Sydnee sat down at the vanity and lined her eyes with charcoal, shadowing them so they appeared to be slanting upward. She finished off her make up with ruby red lips.

"Try your mask," Marie suggested.

After pulling on her long black gloves, Sydnee picked up the black feathered mask with a beak of faux ebony. Holding it by the stick, Sydnee held it up to her face and looked in the mirror. "*Voila*," she said.

There was a knock on the front door and Marie went downstairs to open it. It was Fletcher Locke. "Good evening. Is Mademoiselle Sauveterre in?" he asked, handing Marie his calling card. He was wearing a blue coat, vest and loosely tied cravat, but the front of his white shirt was soaked with perspiration. When Marie escorted him into the parlor, he stopped her. His face was flushed, and he self-consciously ran his hand through his long hair. "Please, I have been at the hospital all day, and my clothes are dirty. May I meet Mademoiselle outside in the garden?"

"Of course, Dr. Locke," she said, taking him out to the courtyard.

Marie went back upstairs and handed Sydnee his calling card.

"What does *he* want? And tonight of all nights," she said, clearly annoyed. "All right, tell him I will be right down."

As she started down the stairs, Tristan and Charles came out of their rooms. They were both dressed in men's formal attire from the previous century. They had on lacy shirts, colorful waistcoats, top coats and breeches. Charles wore the hat of a buccaneer. His mask was black, covering the upper half of his face and had two long braids of hair dangling from it. Tristan wore a smaller, elegant, black satin tri-cornered hat edged in gold lace with a half mask of black satin covered in gold jewels.

"Very nice, gentlemen," Sydnee said, circling them and smiling. "Very handsome, both of you. Will you wait for me in the carriage? I will be there in a moment. Dr. Locke is in the courtyard."

"Locke? What is he doing here? Certainly you didn't forget to invite him?" Tristan said, walking down the stairs behind her.

"No, I didn't *forget* to invite him," she said, sweeping down the hall. "I just didn't," she mumbled to herself.

The sun had set, and Marie lit the Japanese lanterns over the fountain in the garden.

"Welcome Dr. Locke," Sydnee said, in a business-like tone,

stepping out into the courtyard.

He was standing with his back to her and when he turned around, he was stunned at her appearance. Collecting himself he said, "I-I had no idea the ball was tonight."

"How may I help you?"

He looked at her red lips and then ran his eyes over her long graceful neck and arms. He was embarrassed and angry with himself for being dazzled by her. Setting his jaw, he shook his head. "Think no more of it, Mademoiselle Sauveterre. I see that doing charitable works was last year's fancy. You have found other diversions. I won't keep you. Good night."

Taking long strides with his hat in his hand, he started for the gate.

Sydnee's face flushed with anger. "Dr. Locke, you have interrupted my evening. You owe me an explanation. If it is an invitation to the ball you want--"

"Certainly not," he said. "I came here tonight looking for your help. After the fever this season, I have found out that gangs are stealing children, mostly those orphaned from yellow jack, to sell in the north for labor and other unspeakable practices. I have every reason to believe they will be back again this summer."

Sydnee stared at him, absorbing the news. "I see. What do you propose?"

He shrugged. "That is why I am here--to consult with you."

"I would like to be involved--"

"But you cannot because," he interrupted, assuming she would reject him.

"I *said* I would like to be involved, Dr. Locke."

"Indeed," he answered, with raised eyebrows. "Very well, I will call for you tomorrow morning at eight."

"Eight!"

"Oh, forgive me, you will certainly be at Mass," he said sarcastically. "Let's make it nine."

Sydnee scowled and said, "Very well, nine."

Before he left, he turned back and asked, "By the way, your costume. What are you?"

Holding the mask over her face, Sydnee thrust her arm into the air, and Vivian swooped down to perch on her wrist. "Tonight I masquerade as an old friend."

*   *   *

Dr. Locke took the long way home that night. He walked out of his way so he could watch guests arriving at the Orleans Ballroom for the masquerade. He stood in the shadows across the street with his hands in his pockets. Although he did not dance and most of these functions bored him, he would have liked to have attended this event. He hated to admit it, but something stirred within him when he was around that Sauveterre woman. It was mesmerizing to watch her move, and her personality was certainly unpredictable. One minute she was elegant and reserved, the next she was sharp-tongued and derisive.

At last the stream of guests arriving for the ball diminished, and the music began. He heard laughter and saw costumed figures sail past the ballroom windows. Locke thought of Sydnee once more, smiling when he remembered the sharp tone she used with him. He turned toward home wondering if she was like that with everyone, or if Fletcher Locke was the only one who could ruffle those feathers.

*   *   *

Tristan watched Sydnee in the carriage on the way to the ball. She sat stiffly in her seat, staring out the window. "What did Locke say that upset you, my love?" he asked.

"*Pardon?*" Sydnee said absent-mindedly. "Oh, nothing that matters now. We must forget ourselves and attend to our guests tonight."

"Very well, Madame Picard," Tristan teased.

Charles looked at him, confused.

The carriage stopped, and the coachman pulled the door open. Sydnee slid forward, took the driver's gloved hand and stepped out, followed by Tristan and Charles. The three of them stood by the front door of the Orleans Ballroom to receive guests.

Charles dreaded having to talk with strangers and shake

their hands. He was never comfortable around people and when he had to talk, he was often tongue-tied.

He was surprised that Mademoiselle Sauveterre did not seem comfortable either. She stood staring straight ahead, clearly preoccupied. But the moment the first guest arrived, her transformation was miraculous. She smiled gaily and offered her gloved hand for kisses. She cooed and gushed over costumes, laughed and made small talk with everyone young and old. She made every person that walked through that door feel comfortable and welcome. Uncle Tristan had the same knack for hospitality. They both were poised and comfortable.

Charles wished he was like them. He was mortified when someone talked to him, he stammered and blushed and struggled for words. Without fail, Mademoiselle Sauveterre would rescue him, or Uncle Tristan would jump into the conversation.

Mademoiselle Sauveterre was the most beautiful woman Charles had ever seen. He admitted that many of the ladies present were more buxom and full-figured. Many of them were more flirtatious and coy, but Mademoiselle Sauveterre had a grace and charm that enchanted him. Uncle Tristan called her captivating. He guessed that was a good word to describe her.

The Orleans Ballroom was ablaze with candles, casting a golden glow over everything. A massive crystal chandelier was in the center of the ballroom, and the chamber was lined with tall mullioned windows. French doors opened on one side into a courtyard with a fountain where guests could sit and listen to the water or move into the shadows for a kiss.

The orchestra was seated at the far end of the ballroom, and with a nod from Sydnee, they opened the ball with a Polonaise so everyone could display their costumes. The dress was an opulent mix of the beautiful and macabre. There were jesters wearing pointed hats with bells, sultans in gold with turbans, and royalty from the 17th Century. Some of the guests were dressed as Chinamen, or buccaneers in black and gold. There were tropical birds with colorful plumes and hideous creatures with long noses, horns and sharp teeth. Isabel came dressed as Marie Antoinette and spent the night laughing and dancing, hiding successfully behind her white mask and plumed fan. Sydnee looked for D'anton in vain. He could have been anyone hiding behind a costume.

Her first dance was with Tristan, and then she continued on with others, dancing two quadrilles and a cotillion. Staggering over for a glass of claret, she heard someone say, "May I have the pleasure of this next dance?" It was Charles. His face was flushed, and he bowed stiffly.

Sydnee took a breath, smiled and said, "I would be delighted."

She could feel his hand shaking as he put it on her waist. He was so thin that Sydnee felt like she was holding a bag of bones. She looked down at him as he struggled to start the waltz. "You mustn't worry," she whispered. "It is the lady's responsibility to follow whatever step you take. Even if it is wrong, I will not mind. I will follow."

Tristan was talking to a group of people nearby, and Sydnee saw him stop and watch. Charles started out the dance stiffly, stepping on Sydnee's feet several times, but by the end of the waltz, he had mastered the steps.

"Thank you, Monsieur Saint-Yves. That was delightful," she said to him.

He looked up at her with delight. "May I have another?"

"You would like to try it again?"

"Yes, I would!"

They danced another waltz, this time more smoothly, and Sydnee laughed when the boy whirled her around several times. When the music ended, Tristan complimented Charles on his dancing but told him that it was time to go home. Sydnee could see that the boy was disappointed, but he was a perfect gentleman, bowing and asking to be excused.

The rest of the masquerade was a grand success. When Sydnee fell into bed that night she was utterly exhausted. She had consumed too much wine, and her head was filled with the sounds of waltzes, laughter and accolades. But as she drifted to sleep, it was not the success of the party that excited her but the fact that once more her life had direction and purpose, and it would all begin with Fletcher Locke in the morning.

*   *   *

Morning came quickly, but Sydnee was ready when Fletcher came to the door. "It is a beautiful morning," he said. "I left the carriage at home. Is it all right if we walk?"

"Of course," Sydnee said, picking up her parasol. She was dressed in a green and gold plaid day dress. She looked down, and there was Atlantis sitting next to Locke.

"I have prescribed exercise for my patient," he said. "So it is imperative, the dog join us."

Sydnee narrowed her eyes at Atlantis teasingly, and she wagged her tail. "Very well, but you must behave."

"I thought we could walk to market and perhaps pick up some breakfast," Fletcher suggested.

"Good idea." Sydnee said, snapping her parasol open.

They strolled down the street with Atlantis behind them. Locke did not enjoy small talk, so he started right in about his concerns. He told Sydnee about the sudden disappearance of children and about his talk with Mother Baptista. As they approached the market, he swept his arm out and said, "Ordinarily after a summer of fever, there are children of all ages loitering and begging in this area. This year in a matter of days, they disappeared. I would like to believe some were taken to good homes but--" and he shook his head.

"Do you think the kidnappers are taking them upriver?"

"That is what I believe."

"How are they seizing them? Do they snatch them, gag them?" Sydnee asked.

He shrugged. "I don't know."

Thinking of her father, Sydnee said, "Is it possible some of them are surrendered by their parents?"

Fletcher stopped and looked at her. "*Sold* by their parents?"

Sydnee suddenly felt uncomfortable. She cleared her throat and said, "Well, yes. Sometimes parents can no longer feed and clothe their children, so they give them up. But sometimes—yes, there are those that see their young as a financial opportunity."

259

Locke sighed and rubbed his forehead. "So we fight wars on several fronts."

They walked in silence for a while.

At last, Sydnee asked, "If we can stop this, what will we do with these homeless children?"

"Well, there is the Poydras Asylum, but it is badly overcrowded. I would like to start my own orphanage. But how to do it--" He stopped walking and put his fist to his lips, deep in thought.

Sydnee studied him a moment. Although he was naturally fair skinned, he had grown tan in the Louisiana sun. He was a handsome man, but he had lines in his brow from frowning. Sydnee wondered if these were from constant worry about his patients. She had to remind herself that although he was caring and warm to children, he could be difficult and intolerant of spoiled adults and the privileged classes.

"What was your home like in England?" she asked abruptly.

He frowned and shrugged. "It was a house not a home."

Sydnee pressed further. "It is a large estate in Gloucestershire. Am I correct?"

"Yes. Your friend, Monsieur Delacroix should not be discussing my affairs."

"He has not," Sydnee said quickly. "But there has been talk around town."

"None of this is relevant. Let's keep to our topic."

In reality, Sydnee heard very little gossip about Locke, but he confirmed her suspicions. He scorned the aristocracy because his own background had been privileged.

When they arrived at the market, Fletcher bought coffee and beignets for them, and they sat under an awning at a café table. Atlantis sprawled at their feet.

"Are you still helping women?" he asked, taking a sip of his chicory coffee.

"No."

"Good, so you can give this a bit of your attention between the soirees and garden parties?"

"Dr. Locke," Sydnee said firmly.

"Oh yes, my apologies. Where do you think we should start?"

Sydnee put her cup down and stared out over the market. "We must catch the orphans before they are abducted."

"Indeed. From now on, when a patient is admitted to the hospital, I will obtain names of all the family members. That way if someone dies, I know where to find the children."

"And we must determine if there are relatives to take them in," she added. "If there is no one, we must have housing, food and clothing for them."

"Poydras can take them at first, but once summer begins, they will not have room."

"We will need to find a building suitable for an orphanage," Sydnee said. "But most importantly we must put a stop to the abductions. We must dig out the rotten core of this thing and find out who is behind these kidnappings."

He watched the breeze blow a lock of hair across her cheek, and then he ran his eyes over her breasts. He swallowed hard looking away. Damn her, he thought. *I do not need a woman distracting me right now.*

"I have a contact in the North," Sydnee announced. "And I will write to him. He is in Memphis, although if he had noticed anyone selling children, he would have already written."

*   *   *

Over a month later, Mortimer responded to her letter. As predicted, he had no information about trafficking children, but he would watch for anything unusual. Sydnee was at a loss where to find these predators.

She returned to her life at the salon, but this time she was happier; she had purpose once more. After a month of searching Sydnee and Dr. Locke found an abandoned townhome in Faubourg Marigny that would work as an orphanage and they had D'anton draw up papers for a purchase immediately. It was no secret that they were starting another orphanage. In fact they wanted the public to know; they needed patrons. Sydnee used her connections at the salon to solicit funds from the wealthy, and she never hesitated to lord it over Fletcher. "I see you have a double standard," she said as she handed him a hefty donation one afternoon. "You loathe these people but will gladly take their money."

Locke shrugged. "Yes, it's true. It is much like an apprentice who takes wages from a master who is a despicable buffoon."

Sydnee sighed. There was no winning an argument with this man, so she decided to ignore him.

One morning, a boy delivered a disturbing note to Sydnee at her townhome. It was from Clotilde. Sydnee remembered the woman's words when she had consented to helping Frederick, "Someday you will return the favor," and it appeared that now was the time. Clotilde said that there was a woman in need who wanted to meet Sydnee at midnight at the entrance to St. Louis Cemetery.

Sydnee frowned. She did not like going to City of the Dead. Nevertheless she sent a reply saying that she would be there.

Making an excuse that night, she left the recital of a young soprano at the home of Madame Bottineau and returned to the town house. Telling her new coachman, Amaury, to wait, she dressed in modest attire, called Atlantis and climbed back into the carriage. She was grateful that the moon was almost full. She wanted as much light as possible at the City of the Dead.

When they arrived at the gate, there was no one there. Sydnee waited a few moments, and then stepped out of the carriage with Atlantis. She had a sinking feeling that Clotilde and the woman did not want to be seen and were just inside the gate. She did not want to go in.

"Wait here please, Amaury," she said.

Memories of All Soul's Day came back to her, flooding her with fear. Reluctantly she closed her eyes and opened her mind to the spirits. She had to know if that vacuum of despair still churned here.

With her arms at her sides, she turned her palms up and tilted her head back. Sydnee waited for the tumult to begin and the moaning to fill her ears, but there was nothing. She continued to channel the spirits for several moments more, but all was silence and peace.

Taking a deep breath, she opened her eyes and looked around. Atlantis was watching her expectantly. "Very well, my friend, we go inside but not too far."

The black gate towered over her, and Sydnee stepped forward pushing it open. Yawning before her in the moonlight were the rows and rows of tiny white sepulchers. The wind moved the trees slightly throwing shadows over the monuments and statues. Sydnee started down the path, her shoes crunching on the gravel walkway. Atlantis walked at her side stiff-legged and on guard.

They walked only a few steps when there was the sound of a loud rattle behind them. Atlantis jumped and snarled.

"Aye!" a woman cried, jumping back. Sydnee knew her immediately. It was the woman she had seen on All Soul's Day. She was much older, her wild hair was now gray, and she still wore the same flamboyant attire of a gypsy. The dark aura still emanated from her as she crouched in the bushes.

She darted behind one of the mausoleums, watching Atlantis warily.

Sydnee asked, "What do you want?"

"Call your beast off," she hissed in a thick accent. "Or no meeting."

Sydnee narrowed her eyes. *Was this creature part of her rendezvous with Clotilde?* She did not like it. Cautiously she touched Atlantis' head and said, "Sit."

Atlantis sat down but did not take her eyes from the gypsy woman. The wind started again, putting the shadows in motion once more. "What do you want?" Sydnee demanded.

"This!" the gypsy said and with a sweep of her arm, a figure stepped out from behind the crypt.

It was a tall woman with dark skin dressed in a cloak. The figure was silent and motionless. Sydnee's heart was pounding, and she wanted to bolt. *Is this a specter, a voodoo conjuring from this wicked gypsy?*

The hackles raised on Atlantis' back and a gurgling started

in her throat.

"Where is Clotilde?" Sydnee demanded.

"Do you not know me?" the phantom said, stepping into the moonlight.

Sydnee narrowed her eyes, trying to make out the features. The blood roared in her ears as the specter lowered her hood. Sydnee gasped.

"It is Giselle," the woman said.

Chapter 25

Without taking her eyes from the specter's face, Sydnee stepped back, and Atlantis started to snarl again. She knew of the evil that could be done with Voodoo to animate the dead, and now she was a witness to it.

"Stop, please," Giselle said in her island accent. "I did not die that night all those years ago. Maxime and Ninon smuggled me out of New Orleans on the Railroad."

Giselle held out her hand, and Atlantis lunged at her. She jumped back and gasped, "I am flesh and blood."

Sydnee ran her eyes over her and asked suspiciously, "Why are you here?"

Giselle murmured, "I want to see my boy."

The wind sighed through the trees, and the moonlight danced across Giselle's face. Sydnee's breathing slowed. "I will not speak with you here any longer. It is too dangerous."

Giselle called to the gypsy woman over her shoulder in a patois which Sydnee did not understand and then said, "I will come."

They stepped through the gate and out to the carriage. Atlantis walked behind, her hackles still raised. The lanterns on the coach were lit, but before getting into the cab, Sydnee stopped to look at Giselle. There were the cat-like eyes, the high cheek bones, and the regal bearing. Her face was drawn and etched with fine lines, but she had no doubt, it was Giselle. Sydnee swallowed hard. It was beyond unnerving seeing someone she thought was dead, alive once more.

"Where to, Mademoiselle Sauveterre?" Amaury said, glancing suspiciously at Giselle.

"We will stay right here. Thank you, Amaury."

"Very well," he said, opening the door. Putting out his white gloved hand, he helped the women step inside the carriage.

"This is beyond belief," Sydnee murmured, as she sat down. Giselle sat rigidly in the seat across from her. Sydnee was in shock, and she stared at her, wide-eyed. "How did you escape?"

Giselle's face contorted. "That hateful woman, Saint-Yves was too busy stealing my son to come back and check to see to see if I was indeed dead. Instead she signed the papers and informed her husband later that I died giving birth."

"And they smuggled you out that night?"

"The next morning when the mistress did not return to identify a body, no questions were asked. You know how quickly bodies must be buried in this heat."

Giselle looked Sydnee up and down. "Clotilde told me you have become very powerful in this city and that secretly you help women escape."

"Yes, but I am not part of the Underground Railroad."

"That is not why I am here. I want to see my son. I want to just look at him."

"Giselle, this is impossible," Sydnee said emphatically. "If the Saint-Yveses find out you are still alive, they will clap you in chains."

"Do you think I am stupid?" she hissed. "I know the risks. I travel with forged papers saying that I am a free woman of color."

"Nevertheless, it took me a moment, but I recognized you. Besides, your boy is not even here. He resides in Natchez."

"Clotilde told me that he is coming to stay with his uncle in less than week."

Sydnee frowned. It had been over a month since she had spoken with Tristan, and she knew nothing of Charles' visit. Sydnee surmised there must be informants at *Saint-Denis*. "What you ask of me," Sydnee said, rubbing her forehead. "It may be beyond my powers."

Giselle narrowed her eyes and sneered, "Pampered little white girl. You know nothing of losing a child."

Sydnee felt the blood rush to her face. "You know nothing

of me. If you want my help, you will ask for it, not demand it."

Giselle stared at her a moment and then dropped her eyes. Her demeanor softened. "I just want to see him once, just for a moment."

They were silent, and at last Sydnee said, "I will see what I can do. I will not come back to the cemetery though for a rendezvous. You must provide another means of contact."

"Through Clotilde?"

"Very well."

Giselle was about to get out, but Sydnee stopped her. "Where have you been living?"

"North of St. Louis on the east side of the river in Quincy. We are free in Illinois."

Sydnee nodded, considering what she said and how it may benefit *her* cause. "Now I ask for *your* help. Can you read and write?"

"No, but my husband is a free man of color. He can."

"Have you heard of children being bought and sold along the river?"

"Yes." Giselle shrugged. "Everyone in Quincy knows of it. Many buy orphans to help on their farms."

"Well, I want to know how and where they sell these children and who is at the head of this operation."

Giselle nodded. Before she closed the door she said, "I will be waiting, Mademoiselle."

*　　　　*　　　　*

The next day, Sydnee sent a note to Tristan, suggesting they meet at Antoine's for supper. One of the first things he told her was that Charles was coming to visit. He expressed his concern again about his mother smothering the boy and his wish to expose Charles to new experiences. Sydnee said that she was delighted and wanted to be included in things. They agreed on an outing to *Saint-Denis*.

It was a beautiful spring day when Sydnee, Tristan, and Charles rode out to the plantation. With the landau open, they whisked through the countryside enjoying the fresh scent of wildflowers and the breeze. Sydnee was dressed in a light pink-striped gown and carried a white lace parasol.

"Couldn't you have worn something fancier?" Tristan asked sarcastically, looking at her dress.

"*Pardon?*" she called over to him, and Charles started to laugh. Uncle and nephew were sitting across from her, dressed in coarse trousers and boots, ready for a day of fishing. They had removed their jackets and were in their white shirts and vests.

Tristan smiled and shook his head. "Nothing, my dear friend."

The moment they pulled up to *Saint-Denis,* Tristan jumped out and went to the kitchen to have the cook put together a picnic lunch for them. Sydnee and Charles went to the gazebo and sat down to wait.

"Aunt Isabel knows about you," Charles said, looking at Sydnee out of the corner of his eye.

She was adjusting the lace on her sleeve, and she looked up. "Does she?"

"I mentioned you by accident this morning, and she smiled." He wrinkled his nose. "I would think she wouldn't like you."

"Charles, this is a very delicate subject and not the sort of topic a young gentleman should be discussing."

He dropped his eyes and shuffled his feet. "I apologize. I am always doing something wrong."

"Nonsense," Sydnee said. "You are young and curious and in time you will understand our ways."

He nodded his head.

"I tell you this. The reason your Aunt Isabel smiles when you mention me, is that we were best friends many years ago. Life has changed for us both, but there is little animosity between us."

"There are so many things I don't understand. Sometimes I wonder about my parents too."

Sydnee was aware that Charles knew the truth about his mother, nevertheless she was not at liberty to discuss it. "You must ask your uncle. Perhaps he wonders about *his* parents too. You know that he was an orphan."

Charles looked up at her. His eyes were so blue and his lashes so long. Sydnee was certain that he would be a handsome young man someday. He asked eagerly, "Shall I ask him today?"

"By all means and look," she said standing up. "Here he is with lunch and some fishing poles. We are off."

The three walked down to the lake, and Tristan unlocked the boat house. When they pulled the rowboat out, Sydnee gasped. "It looks terrible, Tristan!"

The paint had worn off. It was full of cobwebs, and it appeared as if mice had been nesting in the corners. Tristan frowned and surveyed it. "She's a bit old and in need of paint, but it won't sink."

Sydnee rolled her eyes.

"Besides we can all swim, right Charles?"

"I can, Uncle Tristan."

"You can too, Sydnee," Tristan added.

"With this gown, I will sink like a rock. Nevertheless, let's go."

They brushed it out and pushed the rickety boat out onto the lake. It still floated. Sydnee stepped in and sat down, adjusting her parasol. This reminded her of Isabel when they first met and went boating together. Sydnee smiled wistfully. How little they had known about where life would lead them that sunny day so long ago.

Charles was thrilled to be on the lake. He insisted on being the first to row, sending them round and round in circles until they all laughed, and Tristan corrected him.

The boy was eager to fish too, and his uncle showed him how to bate a hook. When he at last caught a catfish, he was amazed when Mademoiselle Sauveterre reached out and skillfully took the ugly, black creature off the hook. She seemed fearless, and he stared at her in awe. To Charles, she was the perfect woman, elegant and refined but unafraid of life. When Tristan saw the boy gazing at her, he nudged him and murmured, "I told you she was marvelous."

After lunch they relaxed and were quiet, drifting lazily from one end of the lake to the other. They dozed in the sun, listened to the birds or took turns reading out loud.

"Uncle Tristan?" Charles asked, propping himself up on one elbow.

"Hmm?"

"Do you ever wonder about your parents?"

Sydnee opened one eye and looked at Tristan.

He scratched his head and said, "Yes, I have often wondered about them. I used to make up stories about them when I was young. They were always grand and good looking. Why? Do you wonder about your parents?"

Sydnee straightened up and brushed off her lap, swallowing hard.

"Sometimes I wish I knew them," the boy admitted. "I feel like I know my father, but Grandmamma will not talk about my mother."

Tristan sighed. "I knew your mother but not well, Charles. She was quiet and reserved, tall and stately. I was just a little older than you when she died. I wish I could tell you more." Changing the subject, Tristan asked, "Are you having a good time today?"

Charles smiled and nodded.

Sydnee chimed in, "Tristan and I did this sort of thing when we were your age. Do you have friends in Natchez?"

"Not really. Grandmamma does not like boys my age."

Tristan shot a disgusted look at Sydnee. "Well, we will see about that," he said.

As the sun began to set, they rowed back to the big house. Everyone was tired on their return to town, and Charles slept most of the way home leaning on Sydnee's shoulder.

*   *   *

Sydnee did not sleep well that night, worrying about how to arrange a rendezvous with Giselle. She worried that the woman might reveal herself to Charles on impulse, so the next morning, Sydnee wrote to Clotilde insisting on complete restraint and anonymity for everyone's safety. Coordinating anything with a fugitive slave was a risky and dangerous affair.

After several messages back and forth, it was agreed that

Sydnee would bring Charles to the market for a coffee on Sunday morning after Mass. A "chance encounter" was arranged with Giselle who would be known as Madame Montagne. At that time, she could meet Charles, visit briefly and leave.

Sunday morning after Mass, Sydnee had Amaury take her to market where she would meet Tristan and Charles. Since it was Charles' last day in New Orleans, Sydnee requested an outing just for the two of them.

"I will meet you later at the house for cards," Tristan said, as Charles' climbed out of the landau.

"If you dare," said Sydnee. "I am going to take your money."

"You already are," he called as he rode away, waving.

Sydnee raised an eyebrow and then glanced at Charles to see if he understood the double entendre, but he was gazing wide-eyed at the activity in the market. It was almost an hour before Sydnee had to rendezvous with Giselle so they walked through the marketplace first.

There were throngs of people after Mass, and the market was filled with a cacophony of sights and sounds. People of all colors and from all walks of life were crowded together shoulder to shoulder, making purchases, examining meats, inspecting produce, and haggling with vendors.

Sydnee and Charles pushed through the crowds, stopping to watch a juggler, and then turned back under the awning, strolling down the produce aisles where Sydnee bought some okra and onions. She stopped to savor the aroma of boiling crayfish. The steam rolled up thick with spices filling her nostrils with delicious scent. Huge barrels of coffee beans were nearby filling the air with the dark aroma of the tropics. Charles was a few steps away, mesmerized by five parrots sitting on perches in the rafters of the market building. They seemed entertained by the crowds as their owner sang their praises trying to seduce buyers into a purchase.

Sydnee bought cups of coffee for them and stopped a vendor selling rolls and brioche. He had the tray of pastries strapped to his shoulders as he walked through the market.

Pulling out her delicate pendant watch, Sydnee noticed it was time to meet Giselle.

"Let's sit on this bench right here and eat, Charles," she suggested, scanning the crowd. They had agreed to meet at this corner.

Sydnee's stomach was tied in knots, and she could not eat. Being an adolescent, Charles devoured his breakfast quickly and was still hungry, so she gave him her brioche. Giselle was nowhere in sight. Sydnee looked at her watch. She was fifteen minutes late. Her hands started to perspire.

"Mademoiselle Sauveterre, how nice to see you," someone said.

Sydnee turned hoping to see Giselle, but it was an acquaintance from the milliner's shop with her elderly husband. They exchanged pleasantries and then strolled away. Sydnee looked around anxiously. Giselle would never come up if someone was speaking with her, but now the couple was gone and she still she was nowhere to be found.

Sydnee looked at Charles. "Are you still hungry?'

"A little," he replied.

"Of course you are," she said, handing him some money. "There is the baker again with his tray. Buy yourself something else."

He ran and leaned over the tray, trying to decide. Once more Sydnee scanned the crowd. Now Giselle was a half hour late. Sydnee feared the worst, wondering if someone had recognized her.

Thunder rumbled overhead, and she looked up. It had looked like rain all morning, and she was glad she remembered her umbrella. She opened it, resting it on her shoulder.

Charles returned and sat down next to her, eating another brioche. Suddenly there was a flash of lightning, more thunder and then a downpour. The market erupted into pandemonium as customers ran for cover, and vendors pulled their merchandise under the awnings. Sydnee looked around frantically for Giselle. They could not stand in the rain waiting for her any longer.

Sydnee took Charles by the arm, and they bolted for the carriage, splashing mud all over themselves as they ran. When they reached the carriage, Amaury was waiting for them under an umbrella. He opened the door and just as they were about to duck in someone said, "Mademoiselle Sauveterre?"

Sydnee whirled around. It was Giselle. She was dressed in dark cloak with a hood. "Why, Madame Montagne, how nice to see you again," she said, breathlessly.

Giselle was soaked. Rain was running down her face, and she was panting. Amaury gave her his umbrella and scrambled back up onto the driver's seat where he snapped open another umbrella.

As if she was bewitched, Giselle stared at Charles, and he looked back at her, wide-eyed. He looked confused.

Sydnee asked quickly, "You were shopping at market today?"

Dragging her eyes from Charles, Giselle murmured, "Y—yes."

"Oh, forgive me," Sydnee said. "Madame Montagne, allow me to introduce my young friend, Monsieur Saint-Yves." She put her hand on Charles' shoulder.

"How do you do?" he mumbled, but Giselle did not respond. She just continued to stare at him.

The rain poured all around them, drumming loudly on their umbrellas and thunder rumbled.

Giselle ran her eyes over the boy as if she was memorizing every inch of him. "How long are you staying?" she asked him at last.

Charles did not hear her. He could not understand why they were standing outside talking in the rain. Sydnee gave him a nudge. "Madame Montagne asked you how long are you visiting us."

"Oh, I leave tomorrow."

Giselle's eyes filled with tears. Clearing her throat and licking her lips, she murmured, "I hope—I hope you are happy."

Charles was starting to feel uncomfortable. He looked up at Sydnee for help. Sydnee too was starting to feel panicked, and she urged, "Madame Montagne, please come inside the carriage. The weather is too foul to be talking out here."

Giselle looked at the ground and shook her head slowly. Handing Sydnee the umbrella, she turned and walked away in the downpour, her shoulders hunched as if she was a very old woman.

Paralyzed with pity, Sydnee watched her, unsure whether to call her back or let her go. At last she said reluctantly, "Come Charles, get into the carriage."

All the way back to the town house, Sydnee sat rigidly in her seat. She tried to make small talk, but Charles did not want to converse.

After they changed out of their wet clothing, Tristan joined them, and they played cards by the fire the rest of the afternoon. Charles seemed to wake up at last, laughing and chattering once more, but Sydnee could not shake the melancholy.

When they left, she went straight up to her bed chamber and stared out the window at the pouring rain for a long time. It was early evening, but she pulled the covers back and crawled into bed. She wanted this day to end.

Chapter 26

Summer was approaching, and Sydnee was starting to worry. Already several cases of yellow fever had been reported, and they had done little work to the orphanage. Dr. Locke had been gone most of the spring to his estate in Natchez, so they had only visited the new house twice, and it was already the middle of May. Sydnee knew that once the epidemic started, Dr. Locke would be unavailable, so time was of the essence.

He came back in town the last week of May and sent her a note which said, "I commissioned someone to oversee renovation of the orphanage. They have money for supplies and will start tomorrow."

Sydnee breathed a sigh of relief. Something was happening at last. She had finished collecting donations from her friends before the summer exodus, so she could now turn her attention to purchasing furniture and supplies for housekeeping. Everything from bedding, to fabric for clothing, to cooking utensils was needed. Dr. Locke would provide medical necessities.

After a long day of making lists and placing orders, Sydnee decided to take Atlantis for a walk past the orphanage to see how the work was progressing. Only a few blocks from her home, the orphanage looked like any other town house except that it was larger than the other row houses around it. The cream-colored structure had faded, green shutters and a balcony encircling the second story. It was starting to show its age, but that is why they obtained it for such a good price. Some of the stucco was crumbling, and the interior had broken floor boards. There were holes in some of the walls, and it was in need of a good cleaning.

Sydnee cranked the large skeleton key stiffly around in the

lock and opened the front door. The moment she stepped inside she could see that no workmen had been there at all. She threw her head back and gasped with frustration. Walking outside, she sat down heavily on the front step with Atlantis beside her. The sun was starting to set, and she saw Fletcher approaching. He was walking slowly, and she knew that he was probably weary after a long day at the hospital. When he saw her sitting on the front step, he quickened his pace. With long strides he came up to her, frowning. "What is it?"

"They never came," she replied.

He stepped around her and went inside the house. When he came out again his expression was dark. "Damn it! I suspect we will never see them again *or* the money."

Sydnee looked at him out of the corner of her eye. He was staring straight ahead, his jaw clenched. He sat down next to her, and they were quiet for a long time, watching pedestrians and carriages go by.

At last Locke slapped his thighs, stood up and announced, "I will track the bastards down and get every penny out of them someday but for now--" He looked at Sydnee. "Have you ever cleaned a house or made repairs to anything?"

"No, I never get my hands dirty," she said, irritated.

"Well you are about to start. Roll up those lacy white sleeves and let's go."

They worked side by side until late that night, prioritizing repairs and listing supplies. The next day, when Fletcher was at the hospital, Sydnee and Marie started cleaning and taking deliveries. Sydnee went to the saw mill to order lumber and the general store for hardware.

When the sun began to set, Marie and Sydnee returned home. The heat and humidity was oppressive, and she could not stand to work any longer in her corset. She could not bend over without feeling light-headed, and on several occasions she thought she was going to faint. The moment Marie unlaced her, she could breathe again. She sponged herself off, changed into an old, loose-fitting gown, covered her hair with a fresh kerchief and headed back to the orphanage.

Locke was already working when she arrived. Dressed in old trousers, boots, and an old white linen shirt, he had his knee up on a saw horse, cutting a plank for the floor. He raised his eyebrows when she walked in. "Well lo and behold, the transformation."

"Marie sent supper," she said.

"Good, I'm hungry." He put his saw down, opened the basket and helped himself to a biscuit. "There is so much to be done but most importantly we should mend these holes in the floor, or I will be mending children."

"Agreed," Sydnee said, tying on an apron. "I will continue to clean and when you need help, call me."

Locke continued with the floor, but every time Sydnee passed by him, he caught her lavender scent, and it distracted him. He rolled his eyes, disgusted by his schoolboy reaction. Then when she bent over to clean, his eyes ran over her figure, and he found himself wondering what it would be like run his hands over her skin.

He told himself he needed to walk outside and dump a bucket of water over his head, but instead he watched her stretch and run her hands over the small of her back. He reminded himself that she was nothing more than a well-bred courtesan, the plaything of spoiled Southern gentry, but it was oddly sensual working side by side, alone in the house with this woman.

Sydnee turned and asked suddenly, "How is it you know how to do the work of a carpenter, Dr. Locke?"

He was kneeling down working on a baseboard, and he sat back on his heels. "My family owns three collieries. I worked one summer in a mine constructing shafts."

"But you did not go into the family business?"

"No, I did not. Coal mining exposed me to many things and one of them was inhumanity. After witnessing breathing problems, stunted growth in children and catastrophic accidents, I knew then that I had to be a physician."

"And your father? Was he angry you did not go into the business?"

"Ha!" he laughed. "He was. Especially when I demanded he improve working conditions at the mines. I told him while we slept on silk sheets, breathing clean country air, his workers slept in lice-ridden hovels and were suffocating to death."

"So you defied him and enrolled in medical school."

"I did. We always had an uneasy relationship. My oldest brother was the fair-haired child."

"And is your father still alive?"

"If you can call it that. He is very old, and his mind is now addled."

"And what of your family?" he asked.

"They are dead," Sydnee said, turning back to wash the windows.

*   *   *

The routine was the same for the next few days. Dr. Locke would work at the hospital during the day, and in the evening he would meet Sydnee to do repairs. Even though they were making progress on the house, he dreaded going there. He did not like the way this Sauveterre woman made him feel. His eyes followed her around the room too much, and he found himself making amateur mistakes when he worked. When she spoke to him, he found that he could not control his tongue. He either divulged too much information about himself, or he teased her awkwardly.

He believed there was no substance to these feelings and that she appealed only to his baser instincts, but when she swept past him, his chest tightened and something stirred within him that he had never felt before. It was disturbing and kept him awake at night, now when he needed sleep the most.

The final insult came late in the week when he was working on a broken door frame. "Come and hold this for me, will you?" he asked.

Sydnee rested her broom against the wall, walked over and put her arms up over her head to hold the frame as he nailed it. He stood facing her. Perspiration was drenching his shirt, and he was concentrating on his work when he accidentally pressed against her. He felt the soft cushion of her breasts, the contour

278

of her nipples and even the warmth of her skin. He jumped back and dropped the nail.

If Sydnee noticed his reaction, she did not show it and continued to hold the board in place, waiting patiently for him. He fumbled around, found another nail and completed the job with his heart hammering in his chest.

The incident plagued Locke all that night. Women were usually so heavily corseted and padded that, even when he embraced them, there was no sensuality. But this time there was only a thin barrier of fabric between his skin and hers. The sensation was so unexpected that it startled him. He was not only embarrassed but angry with himself. He sighed impatiently, vowing to snuff out the infatuation once and for all. This woman was the courtesan of Tristan Saint-Yves.

Sydnee was having an equally unnerving experience. To her, Fletcher Locke was insufferable. He was opinionated and proud, always deriding her lifestyle or goading her into an argument. When she spoke to him he avoided her eyes, and when she passed near him he withdrew. The night he was nailing a door frame over her head, he brushed against her and jumped away so quickly she thought he had been bitten by something.

She knew that she had been responsible for the mishap. She had inadvertently stepped closer to him without realizing it. Locke's musky scent mixed with the heat of his body was intoxicating, and it made the blood run hot in her veins.

All of these feelings confused her. She would be happy when they were done with repairs to the orphanage, and they could return to their own lives.

*   *   *

By the first of June the repairs were complete and just in time because Dr. Locke was starting to see an increase in yellow jack. It promised to be a particularly virulent year, the death toll was rising early.

Sydnee worked late every night furnishing the orphanage. Poydras House was filling up fast, and she knew that in no time there would be children coming to their orphanage. They could house forty children at their facility, but Sydnee could not do it alone. Dr. Locke had two young women lined up, ready to serve at a moment's notice, and Sydnee hired Marie's mother, Clemence Dugas. She would be their cook, and Sydnee had her stock the kitchen immediately. She salted meat, preserved fruit, and made all manner of foods that would keep for long periods of time.

Everything was falling into place and just in the nick of time. Late one night, there was a knock on the door, and it was a boy with a note from Dr. Locke. Poydras House was full and seven children needed beds. He would meet Sydnee shortly at the orphanage.

"Marie, I may need your help. Will you come?" asked Sydnee, as she wrapped a shawl around her shoulders.

"Yes, Mademoiselle Sydnee," the housekeeper responded. "My mother will be so happy to have children around her again."

Clemence Dugas was living full time at the orphanage.

"Atlantis come!" Sydnee called out in the courtyard. The dog came bounding up to her, eager for an outing. But when Vivian landed on her shoulder, Sydnee had to tell her to go back to her perch. "I'm sorry Vivian. You cannot accompany us tonight. You will scare the children." Sydnee knew Vivian would swoop down and herd them like cattle and that would terrify little ones. She assured her friend that she would make it up to her tomorrow with lots of dried grasshoppers. Vivian still pouted.

Once they arrived at the orphanage, they awakened Clemence. Instantly there was a flurry of activity as they made beds, toted water for baths, and started to make a meal. Just as Sydnee was about to start up the stairs with linen, the front door opened, and there stood Dr. Locke holding a baby wrapped in a blanket. Six children of all different ages and races clung to his pant legs, and the moment they stepped inside one of them retched all over Sydnee's shoes.

Her jaw dropped, and she looked up at Dr. Locke.

"Rotten luck," was his reply.

Clemence swept past Sydnee, took the baby from him and held out her hand to the orphans. "Welcome children, let's get you bathed."

The next few hours were spent washing and feeding the children. Dr. Locke went home after a half hour to catch a few precious hours of sleep before reporting back to the hospital again in the morning.

Clemence orchestrated everything. A free woman of color, she had given birth six times in her life, but only Marie had survived into adulthood. Clemence Dugas had first-hand knowledge of how quickly disease and accidents could take children, so youngsters were precious to her. She was a large woman with gray hair, a pronounced limp and boundless amounts of energy. She was definitely a woman in charge, as Marie had warned Sydnee, and she took over management of the orphanage with a fervor.

Sydnee was neither intimidated nor offended by Clemence's efficiency. She did not have the time to run the facility. She had her own full time job pandering to the wealthy to find and maintain benefactors for the facility. She was quick to remind Fletcher Locke of this fact when he sneered at her lifestyle as a hostess. At last he was limiting his remarks, knowing she was right.

The first part of June there was a steady flow of children coming into the orphanage, and they hired the two girls that Dr. Locke had recommended. Sydnee and Fletcher saw little of each other during this time, but they wrote letters daily. On one occasion though, they met with Mother Baptista for information on how to find safe placement for orphans. They were prepared to house these children on a temporary basis, but they could not take them long term. Every summer would bring more children, and they must find families as soon as possible.

Then in in the middle of the month everything changed. The flow of children stopped as abruptly as it started. Although Fletcher saw an increased death count from the fever, there were no orphans to house. The streets were empty of waifs.

Sydnee knew it had begun. The gangs were back.

"Is it at all possible that relatives are taking them in?" Sydnee asked Locke, late one night when they met at her town house to discuss the turn of events.

"Most of the forms say the deceased have no children."

"All the forms say that?"

"Yes, most of them. Now that I think about it that seems unusual."

"Is it possible you have a clerk or a nurse who is changing the paperwork now that the gangs are back and ready for business?"

Locke collapsed down into a chair and gasped. "I'm ashamed to say that I didn't think of that."

"You have not had a spare minute," she countered.

"Well," Locke said uncertainly. "I can change worker's access to the paperwork."

Sydnee sighed. "They would just find another way. We need to get up north and see for ourselves who is selling these children."

"And follow the trail of money."

"Indeed," said Sydnee.

It was difficult for Dr. Locke to get away, but it was imperative he go. The hospital did not like it, but if he waited until the fever season subsided, all the orphans would be whisked away and already sold up north. They would have to wait another year and by that time more children would be kidnapped. It was a difficult decision, but he took a leave of absence from the hospital.

Sydnee received a letter from Giselle's husband, Gerard Bazile, shortly after they decided to journey north. He had been to St. Louis recently and witnessed one of the orphan sales. He said it was similar to the selling of slaves, and they occurred frequently on Sunday afternoons. The children were displayed in the same atriums of hotels where they auctioned off slaves. The thugs were not allowed to sell the orphans, but they could demand recompense for food and transportation which was greatly inflated. They allowed customers to check their teeth, their bones, and the whites of their eyes. His observation was that the major market, particularly in St. Louis, was for older children who were purchased to help with the wagon trains going west or taken for farming, and the remainder of the youngsters, he suspected, were dumped back onto the street or in houses of ill repute. He admitted that a few people did seem sincerely interested in the adoption of children into their families but most were more interested in low cost labor. Monsieur Bazile added that these orphan sales were nothing new. They had been going on for years in his hometown of Nashville.

Sydnee sighed. They had to act quickly. When Dr. Locke told her that he booked their passage on a steamboat to St. Louis, she was relieved. She was not certain how they were going to ensnare these predators, but she would not stop until they were exposed.

*   *   *

A few days before they left for St. Louis, Fletcher had been seeing Renata Olmos. She was one of the few residents of Louisiana with money who did not leave every summer. She had contracted yellow fever as a child, and her risk of recurrence was slight.

Locke hoped to take the memory of her Creole heat and passion along with him as he traveled to the North Country. He wanted desperately to eliminate these thoughts of Sydnee, but the obsession with her continued to disrupt his life. During the day, work seemed to keep him occupied, but at night when he tried to sleep, his mind wandered back to Sydnee, her large almond-shaped eyes, her quiet voice, and her lithe figure. He tried working longer hours, hoping to fall into bed too exhausted to think of her, but he only succeeded in sleeping less. Occasionally, he took women to supper to distract himself, but this was not successful either.

One evening when he met D'anton for drinks and cigars, he found himself asking questions about Sydnee's relationship with Tristan, but D'anton would only tell him that Sydnee loved Tristan dearly.

These were words Locke did not want to hear. D'anton laughed at him and accused him of being another victim of Sydnee's charms, but this was an accusation Locke resented and denied vehemently.

Ironically it was Renata Olmos who offered the most information about Sydnee Sauveterre, and Fletcher had not even asked for it. The night before he left for St. Louis he dined alone with Renata at an intimate little establishment on Jackson Square. After supper, they sat at a café table outside the restaurant to watch people promenade. Fletcher was smoking, and Renata was sipping on crème de cassis.

The conversation started with his trip. "So you are actually going north with that creature?" Renata said in her thick Spanish accent, wrinkling her nose.

"It is business regarding the orphanage," he said wearily. He was too tired to argue with her and slumped back in his chair, trying to ignore her.

"Everyone is so infatuated with this base woman," she said. "You know nothing of her origins, do you?"

Fletcher was suddenly interested. "I know that she is a distant cousin of Saint-Yveses'."

Renata shrugged. "That may be, but her youth was spent in a backwoods shack on the Natchez Trace, ignorant and barefoot."

"Where did you hear this?" Fletcher asked, sitting up.

"One of my darkies told me. She was raised by an old slave who practiced Voodoo."

Locke thought back to the folk remedy Sydnee suggested years ago for the girl on the paddle wheeler.

Renata adjusted her dress around her knees and looked at Fletcher out of the corner of her eye. She was feeling smug. She was succeeding in enlightening him about her rival. "Everyone is so impressed with how she made herself such a great lady, but she has done nothing more than imitate that concubine, Ninon Picard."

Fletcher's eyes narrowed and he said, "Mademoiselle Sauveterre told me that Saint-Yves trusts her enough to allow her to travel north with me. I find that unusual. What is her relationship with him?"

This was the very question Renata wanted to hear. "Oh," she shrugged. "They are madly in love. No one can ever come between them, and Saint-Yves is aware of that fact. They have been lovers since they were children. They say she taught him everything, if you understand my meaning."

If Renata hoped to steal Locke's thoughts away from Sydnee that night, she failed miserably. He took her home early and walked the streets instead. There was so much he had to consider.

*   *   *

Fletcher and Sydnee left the next morning on *The Mississippi Empress,* a stern-wheeler of moderate size, but as luxurious as any of the grand steamboats in the company's fleet. Sydnee's room was smaller than her last voyage, but just as inviting. It had a light pink stripe wallpaper, white shutters on the windows and a light green spread on the bed. She sat down on the divan and looked around. She would never get used to the beauty of these graceful vessels with their elegant interiors and breathtaking vistas of the river.

After a light lunch of figs and cheese, Sydnee went out onto the deck to read under her parasol and appreciate the cool breeze that the riverboat created as it moved through the water. She enjoyed watching the river traffic go by, even though there was less this time of year because the river was more perilous. Nevertheless there was an endless parade of flat boats bulging with cargo, canoes, rafts and other paddle wheelers. She thought back to her first trip, years ago with Maxime when she traveled in the lower deck with the slaves and poor people. It was a world of difference between her voyage today and that experience so long ago.

Late in the afternoon, Fletcher came out on deck to smoke and noticed Sydnee. Sauntering over, he sat down. He had a book too.

"What are you reading?" he asked.

"*La Fausse Maîtresse,*" she said, flipping the book over so he could see the cover.

"Balzac," he read out loud. "I was trying to read *La Vendetta* in French but without much success. Do you ever read English literature?"

"I do," Sydnee replied.

"This is by a chap named Charles Dickens," he said, handing her his book. "He writes about the suffering of the poor, particularly children. You would like it.'

"I liked *Oliver Twist*. Is this his latest?"

"Yes, *Nicholas Nickleby*. It is an exposé of the English school system." He paused a moment and looked out over the river. Puffing on his cigar, he said, "If I can make a fraction of the impact this man has made on society, I would be satisfied."

The rest of the afternoon they read side by side, commenting on their books or pointing out interesting things on the river. It was peaceful sitting there, watching the water fowl and the shoreline.

"This must be such a change for you after England," Sydnee observed.

He nodded. "It is."

"I know you inherited your uncle's property in Natchez, but why have you not sold it and gone back home? Land there is at a premium."

"I *did* intend to sell it. I was only going to stay here one summer and then return to England."

"But you stayed. Why?" she asked.

"The same reason you stay, Mademoiselle Sydnee."

She wondered what he meant, and then looked away, chuckling. "Because we have nowhere else to go?"

He smiled and nodded, looking back out at the river. "Odd, isn't it? Home has a way of finding us. We don't find home."

*   *   *

The first few days flew by quickly for Sydnee and Fletcher. They were each busy with new friends they made on board the paddle wheeler. More conservative passengers avoided Sydnee, knowing her reputation as an *inamorata,* but the majority of them did not care, finding her a charming enigma.

Sydnee enjoyed the voyage. She visited with her new acquaintances, listened to musicians or sampled the dainties which were always being offered on silver trays. The food was delicious and plentiful, and Sydnee was alarmed when she noticed her corset feeling a bit tighter.

Fletcher made acquaintances on the riverboat as well. Two of the gentlemen who boarded in Baton Rouge were physicians, and they passed the time exchanging stories, smoking on deck or playing cards.

Sydnee and Fletcher informed everyone that they were on the trip to explore possible sites for orphanages along the Mississippi. Once in St. Louis, they would change their story and masquerade as a married couple interested in purchasing children to be domestics.

"I imagine there have been a few raised eyebrows that we are traveling together," said Fletcher one afternoon on deck. "I must apologize for that."

Sydnee smiled. "Dr. Locke, a woman in my position is used to raising eyebrows. Actually, there is a certain freedom in it. No one expects me to be of very high moral character anyway, so I do what I want."

He nodded. This was the first time Sydnee ever talked about herself, and it gave him a taste of something he wanted badly with her--intimacy.

Sydnee had been avoiding talking to him. She sensed an undercurrent of tension in him that seemed ready to ignite at any moment. His passion scared her, yet it attracted her at the same time. He was extremely unpredictable, and she knew this could spell trouble. One minute he was friendly and approachable, the next minute he was cynical and surly.

Every evening before bed, Sydnee walked out to the stern of the boat by the paddle wheel. There was something thrilling about the black water splashing off the paddles and the wild shore beyond filled with night creatures. The landscape smelled of fresh mint, the air was clear, and the stars were more brilliant than back in Louisiana where they were blurred with humidity. Sydnee noticed the spirits seemed closest to her when the skies were clear, and their voices were more distinct as if the clouds had been muffling their words. She gazed upward, dazzled by the panorama.

"Tomorrow we will be in St. Louis," someone said. It was

Locke. He was in evening dress, holding a glass of bourbon.

"Yes, I hope we are successful," she replied.

"It's nice out here at night," he said, looking around. "I like listening to the splashing of the paddle wheel. It's restful, like a waterfall."

They were quiet for a moment. He tipped back his head, finished off his whisky and set the glass down. Putting his elbows on the railing, he looked at Sydnee with a crooked smile. "Well, since we are going to be masquerading as a married couple tomorrow, I think we should know a little more about each other."

Sydnee raised her eyebrows. So Fletcher Locke was a bit tipsy tonight and flirting with her.

"What would you like to know, Dr. Locke?"

"Hmm, I have heard you come from humble beginnings. Is that true?"

"It is. I was raised at a stand on The Natchez Trace by my father and his slave, Margarite, who was like a mother to me."

"Is that where you learned your Voodoo remedies?"

"Yes, and they are very effective. You must learn to keep an open mind about them."

He shrugged. "I am learning. What are all of these Voodoo deities I hear about?"

"The Hoodoo spirits are blend of Voodoo and Catholic saints. It is a mixture of Christianity and ancient African beliefs. I am not ashamed of my background, Dr. Locke, but I am also prudent who I tell. Many people frown on our ways."

He nodded and then ran his eyes over her. The moonlight cast a faint glow on her face and reflected the champagne color of her gown.

"Now, it is my turn," Sydnee said, brushing a wisp of hair away from her face. She smiled and asked shyly, "Why have you never married?"

Fletcher laughed. "Well, you get right to the intimate details, don't you?" He sighed and shrugged. "No great mystery. I have never had time for a wife. I jumped right over the marrying part and went right to children. And will you remain unmarried and forever faithful to your foppish friend, Saint-Yves?"

The smile dropped from Sydnee's face, and Fletcher knew that he made a mistake. "I apologize," he said quickly. "The whisky has loosened my tongue."

"Dr. Locke, I accept your apology, but you lack manners. It is apparent that being busy is not the only reason you're unmarried. Good night."

Sydnee started to her room, but he stepped in front of her. She ran into him and then stepped back with surprise. He was almost a head taller than her. She could smell the liquor on his breath and feel the warmth of his skin.

"What do they tell you about us?" he demanded.

"Who?" she asked.

"The spirits. Your Hoodoo spirits."

"This is ridiculous," she replied, trying to step around him, but he caught her by the arms. His hands felt hot on her skin.

"Ask them about us. They know," he ordered. "But you won't like what you hear."

He reached up and lifted her chin, and kissed her. Slowly he moved his mouth over her lips and then arched her body back so far that her breasts pushed firmly into his chest. Suddenly she felt small, like a rag doll, and a rush of warmth flooded her.

"My God," he murmured as he ran his mouth down her neck, his whiskers grazing her skin. Sydnee felt the blood pulsing in her ears as she leaned back letting him run his lips over the tops of her breasts.

Suddenly she pushed him away. "Stop," she said.

He stepped back from her, looking confused.

"You have the wrong idea. I-I am faithful to Monsieur Saint-Yves," she said.

He frowned. She had been returning his passion. He had felt her heat. Nevertheless, her rejection stung him. He straightened his jacket and said, "Mademoiselle Sauveterre, I would actually have to *think* about you to have the wrong idea about you."

Sydnee felt of rush of anger at the insult. She went into her stateroom and slammed the door.

Chapter 27

Sydnee was furious with Locke. The man had not only stolen her peace of mind but her communication with the spirits. She feared listening to them, filled with trepidation about what they may say about him.

Sydnee was not only afraid of her infatuation for Fletcher but of the ramifications of a serious liaison. If she allowed herself to fall in love with this man, any man, she could compromise Tristan's secret relationship with D'anton. Creoles were tolerant of men having an *inamorata,* but men loving men was another story and extremely taboo. Tristan had Isabel for this masquerade, but they needed a home in which to rendezvous. She could not take a chance by allowing anyone else into this world which was balanced so precariously on secrets and trust.

The next morning *The Mississippi Empress* arrived in St. Louis. Sydnee was packing when there was a knock on her stateroom door. It was Locke. Although he was dressed in crisp, clean clothes, he looked as if he had slept little, with dark rings under his eyes. With a sheepish look, he held out a tussie-mussie of flowers for her.

"I am unfamiliar with the language of flowers," he said. "But I hope there is a flower in the group that denotes apology."

Sydnee gave him a crooked smile and took the bouquet of miniature blossoms that he had just purchased from a peddler onshore. "I am sure there is a hyacinth here somewhere. Thank you."

"Are you ready?" he asked. "I just had our luggage directed to the St. Louis Hotel. I booked adjoining rooms for us there. This way everyone thinks we are married, but we still have separate rooms."

"I too am prepared," she said, holding up her left hand. It

had a ring on it.

They walked down the landing stage of *The Mississippi Empress* arm in arm that sunny afternoon as if they were married. The St. Louis landing was alive with activity. It was loud and smelled of fish, wood smoke, and horse dung. Everywhere Sydnee looked, there were peddlers and draymen, slaves, sailors, and river rats.

Laclede's landing, once a small 18th Century French village, was now the bustling commercial center of the city of St. Louis, Missouri. Cobblestone streets, lined with warehouses and outfitters, all catered in some way to the frantic stampede of westward expansion that swept the country. Prospectors, immigrants, and charlatans pushed through the city, shoulder to shoulder, all in search of a better life west of the Mississippi.

Hawkers sang the praises of their oxen, or recently constructed "prairie schooners", enticing travelers to come take a look at their "exceptional" merchandise. Swindlers, gamblers, and miscreants lurked on every corner, competing and groveling for any opportunity to fleece the naive. Prostitutes lingered in every doorway, displaying their attributes.

Fletcher and Sydnee wound their way through this chaos, not speaking until they reached a quiet residential street. "Where are we going?" Sydnee asked.

"They said at the hotel that most of the sales are at a place on Clark Street."

"Look at this," Sydnee said, bending down and picking up a handbill. It was an advertisement for a slave sale at Murphy's Exchange on Clark Street followed by an orphan adoption meeting. "Every Sunday at the Exchange," she said. "Just like Giselle's husband said in his letter."

"Orphan sales *every* Sunday? That's a lot of children."

"They must be sweeping cities up and down the river gathering youngsters," Sydnee said. "I am guessing they are holding sales as far north as Dubuque. Remember Ruth? She escaped from Hannibal. I think this is a much larger operation than we realized."

Murphy's Exchange was only a few blocks away. It was a

massive domed structure, which was not only a hotel, but an auction house, a *maison de café* by day, and a drinking establishment by night.

Neither Sydnee nor Dr. Locke wanted to watch the slave auction and waited in a doorway nearby until they were finished. "There are many things I detest about England, but at least we don't enslave the African," he said as he watched slaves leave the Exchange with their masters.

Sydnee chuckled cynically. "That's right. Why bother when you have the Irish?"

Locke opened his mouth to argue, and then changed his mind.

At last it was time for the orphan sale, and they entered the building. People were pulling up in wagons, others came on foot. Most of them looked like farmers or settlers traveling west coming to find low cost labor. The men were in work boots, wore threadbare clothing and had tanned leathery skin. The women were equally weather-beaten. They wore shabby bonnets and had dingy shawls draped over their thin shoulders. There were a few smartly-dressed people who Sydnee thought were probably looking for servants. She hoped a few of these people were sincerely interested in welcoming an orphaned child into their home.

The atrium of Murphy's Exchange was a large pillared area with a chandelier overhead, stone floors and a faux marble platform suitable for displaying merchandise. A worker stepped up with a broom, swept the platform off quickly, and then nodded to a man in a dirty black suit coat standing in a doorway. The man in the suit coat had on the collar of a preacher, long shaggy side burns, and dirty unkempt hair.

He stepped up onto the platform and addressed the crowd in a drawl. "Good day, folks. My name is Brother Jackson and God bless ya'll for coming. In a moment you will witness God's finest creation--his children. These children have been dealt cruel blows and orphaned at tender ages in New Orleans, Baton Rouge, and Natchez."

Fletcher looked at Sydnee and whispered, "Multiple cities."

"They have lost their parents but escaped the ravages of disease themselves because of their fine constitutions. Nevertheless they have been rendered destitute and homeless, and I appeal to your hearts today to give them loving homes."

He swept his arm, and a chubby, middle-aged woman directed the orphans onto the platform. The tallest orphans came out first, mostly boys and girls around the age of eleven or twelve followed by younger children. Some of the older girls held the hands of toddlers or carried infants. In all, there were about sixty orphans. Their eyes looked too big for their faces because they were emaciated, and their clothes were hanging on them like scarecrows. It was obvious someone had washed their faces and hands before the sale, but their hair was dirty and matted.

"These poor unfortunates have come a long way to unite with you today. Granted they are thin but with good food and hard work they will be back to full health in a jiffy."

Then Brother Jackson put his hands up in a dramatic gesture. "Now, we ask nothing from you for these dear children of God. They are not for sale. The only recompense we ask is the cost for bringing them upriver to you today. In one easy transaction with my colleague in the back of the atrium, you may take them home. Now step right up and feel free to converse with our angels and examine them. You will find them in excellent health."

Sydnee and Fletcher watched people step up and quickly surround the older boys. They picked up their arms to examine their biceps, had them bend over and touch their toes or jump up and down. Many of the customers had children open their mouths to examine their teeth while others checked the whites of their eyes. Several women took infants into their arms and rocked them. Some customers talked with the girls, but they were not a popular commodity. It was the boys they wanted for labor on the wagon trains or farms.

"Have you noticed there are no mulattos or Negros in the group?" Fletcher muttered to Sydnee. "They don't want anyone accusing them of stealing slaves."

Customers were now taking children to the desk in the rear of the atrium to pay. Almost all of the boys over the age of eight were taken, most of the infants, and a few of the girls. As the crowd thinned out, Jackson stepped off the platform to pressure customers who had not yet made up their minds.

Sydnee felt queasy and stepped over to lean against a pillar. A humming started in her ears and her heart started to pound. She anticipated the sale would sicken her, but this seemed excessive. The humming became louder and louder. Suddenly, with a jolt, she realized that this was the droning that preceded a vision.

Panicking, she appealed to the spirits. *Not now! I must not attract attention. No, please!* Panting, she squeezed her eyes shut and rubbed her temples, trying to block the vision.

Fletcher noticed her, and in two steps he was upon her. "Are you ill? What is it?"

With that, Sydnee's head snapped forward, and her eyes opened. She realized the spirits had been trying to warn her about someone. She looked across the atrium and there he was, looking just like he had looked years ago on The Trace. It was the man who had come for a reading from Margarite in the shed that stormy night long ago when Sydnee was only fourteen. It was the man who Cumptico, the snake, had cornered. There was no mistaking him, tall and thin, rounded shoulders, heavy brow and sunken cheeks.

Sydnee stared at him with horror. Just like it was yesterday, he wore his threadbare greatcoat and heavy boots. His head was down, and his collar was up.

When Brother Jackson finished with one of the couples he started talking to him. They seemed to be conducting a transaction regarding the remaining children.

"What is it?" Fletcher asked.

She reached up and pushed the damp hair from her forehead. "Find out what that Jackson man is saying to that creature," she murmured.

He nodded, looking at the men. "Very well."

Fletcher strolled over casually. When he returned, he told

her that the man in the greatcoat was purchasing the remaining children.

"No," she gasped. "No, don't let him!" she blurted, taking his lapels.

"Quiet," he said, grabbing her arms and whisking her behind a pillar. Locke had never seen her so agitated. Sydnee's eyes were on fire, and she was shaking.

"Don't let him near those children. This man is evil, capable of anything. You must stop him!"

"Hush," he said. "Lower your voice."

Tears started to run down her cheeks.

"There, there," he murmured, pulling her into his arms. "Be still. Don't worry. I will take care of it."

As Sydnee buried her face in his jacket, Fletcher frowned. He had to think of something and think fast. Pulling out his handkerchief, he bent over, dried her tears and said, "Stay here."

Stepping onto the platform, he approached one of the girls and asked her to open her mouth. He looked down her throat, felt the glands in her neck and then approached the next child.

Brother Jackson came over. "Hello friend," he said to Locke. "Do you see someone who interests you?"

Locke ignored him. He went to the next child, looked down the boy's throat and felt his neck as well. He turned to Brother Jackson and said abruptly, "No one is taking any more orphans. These children have diphtheria."

Jackson's eyes grew large, and he barked, "Impossible! They are as healthy as horses. Just exactly who are you, sir?"

"I am a doctor, and these children are going to the hospital. They need to be quarantined immediately."

"How dare you!" Jackson roared. With a flourish, he signaled to the woman to start taking the children off the platform.

In a flash, Locke grabbed Jackson by the jacket and snarled, "I'll let the constables know that you are contributing to a contagion."

Jackson's eyes grew wide, and he babbled, "No, no, not necessary. Take them. Take them all. I have no use for sick children."

Dr. Locke stepped back. Never taking his eyes off Jackson, he motioned to Sydnee saying, "Mademoiselle, if you please!"

Sydnee scurried up.

"Take these children to the hospital," he said.

"Very well," she murmured and began to direct the children to come with her.

Locke dragged his eyes from Jackson's face and looked at the orphans. Instantly his demeanor softened. "You will be just fine," he said, going from one to the other. "Do not worry. We will take care of you."

When Locke turned around, Brother Jackson, and his assistants were darting out the door. The man who terrified Sydnee had disappeared as well.

"What the hell are we supposed to do with all these children?" Fletcher said to Sydnee. "There must be thirty of them."

Sydnee smiled, looking relieved. "I don't know Dr. Locke. This was your idea."

He mustered a smile, running his hand through his tangled hair. As quickly as possible they whisked the orphans out of The Exchange. With Sydnee in the back and Fletcher in the front they hustled the children down several blocks to a quiet street and stopped. "Where are we going?" Sydnee asked.

"I don't know. I can't think," Locke said. The toddler he had on his back was crying. Sydnee handed the child to an older girl. "We need to get them back to New Orleans somehow," he said, straightening his shoulders.

"A paddle wheeler?" she suggested.

"I haven't the fare for thirty children. Besides, once Jackson and his thugs see that we aren't at the hospital, the first place they'll look is the landing."

"I have a friend in Memphis who could help us. He could certainly lend us the fare for the rest of the way," Sydnee stated.

"Memphis is a long way!" Fletcher exclaimed, but after a moment's consideration, he sighed and said, "Very well, there is little choice. We will travel overland until we can hire a flat boat."

"It will be a long walk, but we can do it," Sydnee said. "People have walked The Trace for years with children."

"This is going to be difficult."

Sydnee put her fist to her lips, thinking. "We will need supplies. It is a stroke of luck that we have hundreds of outfitters here in St. Louis for overland travel."

"Until we get organized, we need to hide them somewhere," Fletcher said, looking up and down the block. "A warehouse or a school."

"What about a church?"

"That's it!"

After making a few inquiries, they found that they were not far from The Basilica of St. Louis, a large cathedral by the river with an imposing spire and four huge stone pillars at the entrance. Sydnee and Fletcher rushed the children inside and sat them down in the pews. After quieting them, Sydnee counted heads while Fletcher tended a skinned knee.

"I will go out to get the supplies we need for the journey," she said stepping up beside him.

He nodded, patted the boy on the head and stood up. He stuffed a wad of bills into her hand and added, "Hurry."

When Sydnee turned to go, he caught her arm and whispered, "Buy rifles for us."

She nodded and dashed out onto the street, afraid she would see the man from The Trace again, but he was nowhere in sight. Squaring her shoulders, she pushed on. It did not take long to find an outfitter and after inspecting several packages she bought fifteen knapsacks suitable for people traveling on foot, complete with supplies. She also purchased food and two rifles. Sydnee and a clerk from the outfitters hauled everything in a wagon and unloaded it outside the church.

"Has anyone been in the church?" she asked Fletcher as he helped her haul the packs inside.

He shook his head. "Only a few old ladies came in to light candles."

"Good," she said as she opened a large burlap bag and began to pass out bread, apples, and cheese to the orphans.

"Eat quickly now, children, and you must be quiet," she said.

Locke went outside to inspect the rifles and then left to make inquiries about trails to the south. It turned out there was only one which followed the Mississippi to St. Genevieve, and there they could hire a flatboat.

"It should be quiet along there," he said. "Most of the traffic is steam travel now on the river."

Fletcher took a bite of an apple and looked down at the children's feet. Many of them had no shoes. "Look there," he said with a scowl. "They cannot walk any distance barefoot."

Sydnee shook her head. "That's not true. If you have gone barefoot your whole life, shoes are worse. I walked to Natchez barefoot."

Fletcher stopped chewing and looked at her. There were so many things that he did not know or understand about Sydnee. "I must fetch my medical bag. Is there anything you need from the hotel?" he asked.

"No, leave my things. There were just a few useless gowns anyway. By the way, I just purchased some clothes for overland travel for all of us," she said, picking up one of the packs and pulling out some garments. "They are a bit worn but more suitable than what we are wearing now." She tossed him a pair of cotton duck trousers, a dark red shirt and a black vest.

Fletcher took the clothes and left. He changed at the hotel, settled the bill and returned to the church with his medical bag. Sydnee had changed by that time too. She was dressed in a faded, yellow print gown.

"Very well, let's go," Fletcher said. "We still have several hours of daylight left."

The surrounding area of St. Louis became rural quickly, and at last Sydnee and Fletcher could relax. They followed a wooded trail along the shore. They walked in a line with Fletcher in the front and Sydnee in the back. They would alternate with the older children carrying either packs or toddlers because no one could ever manage both. Just about everyone who could walk carried something.

Sydnee observed a few abandoned stands along the way, but the trail was nothing compared to the Natchez Trace. It was obvious this thoroughfare had not been as heavily traveled.

After several hours of walking they stopped to rest on the shore of the river in the breeze away from the bugs. Sydnee and Fletcher knew that the children were anxious to know where they were going. In their haste to escape St. Louis, there had been no time for explanations. Everyone sat down on the sand or rocks looking up expectantly at Fletcher and Sydnee while the older children kept an eye on the toddlers.

For the first time, Sydnee was able to look at each one of the orphans individually. There were thirty-two children in all. Eight of them were girls around the age eleven, and they were of great help. They carried the infants and toddlers, helped with food and with discipline. There was only one older boy in the group, about the age of twelve, who was passed over by the customers because he was blind in one eye and had a paralyzed right hand. The younger children were a mix of ages including two infants.

Fletcher and Sydnee called for everyone's attention. "Children, I want you to know that you are safe now," Fletcher announced. He paused while Sydnee translated into French. Some of the children spoke English, others did not. Fletcher had been learning French, but his skills were limited. "We are taking you home, and we will try to find someone kind to take care of you. We want you to be safe and well cared for. If you are wondering, my name is Dr. Locke, and this is Mademoiselle Sauveterre. Her name means 'safe haven'."

Sydnee looked at him with surprise.

He muttered, "You're not the only one who knows French."

It pleased her.

"We are going to be walking during the day," he continued. "And sleeping at night under the stars for many nights. But do not worry, you will always have enough to eat, and we will keep you safe."

Looking at Sydnee, he asked, "What do you want to say?"

"This will be a long journey, and we will eventually be taking a boat," she added. "You will get tired, but we all must stay strong and help each other."

The toddlers were growing restless and starting to squirm. "We will walk until it gets dark tonight and then camp outside," she said in closing.

Fletcher put his felt hat on, slung a rifle over his shoulder and picked up the heaviest pack as Sydnee dropped to the rear of the line to make sure there were no stragglers. One of the girls helped her strap a toddler onto her back with a large scarf, and Sydnee slung a rifle over her shoulder. She hunted only minimally on The Trace for rabbits and squirrels before her father lost the shotgun gambling, but she would not hesitate to use the weapon if necessary.

At sunset they stopped at a clearing by the river where, once again, the breeze would sweep the bugs away. They built a fire and cooked side pork, potatoes and some collard greens. They were amazed at how much the children ate.

"I hope they slow down or we will be boiling bark," Sydnee said.

"Right now they are panicked about food. When they see they are getting enough to eat regularly, they will slow down."

"Really?" she said, feeling relieved.

"Actually I'm not sure. Did I sound convincing?"

Sydnee rolled her eyes and laughed. "Let's pretend you know what you are talking about."

Before the sun set they tied their food in the trees and distributed bedrolls pairing older children with younger children for the night. Everyone was near the fire for safety and warmth, and they stretched two large tarps between trees for shelter in case it rained.

It was late before the last child was settled for the night. Sydnee sat down by the fire. She was still on edge even though she was exhausted. Fletcher came out of the shadows to join her. He took his hat off and sat down cross-legged beside her. "It's hard to believe all of this, isn't it?"

"My head is spinning. So much has happened."

They were silent for a moment watching the blaze send sparks high into the sky.

"You have more experience with overland travel than I," he said. "Given the distance, how many days walk is it to Cairo, if there is not a flatboat for hire in St. Genevieve?"

"With this group? Longer than normal. Probably five or six days."

Fletcher nodded. "Keep your rifle by your side all night. Do you know how to shoot?"

"Not really. I hunted a bit on The Trace, but I am not afraid to use it."

"Good, now get some rest," he said standing up stiffly and retiring to his bedroll.

*   *   *

The following morning after breakfast, they set out again promptly, and by late afternoon of the third day they were in St. Genevieve. They inquired about a flatboat, but there was nothing available, so they bought more food and pushed on for Cairo. They put as many miles behind them as possible, but it was slow going. They had to stop every half hour to have the children line up for a head count, to change rags on the bottoms of the infants, and allow the other children to go behind the trees to relieve themselves.

Fletcher was constantly attending to bruises, skinned knees or bee stings. A few of the children had persistent coughs which caused him to get up at night. At last he listened to the Hoodoo remedies that Sydnee suggested and started using them. She had a bag full of herbs, bark, and plants which she had collected along the trail, and he watched her grind powders and boil leaves to make healing teas and balms. Eventually he started doing it himself.

Although most of time the children trudged along in line obediently, sudden bursts of energy would flood them, and they would skip, run, or dash in and out of the brush playing tag. Boys frequently had sword fights with sticks, and on one occasion a child poked himself in the eye. Alarmed, Sydnee put her fingers to her lips to whistle for Fletcher. When he heard her, he ran back quickly. The child was unhurt and when Fletcher finished the examination, he looked at Sydnee and said, "Good lord, was that you who whistled?"

"Yes."

"The first lady of New Orleans," he chuckled, shaking his head. Fletcher picked up the boy and swung him back in line. "Now you behave yourself," he said to the child.

The little boy gave him a toothless grin.

Sydnee and Fletcher tried to remain tolerant of the children. The journey was arduous and sometimes there were arguments, but Fletcher and Sydnee knew they were all under great strain and needed to blow off steam, sometimes with fights, sometimes with play.

The next day they walked many miles and in the evening, they stopped at a stream on the other side of Perryville to bathe. Fletcher couldn't stand seeing so many dirty children. It had been a hot day, and everyone was sticky with perspiration.

It was all Sydnee could not to run and plunge into the water, drenching herself in the cool stream. Fletcher hung his rifle high in a tree and instructed the older children to undress the younger ones, wash them from head to toe and then scrub themselves and their clothing too.

Everyone was screaming, laughing and splashing in the cool water. After distributing soap, Sydnee stepped in, ankle deep, swinging a toddler back and forth between her knees. The little boy was laughing with delight as his feet dragged through the water. Several children plunged into the brook, others crossed the stream, balancing from one rock to the other. It was soothing to hear the rush of water and the laughter.

Fletcher sat down in the stream with an infant in his arms. He cupped water in his hand and drizzled it over the baby, and then gently eased the child down into the water, soaping its hair and body. The tiny girl smiled up at him, wiggling and kicking her chubby legs.

He looked across the stream at Sydnee. She had unpinned her hair and her tresses tumbled over her shoulders as she swung the toddler back and forth. When she looked up, Fletcher was staring at her.

The smile gradually dropped from her face, and she flushed. She drew up the corner of her mouth into a crooked smile and then looked away.

All afternoon the memory of Fletcher's look stayed with her, and when she thought of him she flooded with pleasure. The next day he locked eyes with her again, but this time she stared back until one of the children began tugging on her skirt, and she had to drag her eyes away.

Sydnee told herself that she could not fall in love with this man. There was too much at stake, but she knew she was fighting a losing battle.

Chapter 28

The next few days, it rained and everyone was miserable. The children whined and clung to Sydnee's skirts wanting to be carried, and Fletcher struggled desperately to keep the infants from getting chilled. Everyone was covered with mud from head to toe. They had to dry off their clothing by the fire before bed each night, and Sydnee strung rope between trees to dry bed rolls as well.

One evening when Sydnee was pulling the blankets from the line, she saw someone standing in the trees watching her. Instantly she recognized him, and her heart jumped into her throat. It was the man from The Trace. He glared at her, his eyes on fire and then disappeared into the shadows.

Paralyzed with fear, Sydnee was too stunned to scream and stared into the black depths of the woods. Swallowing hard, she looked around to see if anyone else had seen him, but everyone carried on as usual, chattering, arranging blankets, and changing clothes. She said nothing and returned to her work. She knew that she was tired and on edge, and she knew that it was improbable anyone had followed them this far down the Mississippi, but a deep fear nagged her. Had she really seen that monster, or was her mind playing tricks on her? Should she tell Fletcher, or would he put it down to fancy?

Rubbing her forehead, she told herself that she was delirious from fatigue and worry, but the rest of the night she slept little, constantly scanning the dark woods.

*   *   *

"Cairo? Oh, it's only a day from here," a grizzly traveler told Fletcher on the trail the next morning."

Sydnee sighed with relief. They were almost there. Although she now believed the man she had seen in the woods was a figment of her imagination, she welcomed a flatboat voyage that would whisk them quickly downriver.

Late in the morning, they decided to bathe the children again in a creek and wash all their muddy clothing. Fletcher and David, the oldest boy, sat on the shore of the stream, working on a project. They were whittling something, and Sydnee saw Fletcher unfold a large handkerchief from his pack.

After lunch, the group walked for several more hours following the river. The sun was shining again and drying the earth. Everyone's spirits were improving.

Late in the afternoon, Fletcher led them to a clearing by the Mississippi. He told them to rest because they would be pushing hard to get to Cairo by sunset. A breeze blew strongly off the river, and Sydnee brushed the hair from her face to watch an eagle coasting on the wind currents overhead.

Suddenly something white caught her eye. She put her hand up to shade her face and squinted. It was a kite, and Fletcher was running along the shore holding the string. It bobbed and stitched across the bright blue sky and when at last it was soaring high enough, he handed the string to David, who had been running along behind him. Since he only had the use of his left hand, Fletcher tied the string around his wrist, stepped back and let the boy fly the kite all by himself.

The children dashed up and crowded around David, begging for a turn. "No, not now, this is David's time," Fletcher said, holding them back. "When we get home I will take you all out, and you will have a turn."

David gazed up at the kite, grinning from ear to ear.

The children continued to whine and beg, so Sydnee told them firmly to pick berries until Dr. Locke said it was time to be on the road again.

At sunset, they arrived across the river from Cairo, Illinois, a small river town at the confluence of the Mississippi and Ohio rivers. On their side of the water there was only a small cluster of cabins with a few flatboats. Fletcher planned to approach someone in the morning about transportation.

That night, for the first time in a long time, Sydnee did not retire immediately. Instead she walked out to the fire to enjoy the quiet. Sitting down, she sighed and rolled her head back and forth to loosen the tight muscles in her neck, muscles that were sore from carrying packs and children.

"So tomorrow we travel by water," Fletcher said walking up and sitting down as well.

"You couldn't sleep either?" she asked.

"No, I was kept awake wondering if you know how to navigate a flatboat."

She smiled. "Walking I know, river boating I do not."

"Will you know if we are getting fleeced by a boatman?"

"Maybe," she replied. "What worries me is keeping thirty-one children from falling overboard."

Fletcher nodded. "Indeed, that will be a challenge. We will think of something. We always do." He stood up and threw another log onto the fire. It exploded into sparks and golden flames. "I have been meaning to apologize to you about something," he said.

Sydnee looked at him with surprise. "About what?"

"I have misjudged you. You are not--" and he hesitated. "You are not the spoiled, selfish woman I thought you were. In fact, I am the one who has been spoiled. I spent my entire youth oblivious to my good fortune, and my entire adult life scoffing at it. I condemned the privileged without first considering their character. I want to say thank you for changing my outlook."

He leaned over and kissed her gently. Three of the girls on bedrolls behind them, jerked blankets over their heads and squealed with laughter.

Fletcher sighed and said, "Good night, Mademoiselles!"

But there was no reply, only more giggling.

*   *   *

The next morning, in their usual formation, they walked down the hill to the cluster of shacks by the shore. A blowsy woman in a low cut gown, put her hand on her hip and watched the group parade down the slope. She was well past her prime, but she had a broad good-natured face and generous smile. "Will ya look at that!" she called to a man down by the river.

He straightened up and shaded his eyes. He was of short

stature, his frame was broad, and his arms were like sides of beef. He had black curly hair laced with gray which poked out of the top of his shirt.

"Well, I'll be goddamned," he muttered.

The group continued to wind their way down the hill. When they finally reached the shack, Locke took off his hat and introduced himself as the children gathered around the couple, staring up at them. Other residents of the hamlet stopped their chores to look at the unusual sight.

When Sydnee finally joined them, her jaw dropped. "Monsieur? Monsieur LaRoche?" she cried.

The man leaned forward and squinted at her.

"It's Sydnee Sauveterre," she said, touching her chest. "Victor Sauveterre's daughter."

"Huh?" he said, stepping back, looking her up and down. "You're all grown up!" he roared.

Sydnee smiled and nodded.

"How is it you are way up here and with all these pixies?" he said as he shook her hand.

"We are taking them south to find homes."

"On foot?"

"*Oui.*"

"You are very brave," he chuckled.

"But now we wish to hire a flatboat to carry us to Memphis. Do you know of anyone?"

He scratched his head and looked at Madame LaRoche who raised her eyebrows. "I have a flatboat," he said reluctantly. "But it is loaded with whisky and soon with produce."

"*If* the farmer ever arrives," his wife added.

"He is almost a week late," LaRoche agreed, scratching his jaw.

Fletcher jumped forward. "We are prepared to offer you double what you would charge for the transport of produce."

"Yes," LaRoche said, looking at the children. "I will charge you double most certainly. Because produce doesn't jump around, whine and cry. You think you can squeeze in around the whisky?"

Locke looked at the broadhorn and said, "We can."

"It's three days to Memphis," LaRoche warned.

"These children have endured much worse," Locke said. "But have you?"

LaRoche's stomach jumped with silent laughter. He spit his tobacco juice and held out his hand for Locke to shake. "Done."

Sydnee and Sapphire LaRoche went into the cabin to cook sausage, biscuits and gravy while Dr. Locke and the children helped load the flatboat.

While they were eating, Fletcher asked Sydnee, "How do you know this man?"

"John is a Kaintuck who used to transport goods from Nashville downriver to New Orleans," she said, wiping her mouth. "After unloading his goods, he would walk The Natchez Trace back to Nashville, and do it all over again. We would see him on the trail, two or three times a year. He comes from a long line of boatman. His grandfather was a voyageur in Canada."

LaRoche's craft was a mid-range flatboat. Constructed of green oak plank, it was fastened with wooden pins and caulked with pitch. Along the sides were sweeps for steering the craft. There was a pen for animal transport and a cabin for shelter. Sydnee and Fletcher planned on using these two structures to contain the small children. The cabin would be for sleeping, use of the pot and changing clothes. The pen would be for outside play and to contain the youngsters who could easily fall overboard. Just outside the cabin there was a sandbox fire pit for cooking, utensils, and a large cast iron pot for boiling water to wash dishes and do laundry.

Grady MacFarlane, LaRoche's steersman would man one of the sweeps. He was an elderly Scot with a wiry frame, and a long tangled beard. Locke and David would help steer the flatboat as well.

The group left early that afternoon. The children were difficult to contain because they were so excited to be on the river. "Why are they so excited?" Sydnee asked one of the older girls. "You came up here on the river, didn't you?"

"Yes, ma'am but we were locked down below with the

slaves," she said. "We never saw the light of day."

Sydnee frowned and nodded. Every day she found out a little bit more about the hardships these children had endured at the hands of their abductors, and it sickened her.

When the sun set, they steered the flatboat to shore and camped. Sydnee was not sure how the two men would respond to having that many children onboard, but so far they seemed amused.

Sydnee had good memories of John LaRoche, remembering him as being good-natured and generous. His companion, Grady MacFarlane seemed equally amiable.

"MacFarlane don't talk much," John said. "But he works like a dog. He's just like that boy of yours there," he said pointing to David who was holding a lantern for Grady as he repaired the boat.

Sydnee nodded. "You would never know he only has one hand and is blind in one eye."

"He's got gumption. That there is a nice boy."

The next day on the river, the children settled down at last. The novelty of flatboat travel was wearing off. Many of the orphans spent time sleeping and catching up on their rest after the long journey. Others spent quiet hours watching the river, fishing or listening to John LaRoche. He had hundreds of stories about his adventures on The Mississippi and The Trace. He had tales of river pirates, scalawags, and wild animals. Of all the children, David was the most attentive to these yarns. He seemed to idolize LaRoche, hanging onto every word and constantly asking him questions about navigating the Great River.

The leisure of riverboat travel over the three days also gave Dr. Locke time to examine the children thoroughly. At last he could attend to the illnesses that had plagued them from being starved and abused for so many weeks.

The weather could not have been better. The sun was out every day transforming the muddy Mississippi into a sparkling blue waterway alive with otters and heron, eagles and musk rats. There was also the traffic on the river to entertain them; canoes, keelboats, flatboats and an occasional paddle wheeler.

On the afternoon of the third day, a flatboat came up alongside them with a colorful flag and a boy on deck playing a fiddle. All the children strained to see. Upon closer inspection, Sydnee realized that it was a floating tavern and whore house. Women lounged on deck dressed in flashy, low-cut gowns with their skirts pulled up high above their knees. Three of the women wore nothing at all. Several burly river boatmen stood at the bar, lifting glasses and smoking cigars.

As the boat coasted up, the ladies called over to LaRoche, MacFarlane and Locke, "Hello boys!"

"Are you thirsty?" one of the girls asked.

"Looking for a little slap and tickle?" another one said.

"No thank you, ladies," LaRoche called back. "We have special cargo this time."

When the women saw the children, they screamed with delight at the children. "Oh, looky there! Can they be any more goddamned precious?"'

"Hi honey!" one cooed.

"I got a baby at home just like you!" another said.

LaRoche laughed and waved them on their way. "Some other time, ladies!"

"Ohhh," they said with pouting red lips. "See ya'll later, pumpkins."

The children stared at the whores wide-eyed as they coasted on ahead of them.

That night onshore after the children left to wash their supper dishes, MacFarlane asked LaRoche if they ever found the man who killed two of the whores from that flatboat a few days back.

Sydnee looked up with alarm. "What happened?"

"Well," said LaRoche. "The whores went ashore at Cairo to look for customers, and a john no one knew, bought two girls, took them into the caves and cut off--"

"LaRoche," MacFarlane muttered.

"Oh, beggin' your pardon, Miss Sydnee," LaRoche said. "Let's just say, he was cruel to 'em then killed them."

Sydnee's mouth went dry. "What did he look like?"

John shrugged. "No one got a good look at him, but he was tall and wore a greatcoat."

Paralyzed, Sydnee stared at him and then looked over at the fire.

The men discussed the murders a bit more and then stood up, taking their dishes over to the tub to be washed. Fletcher had been preparing balms and salves and missed the conversation. "We arrive in Memphis tomorrow," he announced loudly to the children. "Everyone off to bed."

He looked at Sydnee sharply. "What's on your mind?" he asked, sitting down beside her.

She blinked as if waking from a trance and looked at him. "I-I probably should tell you," she said, swallowing hard. "Several days back, I thought I was seeing things, but now I know the man from the orphan sale is following us."

Locke sat up straight. "What the hell are you talking about? That Jackson character, following us way down here?"

"No, the creature who wanted to buy the remainder of the orphans. I saw him in the woods a few nights ago."

"What!" he said, jumping to his feet. "Why didn't you tell me?"

"I didn't think you'd believe me."

"Sydnee, you need to trust me."

She nodded and rubbed her forehead. "The men just said that someone killed two whores in Cairo, someone who looked just like him."

Fletcher stared at her a moment absorbing the news and then looked at the fire, his jaw clenched. They sat in silence for a long time, both wrestling with the implications of someone stalking them.

At last, he took Sydnee's elbow and helped her up. "We are in good hands here tonight with LaRoche and MacFarlane, and tomorrow we will be in Memphis. Now try to get some rest."

Sydnee nodded and went to bed, but once again she slept poorly, scanning the dark woods all night, watching for the creature who she knew was watching them.

*   *   *

In the middle of the afternoon, they arrived in Memphis. They moored the flatboat and LaRoche jumped out, whistling for stevedores to come deliver the whisky to the proper warehouse. While they were unloading, Fletcher stayed on shore with the children while Sydnee dashed off into town to find Mortimer.

When she arrived at the livery, there was a sign saying it had moved to a different location, so she ran over to the new stable a few blocks away. It was a large two-story building, meticulously kept with a sign that said, 'Gish Livery' in fancy gold letters. It was apparent that Mortimer's business was thriving.

Sydnee found him immediately, and without a moment's hesitation, he agreed to loan them the fare for a paddle wheeler. He told her they could stay in the livery and had his stable hands start to clear out an area upstairs where the children could sleep.

When Sydnee returned to the landing, Fletcher was paying LaRoche and MacFarlane for delivering them safely to Memphis. The men said their goodbyes and started for the boat, but LaRoche stopped and turned around, taking his hat off.

"Mademoiselle Sydnee, Dr. Locke?"

"Yes, Monsieur LaRoche?"

"I-I was thinking--you know I think highly of your boy, David--"

They looked over at David who was leaning on a barrel, looking glum.

"Well, I—the Missus and me never had youngins' and--" he hesitated, his face flushed. "Ah--"

"Mr. LaRoche," Dr. Locke said. "Shall we ask David if he would like to go home with you?"

"That's it! That's just what I was tryin' to say."

Sydnee smiled.

They approached David, and he was frowning, shoving his toe around in the dirt.

"David," Fletcher said. "We want to ask you something. Would you like to go back upriver and live with Mr. LaRoche and his wife permanently?"

David looked up, his eyes wide. He looked from Locke to LaRoche and back again. "Can I?"

"Yes," said Dr. Locke. "But I'm afraid you can't take the kite."

David jumped up and said with a grin, "I don't want no kite."

LaRoche rumpled the boy's hair. "Come on then. We got work to do before we shove off."

The man nodded to Fletcher and Sydnee and said, "Grateful to ya."

As they started down the landing together, Sydnee heard LaRoche say to the boy, "Did I ever tell ya the one about the Chickasaw and the gator?"

*   *   *

That evening after settling the children in for the night in the livery, Sydnee and Fletcher met Mortimer downstairs to explain everything. Mortimer shook his head in dismay at the size of the abduction operation. He said that he recently learned the group had been banned from Memphis because they had been marketing kidnapped slaves along with the street urchins.

"Did they catch any of them?"

"Not a one," Mortimer said. "They slithered away like serpents."

After that Dr. Locke asked to be shown around the livery which pleased Mortimer immensely. It was apparent from the start that the two men had much in common. They compared notes on everything to do with medicine. They discussed diseases, treatments, and folk remedies. Even though their patients were different, their love of healing was the same.

Sydnee followed behind them and after an hour of listening, it became clear that she should simply retire for the evening. They had forgotten about her entirely. The men talked late into the night.

"When I first started out," Mortimer said, bending down to change a dressing on the leg of a mare. "Sydnee gave me remedies that she acquired on The Trace as a child. Most of them I use to this day, and they are very effective."

"Yes, I have much to learn about this Hoodoo," Fletcher said. "How long have you known Mademoiselle Sauveterre?"

"Since I was quite young."

Fletcher looked over his shoulder furtively. "Do you know her well?"

Mortimer stood up and looked at Fletcher through the strings of his hair. "Yes."

Locke swallowed hard and asked, "Is she—is she in love with this Saint-Yves?"

Mortimer studied him a moment and then squatted back down again. "She doesn't look at him the way she looks at you."

Locke's palms began to sweat with anticipation. What did he mean by that comment? He longed to ask Mortimer a thousand questions, but he did not dare. Just like D'anton, Mortimer had given him a glimpse inside the secret world of Sydnee Sauveterre and then slammed the door shut. So he swallowed his words and did not pry. He thanked Mortimer for his hospitality and said good night.

Mortimer watched Dr. Locke climb the stairs to bed. He liked this man and was sorry to see yet another victim of their charade. He wanted to tell him that he believed Sydnee was in love with him, but he could not. Mortimer knew that one day the grand masquerade would be over and everyone would know the truth about them all, but he was not about to hasten its coming.

*   *   *

Dr. Locke chose the most inexpensive paddle wheeler he could find the next morning. It was an old run-down boat used mainly for cargo but completely adequate for their purposes. They purchased a block of rooms and slept as many children per room as the steward would allow.

Even though the journey took several days, it passed quickly for everyone. After the hardships endured, the dirty second class riverboat seemed like the height of luxury.

"We have too many children for the orphanage, Sydnee," Dr. Locke said late one afternoon.

"I have been wondering about that as well," she replied.

"Tomorrow when we arrive in Natchez, I propose taking half the children to my home. It may take several months, but we need to set up an orphanage there too."

Sydnee dropped her eyes and nodded. Something inside of her tightened. "It is a good idea."

The rest of the day, Sydnee felt lost. A year ago, she would have put as much distance as possible between her and Fletcher Locke, but now the thought of being without him filled her with emptiness. Their arduous journey was coming to an end, and she realized she was more miserable than when they had started in St. Louis.

Her sleep was fitful that night. She refused to listen to the spirits, but they were omnipresent, whispering to her and nudging her to go to Fletcher. This time she believed common sense and logic were the best guides and must dictate her actions. She reminded herself that she enjoyed masquerading as Tristan's *inamorata,* and nothing was going to upset that arrangement. Indulging in a casual liaison with Locke must not happen. She may lose herself in a whirlwind of emotion and possibly fall in love with him, and then everyone's safety would be compromised. No, she would stand up straight, square her shoulders, and say goodbye to him in Natchez.

The next morning when the paddle wheeler edged up to the landing, Sydnee distracted herself by helping fifteen of the children get ready to go ashore. Fletcher was taking a variety of ages with him to Natchez, keeping as many children as possible together who had grown close during the journey.

When they informed the children that some were leaving, there were tears and protests, but Fletcher said when they were settled perhaps they could organize a visit to see each other again.

It was a somber moment when they walked down the landing stage to shore. The children were dirty and in ragged clothes carrying packs on their backs, tears streaking their faces. None of them were talking. Even the little ones were quiet. Several of them sucked their thumbs sensing something was wrong.

Fletcher placed his battered hat on his head and slung his rifle over his shoulder. He had not shaved in several days, and his face was sunburned. He picked up a toddler and took the hand of another who waddled down the landing stage beside him.

Sydnee and the children who remained on board lined up along the railing watching the group walk to shore. When the last child stepped on land, Fletcher turned around and pushed his hat back. He looked into Sydnee's eyes for a long time with an unspoken farewell, and then he turned and started up the hill with children tagging along behind him.

Sydnee watched until he was out of sight, a sickening ache clutching her stomach. At last the whistle blew, and the grimy old paddle wheeler backed out onto the Mississippi heading for New Orleans.

Chapter 29

Sydnee tried to return to her life in New Orleans, but she was fundamentally changed. She pushed thoughts of Locke to the back of her mind, but the emptiness inside her grew with each passing day. Weeks dragged on with only a few letters from him with news about the orphanage in a business-like tone. He was busy looking for a building, taking care of children and acquainting himself with Natchez society. She burned with jealousy to think that maybe some attractive, well-educated coquette had caught his eye.

More than ever Sydnee's life as hostess seemed shallow and superfluous. She was bored and unfulfilled, preferring the dirty, uncertain life on the trail to the heavily perfumed illusions of the salon. Although she knew that generating income for the children was of the utmost importance, she was tired of entertaining witty, sharp-tongued intellectuals.

Nevertheless, by September, it was becoming apparent that funds were depleting. It was time for a benefit. Sydnee made arrangements with a friend who had a plantation just outside of town to host an all-day affair. There would be a picnic in the afternoon and a ball in the evening. Everyone was returning to the city now, and Sydnee would promote it as the social event of the season, generating anticipation, curiosity and hefty donations.

She threw herself into planning the event. She made many trips out to the Fontaine plantation to discuss food, entertainment and a guest list. One evening when she returned, Marie met her at the door looking anxious. Sydnee was pulling off her gloves when the young woman said, "He was out there again today, Mademoiselle."

"Who?"

"The man. The man in the greatcoat," Marie said.

Sydnee thought she would faint. "What are you talking about?"

"I thought nothing of it the first time. He stood on the sidewalk petting Atlantis, but he came again today and brought a bone. I watched him from the window. He rubbed it all over his neck and then handed it to her."

Sydnee's jaw dropped. She darted to the window and looked outside. Even though the street was empty, she called Atlantis in, locked the doors and had Marie check the windows. "From now on Atlantis stays in the courtyard. This man is trying to gain her trust so he can--" and Sydnee checked herself. "He is not to be trusted."

"You know him?" Marie said, wide-eyed.

Sydnee nodded. "I met him once years ago."

"What is he up to?"

"That is what I would like to know."

A few days passed by, and they did not see the shadowy creature again, but Sydnee felt his presence. She could feel the hatred emanating from him, and her intuition told her that this man was familiar with the dark arts. She realized that is why his presence at the stand, so many years ago, had signaled immediate danger.

*   *   *

The last week of September arrived, and it was the morning of the benefit. It was a glorious day and a perfect temperature. Tristan and Sydnee took the landau out to the Fontaine plantation that morning, and they were in high spirits. "This is a wonderful idea," Tristan said to Sydnee.

"I hope everything goes well. Any word from Isabel?"

"She returns in a few days. She said that she is eating a bit more, but I am not sure I believe her," Tristan said.

Sydnee nodded, and they were silent for a while. Isabel's health was in decline again. She had gone to her parent's plantation with Delphine to recuperate for a few months.

At last, Tristan said with a smile, "You will never believe this, but D'anton will be out later with his wife."

"Paula Devereaux is actually coming to an affair that I host?" asked Sydnee.

Tristan laughed. "Hard to believe, isn't it? Her friends pressured her to come, and she yields only because it is for a good cause."

Sydnee rolled her eyes.

The landau pulled up to the front steps of the Fontaine house, a glorious plantation home. Lush sprawling lawns led down to a cargo landing on the Mississippi which had been transformed into a terrace for guests decorated with Chinese lanterns.

The wealthiest and most influential residents of New Orleans and the surrounding parishes began to arrive by midafternoon. Sydnee and Florence Fontaine had tables and chairs set up outside for the barbeque, or guests could take blankets and sit on the lawn. Slaves roasted pork and beef on a spit near the kitchen as freshly baked breads were pulled from the oven and salads prepared. Cool juleps stuffed with mint were served as well as gin, absinthe and iced tea.

Florence Fontaine was a consummate hostess. She was an attractive woman about Sydnee's age who was unflappable and poised. With a talent for making each guest feel completely at home, Madame Fontaine genuinely enjoyed entertaining.

After the picnic, guests lounged in the gardens or in the gazebos. Some couples took rowboats out onto the lake while others played lawn games. Early in the evening, everyone changed into formal attire for supper and when the sun set, the ball began. The Fontaines had a huge ballroom on the second floor with French doors that opened out onto a gallery that wrapped around the house. After dancing, guests could stroll out to enjoy the night air or walk down to watch the moonlight on the river.

Sydnee especially liked the landing by the river. It looked beautiful in the muted light of the lanterns, their orange glow reflecting in the water. A light breeze carried strains of music down to the river along with the scent of autumn flowers.

It was not until late in the evening that Sydnee danced with Tristan. She was wearing a copper-colored gown of embroidered silk, and her hair was dressed with pearl combs.

"You look beautiful tonight. I have not seen this gown before, have I?" he asked.

"No, you have not, thank you." He twirled her around in the waltz, and she asked, "Have you talked with Paula yet?"

"I have been putting it off."

"I spoke with her briefly, but she--" Sydnee broke off, looking suddenly over her shoulder.

"What is it?" Tristan asked.

"I thought I saw—oh, never mind."

On the next turn around the floor, Sydnee looked again and gasped. It was Fletcher Locke, dressed in formal attire, standing by the French doors speaking with a couple. When Tristan waltzed her again around the floor, she flashed Fletcher a dazzling smile.

He glared at her, took his drink and went outside.

When the waltz ended, Sydnee fought the impulse to chase after him. She was confused and angry. What was the problem? Why was she met with such animosity? They had parted on good terms in Natchez, and she had answered all of his letters. Sydnee ground her teeth. *The man is not even back an hour, and already he is upsetting me.*

She visited with a few other guests before walking out onto the terrace. It was getting late. There were few people outside, and thunder was rumbling in the distance. Following the lamp lit walkway down to the river, she found Fletcher alone on the landing, smoking and looking out at the water. In the dim light of the Chinese lanterns it was hard to see his expression, but Sydnee could feel his anger.

"I had no idea you were coming tonight," she said. Her mouth was dry, and she was on edge.

"Word travels far about Mademoiselle Sauveterre's soirees," he said sarcastically. He ran his eyes over her gown and then took a puff of his cigar. "You and Saint-Yves make a striking couple."

321

Sydnee realized at that moment that Fletcher had never seen her with Tristan before.

Ignoring his comment, she asked, "Are you staying long in New Orleans?"

"I leave tomorrow," he said flatly and then threw his cigar in the river.

Thunder rumbled again and Fletcher looked up at the sky. He took his dress coat from the railing and started to roll down his sleeves. "It's going to rain. I'm heading back to the city."

As he brushed past her, Sydnee said, "You are with children far too much, Dr. Locke. You are starting to act like one. Why exactly are you angry with me?"

In a flash he turned around and was upon her.

Startled, Sydnee stepped back. He put his hands on the railing on either side of her, locking her in. "I will not touch you," he growled. "I dare not, but tell me this, do you love him?"

He was pressing himself firmly against her, looking down into her eyes. "I want an answer."

Sydnee stared at him paralyzed and then murmured, "I do love him."

Fletcher blinked and then stepped back, stunned. He shook his head as if he just received a blow and then picked up his coat again, starting off the landing.

"But not the way I love you," Sydnee called.

He stopped with his back to her.

"He is my friend, just my friend," she continued. "But with you it is different. Somehow my soul, my very being is linked to you."

He turned around. "It is indeed," he murmured.

In three strides he was back to her, taking her face into his hands and pressing his lips onto her mouth roughly. Between kisses he would say, "I love you. I love you, Sydnee. I love you."

"And I love you," she murmured.

Lifting her off her feet, he kissed her again and again, turning her around while Sydnee ran her hands through his hair and over the muscles in his back. Setting her down gently, he ran his lips down her neck. Her skin smelled of lavender, and he pushed down the shoulders of her gown trying to reach her breasts.

Thunder cracked, and it started to pour. They looked up, rain pelting them in the face. Fletcher held his coat over Sydnee's head, and they ran up the lawn and around the house to Fletcher's landau which was sitting in the stable.

The driver opened an umbrella and handed it to Fletcher. "No, you keep it, Henry."

Sydnee asked, "Why don't you put up the top?"

"It won't go up," Fletcher said with a sheepish grin. "I gambled on good weather tonight and lost."

"At least it is a short ride," Sydnee laughed as she stepped into the carriage.

"And I have several blankets for shelter," he said, climbing in beside her.

He held an old quilt over their heads as they pulled out into the rain. With one arm propping the cover up, Fletcher told Henry to set off for New Orleans. They could hear the horse's hooves splashing the mud and the wheels turning on the wet road, but they were warm and dry in their little enclosure. Fletcher encircled Sydnee's waist and leaned forward kissing her. "We are like two children in our little tent," he said as the rain splashed all around them.

"Playing doctor," Sydnee whispered.

Fletcher raised his eyebrows. "Yes indeed," he said, bending her back onto the seat.

*   *   *

For three days, Sydnee and Fletcher were inseparable. All responsibilities were put on hold. Sydnee sent word to Marie that she was with Dr. Locke and that the date of her return home was undetermined. Fletcher was not due back to the hospital for several weeks so he was free of obligations as well.

"Please don't tell me you have to go back to the orphanage in Natchez soon," Sydnee mumbled, pulling the sheet up closely around them as they lounged in bed. She was resting on Fletcher's chest while he ran his hand through her hair.

"Not for a few days, but it doesn't matter because you are coming with me."

Sydnee propped herself up on one elbow, her hair spilling over her shoulders. "That is a wonderful idea! I can see your home, the new orphanage *and* the children."

"I won't have you away from me for a moment, Sydnee. I want you near me always."

She dropped back down and hugged his chest, burying her nose in his skin. Sydnee loved his scent. His skin was warm and smelled of fresh soap with a hint of musk.

"At last I feel safe again," she said. "It has been a very long time."

"Since Margarite?" he asked, stroking her hair again.

"Since Margarite."

Sydnee stood up, wrapped a blanket around her and walked to the window. Locke's house made her think of drawings she had seen of English manor houses. It had dark furniture fitted with brass fixtures, rich upholstery, heavy bedding, and plush carpets.

"It's going to be a beautiful day," she said, looking out at the cloudless sky.

Fletcher jumped out of bed, pulling on his trousers. "I think we should take Atlantis on a picnic. I'm sure she misses you."

"What a wonderful idea!" Sydnee said, whirling around.

"I will have Suzanne pack us a meal while you dress," he said. "And—ah, don't wear a corset."

Sydnee narrowed her eyes at him and then laughed. "It's time you meet Vivian too."

"Vivian? I don't know if I'm ready," he said. "It's a little like meeting a mother-in-law."

"Nonsense, she'll love you—I think." Sydnee said uncertainly.

*   *   *

When Sydnee and Fletcher stepped out into the courtyard of Sydnee's townhome, Atlantis bounded up to them, wagging her tail. Fletcher squatted down to pet her, and the dog immediately rolled over, presenting her stomach.

"Vivian?" Sydnee said, walking to her perch over Baloo's grave. "There is someone I want you to meet."

Fletcher raised an eyebrow, watching from the kitchen steps.

"Vivian," Sydnee called and raised her arm for the bird to fly down. The crow sat stubbornly in the tree, looking at them.

"Vivian, now!"

"I told you, Sydnee," Fletcher called.

"We are leaving on a picnic," Sydnee coaxed. "We will buy you grasshoppers."

Still the old crow would not move.

Sydnee sighed. "Very well. Miss all the fun," she snapped. Turning to Fletcher, she said, "I apologize. She is set in her ways."

As they left the courtyard, she whispered to Fletcher that Vivian would probably follow them, but the bird did not follow. She stayed in the tree the rest of the afternoon, pouting. She did *not* like Fletcher Locke.

They took Fletcher's two person gig down the River Road to a little lake on the property of a friend. Atlantis jumped out the moment they stopped and put her nose to the ground, ready to explore. It was a peaceful spot and private. Their only company was water fowl and frogs which delighted the dog.

Fletcher played fetch with Atlantis, throwing a stick repeatedly into the lake while Sydnee spread a blanket on the grass and set out the food. They ate under a weeping willow tree which reminded Sydnee of her hideaway when she was a child. The long green tendrils sheltered them like a rippling green curtain.

Sydnee told Fletcher many things about her childhood that afternoon, and he was eager to listen. He wanted to know everything about her, and she told him a great dealt, but it was apparent that there were many things she was hiding. He guessed that she had been treated cruelly by her father and that she harbored some secret about his death. She shared details about her life on The Trace, but when he asked her if he could see the stand one day, she said that she burned it down, offering no more information. *What had happened out there to her? What had been so hideous that she had been compelled to set fire to her home?*

Fletcher knew it would take time for Sydnee to tell him everything, and he was willing to wait, but he was not patient about her relationship with Saint-Yves. He burned with jealousy when he pictured her in that man's arms, but when he approached her about it, Sydnee refused to discuss the arrangement.

"Tell me about your life in England," Sydnee said, as she popped a pecan praline into her mouth. "Did you practice medicine there as well?"

"I did," Fletcher replied. He was stretched out on the grass with his head on his hand. "I worked with miners in Wales, and then I practiced in London at a hospital."

"Did you leave a woman behind?"

Fletcher's eyebrows shot up. "And how is that a fair question, when you tell me nothing of *your* love affair?"

Sydnee looked down. "That is true. I apologize."

Fletcher laughed and rolled over onto his back. "I will tell you. There have been women, but no one like you. You are a beautiful enigma, Mademoiselle Sauveterre, and when you finally decide to tell me the truth about your life and your loves, I will still love you."

He reached up and pulled her down into a kiss. Fletcher's desire for Sydnee was like nothing he had ever known. She could ignite him with a smile, a look or by simply brushing past him. He adored her lithe, wispy figure, her large eyes, and her lavender scent. He took her repeatedly throughout the day, each time feeling even closer and more connected to her than the time before.

Sydnee's feelings were the same. Fletcher stirred a fire in her that was beyond anything she ever imagined. When he was tender, she answered him with caresses. When he was intense with lust for her, she met him with passion. Yet, once their thirst for one another was quenched, it was the quiet moments in each other's arms that were truly satisfying to her.

"We must get back. It is twilight," Fletcher said, and he called to Atlantis.

"Yes, I will gather everything up."

It was a short drive back to town and when they arrived at Sydnee's home, Marie handed her a note. Sydnee read it quickly, the blood draining from her face. "It's from Tristan. His daughter is gravely ill. He knows of your skills with children, and he asks you to come quickly."

Fletcher clenched his jaw. He didn't like it, but he nodded and said, "Very well. I must return to the house to get my bag."

When they arrived at the Saint-Yves home, they were taken directly to the nursery. Tristan was pale with a look of panic in his eyes, "Thank you for coming Dr. Locke," he said, shaking Fletcher's hand. "This is my wife, Isabel."

Isabel did not get up from her chair and merely nodded.

Sydnee was startled at what she saw. Isabel looked like a phantom. Her face was colorless, her figure was skeletal, and her hair had grown thin falling in wisps around her face. Her skin was as dry as parchment, and her voice was weak. "Thank you, Dr. Locke," she whispered.

Fletcher walked over to Delphine's bed. The child was on her back, her eyes were closed, and her face was flushed. While he was examining her, Sydnee sat down and took Isabel's hand. "Isabel, you are ill too. What is it?"

Isabel shook her head. "It's nothing, just fatigue."

"I need cool cloths to bring the child's fever down," Locke stated.

Tristan ran out of the room as Dr. Locke took the covers off the little girl. Isabel strained to look at Delphine even though she could not stand up.

As Fletcher was rolling up his sleeves, he said, "Madame Saint-Yves, your daughter's lungs are clear, and her heart is sound so that is good news, but my concern right now is the fever."

He looked down at Sydnee holding Isabel's hand and then went back to Delphine immediately.

Tristan returned with cold water and towels. "Ice is on the way," he said.

"Good," said Locke.

They undressed the little girl and bathed her repeatedly in cold cloths.

Suddenly Isabel slumped forward, and Sydnee caught her. "Isabel!"

"I'm a little light-headed," she murmured.

"I will help you to your room," Sydnee said, taking her arm. Isabel was unsteady, but Sydnee was able to help her to her bed chamber. Isabel sank down onto the bed and said, "Sydnee, thank you. Thank you, my friend."

Sydnee covered her with a blanket and asked, "How long have you been sick?"

"I am not sick. I simply have no appetite." Isabel's eyes filled with tears. "That child keeps me alive, Sydnee. If something happens to her--"

"I know Isabel. I know," Sydnee murmured.

Isabel closed her eyes, and Sydnee sat by her side. She prayed fervently for the fever to break and at last Tristan opened the door. "It is down!" he announced. "The fever is down."

Isabel started to sob, and Sydnee's eyes filled with tears. "Is she out of danger?"

"Yes, Dr. Locke says she is out of danger."

Sydnee sighed deeply and sank back in her chair as Tristan hugged Isabel.

Fletcher was just snapping his bag shut when Tristan came back into Delphine's room. He handed Locke a generous sum and said, "How can I ever thank you? Madame Saint-Yves and I will be forever grateful."

"Watch her carefully and contact me if anything changes," Locke replied.

On their way home in the carriage, Fletcher and Sydnee were quiet. Both of them felt drained. Holding the reins loosely with his elbows on his knees, Fletcher said at last, "Sydnee, the health of that little girl does not worry me. It is the mother who is seriously ill. Do you know what ails her?"

Sydnee sighed. "I believe it is a sickness of the heart."

Locke frowned. "Why?"

Shaking her head, Sydnee shrugged slightly and turned away. Locke went back to brooding, watching his horse wind its way through the streets. The mystery seemed to be growing deeper and deeper for him. *What is the truth here? I saw the women holding hands tonight. Why is the wife friends with the mistress? What manner of illness plagues Madame Saint-Yves, and who is Tristan Saint-Yves really?*

Fletcher spent most of that night staring at the ceiling with his hands behind his head.

*   *   *

By the next day, Delphine had recovered completely. Locke examined her in the evening and found the little girl in excellent health, much to everyone's relief. When he returned home he said to Sydnee, "It is time we go to Natchez."

"I will speak with Tristan immediately," she replied.

"Will he be angry that you are traveling with me?"

"No," she said, shaking her head. "I will tell him it is a matter of business regarding the orphanage."

Flletcher nodded uncertainly.

The next day they boarded a riverboat and cruised up the Mississippi once more. When they arrived at Fletcher's estate, Sydnee fell in love with the house instantly. It was a white Italianate style structure with thin pillars and three white decorative arches over the first floor portico. There was lacy detail on the eaves, black shutters and a marble fountain near the entry. Fletcher sold the fields a year ago but retained the house, the sprawling lawns and gardens filled with magnolias, pecan trees, and topiaries.

The interior was equally as grand, although somewhat outdated. Fletcher's aunt and uncle decorated the plantation home twenty years earlier with quality furnishings, that were the height of fashion at the time, but today seemed passé. Sydnee chuckled to herself as she looked around. Fletcher would never notice such a thing or even care.

For several weeks they lived as a couple, waking late every morning, having coffee by the fountain, strolling in the gardens or reading. Sydnee loved watching the birds and realized she had been so caught up in the details of life that she had taken little notice of the things she loved.

The spirits were swirling all around her during this time, echoing the joy and ecstasy she felt at last. Sometimes, when she walked alone in the gardens, she would cup her hands upward to capture the white light flowing down to her from above.

Fletcher's experience was equally intense. All of his instincts were to shelter and protect his rare find. He was in awe that a woman of such exceptional quality would turn her eyes toward him and love him.

He watched Sydnee closely, memorizing everything about her. He loved the way she moved so gracefully and her peaceful demeanor. He was almost ashamed when passion flooded him violently, and he would pull her roughly into his arms. But she would accept him always, calming and diminishing his waves of desire.

Her second day in Natchez, Sydnee visited the new orphanage. It was a large structure in the middle of town, not far from the plantation home she approached for work when she was young. The house was originally in poor condition, but Fletcher renovated it quickly, having better luck hiring workers than he did in New Orleans.

The children were delighted to see Sydnee after so many months. They crowded around her, bidding for her attention. Several of the orphans were missing, and Fletcher told her that they found new homes. "I recently hired a woman who is a wonder," he explained. "She is efficient, has connections around Natchez, and a knack for finding safe and loving placements for the orphans."

"Well, they all look as if they have grown taller too," Sydnee said with amazement. "And I had no idea they had faces under all that dirt."

He laughed. "With rosy cheeks too."

The closer the time came for Fletcher to return to the hospital, the unhappier he felt. The thought of ending his blissful days with Sydnee and returning to everyday life seemed abhorrent. But most of all, he did not want her to return to life as Saint-Yves' mistress. He wrestled with the prospect, and even though it was impulsive and rash, he decided to ask her to marry him.

A week before they were scheduled to return to New Orleans, he took her for a walk in the gardens and proposed. Sydnee stared at him thunderstruck. She wanted to throw her arms around him and say yes, but she could not. Grappling with the uncertainties and secrets, she stood before him speechless. The very reason she avoided a liaison with him in the beginning was now before her once more.

Sydnee saw the hurt in Fletcher's eyes turn suddenly to anger. He jumped up and started to pace. "What is it?" he snarled between his teeth. "What *is* it that you are hiding?"

With clenched fists, he walked back and forth while Sydnee sat rigidly on the stone bench. "Your secrets will destroy us," he ranted. "I must know who you are. Do you think I'm stupid? I saw you comforting Madame Saint-Yves the night her child was ill. Do you think I didn't notice that we used the back entrance to their home? And what secret is killing her? There is no doubt this little intrigue of yours will end badly, Sydnee."

Rising to her feet slowly, Sydnee said, "I am willing to tell you everything, Fletcher, but I must speak with—with the others. These are not my secrets to divulge."

Fletcher studied her face and then nodded. "Very well, will you do it when we return to New Orleans?"

"Yes," she assured him.

There was little rest for either of them that night. When the sun rose, Sydnee heard Fletcher's deep regular breathing. She knew he was asleep. Silently she slipped out of bed, dressed, and left the house. She wrote a note explaining that earning his trust was so important that she could not wait until they returned to

New Orleans in a week. She must resolve it immediately or go mad. When they met again, she would have answers.

Sydnee walked to the landing and booked passage on the next riverboat to New Orleans. With an hour to wait before boarding, she decided to look around Natchez Under-the-Hill once more. It was still a loud and busy landing lined with dilapidated taverns and warehouses perched on pilings. She walked past the whorehouse where she met Maxime, watched flatboats unload, and draymen fetch cargo. There were few miscreants on the street at this hour, but occasionally a man would stumble out of a rundown hotel and spit or retch.

Suddenly Sydnee swung around into a doorway, pressing herself against the doorframe. She had just seen the creature step out of a whorehouse and start up the hill. With her heart in her throat, she watched the man in the greatcoat trudge up the road towards the residential district of town.

Every fiber of Sydnee's being was on alert. What was he doing here? Was he following her, or was it something to do with the abductions?

Wiping her hands on her dress, she put up her parasol to hide her face and started up the hill after him. The sun suddenly felt unbearably hot and her mouth parched. When he reached the summit, the man turned down one of the grandest streets in Natchez and continued walking. Sydnee followed him past huge plantation houses to the end of town. It was early, and the roads were quiet, so she was surprised when a carriage came down the road. The driver was traveling at a leisurely pace, and she could see the passenger inside. He was a well-dressed, elderly gentleman who looked vaguely familiar to her. Suddenly she realized with a jolt that it was Cuthbert Saint-Yves. She had forgotten he resided here with Tristan's mother and Charles. He had not seen her, nevertheless, she quickly covered her face with her parasol.

Sydnee watched the carriage roll down the road and stop alongside the man in the greatcoat. When the door opened and he crawled inside, Sydnee thought she would faint. *How can this be? How does Saint-Yves know this hideous beast?* Sydnee clawed at her corset, gasping for air. Staggering into the shade of a tree, she caught her breath as the carriage moved on down the road away from her.

Frantically she tried to gather her thoughts. What should she do? Her first impulse was to run back to Fletcher, but she realized that there was more to gain by returning to New Orleans to talk to Tristan. Her legs felt like butter, and her hands shook so violently that her parasol quivered. Nevertheless, she found the strength to return to the landing. Taking a deep breath, she reached inside her drawstring bag and handed the attendant her ticket, boarding the paddle wheeler. The first thing Sydnee did when they blew the whistle and pulled away from shore was to order two whiskies and swallow them one after the other.

Chapter 30

The riverboat arrived in New Orleans late that night. Without regard to the hour, Sydnee hired a hackney and went to see Tristan. She looked up and saw a light in his room, so she knocked loudly. He opened the window and leaned outside. "Sydnee, what on earth! I'm on my way down."

When he opened the door, she stepped inside and whispered, "No one is ill. Everyone is safe, but it is a matter which cannot wait."

Tristan was still dressed, and he picked up a candle ushering her into the library. Sydnee pulled off her wrap and threw it on a chair. He stood before her, looking at her anxiously.

"It is about your father. I believe he is in some way connected to the abduction and sale of orphans."

Tristan's jaw dropped. "What are you talking about? Father?"

"I was as stunned as you."

"Why?"

Sydnee explained everything and then asked, "Have you ever witnessed anything unusual in who he meets, in his accounts?"

Tristan walked to his desk, shaking his head. "I know a little about Father's finances, but of course, not everything. I was helping him a while back when he was having some financial difficulties, but he told me that he made some new investments and corrected the downturn."

"What year was that, Tristan?"

He frowned, thinking back. "It was the year we went to see Mortimer. That was--forty two."

"That was when the kidnappings started in New Orleans," Sydnee said.

Tristan gasped. "Are you saying that is how he pulled himself out of debt? By selling children?"

"Quite possibly," Sydnee replied.

Tristan paced back and forth, rubbing his forehead. "I detest my father, Sydnee but I don't think he is capable of such a thing."

"I understand Tristan, but can you look the other way?"

He stared at her and then said at last, "You're right. I will not rest until I know for certain. We must go to his office."

"You have keys?"

"Yes. Let's walk. If we take the carriage out, we will wake the household."

Cuthbert Saint-Yves' office was near Jackson Square, only a short distance from Tristan's home. Several planters, attorneys, and merchants had offices in the building. It was late, and the streets were deserted. When they arrived at the building, Tristan turned the large skeleton key in the lock, and it ground open. He held the lantern high as they walked down a corridor. Tristan opened another door, and they were in his father's office. He set the lantern down on the desk as Sydnee untied the drapes, letting them drop over the window.

Sitting down at his father's desk, he started opening drawers and taking out files. Sydnee pulled up a chair, and together they began the arduous task of examining documents. There were years of transactions, receipts, and miscellaneous ledgers. For hours they pored over records of slaves bought and sold at *Saint-Denis;* births, deaths, and illnesses, but there was never anything about the trafficking of orphans.

When they examined the last document, Tristan sat back and sighed. "Well this has told us nothing."

"Perhaps he did not keep files."

Tristan shook his head. "My father? Not likely. Let's try to get some sleep. We are exhausted. It is still several hours before sunrise, and I don't want Isabel to wake up and ask where I have been."

"You're right," Sydnee said.

They put the files away, locked up and started home. When they reached Sydnee's house, she told him to come in and have a drink.

"Good idea. I need something strong to help me sleep," Tristan said, as they walked in the door. Sydnee picked up her mail on the hall table and walked into the parlor with Tristan. She lit a lamp and poured them each a strong drink.

"Just what I need," Tristan said, taking a sip and slumping back into a chair while Sydnee opened her mail. She read and tossed several letters on the table, took a sip of bourbon and opened another letter.

"I have been wanting to ask you more about Fletcher Locke," Tristan said. "He seems--" He stopped mid-sentence, staring at Sydnee. "What is it?"

"It is--" she hesitated, reading the letter again. "Of all things, this is a letter from Madame Picard."

"What! After all of these years?"

She looked up from the letter and said, "It seems she knows of my work with kidnapped children. Gis--," Sydnee stopped. She almost said, "Giselle" and then caught herself. "—a friend told her." She continued, "Madame Picard believes Maxime's last words may help us find the ringleaders. She read Ninon's words to Tristan. "Maxime whispered several disjointed words to me before he died. For years, I did not understand the meaning. I thought he was delirious, but now I am not so sure. He mumbled, 'abduction', 'mask' and the book, '*La Vendetta.*'"

Tristan was stunned. "Is it possible he knew something about father, Sydnee? Maxime always did his bookkeeping for him."

"Maybe, but what does it mean? Mask? *La Vendetta?*"

"Isn't a mask sort of like a stencil?"

"Yes, you are right," Sydnee exclaimed, her eyes widening. "But the difference is with a mask you place it over a letter to read a hidden message. Is it possible there is a mask hidden somewhere that will reveal the truth when it is placed over certain documents? A mask which is hidden perhaps in a copy of *La Vendetta?*"

Emptying his glass, Tristan said, "Let's go."

They rushed back to the office and went through Cuthbert's bookcase, but there was no mask and no copy of *La Vendetta*.

"If it is hidden in a copy of a book, it is probably in Natchez," Tristan said, disheartened.

"Maybe Maxime was the one to hide it, but again, it is probably at the house in Natchez."

"Just a moment, Sydnee," Tristan said. "You found Maxime in the *garçonnière* the night he died. Could *he* have hidden the mask in there somewhere?"

"If he was strong enough," Sydnee said.

"We must look."

They rushed out into the night once more but this time to the abandoned property on Rue St. Louis. The *garçonnière* was a melancholy sight indeed. It had fallen completely into disrepair. The stucco was crumbling, the shutters were unhinged, and the weeds had taken over the courtyard. Rodents had infested the little building and much of the furniture had been stolen. It smelled musty, and they had to brush cobwebs away from their faces when they entered. They walked carefully across the floor because of rotten floor boards. A heavy layer of dust covered everything, and they could hear mice scurrying in the walls. When Tristan held the lantern up, Sydnee saw the bed where she had found Maxime.

"There are still books in the bookcase, Sydnee," Tristan exclaimed with relief. "I am amazed they are not gone."

Blowing the dust off the volumes, they started to scan the titles. Sydnee squatted down to look at the lower shelves. Suddenly she yanked a book out and opened it. The pages parted and there was an envelope. "Tristan," she said, standing up. Pulling out a heavy piece of paper, she unfolded it. It was a blank sheet with holes cut in it. "Look," she said, flipping over the book. The title was *La Vendetta*.

They looked at each other, their eyes wide.

Once more they dashed to the office, but this time the sun was rising, and the city was stirring. Vendors and farmers were winding through town with their wagons and pedestrians were stepping out of their homes, ready to start their day. One more time, Tristan and Sydnee entered Cuthbert St. Yves' office.

Tristan yanked open a drawer and said, "I noticed earlier that there were a few ledgers that looked different from the rest, perhaps--" and he opened one, placing the mask over different pages.

Sydnee held her breath.

Nothing. No coherent pattern emerged. They tried it on several more ledgers, and the words were just a random assortment of text. Tristan opened another one, put the mask down and like magic, names and dates appeared.

"Oh, *Mon Dieu*!" Sydnee gasped.

Document after document held lists of children bought and sold. There were over twenty years of records.

"It appears my father has been doing this for years, up and down the Mississippi Valley and as far east as Nashville."

"But not until 1842 in New Orleans. Why?"

Tristan shrugged. "Maybe too close to home, but when his finances took a downturn, he grew desperate and started here too."

They continued to examine the files. There were parent's names and how much they received for the sale of their children. Other ledgers recorded the names and addresses of the people who bought the children. There were even accounts of money paid to workers in the organization. Tristan and Sydnee scrutinized these lists closely but did not recognize any names.

"Oh, Sydnee," Tristan said, sitting back and sighing. "My father did this hideous thing, and unwittingly I benefited from it."

"We both did," she said, pulling the drape back and looking out. "We must go before someone sees us. The workday is starting."

They gathered everything up, opened the drapes again and left the office. When they reached Sydnee's front door, Tristan handed her the envelope with the mask. "We must keep these separate. You take the mask. I will give the ledgers to D'anton."

Sydnee nodded.

"My father is coming to New Orleans on the packet from Natchez tonight. I am going to confront him with everything."

"No, Tristan!" Sydnee gasped.

"I need to give him a chance to explain himself."

"Why? Why does he need a chance? The man is dangerous."

"I'm not afraid of him."

"I think you should be."

Tristan looked into Sydnee's eyes and then took her hand. "I will be fine."

Sydnee walked into the house and called Atlantis. Wearily she climbed the stairs to her bedroom with the dog by her side. She drew the drapes, locked the door and tried to sleep, but nightmares of the man in the greatcoat haunted her. Several times, she sat up in bed drenched in sweat and terrified.

She looked down at Atlantis, grateful the man had been unsuccessful in befriending her, but Sydnee was not naive. She knew that after Tristan confronted his father, that creature would be relentless in exacting his revenge.

*   *   *

At last Sydnee was able to sleep, and she did not wake until the sun was setting. She dressed making sure to put the mask deep inside her bodice. Marie had been working most of the day downstairs, and she gave Sydnee a cup of coffee, telling her that everything had been quiet while she was in Natchez.

Sydnee sat down in the dining room. The setting sun sent streaks of gold through the shutters and onto the carpet. She picked up the letter from Madame Picard. Without her they never would have traced the abductions to Cuthbert Saint-Yves. Once again this woman had changed her life.

As she bent over the hearth burning the letter, Sydnee wondered how she fared and if the pain from Maxime's passing had eased for her.

Suddenly she gasped, jumping up. *Is is possible?* She stared straight ahead, wild eyed. *What if Maxime had not contracted cholera? What if Cuthbert Saint-Yves had poisoned him for his discovery? The symptoms of cholera and poisoning are similar, vomiting, the flux and cramping.*

Sydnee put her fist to her lips. *That would explain Maxime's frantic last words to Ninon.*

"I must stop Tristan," she said out loud. "He cannot meet with that man."

*　　　　　*　　　　　*

"What is so important that it cannot wait until morning," Cuthbert Saint-Yves said to Tristan. He was sitting at his desk in his office, looking at Tristan with distain.

"Before I go to the authorities, Father," Tristan said, standing before him. "I want the satisfaction of telling you exactly what I know and how ashamed I am to have benefitted from such loathsome activity."

Cuthbert's eyes narrowed. "What are you babbling about?"

Tristan threw one of the ledgers down on his father's desk. Cuthbert grabbed it and opened it. "So?" he said impatiently. "These are slave ledgers."

"No, Father. These are not slave ledgers. These are records of the sales of children, children sold into bondage for labor and other unspeakable practices."

Cuthbert did not move, his eyes on his son.

Tristan continued, "I have your little instrument of intrigue as well, the mask. It is hidden away in a safe place separately from the documents."

Rising to his feet, Cuthbert's nostrils flared. He was furious and wanted nothing more than to place his hands around his son's neck and squeeze.

Tristan met his gaze head on.

Cuthbert's face looked gaunt and his cheeks sunken in the dim light. His eyes darted to the window. He saw movement outside. Turning back to Tristan, he sneered, "Beware my son. You are in over your head."

"It is too late for threats, Father."

"What is it you want?"

"I am not here to blackmail you," Tristan said. "The good Lord knows why I came here at all." He picked up the ledger and started for the door. But I have one more question. Is mother a party to this?"

His father chuckled cynically. "She has her alcohol and Charles. She cares not how I obtain my money."

Tristan opened the door.

"Beware," Cuthbert snarled. "I will unleash my wrath upon you."

"That is nothing new," Tristan replied, unconcerned. "You have been doing it for years."

*   *   *

Sydnee was too late. She watched from across the street as Tristan climbed into his carriage and left his father's office. She sighed. In her heart she knew Cuthbert Saint-Yves had poisoned Maxime. The man was capable of anything and murdering a slave was the least of his worries. She would see Tristan that afternoon at her townhome when he rendezvoused with D'anton, and at that time she would tell him about the possible murder.

D'anton was the first to arrive at Sydnee's house that afternoon. He was smartly dressed in a dark blue coat with grey trousers. Taking off his hat and dropping his cane in the rack, he asked, "What's wrong with you Sydnee? You look pale." He moved his hand up and cupped her cheek.

"Tristan and I have something to discuss with you," she replied.

When Tristan arrived, they told D'anton everything. "Here are the documents for you to lock in your office," Tristan said, handing D'anton the ledgers.

"You have the mask, Sydnee?" D'anton asked.

She nodded.

He stood up, reached in his pocket and took out a calling card. On the back he wrote a name. Handing it to Sydnee, he said, "This is the name of a judge in Natchez. Take the mask to him as soon as possible. We must keep these items far apart."

"I will go now and purchase a ticket on the next packet," Sydnee said, picking up her gloves and calling for Atlantis.

When Sydnee left, D'anton said, "You look weary, Tristan. Let's go upstairs and try to rest for a while."

Tristan nodded. "I don't believe I slept at all last night."

"You will need to be alert. Anything can happen," D'anton said as they climbed the stairs to their room.

Tristan fell asleep instantly, but D'anton lay on the bed staring at the ceiling with his hands behind his head. It was hard to absorb everything, and his mind was racing. He was so preoccupied with his thoughts that he did not hear his wife walk into the room, not until she gasped.

"What the hell!" he cried, bolting upright, trying to cover himself.

Paula Delacroix stood over him wide-eyed. A big-boned brunette, she towered over the bed.

Tristan woke up with a jolt, yanking the sheet up over his legs.

Lucy Franklin, a thin lipped busy-body, was standing behind Paula gawking at them.

"Oh!" cried Paula, putting a hanky to her face. "Oh, how could you, D'anton?" She dashed from the room and down the stairs with Lucy behind her.

"Oh, Mon Dieu!" exclaimed D'anton, jumping out of bed and grabbing his trousers. "I must stop them, or we are ruined."

Madly pulling on clothes, Tristan ran out after him and down the stairs too.

Neither one of them remembered to take Cuthbert Saint-Yves' ledgers.

*　　　　*　　　　*

When Sydnee arrived home, Marie was crying. "They pushed past me, Mademoiselle. I could not stop them!"

Grabbing Marie by the arms, Sydnee demanded, "Who? Who came in?"

"Monsieur Delacroix's wife and another woman. They went upstairs, and then I heard shouts. The women ran out and then the men after them. I rushed down to market, hoping to find you."

Sydnee covered her face with her hands and moaned. "It has happened," she mumbled. "It has finally happened. Oh, Marie, I know who is behind this."

News of the discovery was all over the city in a matter of hours. Pedestrians were walking past Sydnee's town house, pointing and shaking their heads.

Well after sunset, Sydnee went to see Tristan and Isabel. Atlantis came with her. After telling the dog to wait on the step, Sydnee was shown into the parlor by the Saint-Yveses' house slave.

Tristan gave Sydnee a weak smile when he walked into the room. "Delphine is fussy tonight, and Isabel is rocking her to sleep."

"I understand."

The fire was dying in the grate, and she noticed Tristan's hands shaking as he lit candles. When he looked at her, she saw dark rings under his eyes.

"Your father is responsible for this, Tristan. All it took was a simple note to Paula."

He nodded. "It is the perfect way to discredit me about the orphan sales. No one will believe a sodomite."

He started for a drink and then, with a jolt, he realized something. "Oh no! Sydnee, in my haste, I left the ledgers at your house!"

Sydnee's jaw dropped. "Where?"

"In the bedroom on the nightstand."

Sydnee stood up and took his arm. "I must go immediately, but listen to me. You and Isabel must flee. You need to escape to safety tonight. There is talk of imprisoning you."

He looked at her glassy-eyed.

"Tristan, they hang people for this!"

Blinking several times, he said, "Y-yes, but where do we go?"

"To Memphis, to Mortimer. The authorities will never pursue you upriver. They will be satisfied that you have left. There is boat at dawn. Take Isabel and Delphine with you."

Tristan ran his hands through his hair. "But what should I take? My business is here, our lives."

"That is all you need to take with you, your lives."

"What about you, Sydnee? Surely you are coming with us," he said.

She shook her head. "I will leave later. We cannot carry the ledgers and the mask together. I will meet you at the landing in the morning to give you the documents and to say goodbye. Now I must go."

Squeezing his hand, Sydnee ran out the door and back to her house. Taking the stairs two at a time, she dashed into the bedroom and hastily lit a candle to look for the ledgers. They were not on the nightstand. She flipped the bed linens back, looked under the bed and in the wardrobe. She opened drawers and then ran down to the parlor and the dining room to search. She called to Marie. The young woman had not seen them.

"Did you tell me that you left the house to look for me this afternoon?"

"Yes, Mademoiselle Sydnee. I went to the market."

Sydnee threw her head back and sighed. The house had been empty. Even Atlantis had been gone. The dog went with her to the landing when she purchased a ticket. Saint-Yves must have been watching the house and entered when no one was home to take the ledgers. She put her head in her hands and moaned.

"I am sorry, Mademoiselle Sydnee," Marie said.

Sydnee shook her head. "No, Marie. You have done nothing wrong."

Dismissing her, Sydnee, went to her bed chamber to think. Pacing, she tried to gather her thoughts. *Without the ledgers and the mask together, we are lost. There is absolutely no proof against Saint-Yves, and he has won.* She clenched her fists and growled. *But it cannot be. There must be a way.*

Sydnee realized suddenly that she was completely alone. Tristan and D'anton could no longer offer their help. She knew that she must go to Natchez immediately. She must get away from the dangers in this city, and once there, she would tell Fletcher everything. Together they would continue the fight.

The night seemed endless, and Sydnee slept little. Just before dawn she set out with Atlantis for the landing to find Tristan, Isabel and Delphine. The sun had not risen yet, and the streets were still quiet. The sound of her heels on the pavement was deafening and a heaviness was upon her.

As she approached the landing she noticed a crowd gathering at the end of the street in front of D'anton's office. Filthy gossips, she thought, taking pleasure in other's misfortune. But as she came closer she saw the look of concern on their faces. People were murmuring to each other and pointing.

"What is it?" she asked one of the men.

"The lawyer, Delacroix hanged himself last night."

Sydnee stood paralyzed, staring at the man.

"Madame?" the stranger said anxiously. "Madame, are you well?"

"H-how do you know?"

"They just brought him out. Someone found him hanging in his office."

Elbowing her way through the crowd, Sydnee asked a constable, "What's happened? I am a friend of Monsieur Delacroix."

He said, "I am sorry for your loss, madam," and pointed to the door. "They are about to put him in the hearse."

He helped Sydnee move through the crowd and just as she reached the front, she saw the undertaker reach down and fold back a sheet for Paula Delacroix to see the body.

It was indeed D'anton, his head rolled to one side limply. A sob escaped Sydnee, and she clutched her stomach. Paula said nothing. She just turned and walked away. The undertaker's assistants put D'anton's body in the hearse, shut the door and drove off.

Sydnee staggered to a tree and began to retch. Dark spirits swirled around her like a vicious maelstrom. There was ringing in her ears and darkness before her eyes. *I must not let them win. I cannot. This will not happen!*

Straightening up and opening her eyes, she saw Atlantis watching her anxiously. "It's all right, my friend," she murmured.

Taking a deep breath, Sydnee collected herself. She had to get to Tristan and Isabel before the boat left. Picking up her skirts, she ran toward the landing, clutching her side with Atlantis at her heels. She wanted nothing more than to tear her corset off and run full speed. Nevertheless, as difficult as it was, she reached the paddle wheeler without fainting.

The sun had just broken over the horizon, a blaze of angry red as passengers filed up the landing stage. Sydnee scanned the crowd and found the Saint-Yveses at the end of the line. Tristan was holding Delphine, and Isabel was standing beside him.

When Isabel saw Sydnee, a look of relief spread over her face. Sydnee dashed up and hugged them. "My friends, my dear friends," she said.

When she looked into Tristan's face, she knew that she could not tell him about D'anton's death. In his agony and despair she knew that he would stay in New Orleans to bury his friend, and it was far too dangerous.

"Bon voyage, my friends and be safe," Sydnee said.

"You will join us shortly?" Isabel asked.

"Indeed I will."

"Sydnee," Tristan said. "Did you bring the ledgers?"

She grimaced and hesitated.

"What is it?" he urged anxiously. "Tell me."

"They're gone."

"What!"

"I believe your father came to the house yesterday and took them."

"Oh, *Mon Dieu*," he gasped. "Are you certain? Did you look everywhere? I left them on the nightstand."

Sydnee nodded.

"Then it is over as soon as it starts," he said, shaking his head in disbelief. "Oh, Sydnee, what now?"

The whistle blew, and she pushed them toward the landing stage. "We will think of something, but you must go. There is too much danger here."

They moved back into line. Two gentlemen standing next to Tristan were smoking and gossiping. "They found his body at his office," one of them said.

"How did he do it?" the other man asked, taking a puff of his cigar and adjusting his gloves.

"Hanged."

"Hanged? What was his name again?"

"Delacroix. You know the one who they were about to arrest for--"

Sydnee looked sharply at Tristan hoping he had not heard, but it was too late.

"W-what did you say?" Tristan asked the men.

"You didn't hear about it, sir? A lawyer by the name of Delacroix killed himself last night. Just down that street over there."

"What!" Tristan cried, shaking his head with his mouth open. "No!"

The gentlemen looked at each other and edged away.

Delphine was watching her father, and suddenly burst into tears. She was terrified. Isabel took her immediately.

"It cannot be!" Isabel said. "Our D'anton."

Wild eyed, Tristan looked at Sydnee for an answer.

She murmured, "It's true. I just came from there."

Tristan clutched her arms. "But how do you know? Are you sure?"

"I saw him. I saw his body. He is gone, Tristan."

Delphine was shrieking, and passengers were turning to look at the uproar.

"I must go," he said.

"No Tristan!" Isabel exclaimed. "You cannot go back to the city. We must leave here."

Sydnee grabbed his arm. "There is nothing you can do."

"Are you mad, Sydnee? I must go to him!"

He yanked away, but Sydnee held her ground. "You will not go back," she ordered.

When he tried to move around her, she stepped in front of him. "You are getting on that boat," she said.

Tristan towered over her petite frame, but she did not move. Atlantis sat nearby watching anxiously. Tristan pushed Sydnee out of the way, and she grabbed him again.

With madness in his eyes, he raised his hand to strike her. "So you will hit me, Tristan? I will take it and stand firm. Get on that boat."

A sob escaped him, and he dropped his hand and then his head.

Isabel came forward and put her arm around him. Delphine stopped crying and touched her father. "Papa?" she said.

He looked up. "Papa is coming now," he murmured.

Wiping his face with the heels of his hands, he nodded to Isabel.

The whistle blew a final time, and Sydnee ran ahead to tell the steward that they were still coming.

The Saint-Yveses walked up the landing stage and onto the paddle wheeler headed for Memphis. The only one who waved goodbye to Sydnee was Delphine.

Chapter 31

Sydnee stepped off the landing stage into Natchez. It was good to be out of New Orleans and close to Fletcher once more. With him, she was safe, but when she arrived at the house he was gone. Her first thought was that they had crossed paths, and now he was in New Orleans, but his housekeeper said otherwise. "There was a change of plans, Mademoiselle Sauveterre. He had to go to Vicksburg yesterday to help with a breakout of fever."

Sydnee was sorely disappointed. "Did he say when he would be back?"

"No, Mademoiselle. Please come in by the fire. There is chill in the air. I will make you something to eat and prepare a room."

"Thank you, Questa," she said, pulling her gloves off. "Don't go to any trouble."

The woman built a fire, curtsied and left Sydnee alone in the parlor. A steady mist fell the rest of the evening which added to Sydnee's malaise. She grieved not only for D'anton but for the sake of Tristan. She knew that D'anton had been the great love of his life, and he would never fully recover.

She ate and retired early, hoping that when she awoke, Fletcher would be home. Although Questa made up a room for her, Sydnee slept in Fletcher's bed. It was comforting to have his scent all around her.

She rose late, the morning sun being obscured by gray clouds and rain again. When Sydnee reached for the mask to tuck it into her bodice, she hesitated. Even though the ledgers were in Saint-Yves' possession once more, the mask was still of importance, and she no longer felt comfortable carrying it. The judge in Natchez would not want it without access to the ledgers, so she decided to hide it somewhere at Fletcher's house.

Walking down to the library, she scanned his books. She remembered him saying once that he was reading *La Vendetta*, and she found it. She smiled when she opened it. His bookmark was only one quarter of the way through the book, and she deduced that reading in French proved too challenging for him. She slipped the mask inside the book and replaced it on the shelf.

After breakfast, she walked into town and posted a letter to Fletcher, telling him the location of the mask as well as a full explanation of her discoveries. The letter could only be picked up by him. This way if something happened to her, the mask was safe.

She took a deep breath, put her umbrella up and walked back home. She wished Atlantis was with her. The thought of Cuthbert Saint-Yves and the man in the greatcoat sent a shudder through her. She scanned the rainy streets of Natchez for the Saint-Yveses' carriage but saw nothing.

The rest of the afternoon, Sydnee sat by the fire in her day gown and slippers, reading. She was restless though, continually walking to the window looking for Fletcher. A sick feeling in the pit of her stomach accompanied her all day; and she knew it was not only anxiety, but grief. The grand masquerade had finally ended. It had protected and sheltered them for years, but inevitably it came crashing down around them.

Sunset came early and rather than bother Questa for food, Sydnee went to the kitchen to help herself to some soup. She brought it back to the parlor to sit in front of the fire.

Sydnee did not see the man in the greatcoat behind the door.

As she walked into the room, he lunged forward and clapped his hand over her mouth. Her bowl of soup crashed to the floor. Like a band of iron, he wrapped his arm around her waist and growled in her ear, "Cry for the servants and I will slit their throats."

Sydnee's terror was so great, she thought she would swoon. "Where is it?" he demanded removing his hand from her mouth. His arm was so tight around her that she could not speak. He groped her body for the envelope and when he found nothing, he took a handful of her hair, yanked her head back and held a gutting knife to her neck.

She took short gasps of air.

"Where *is* it?" he snarled.

"M-mailed it."

"To who?"

"A judge," she said, choking.

"We'll see if you're lying," he said in a hoarse voice.

He kicked the door aside and backed out of the room, dragging her with him. Looking up and down the hall, he pulled her through the kitchen and out to the carriage house. After gagging her and lashing her hands tightly, he put her on the bed of a utility wagon and threw a tarp over her.

With her heart beating madly, Sydnee listened to him hitch a horse. There was little doubt that he was taking her somewhere to either torture her or kill her. She closed her eyes and called on all the power of the spirits, "Lord God, Jesus protect me. All the angels and saints please shelter me from harm. Danbala, who delivered Margarite from this monster, please help me now!"

Sydnee waited in terror as he drove her down the streets of Natchez and out of town. Her hands grew numb, they were bound so tightly. She knew that he was taking her far out into the surrounding wilds of Mississippi probably onto The Trace where no one could hear her. She slipped into a swoon, and when she awoke she was unsure how far they traveled.

The wagon stopped with a jolt, and she heard the crunch of his feet. He flipped back the tarp and then rolled her over untying the rope on her hands and pulled off the gag.

Taking her arm, he yanked her off the wagon and dragged her into the brush. They were indeed on The Trace in a swampy area thick with vegetation. The ground was soggy and littered with fallen trees and moss-covered logs. A swamp lay nearby filled with cypress, tupelo, and standing water. In the gloom she saw a shack across the road.

Grabbing her from behind, the man put the gutting knife to her throat once more. "Where is it?" he said.

Sydnee tried to speak but she could not. Her terror was too great.

"Tell me or I will--" Suddenly there was a loud crack, and the man grunted. Releasing her, he stumbled backward and clutched his arm.

Sydnee saw Cuthbert Saint-Yves climb down from his horse, holding a gun. "So you'll blackmail me, Underwood?"

Wide-eyed, Sydnee backed away.

Saint-Yves continued, "You think I didn't see you listening outside my office window that night? I watched you, and when you stole the ledgers I knew what you intended. Now you will have the mask too."

"You smug bastard," Underwood growled, and he charged Saint-Yves.

The old man raised his gun, but it misfired. When Underwood slammed into him, the weapon fell to the ground, and the horse bolted. They locked together in a struggle. Underwood's coat was soaked with blood from the gunshot. They staggered down the embankment slogging through the mud, each trying to break free. Underwood was weakened from the wound, and when his grip slipped, Saint-Yves put his hands around his neck. The two men dropped into the water.

Sydnee backed up the embankment, watching, and then turned and ran. She ran down The Trace around the edge of the swamp and looked back. The two men were still wrestling in the water, splashing and kicking. She saw Saint-Yves try to stand, but Underwood pulled him back down and pushed his head under water.

Something along the shore caught Sydnee's eye, and she saw an alligator slip into the water. Across the swamp, another one crawled in as well.

Cuthbert broke free and staggered to his feet, drenched and covered with weeds. The men continued to struggle and then fell back into the water. All at once there were garbled screams, a heavy churning of water and then silence.

*　　　　*　　　　*

Sydnee ran and continued to run for what seemed like hours. Even though she knew the men were dead, she was still terrified and would not feel safe until she was inside Fletcher's home with the doors locked.

When she was too spent to run any longer, she staggered down the road by the light of a full moon. The rain had stopped, and the skies cleared. She was not afraid of the The Trace after dark. It would always be her home.

The spirits accompanied her all the way back to Natchez, urging her forward and guarding her. She was deeply thankful to them for rescuing her and promised good works and offerings as gratitude.

It was late by the time she stumbled up to Fletcher's house. She knew that at this hour it would be locked, so she went around to the kitchen where she saw a light.

"Mademoiselle Sauveterre!" Questa exclaimed when she opened the door. The servant was banking the fire for the night. "What happened?"

Sydnee told her nothing, saying only that she visited someone on The Trace and had gotten lost. Questa brought water, and after bathing, Sydnee dropped into Fletcher's bed, sick with exhaustion.

She slept late into the next day, and when she opened her eyes Fletcher was standing over her. He sat down on the bed and put his hand to her cheek. "What is it? Are you ill? I have been so worried."

Sydnee sat up and hugged his neck, overjoyed to see him.

"When did you return?" she asked.

"Early this morning. Questa said that you were lost on The Trace, and I knew that was a lie. What happened?"

She pushed the hair from her face, sat cross-legged on the bed and told him everything. Fletcher listened wide-eyed. In less than an hour, he learned about Sydnee's relationship with Tristan, the love affair between Mortimer and Isabel and the death of D'anton. When she told him about Cuthbert Saint-Yves and Underwood, he grew pale. Overwhelmed with all the information, he would pace and then sit back down, then pace again. He shook his head in disbelief and would gasp with astonishment.

"All this happened in just a few days, Sydnee. I am in shock." He looked her over anxiously. "Have you been hurt in anyway?"

"Mosquito bites, and that's all," she said with relief.

Fletcher was dumbfounded. Standing up, he went to the window. "Tomorrow I will retrieve the horse and wagon, if they haven't been stolen."

"I want to go with you," Sydnee said.

"No, you should not go back there."

"That shack on The Trace was probably Underwood's hideout," she explained. "I believe he may have taken the ledgers there. Even though the ringleaders are dead, I want those ledgers, and I want the authorities to know of the operation so others like Brother Jackson cannot resurrect it."

Fletcher sighed. "Very well."

They pored over and over the events throughout the day and slept in each other's arms that night. Fletcher could at last put his mind to rest about Sydnee's devotion to him, and Sydnee felt secure once more.

The next morning they rode out to where Underwood had taken Sydnee and found the horse grazing along the road still hitched to the wagon. "I am surprised she wasn't stolen or attacked by a panther," Fletcher said, dismounting.

"I am surprised too," Sydnee said, looking around the area with a frown.

"Where were they fighting, Sydnee?"

She pointed to the edge of the swamp. Fletcher walked over and looked at the water. There was no trace of clothing and no signs of a struggle. He murmured, "Gone, just like that. Good riddance."

Sydnee dismounted. "I am going into the shack."

"Are you sure?"

She swallowed hard and nodded.

It was a one room broken down hovel which was filthy, smelled of urine, and unwashed bedding. Sydnee put her sleeve to her nose and scanned the room. There was just a rickety bed, table, one chair, and a few cooking implements.

Fletcher put gloves on. He pulled the mattress up and looked underneath it, opened a dusty cupboard and then scanned the rafters. Sydnee pulled up some loose floor boards, but there was nothing under them but damp earth.

They walked around the outside of the house which was overgrown with weeds, and Fletcher looked down into an old dried up well. He pulled the bucket up and inside was a burlap bag. "Sydnee!" he called.

She ran over as he opened it. The ledgers were inside. "Oh!" she gasped with relief. "Thank God!"

"Let's go home and look at these things."

They took their midday meal to the library, pulled the mask out of the book and started looking at dates and names. "I recognize some of these names," Fletcher said. "Relatives have contacted the hospital looking for these children. With any luck we can reunite them."

For hours they examined the documents and then in the middle of the afternoon, Sydnee thought of something. Saying nothing to Fletcher, she grabbed the earliest ledger that they had recovered, from years ago. Placing the mask over several pages, she scanned the entries. Her palms were sweating, and her heart was pounding. She stopped at the bottom of one of the pages. It read,

Newborn, Victor Sauveterre, Natchez Trace, July 1831.

Sydnee stared at the page. Her baby had not died at birth. Holding her breath, she read the next line,

Purchased, Denis and Magali Germain, St. Louis, Missouri, August 1831

When she looked up, Fletcher was watching her. "What is it?"

With clenched fists, she walked to the window. Now she knew that her father had sold her baby to the man in the greatcoat. Sometime that night when she had given birth, he had sold her child.

Sydnee turned to Fletcher and said, "I have something else to tell you."

*   *   *

Later that day they turned the mask and ledgers over to the authorities. Sydnee told them of the struggle and the alligator attack, and after hours of questioning, they allowed her to go. The constables said they would inform Madame Saint-Yves of the death of her husband and begin monitoring the streets for abduction operations.

"Shall I purchase our tickets for Memphis?" Fletcher asked Sydnee.

"Yes, I know Tristan, Isabel and Mortimer are anxious for information," she said.

"And you are anxious to find your child."

Sydnee bit her lip. "Yes, I am anxious indeed," she said.

"This morning I was combing the ledgers, and four children that were abducted this past year were purchased by people in the St. Louis area," he added.

"And their relatives are looking for them?"

"Yes, so I will search for them too."

They arrived in Memphis a week later and checked into the hotel where Tristan and Isabel were staying. It was a reunion filled with tears and sorrow but also of hope.

They decided they would discuss everything over supper in Mortimer's lodgings that night. He was still living over the livery, but his furnishings were greatly improved. In the past few months, he had added new furniture, a plush Turkish carpet, and countless leather-bound volumes to the bookcases lining the walls. It warmed Sydnee the moment she stepped into the room.

They ate first, and Tristan and Isabel made small talk with Fletcher trying to make him feel comfortable and welcome. Although they were gracious and warm, Sydnee could see they were on edge. They were anxious for news from New Orleans.

After Delphine went to bed, they gathered around the fire. Isabel sat with her hand on Mortimer's arm, looking stronger than she had in years with Mortimer stealing looks at her as if he was an infatuated schoolboy. Sydnee knew their love would never waiver, and she was glad, but Tristan had changed. He looked drawn, and his eyes were no longer the brilliant blue she loved. Now they were a lifeless gray. He had aged, and Sydnee knew that he would never fully recover from D'anton's death. She dreaded telling him about his father's demise, but when the time came, he showed no sign of emotion. "I am sorry I brought you more distressing news, Tristan," she said.

"Don't be sorry, Sydnee. He was never a father to me. I can honestly say that I am relieved he is gone."

"And what now?"

He sighed and sat back in his chair. "Well, I will have to meet with mother to discuss selling our properties and holdings in Louisiana and Mississippi. I assume she will not want to stay in the area.

"Have you decided yet where you will live?" Mortimer asked.

"As you know, I have been giving it a lot of thought," Tristan said. "And for now, I will travel and possibly get involved in some new business ventures. I believe rail transportation is the future of this country, and I am going to invest heavily in it." Then Tristan looked at Sydnee. "Just as steamboats put an end to The Natchez Trace, so too will railroads be the end of the paddle wheeler. I plan on being the first to make money on it."

"But you must not stray too far from Delphine," Isabel added.

"I could never stay away from her or from Charles. I think I will start out in Saratoga. If mother refuses to come with me, that is her choice, but I will bring Charles. He is of age and ready to spread his wings."

"And we too are spreading our wings," Isabel said, smiling. "We are moving to St. Louis."

Sydnee's eyebrows shot up. "Leaving here?"

"Oh no," Mortimer said. "I am opening another livery up there. The city is bursting at the seams, and needs care for all the horses and oxen going west."

"And it is a town with all sorts of people coming and going all the time," Isabel said. "I will live there as Mortimer's wife, and no one will care. There will be no more insular Creole society choking us to death. Now more than ever I realize that we must cling to happiness while we can."

Everyone was quiet for a moment thinking of D'anton.

"And what of you, Sydnee?" Isabel asked.

"Oh, my life is still in New Orleans," she said looking at Fletcher. "But first I must pay a visit to St. Louis."

*   *   *

A few days before they left Memphis, Sydnee posted a letter to Giselle telling her about Tristan's plan for Charles, the discovery of Cuthbert Saint-Yves' involvement in orphan sales, and his demise. She also told her she would be visiting St. Louis soon, where she was staying, and her reason for coming. "Just like you, I am searching for a child. Now more than ever, I understand the grief and pain you have endured over these years."

It was early November when they arrived in St. Louis and gray clouds hung over the city. After settling into the hotel, Sydnee put on her blue plaid dress and navy jacket with braid.

"You really think it is cold?" asked Fletcher. "You would not do well in England."

"I think it would be very difficult for me," she admitted. "I am born and bred a Southern girl."

"Are we ready?" he said, offering his arm, and they started for the courthouse to search public records. Sydnee was anxious about what they might find and wondered how she would feel if she found her daughter after so many years. She realized that she didn't even know her name.

It did not take long to locate the Germains. They owned a home in a respectable neighborhood of St. Louis, not far from the city center. "Well?" Fletcher said. "What would you like to do?"

"Let's walk past the house," Sydnee replied, swallowing hard. "We will take a look."

It was a short walk along the river and past the cathedral. They wound through the streets looking at addresses. Sydnee had been too distracted the first time they were here to notice the houses were very different from New Orleans. They were constructed of wood and did not have enclosed courtyards, galleries or balconies. Most of them were flat-faced dwellings with shingle siding and dark shutters. Although they looked new and were very practical, she thought they were plain and lacked style.

Fletcher stopped in front of one of the houses. "Here it is, Sydnee."

The Germain home was a tidy wood frame dwelling with white-washed siding, green shutters and lace curtains in the windows. Instead of standing in front of it staring, they walked across the cobblestone street and stood under an elm tree. Pedestrians walked back and forth, carts and wagons rolled by, but no one emerged from the house.

Fletcher wondered how long Sydnee would stand there in silence. She stared at the house as if memorizing every detail. She wondered if her daughter was still there, if the family was good to her, or if they passed her off to someone else who was in need of low cost labor. Sydnee longed for a glimpse of someone, but no one emerged. The longer she waited, the more melancholy she became. At last she gathered her jacket around her as if she was chilled and said, "I am done."

As they walked back to the hotel, Fletcher waited for a reaction. He watched her closely, but her face was inscrutable. He worried that hideous memories may flood her, or maybe she would burst into tears, but she walked beside him quietly, revealing nothing. He wanted her to talk with him, but he knew he should not press her. For all of her warmth and gentle charm, he understood that she was a private person.

When they arrived at the hotel, the clerk handed Sydnee a note. Sitting down on the edge of a circular divan in the lobby, she read it. "It is from my friend, Madame Picard!" she gasped, looking up.

"Your teacher?"

Sydnee nodded. "She wants us to come to supper tonight."

"She is here in St. Louis?"

"Yes indeed, to my surprise!" Sydnee exclaimed, the color returning to her face.

Fletcher was relieved. It was good to see her smile again.

Sydnee fluttered around her hotel room that afternoon doing her hair and trying on gowns. Everything had to be perfect. She was seeing Madame Picard again. Suddenly she dropped her arms. Giselle had been responsible for this reunion. Ever since the meeting with Charles, Giselle had helped Sydnee over and over again. For all of her cold reserve, Giselle had a generous soul indeed. She sighed and shook her head. She hoped that somehow the woman had found some peace.

When they stepped out of the hackney in front of Madame Picard's house that evening, Sydnee smiled. Ninon had the finest home on the block. It was not the biggest house on the street or the most opulent, but it reflected the finest taste and refinement of any dwelling in the neighborhood. It did not surprise her.

When they started up the walk the door flew open, and Madame Picard rushed out to embrace Sydnee. Fletcher removed his hat and stepped back, smiling. He watched the women cry and laugh and babble incoherently.

At last Madame Picard, wiped her eyes and said, "Oh, my goodness, how do you do, Dr. Locke? I apologize. My students would be appalled if they saw me. I believe I have broken every rule of etiquette today. Please come inside."

Madame's housekeeper met them at the door. "I am sorry, madam. I didn't hear them knock."

"They did not have a chance to knock, Francis," Madame Picard said, laughing. "I bolted out the moment I saw them."

The housekeeper curtsied and went back to the kitchen to attend to supper.

Ninon Picard showed them into the parlor, a cozy room, decorated in soft olive greens with pearl accents. After pulling the doors closed, Madame Picard said quietly, "The name I use now is Mrs. Prouveaux. Although it is unlikely my past will follow me this far north, Missouri is still a slave state, and I must be careful."

Although she was still a beauty, Sydnee noticed fine lines around her eyes, and her hair was streaked with more gray. She knew it had been years since she had seen her, but she suspected Madame was still involved in the Underground Railroad.

With her usual grace and charm, Madame Picard made Fletcher feel at home. She asked him about his life in England and his work with children in Mississippi and Louisiana. There was so much to share, and they talked about everything from Madame's escape, to smuggling women to safety, to the opening of orphanages and at last Cuthbert Saint-Yves' involvement in child abductions.

"And you have a finishing school up here?" Fletcher asked at supper.

"I do indeed. The parents are quite different from the New Orleans' Creole, but they are just as eager for their children to learn social graces."

"Do you participate in St. Louis society?" asked Sydnee.

Madame Picard took a sip of wine and shook her head. "I lead a quiet life. It is very different here and much of the population is transient. Many of their customs are alien to me, and I prefer to stay at home with my books and my needlework."

After their dessert soufflé, Madame Picard said carefully, "Forgive me my dear, but Giselle said you are here to search for your daughter."

The smile faded from Sydnee's face, and she nodded. "We found the home of the couple who originally purchased her, but we know nothing about them or if she is with them any longer."

"What is the name?"

"Germain. Denis and Magali Germain."

Madame Picard started. "Germain?"

"Yes."

Blinking, she looked from Sydnee to Fletcher and back again. "I know them. I have their child in my class."

Sydnee's heart jumped.

Fletcher asked, "A girl or a boy?"

"A girl. She is twelve. She is their only child."

Sydnee stared at Ninon, stunned. "Are--are they kind to her?"

"They are indeed. They are good parents."

"Can you tell—is there any way--how will I know if it is her?" Sydnee stammered.

"Come tomorrow to class. Her name is Justine."

*   *   *

Sydnee was nervous about her reaction. When she saw the girl would she cry? Would she feel cheated? Would she dash out of the house overcome with emotion? It occurred to her that perhaps this Justine was not even her daughter, and she would have to continue searching. Either way having Fletcher by her side calmed her. He never pushed her and was always ready to listen when she needed to talk.

When they arrived at Madame's Picard's home the next morning, class was in session. Francis, the housekeeper, took them into the parlor where the young people were practicing correct posture and walking around the room with books on their heads.

Sydnee and Fletcher stood in the doorway as Madame Picard continued with class. There were fewer students than in her New Orleans school, five girls and four boys.

Instantly Sydnee recognized the girl named Justine, and Fletcher did too. She was the picture of Sydnee with cinnamon-colored hair, high cheekbones and freckles. Her figure had not developed yet, but it was apparent that she would have the graceful appearance of her mother. The only difference was that she was tall.

Suddenly the book slipped off Justine's head, upset a small table and fell on the floor. Embarrassed, she started to laugh, and then stopped abruptly when Madame Picard raised an eyebrow. "Try it again, Justine," she said.

Some of the other students snickered as Justine set the table upright, picked up the book and tried balancing it again. She looked at them and grinned.

The class practiced again for a while, walking around the room carefully, and then Madame Picard announced, "That is enough for today. Please stack your books on the table and line up. There is someone here that would like to meet you. Let's use our best manners please."

The students lined up with Justine at the end. Fletcher noticed one of the boys nudge her and she nudged him back flirtatiously.

"Mademoiselle Sauveterre, Dr. Locke," Madame Picard said. "I would like to present my students," and she went down the line introducing them all. The boys stepped forward and bowed, and the girls curtsied.

Although Sydnee greeted each young person, her eyes always returned to Justine who seemed to be having trouble paying attention. She was more interested in looking out the window. When her name was called, she jumped forward as if surprised and curtsied.

"Thank you, class. Now please select a book and read quietly until I return."

Sydnee noticed Justine take a book and sit in the window, stealing glances outside, unaware of how closely she was being observed.

Affection welled up in Sydnee as she watched the girl. She understood her. She knew how she felt. She longed to be outside, near the birds, the trees, and the sky. Sydnee longed to tell her everything about the wonders of the world and open her heart to the spirits, so she could hear them whispering to her in the rain, the trees, and in the wind.

Madame Picard joined them in the doorway and looked over at Justine. "She looks like you," she said gently.

"She does," Fletcher added. "She has your eyes."

Sydnee nodded still watching the girl.

Ninon added, "But her character is quite different. You were timid and withdrawn. Justine is gregarious and sometimes even wild."

"I'm glad. She has spirit," Sydnee said.

"Shall I call her over?" Madame Picard asked.

Sydnee shook her head. "Thank you, Madame but no. Someday I will return. Justine needs to keep her innocence as long as possible."

They knew that Sydnee was referring to her own lost childhood.

"*Au revoir*," she said, taking Ninon's hand.

"*Au revoir*, my dear friend."

Chapter 32

The next day they set out to find the other children. Fletcher and Sydnee dressed in simple clothing and hired a wagon from a livery in St. Louis. They had three locations to visit all of which were across the river in Illinois. They had to take a ferry and then travel out into the country.

The first home was nothing more than a run-down shack on the river with uncultivated fields. It reminded Sydnee of an abandoned stand on The Trace. The roof was full of holes, the porch was sagging, and there were rags hanging in the windows. It overlooked the Mississippi and was surrounded by trees and thick foliage. A grizzly old man sat on the front steps with flies buzzing around him. His eyes narrowed when the wagon pulled up, and he laid a shot gun across his lap.

Fletcher did not want Sydnee to accompany him so she stayed in the wagon, holding her breath. He jumped down and strode across the yard with a ledger in his hand. He did not approach cautiously or politely. The nearer he came to the porch, the wider the old man's eyes became. By the time Fletcher was in front of him, he was on his feet backing up toward the door of the house.

Fletcher opened the ledger and barked, "Are you Clay McCoy?"

"I am," the man replied, tightening the grip on his rifle.

"On October 8th, 1842, did you give money in exchange for a boy named Andrew Greely?"

The man frowned and said, "I did."

"Where is he?"

"Why you wanna know?"

"Where is he?" Fletcher snarled, taking a step forward.

"Out back."

With a scowl, Fletcher snapped the book shut, turned and walked to the back of the shack. He ran his eyes across the fields and saw no one. He looked in the shed and in the chicken coup. There was no one. He walked around the wood pile and came back, seeing no boy. At last he walked behind the outhouse and there he saw it. It was a grave, a fresh mound of dirt with no headstone.

Fletcher stared at it thunderstruck. This child never had a chance. This nine-year-old boy had been nothing more than a commodity, a tool, a beast of burden and like the slaves when he was used up, he was thrown away.

Enraged, Fletcher started back to the front of the house. When Sydnee saw the fury on his face, she jumped down from the wagon. He was headed straight for the old man. McCoy raised his rifle, but Sydnee jumped in front of Locke. "No, Fletcher. You will *not!*"

Fletcher grabbed her arms ready to push her aside, but she was stronger than he realized. He struggled with her and yelled, "You son of a bitch! You killed him!"

"It war not me. It war the fever. I cared about that youngin'!"

"Liar!" Fletcher spat. "You couldn't even give him a godammed headstone."

With all her strength, Sydnee pushed Fletcher back toward the wagon, digging her feet into the dirt and pushing.

"Git off my land!" the old man called in a shaky voice.

At last Fletcher stopped struggling and stood by the wagon, panting, never taking his eyes from McCoy. He straightened his coat and helped Sydnee into her seat. Crawling up beside her, he snapped the reins, and they left.

No words were exchanged as they traveled to the next residence. Although it was a several hour drive, they stopped only once by a stream to refresh the horse and to try to eat something, but neither of them were hungry.

By mid-afternoon they arrived at the next farm. This one was well-kept and appeared prosperous. The house was a white-washed two story dwelling with a tidy yard, flower garden, sturdy barn and several outbuildings. Sydnee noticed a curtain flutter in the window when they drove up, and a man in his middle years came out of the barn, wiping his hands on a rag.

"*Ja?*" he said. The farmer was wearing a homespun shirt and trousers with suspenders. He ran his eyes over Fletcher as he jumped down from the wagon. Sydnee noticed several children and adults working in the fields and two girls taking turns churning butter.

Sydnee was on guard. She knew Fletcher had not yet recovered from his encounter with McCoy, and he was taut as a bowstring.

"Good afternoon. My name is Locke and--"

"You're from England," the farmer said with a grunt.

Fletcher raised an eyebrow, ignored his comment and opened the ledger. "Are you Carl Reichman?"

The man did not respond.

"You bought two orphans by the name of Hannah and Theobold Claus on August 29th of this year."

"So?"

"They were stolen from the streets of New Orleans, and their families are looking for them. I am here to take them home."

"You will *not*," was the man's terse reply.

"I will reimburse you what you paid for them," Fletcher said, putting his hand in his jacket pocket.

The farmer turned his back on Fletcher, and started to walk away. He said over his shoulder, "They are not for sale."

Sydnee tensed up.

"Mr. Reichman," Fletcher called. "That sale was illegal. Now you can take my offer today and recover your expenses, or I will send the authorities out here to get them."

The man stopped.

Fletcher continued, "I assure you there will be no compensation for your loss when *they* come."

Reichman turned around. Narrowing his eyes he considered what Fletcher said and then walked back and held his hand out for payment. "I want to see the money."

Fletcher jerked his head toward the field. "I want to see the children."

The man whistled and called, "Claus twins, here now!" A boy about the age of eleven came running with a girl behind him who was a few years younger. They were extremely thin with dirty, dark hair and skin darkened from the summer sun.

"Are you Theobold?" Fletcher asked the boy. He looked up and nodded. "And is this your sister, Hannah?" Again the boy nodded. They both looked scared.

Fletcher pulled a wad of bills out of his pocket and stuffed it in the farmer's hand. He lifted the children up next to Sydnee, climbed up beside her and snapped the reins. "One more to go," he said as they pulled out of the yard.

"Could you really send the authorities out here?" Sydnee asked him.

"No," Fletcher said with a chuckle. "But that bumpkin didn't know that."

The first thing they did was find a shady spot and give Hannah and Theobold something to eat. They made small talk with the children to put them at ease and explained to them that they were taking them home to their aunt and uncle in New Orleans. Gradually the children relaxed.

"You will be staying in a hotel and riding in a paddle wheeler. Will you like that, Theobold?" Sydnee asked.

"He likes to be called Theo," Hannah said.

"Oh, very well, Theo," she said smiling. "We have one more child to find today before we return to the hotel for the night."

"In fact we are here now," Fletcher said.

He turned the horse down a lane, but when they arrived at the homestead, it was abandoned. They asked a neighbor where the family had gone, and the woman said they had moved west.

Disappointed, Sydnee asked Fletcher, "So what now?"

Fletcher shrugged. "There is nothing we can do."

The sun was setting as they crossed the river back to St. Louis on the ferry. "I want to stop briefly at St. Anne's Home for Children tonight," stated Fletcher.

"Yes, and then tomorrow let's go home," she said quietly. "We are all weary."

It was dark by the time they reached the orphanage, but Sister Hortense had been expecting them. She welcomed them inside immediately. It was a large residence in the middle of town in bad need of repair. The dedicated nuns worked around the clock trying to feed and clothe the children and had little time for renovations. "We opened our doors recently," Sister Hortense explained. "God will provide everything we need in time."

The young nun explained their mission, introduced them to some of the children and listened as Fletcher explained their recent endeavor rescuing orphans.

"We need to eliminate this outrage," Sister Hortense said. "I have witnessed these sales right here in the city."

"We are not always successful doing rescues," Fletcher added. "The last house we visited was empty. They had gone west."

Sister Hortense shook her head. "It is hard to believe, but many people abandon children on their way west. They want as little as possible encumbering them on their journey, including children. What is the child's name?"

"Adele Toussard. She is only three."

"No one here by that name," she said sitting down at her desk.

"The people that purchased her were Charles and Louise Bertrand."

"Well, let me see," she said, opening a ledger.

She ran her finger down the first page and then flipped the leaf over and ran her finger down another row of names. "Yes!" she exclaimed. "Here she is! We know her as Adelaide."

Sydnee gasped, and Fletcher heaved a sigh, slumping back in his chair. "I cannot believe it. We have found another."

*   *   *

The next day they boarded *The Belle of St. Louis* bound for New Orleans. As usual Sydnee and Fletcher took separate staterooms. The twins stayed with Fletcher, and Sydnee took

Adele. She spent most of the day chasing the toddler around the riverboat, making sure she did not climb the railings, topple into the water or fall down the stairs. Since the weather was cool she tried to stay inside, but the toddler's attention span was short, and inevitably she would want to run outside on deck to explore.

By afternoon, Adele had worn herself out and fell asleep in Sydnee's stateroom. Fletcher taught Hannah and Theo how to play checkers and then joined Sydnee on the deck to smoke.

"That child exhausts me," Sydnee said, leaning on the railing.

"I will take a turn with her when she wakes up," Fletcher said, lighting his cigar. He looked out along shore. It was early November and many of the leaves had dropped from the trees, but the sun was shining, and the sky was a bright blue.

Fletcher took a deep breath of the crisp autumn air. "For the first time in my life, I feel at peace. I seem to have found everything I have been looking for," he said taking her hand and kissing it.

"I have too. I have so much to be thankful for," Sydnee said, smiling. "I have found you *and* my daughter."

"But I'm afraid you have lost your friends."

"No, they will be with me always," she said. Shaking her head, she added, "I have to admit I am glad the masquerade is over. I realize now there would never have been a happy ending. Keeping the secret almost killed Isabel. Revealing it, did kill D'anton."

They were quiet a moment and Fletcher asked, "And Justine?"

"I will come back one day to meet her. When we are both ready."

An elderly man dressed in evening attire, strolling on deck, paused and asked Fletcher, "Did you feel it, sir?"

"Feel what?" Fletcher said.

"The tremor?"

"What tremor?"

"When we were boarding in Cairo, the earth shook."

Fletcher looked at Sydnee, and she shook her head. "No, we felt nothing here on the water, sir," Fletcher replied. "Do you refer to a mild earthquake?"

"Yes. I am sure you think I am daft, but we do have tremors here," the man said. "Thirty years ago there were massive quakes here." Pointing his cane toward shore, he explained, "This whole area was devastated. The ground opened and cabins slid into the river. The town of New Madrid was obliterated, and the Mississippi ran backward."

"Surely you jest," Fletcher gasped.

"I do not. I was here," the gentleman said. "One is never the same after witnessing the wrath of the Lord."

"Indeed," Fletcher said.

Puffing on his cigar, Fletcher watched the man walk away. "Have you ever heard of such a thing?"

Sydnee shook her head. "Hurricanes yes, earthquakes no," was her reply.

*   *   *

The sun was starting to set as Fletcher and Sydnee took the children in to supper. Fletcher was weary from chasing Adele for hours so he tied her onto his back with a belt and carried her. The toddler was overjoyed. She was at everyone's eye level and babbled and flirted with every passenger she encountered.

As they walked along the deck, the child put her chubby hand in the air and pointed. At the same time Hannah exclaimed, "Look up there. Look at the birds!" The sky was peppered with birds flying overhead, screeching and squawking wildly.

Fletcher cocked his head and listened to a rumbling in the distance. "Is that thunder?"

There was not a cloud in the sky, but the rumbling came closer, and it was growing in intensity. Sydnee saw the shoreline start to shake and then it rolled as if someone was turning under bedclothes. Then the river rose in a great black wave heaving the paddle wheeler to one side, throwing everyone off their feet. The children screamed in terror, but when they tried to stand up the riverboat lurched in the other direction, sliding everyone toward the railing. Sydnee fell face down and started to slide,

371

catching a post in time before falling overboard. Fletcher fell onto the stairs and grabbed onto the railing.

China smashed in the dining room, and a table crashed through a window sending shards of glass everywhere. Sydnee clutched Hannah around the waist, hanging onto a pole with her other hand as the river heaved the paddle wheeler up and down. A woman lost her balance, clawing frantically at the air and then toppled over into the black water.

"Where's Theo!" Hannah screamed.

Before Sydnee could look, a huge log surfaced from underwater and slammed into the side of the boat, splintering the hull and the deck. Trees were uprooted on shore falling into the river as the ground split, and the Mississippi surged over the banks. The sound of rumbling, cracking and screaming was deafening. Huge chunks of earth split and dropped into the water.

Fletcher staggered to his feet with Adele on his back as the paddle wheeler pitched. Passengers were shrieking and running wildly on deck trying to get to the safety of their staterooms.

Theo was clinging to a column by the stairs, soaked and trembling, and Fletcher stumbled over to him. With Adele on his back, he wrapped his arms around Theo and the column, holding on tightly. At that moment the paddle wheeler lurched forward and careened down a newly formed wall of water. It hit the water below with such force that everyone on deck lost their grip and were catapulted forward. Some passengers crashed through the dining room windows, others hit the railings and toppled over, and several flew directly into the river. The riverboat was smashed apart on impact and the pieces hurtled in every direction.

Some passengers were killed instantly, others clung to debris. Women in heavy skirts who landed in the water were sucked under instantly. Sydnee fell into the river, and the raging current tossed her like a rag doll. She was gasping and flailing, trying to find something to cling to, but the water pushed her along so quickly she was helpless. She slammed abruptly into a tree that had fallen along the shore. Holding on with every bit of strength she had, she clawed at the slippery trunk, trying to get a firm grasp. Fortunately she had shed her petticoats to chase Adele, so she was able to hook a leg around a branch and drag herself on top of the tree.

Panting, she pushed the wet hair from her face and looked around. The ground had stopped shaking, but the river was still running a mad course. Dazed and shaken, her eyes gradually focused, and she saw a massive chunk of the paddle wheeler on shore. It had run aground, and people were standing on the river bank.

Sydnee crawled along the tree, yanking at her skirt as it caught on the branches. She managed to stand and stumbled toward the other passengers. Hannah burst from the group and ran toward her with Theo behind her. When they met they almost toppled her over, hugging and sobbing.

"Have you seen Dr. Locke or Adele?" Sydnee asked frantically.

Theo pointed out to the river.

To Sydnee's horror, Fletcher was standing on a tiny island with the toddler still strapped to his back. He was clinging desperately to a tree as the torrent raced around him, washing away the soil at his feet. Just as Sydnee was about to call to him, the earth collapsed under him, and he tumbled into the river with the child.

Sydnee screamed and ran along the shore, climbing over debris and crawling over upturned trees and rocks trying to follow them downriver, but they were gone. She stood for a long time, staring at the river and sobbing.

"Mademoiselle," a little voice said at last. "Mademoiselle Sauveterre."

Dazed, Sydnee turned around. It was Hannah. "They are gone."

Sydnee blinked. "What?"

"The other passengers. They are gone. They started walking a long time ago. It is just you and me and Theo left."

Sydnee closed her eyes and took a deep breath. Stunned and delirious, she wiped her nose on her sleeve and stumbled forward. Taking the children by the hands, she started walking down a deer path to try to find help, but there was no one.

The area was devastated. Trees were uprooted, large rifts were gouged into the ground, and the river was foaming and churning. In less than five minutes, the Mississippi found a new course and ran over land previously dry. Cabins lay in ruins with chimneys crumbled. The river was littered with debris, trees and smashed flatboats. The ground was still trembling with aftershocks, and each time one occurred the children would drop into a crouch, terrified.

Sydnee was too stunned to care about the tremors. All of her thoughts were on Fletcher and Adele. Had they survived, or had the water claimed them? Had someone rescued them, or had they been smashed to bits by debris and fallen trees? Over and over she thought of ways they may have survived, but there was a sickness in her stomach that told her otherwise.

They stopped at last to rest, too exhausted to walk any longer. Sydnee tried to clear her mind to appeal to the spirits for answers but try as she might, she could not hear their voices. She could feel them swirling all around her though, mad with pain and confusion. They were too unsettled to glean any answers. Tears rolled down her cheeks.

When the sun set that evening, they slept in the remains of a cabin. It was likely the family had fled to higher ground. A tree had fallen through the roof, and although there were holes, it was still shelter for them, and they found everything they needed, food, firewood, and beds.

Although she was weak from exhaustion and anxiety, Sydnee could not sleep. She looked through the roof and stared at the full moon above her bed. Again she appealed to the spirits, but they were silent, and she feared the worst.

In the morning they continued on the deer path. By sunset Sydnee noticed a bit less damage. There were fewer trees down, and the earth was not as scarred and gouged. They came to a cluster of cabins on high ground overlooking the river, and the residents rushed forward to welcome them warmly, offering food and shelter.

"This was nothing like the one thirty years ago. Mild in comparison," a leathery-skinned old woman told Sydnee. "But it was hell for y'all, either way. You'll get home soon. Men come down from the north in flatboats all the time. Once they see the devastation, they'll stop here to ask questions. Don't worry, dear. We will get you and the youngins' on a flatboat bound for Memphis tomorrow."

Sydnee almost collapsed from relief, and tears of gratitude filled her eyes. Tristan, Isabel and Mortimer were in Memphis. They would know what to do. They would help her find her way. They loved her and would always take care of her.

Chapter 33
New Orleans, December 1843

New Orleans had lost its luster for Sydnee. The city that had dazzled her for years with its flamboyant good-nature and carefree ambiance, now seemed gray and lifeless. Fletcher and Adele had not returned home, and every day that passed Sydnee fell deeper into despair. It had been weeks since the quake, and although Sydnee knew that travel was difficult in the area, they should have been home by now.

Sydnee spent many anxious days in Memphis with her friends waiting for news, but there was nothing. Reluctantly, she returned to New Orleans to take Theo and Hannah home. Their aunt and uncle were overjoyed to see them again, but even the happy reunion failed to move Sydnee. She felt empty and lost.

News about the earthquake was on everyone's lips. The major cities experienced heavy tremors and flooding, but nothing compared to the stretch of the Mississippi they had been traveling.

The strain of waiting for news about Fletcher and Adele drained her over time, and she moved from anxious agitation pacing the floors every night, to a deep despondency where she slept for hours on end like D'anton. She would drag herself from bed long enough to attend to the needs of the orphanage and then return to her room with Atlantis where she drew the drapes and kept the outside world remote. Vivian and Atlantis sensed her despair and were at her side every minute.

"Mademoiselle Sydnee," Marie said one rainy morning, knocking at her bed chamber door. "I just returned from the orphanage, and my mother said you should come quickly. The roof is leaking."

Sydnee sat up in a stupor and rubbed her eyes. "Very well, I will be right there," she mumbled.

After examining the roof and reviewing the books, it was apparent a benefit was needed once more. Sydnee did not have the interest or the energy for a large affair, so she decided to have a small soiree at her town house with her closest, wealthiest acquaintances. She would raise just enough money for the roof and be done with it. She would serve delicacies and drinks. There would be dancing in the courtyard if the weather was fair, and tables for faro in the parlor with the winnings going to the orphanage.

The morning of the benefit, Sydnee had trouble rising from bed. She was tired of the endless parade of witty intellectuals and bejeweled matrons through her home. There was a time when her only thought was to entertain, but now it was a burden. When she looked at her future, it seemed to hold only endless days of loneliness and despair. She had found love and complete happiness for such a short time, and it had been ripped from her grasp. Her friends were gone, pursuing new lives elsewhere, and even the spirits had abandoned her. She called to them repeatedly, but they never answered her anymore.

Angry and bitter, Sydnee threw off the covers and stood up. She had made a decision. She was leaving New Orleans. There were too many memories here, and it was time to make a new life elsewhere. She would relinquish the responsibility of the children's home in Natchez to the citizens of Mississippi and give the New Orleans orphanage to the Ursulines.

She sighed. It was one less burden for her and a huge relief. She was tired and wanted nothing more than to pull back into herself and retreat from life permanently.

Sydnee spent the rest of the day getting ready for the benefit. She dragged herself through the preparations, consoling herself with the fact that this was the last time she would have to orchestrate an event. There would be no more parties, no more responsibilities and no more worries. It was just like the day she burned her father's stand on The Trace. She would be done forever.

After helping Marie and her mother with food and set up, Sydnee stepped outside in the courtyard to make sure everything was ready for the musicians when they arrived. The evening was fair, and the temperature extremely mild for a December day. She sat down by the fountain and thought back to the first day at her town house. She was going to be the first lady of New Orleans. Tristan was going to be a distinguished gentleman; Isabel a wife; Mortimer a business owner; and D'anton an attorney. She chuckled cynically. They accomplished all of those things, but it was not what any of them really wanted in the end.

Life turned out to be nothing more than a bitter disappointment, she thought. Dreams, they were only pipe dreams.

She noticed Vivian watching her from the tree. There was something about the way the crow looked at her that made her feel guilty, and she frowned. Usually Sydnee would raise her arm to have the bird come and perch, but this time Sydnee turned away and went to the house. She was even tired of Vivian.

The crow watched her walk up the steps and then cocked her head to the side. The wind chimes were tinkling, but Sydnee did not hear them. She passed right by and went into the house. They had been calling to Sydnee for weeks, but she had not been listening.

*   *   *

Marie helped Sydnee into her green brocade gown and dressed her hair with tiny faux gems and a ribbon. Hannah and Theo came over to help with serving. Once a week they would come by the town house to visit with her, and she asked them if they were interested in earning some money by helping at the benefit.

Sydnee greeted the guests, started the faro and served refreshments. After a few hours, Marie lit the Chinese lanterns in the courtyard, and the musicians begin to play waltzes. The courtyard looked magical to Hannah and Theo. The lanterns cast a golden light over everything, and the water splashing in the fountain looked like jewels. Sydnee saw the delight in their eyes and remembered a dream she had long ago where beautiful flowers magically turned into dancers at a ball. She blinked and tried to remember more, but it would not surface.

"You may stay to watch the dancers for a half hour, and then it is time to go home," she said to the children.

After several rounds of faro, Sydnee returned to the courtyard. It was crowded with dancers. Looking across the garden she saw Theo, and he was holding a little girl in his arms and bouncing her. Sydnee frowned. It seemed unusual that someone would bring a child to the soiree.

The waltz ended, and the dancers drifted off. Theo was gone, but there was a gentleman with his arm in a sling staring at her across the courtyard. She looked, and her lips parted. It was Fletcher Locke, and he was dressed in evening attire.

The music started again, and the courtyard crowded with dancers. Sydnee was too stunned to move as he wound his way through the guests, trying to reach her. Her chest heaved when he stopped in front of her, and her eyes filled with tears.

"Your friend LaRoche, the boatman found me on the riverbank with Adele still strapped to my back. We were both unconscious," Fletcher said, and then he chuckled. "Damned if I know how we survived, but they nursed us back to health. David helped too."

Sydnee could find no words. She looked him up and down. Aside from his arm being in a sling, Fletcher was unscathed. It seemed like a miracle and suddenly, in a rush, she knew that her life was back once more. The luster had returned to everything. She collapsed into his arms, and he held her so close she could barely breathe. He kissed her and told her over and over how much he loved her.

At last Fletcher stepped back, took out his handkerchief and dried Sydnee's tears. The musicians began a new waltz, and he held up his one good hand saying, "May I have this dance?"

Sydnee raised her eyebrows. "But you don't dance."

"No, but my wedding is coming up. I need to practice."

She smiled slowly. Taking his hand, they started to waltz. Fletcher moved stiffly around the floor with a sheepish grin on his face.

"You're stepping on my feet," she teased.

"I'm sorry, but I am just learning," he said defensively.

They waltzed around the courtyard bumping into people and apologizing when suddenly there was a fluttering of wings, and Vivian landed on Fletcher's shoulder. He stopped dancing, and his eyes grew large. "What should I do?" he whispered to Sydnee.

Sydnee grinned. "Just keep dancing."

Author's Note

All of my work is fiction, and it is set within the historical backgrounds of the 18th and 19th Centuries. Although some of my secondary characters really lived, my main characters are always fictitious, as well as their accomplishments and experiences.

Seldom do I feel the need to explain the events of my novels. My readers are generally well-versed in history, so there is little need for clarification, but in *The Grand Masquerade*, I feel compelled to share what I learned about the New Madrid earthquake of 1811-12.

I have lived most of my life in the Midwest and always thought earthquakes in the U.S. were restricted to the states bordering The San Andreas Fault. When I was researching life on the Mississippi in the 19th Century, I was floored to learn there had been several major earthquakes centering in Missouri called the New Madrid Earthquakes.

These were no minor tremors. The New Madrid earthquakes of 1811-12 rank as some of the largest quakes ever recorded in North America. It is said the range of shocks were two to three times as large as the 1964 Alaska earthquake and ten times as large as the 1906 San Francisco earthquake. People reported tremors from the New Madrid quakes as far away as Montreal, Boston and Washington D.C.

Since there were few major European settlements on the Mississippi at that time, there was little residential and commercial damage, but today it would be another story. I have downsized the magnitude of the fictitious earthquake that Sydnee, Fletcher and the children experienced in *The Grand Masquerade* in 1843. Nevertheless, it would be terrifying indeed to be on a riverboat during such a natural disaster. If an earthquake that size hit the Midwest today, the devastation would be enormous. It would only be matched by the shock and surprise of residents of the area. I certainly hope we never experience it.

Please look for my other novels on Amazon.com: *Beyond the Cliffs of Kerry, The Pride of the King,* and *The Sword of the Banshee*

And don't forget to visit my website and join my mailing list at: www.amandahughesauthor.com

Amanda Hughes

ABOUT THE AUTHOR

All her life Amanda Hughes has been a "Walter Mitty", spending more time in heroic daydreams than the real world. At last she found an outlet writing adventures about audacious women in the 18th and 19th Century. Her debut novel, *Beyond the Cliffs of Kerry* *http://www.amazon.com/dp/B004V12JIK* was published in 2002, followed by *The Pride of the King* *http://www.amazon.com/dp/B0056QJOVE* in 2011 and *The Sword of the Banshee* *http://www.amazon.com/dp/B00BB0NR9E* in 2013. Amanda is a graduate of the University of Minnesota, and when she isn't off tilting windmills, she lives and writes in St. Paul, Minnesota. Please visit her at *http://www.amandahughesauthor.com*

Made in the USA
Middletown, DE
06 January 2015